# The
# Holiday

Lucy Dickens is the pseudonym for Lisa Dickenson. Lisa lives by the Devon seaside with her husband and one very boisterous Bernese Mountain Dog.

Also by Lucy Dickens

*The Broken Hearts Honeymoon*

# The
# Holiday
# Bookshop

### Lucy Dickens

PENGUIN BOOKS

PENGUIN BOOKS

UK | USA | Canada | Ireland | Australia
India | New Zealand | South Africa

Penguin Books is part of the Penguin Random House group
of companies whose addresses can be found at
global.penguinrandomhouse.com

Penguin
Random House
UK

Published in Penguin Books 2022
001

Typeset in 10.5/15.5 pt Palatino LT Std
by Integra Software Services Pvt. Ltd, Pondicherry

Map © Darren Bennett at DKB Creative Ltd
(www.dkbcreative.com)

Printed and bound in Great Britain by Clays Ltd, Elcograf S.p.A.

The authorised representative in the EEA is Penguin Random House
Ireland, Morrison Chambers, 32 Nassau Street, Dublin D02 YH68

A CIP catalogue record for this book is available from
the British Library

ISBN: 978–1–529–15763–5

www.greenpenguin.co.uk

*Dedicated to*
*Phil, for all the fun holidays.*

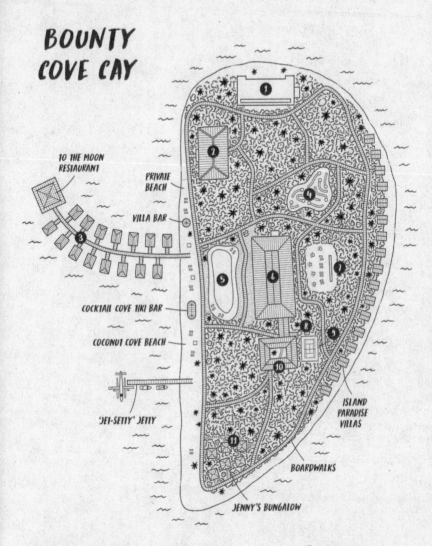

# BOUNTY COVE CAY

**TO THE MOON RESTAURANT**

PRIVATE BEACH

VILLA BAR

COCKTAIL COVE TIKI BAR

COCONUT COVE BEACH

'JET-SETTY' JETTY

ISLAND PARADISE VILLAS

BOARDWALKS

JENNY'S BUNGALOW

1. STAFF ACCOMMODATION
2. BOUNT ECO & TURTLE SANCTUARY
3. LAGUNA PRIVATE WATER VILLAS
4. MINIATURE GOLF
5. POOL
6. COVE PAVILION
7. CINEMA UNDER THE STARS
8. JENNY'S BOOKSHOP
9. TENNIS COURTS
10. DIVINE OCEAN SPA & GYMNASIUM
11. BEACH BUNGALOWS

# Chapter 1

# Jenny

'Opening night,' the reporter declared with gusto, despite the beads of rain still dripping from his forehead. 'Are you ready?'

I pasted on a grin and stared at him, trying to squeeze out a 'Yes' through my teeth. *I'm not ready at all for this,* I thought. *What the hell do I know about owning my own business? About running a bookshop?* I felt my eyes widen, causing the reporter's eyes to widen back at me, his pen hovering in the air. Somebody shuffled past me to my left, making their way to the table of free wine, their wet umbrella tickling my leg as they passed. *I put the wine out, right?*

The reporter, having driven more than thirty minutes through the impending storm from the office of the local paper, cleared his throat, blinked and said, a little slower, 'Opening night—'

She materialised on my right. I felt her hand in mine before I saw her, before I smelled the familiar waft of coconutty body mist she stocked up on from Hollister. Marianne, my best friend, here to save the day.

1

She squeezed my hand and enthused, 'We are *so* ready.'

The reporter, visibly relieved, turned to face her. 'You must be Jenny's business partner. Marianne, is it?'

'It is. Thanks for coming all the way over here for our big night, even through that ...' She gestured to the dark night beyond the shop windows, where late winter rain was beating to be let inside and a thunderstorm was brewing over the ocean that watched over our small coastal town in North Cornwall.

It was incredible, really, that so many people had shown up to our opening night, albeit mostly family, friends and locals who'd been bombarded with the irresistible promise of free bubbly and a one-night-only discount of twenty per cent off book purchases. Even weather like this couldn't stop people from enjoying freebies and discounts.

I refocused on the reporter, whose forehead was drying under Marianne's warm gaze as she regaled him with tales of how we'd grown up together here in Bayside and had been as close as sisters all the way through school. She told him how after I'd finished university and she had finished travelling the world as part of the entertainment crew on a cruise ship, we had moved back to our home town with big dreams of opening a business, and doing it together.

I was so glad she was here with me. Marianne thrived in situations like this, while I always lost my train of thought three words in and had a tendency to apologise for my successes. I sent her thank-you vibes through our palms.

'And here it is,' the reporter commented, glancing around our small, brand-new bookshop. 'The Book Nook on the Beach.'

'Best bookshop you'll ever visit, Mike,' Marianne declared, though I was pretty sure that he'd said his name was Steve.

Steve or Mike zoned in on me again and asked, 'Are you worried about the two of you working at such close quarters?'

Marianne gave my hand a squeeze again, a little harder this time, and I glanced at her reassuring face before I spoke. 'No, not at all. We've spent so much of our lives together, we live together now in a tiny flat across town, and we never argue. We've always been a good team, I think. We're going to be just fine.'

She threw me one of her biggest grins and added, 'I second that! Besides, Jenny is *the best* business partner a girl could ask for. She's so organised, so on the ball, and she always seems to find a way to make my crazy ideas work!'

'Such as this place,' I joked.

'The Book Nook was both our idea.' Marianne faced Steve/Mike again, adding, 'I knew I wanted to be my own boss and start my own business. But a *bookshop* was this one's big dream.' She gave me a conspiratorial wink.

'It was Marianne's idea to go into business together,' I added, 'but, yep, I've always kind of wanted to run a bookshop. I used to read non-stop growing up, and through uni I worked in a bookshop part-time. I love

3

helping people find that perfect book that lets them drift away from their busy lives. That makes me happy.'

Steve/Mike scribbled down some notes, nodding. 'Any fears about starting a new business, especially at your age?'

I nodded. 'Yes, lots, though I'm not sure that's anything to do with being in our twenties ...'

'No,' Marianne said at the same time. 'If you're scared of everything, you'd never do anything. I don't let fear in, ever, so I'm not letting my girl here get scared either.'

I sneaked a look around our shop, at the full shelves, the vintage book-cover posters, the mood lighting, the warm ambience, the kids' corner, the window seats. The air, though currently a little full of the aroma of damp umbrellas and red wine, had taken on the unmistakable scent of a whole bounty of books. It had come a long way from the run-down empty space we'd leased nearly six months ago. Marianne had found it – a tiny unit right on the seafront with views out over the single-lane road and pavement to the ocean beyond. The only source of natural light came from the glass door framed by two tall, arched windows at the front, but the shop stretched back a decent way. However, it needed *so* much work that I had almost backed out in favour of a wide, ex-charity shop in the centre of the town, which had electricity and shelving and everything. As usual, though, I'd trusted Marianne's gut over my own and, as usual, she was right. It felt like it would work perfectly, it could (hopefully) pull in customers from the beach, and it felt magnificent to know we'd have that view every day.

'Don't you want to stand here,' Marianne had said to me six months ago, the day our loan had been approved, 'and every single day be able to look out there? Isn't that the office life you'd give your everything for?' That day the sun had been shining, sparkling off the sea, winking at me as if to agree with my soon-to-be partner.

'Imagine the customers,' Marianne had whispered, sidling up to me. 'Imagine them coming in here and being so entranced by the ocean that they buy our whole stack of seaside-themed romcoms in one … fell … swoop.'

'OK!' I'd laughed, and she'd pulled a bottle of pink Prosecco from her bag in glee.

'Hooray, we've found our shop, our slice of heaven!'

Despite everything she'd been through, she was always vibrant and full of love for life. I hoped she'd never change. Smiling at the memory, I was pulled back to the present again by the reporter, who asked, 'And finally, what about the future?'

'God knows,' Marianne laughed. 'See the world? Own a shit ton of shops? Buy Amazon?'

Phew, this was a question I knew how to answer. Thanks to a lot of late nights devouring business-management modules online, and reading every book on the topic I could get my hands on, I was clear about how I wanted us to run things. Marianne had tried to get involved in our business plan, but we knew from early on she would flourish more on the practical, creative side of the bookshop, so we divided up the labour in that way. Not that it was particularly *equal*, but that was fine with me, we were both more than happy playing to our individual skills. And so I said, 'I'd love to see a steady growth across the next five years. Christmas next year will be a key time for us, so we'd like to have a real place in the community by then, with lots of fun events and interesting stock to keep our customers happy.'

Steve/Mike smiled at me. 'No seeing the world for you, then?'

'Well ...' I gave a quick wave to Marianne's hot brother, Evan, who'd just walked in the door, shaking the rain from his coat. My hand instinctively moved to smooth my hair, something I'd been doing on seeing Evan since I was a teenager, checking my strawberry-blonde locks weren't escaping the short braid I'd twisted them into. Then I focused behind him, where a car was crawling past in the dark, lashing rain, its headlights beaming, illuminating a wave that was leaping over the sea wall to crash onto the top of it. 'Maybe opening a second branch somewhere abroad would be fun. Somewhere sunny and tropical.'

We all laughed, but none of us really knew, back then, what was on the other side of our little bookshop's door, now that it had opened.

# Chapter 2

# Jenny

**Three years later ...**

*Whoosh!* Oh, Christ. The door flung itself open yet again, sending in a hard smattering of rain, the wind dashing about the bookshop, making covers gasp open, pages tremble and jump over each other, coffee cups rattle and customers scurry deeper towards the back section, covering their drinks with their hands and taking a great interest in the Local History shelves.

February in our little seaside town in Cornwall wasn't known for its postcard-perfect weather, however this storm was something else. I'd lost power twice already today, and I was sorely tempted to just close up and head home for an afternoon bath and a wine party for one. But, on this, the third day of the storm, it seemed the residents of Bayside were getting cabin fever, so had ventured out of their own homes for a slow stroll around my store. Besides, tonight was the first of our new series of events, the Meet the Author evenings, and Marianne wasn't budging over my suggestions to cancel.

'This storm is wild,' Marianne boomed to the whole shop, leaving her position behind the desk to help me push the door back into place, the Book Nook on the Beach sign creaking as it flapped back and forth above the door in the wind. She stood with her back to it, wiping her damp, dark curls away from her face with her hand. 'Fancy chucking this all in and going to work at a Club Med instead?'

'Yes, please,' I replied, but I straightened the books with a careful fondness, and adjusted the string of fairy lights over the window back into place.

Marianne came and stood next to me, leaning her head on my shoulder and watching the waves crash against the sea wall and up over the railings on the opposite side of the road. 'Remember when you came and met my cruise ship out in Crete, and I was so annoyed because it was forecast for rain the whole week you were there—'

'—but it was wall-to-wall sunshine?'

'I miss trips with you,' Marianne sighed.

'Me too.' I did miss holidays, I really, truly did, but I worked here pretty much six days a week. Plus a few evenings. And early starts. There just wasn't any time any more. At least, that's how *I* felt.

'Rain, rain, go away,' Marianne sang, seemingly not wanting to push her point right now.

I went back to straightening books, tidying coffee cups, wiping rain off surfaces, while Marianne followed me, rearranging displays I'd just neatened. 'How's Drew feeling about tonight?'

It was Marianne's latest boyfriend who was responsible for us starting the author events. When Drew Inkbridge, author of one of last year's big thrillers, had appeared in our shop shortly before Christmas and bashfully asked if we'd like him to sign the two copies of his book we still had in stock, it was smitten at first sight for Marianne. Luckily, he'd just moved to Bayside to write the follow-up, which was to be set in a fictional coastal town, though from what I could tell he spent most of his time here smooching my best friend and drinking our coffee. He was a nice guy, from what I knew of him when he came up for air, and he was into books, which was a tick in both of our boxes. Plus, he seemed completely besotted with Marianne – and she with him, so far – which made a change from her usual nonchalant kinda partner.

And so, hosting Meet the Author events became Marianne's latest idea. Most of the marketing and PR ideas around here were Marianne's. To put it bluntly, she was still the creative, ideas woman, and I was still the one who made them happen. Sometimes she needed reigning in, but I suppose sometimes I did need the push.

For example, back when she'd first presented the idea of the Meet the Author events, I'd argued, 'But we don't get many authors down here.'

'We'll invite them, Jenn – that's like saying we shouldn't have got the coffee machine because we didn't have any coffee beans. We make these things and the necessary people will come. It'll be fine. Besides, who cares if it fails? It's fun to take a chance.'

She got her way, of course, because even though it would mean more work for me, more late nights at the bookshop, more advertising and promoting and organising, Marianne's ideas had a sparkle about them, a vibrancy, a life of their own, much like her. They attracted more customers, and they continued to cement the bookshop's place as a fixture in the community and a precious presence. And *that* meant our regulars were loyal and supportive and rarely attracted by the big-light discounts of the massive online retailers.

We still made a good team, though lately … I wasn't sure … I felt like we were getting scratchy with each other. Arguing a little more. Finding annoyances in shadows that weren't there before.

Maybe it was just me. I was a little burned out. Owning a business was *hard*.

'Hmm?' Marianne asked, her gaze dissecting the display of Drew's novels that we'd bought for tonight.

'Drew,' I repeated, my thoughts returning to the present. 'How's he feeling?'

'Oh, yeah, he's fine, I think. I doubt he gets nervous about this kind of thing, he's done so many.'

Marianne sauntered back over to the counter, where two small faces were peering up, their pocket-money-filled hands waving in the air while they clutched colourful books to their damp raincoats.

'Do you know if Evan's coming down for tonight?' she called over to me.

I turned my face away so I wouldn't do something as obvious as blush. 'I don't know, I haven't seen him today.'

Things had changed a little in the last three years, one of those changes being that Marianne and I no longer lived together. The two-bedroom flat above the bookshop opened up earlier last year and the thought of living a) with an ocean view and b) with such a tiny commute had been too tempting for me to resist. Marianne loved the teeny flat we'd shared, so she was happy to stay put. I wondered if both of us had needed a *little* space from each other, which was why we'd agreed so readily. I thought it was good for us and our friendship, but it also meant I found myself toiling away in the evenings and Sundays because work was just *right there*.

Evan – Marianne's hot older brother – had also returned to Bayside recently from London, having missed the waves too much, and was looking to follow his dreams of working for the RNLI. Marianne, with her spontaneity that I just *flippin' love*, had suggested that he take my spare room! *I have plenty of space! Why wouldn't I want to split the cost with a flatmate I knew so well?!*

I'd known Evan for ever, of course, and everyone – even Marianne – knew I had the almightiest crush on him when I was at school. When I was over at her house I used to sneak down to watch him and his friends rinse the sand from their hair under the outdoor shower. Their lovely mum caught me once. Cringe.

Anyway, he needed somewhere to live; how could I say no? When he asked if I wanted to join him on the beach for a beer after his first surf back in Bayside, even though it was freezing outside, how could I say no? And after treating myself to a gawk of that same man peeling his wetsuit off to his waist and then sit beside me and clink beer bottles together under the warmth of a blanket, how could I not develop my crush again?

Suddenly, he wasn't just Marianne's delicious but out-of-reach big brother, but a guy, only a couple of years older than me, with whom I had a lot in common, who made me laugh and who seemed pleased to see me after all this time. Though nothing happened, I felt something shift. We saw each other in a new light. At least, I thought he felt the same way.

'Good evening, ladies and gentlemen,' Marianne announced in her most charismatic voice. She'd raced home through the rain to change, and I got the feeling she was going for the Gothic Party Host vibe this evening to match the darkness of Drew's novel, with her black and red ensemble and her dark wavy hair, inherited from her mother, gleaming.

'Good evening,' I replied, then felt like an idiot because I was the only one, which caused a snigger from one of the fold-out chairs in the back, but a grateful smile from Drew on his raised stool.

We'd closed the shop to the public an hour early and decked it out with mood lighting, and had small measures of red and white wine available for the thirty customers. My mum shuffled in her seat next to me, clasping her copy of Drew's book, which she'd asked me to set aside for her and wanted him to sign. Around me were some familiar faces. Locals who came to everything, especially when there was free wine. Bella from the bakery, who was a massive Drew Inkbridge fan, was there, sitting in the front row, leaning forward, gazing up at him unabashedly. Scattered around were other thriller fans and people just keen for an interesting evening out during a long, drab February. And I was trying not to glance over at Evan, who had crept downstairs and was leaning against a bookshelf near the back.

Marianne flashed me a wink before continuing. 'Tonight, the Book Nook on the Beach is very pleased to welcome our new local author – *andmyboyfriend* – Drew Inkbridge, who will give us a reading from his blockbuster bestselling creepy novel from last year, *A Cliff to Die On.*'

Not sure I would have added the boyfriend part, but Marianne could say whatever she wanted if she was willing to host these things and I didn't have to get up there and flail about trying to remember how to form a sentence in public. I joined in with the welcoming clap as Drew stood and Marianne took the seat on the other side of me and we shared excited smiles.

As Drew read aloud, his voice deep and enthralling, I kept glancing at Marianne. She was hanging off his every word, smitten with her latest flame, and I was happy for her. She loved hard and lived hard – and I'd always loved that about her.

'Isn't he lush?' Marianne whispered to me as Drew leapt off his chair and dragged a hand through his hair, getting into the scene he was reading as if he was auditioning for Macbeth up there.

'He's doing great,' I replied. The audience thought so too, and I could see one or two plotting the route from their chair to the book stack so they could be first in line and avoid missing out.

'Shall we all have dinner sometime?' I whispered to her, all of a sudden awash with the feeling of having been a bad friend by not really getting to know her new man very well, despite him being in the shop so often I wondered if he should be added to the payroll.

Marianne tore her eyes off him to beam at me. 'Bloody *yes*,' she hissed. 'Maybe we could shack you up with someone and make it a double date.'

I was quite happy being the gooseberry, actually, but I was pleased she was up for the idea, and trained my eyes back onto Drew so as not to let them slide back towards Evan. Maybe it would help us reconnect if we put some effort into having fun together rather than making everything about work.

After the last customers had gone, Marianne, Drew and Evan braved the rain and went out for celebratory drinks, but I shied off, saying I'd get the shop cleaned up and then have a bath while I had the flat to myself for a couple of hours. I didn't say that to Evan, of course, just Marianne as she leaned in for a quick, buzzy hug before grabbing Drew's hand.

I could have joined them for drinks. Maybe I *should* have joined them, I thought, as I stacked the foldaway chairs back in the stockroom. Three of the buggers tumbled back onto my shin and I cursed into the darkness. It had been a successful night, though, so I should try not to feel resentful about clearing up on my own when I'd explicitly told them all it was fine and to go ahead. Even after Evan said to at least leave the chairs and he'd pack them up when he came back in, and I shook his hand on it just for an excuse to touch his skin, I'd still taken it upon myself to finish the job, so I only had myself to blame.

I took that bath, sinking into the warm water until just my nose poked out from the surface, and I watched the steam rise as if I was an alligator. I stayed there in the tub for a while, giving my feet a break, giving my back a chance to un-hunch. Afterwards, wrapped in a towel, I put some fish and some veggies in the oven to start cooking, made myself a warming cup of tea and drew my curtains, shutting out the storm for the day, once and for all.

Briefly, I considered putting clothes back on in case Evan reappeared, but I was too sleepy to care what he thought of my outfit (and he never seemed to be one to care about outfits, seeing as he was most often in half a wetsuit or a pair of board shorts), and I changed instead into my most luxuriously comfortable PJs. On went my home-made playlist of hygge music and I opened my laptop, navigating to the first of my bookmarked pages.

Filling my screen was an image that made me salivate. A big, beautiful beach with a palm tree lolling over the sand, the sun glinting off the sea, the headline 'Ten Reasons to Tempt You to the Cook Islands'. I scrolled the page, skimming the words, drinking them in: *coconut, relax, South Pacific, sundowner, massage. Mmm, now we're talking.*

When I got to the bottom I hungrily clicked through to another article. 'One Year in China: Adventures on a Bicycle'. I bit my lip looking through the photographs of temples and rice terraces.

I spent the next twenty minutes opening and closing tabs, pausing only to grab my dinner from the oven, flitting between pages of online travel magazines, reading any new stories and revisiting some favourites. Scrolling through travel-blogger feeds on Instagram. I was bordering on obsessive, like some kind of tourism pervert.

This had become something of a habit over the past year, a guilty pleasure sparked by a range of big hardback books we'd got in stock that sang about all the destinations you should visit before you die. It was a long time since I had last taken a vacation. At least since the shop opened, and doing this was like a harmless little reminder of the trips Marianne and I used to make together. That felt like so long ago now, though she still took time off occasionally. She'd gone to Madrid for a long weekend last autumn, on her own, and she'd asked if I wanted to come but we couldn't both have left the shop. This was my way to escape, my peephole into another world while I was way too tied down to go and see it for myself.

It wasn't something I did every night, just sometimes when I needed some brain TLC.

I remember this next moment so clearly, everything about it. The taste of the oil and salt on my tongue from the flake of local mackerel I'd just put in my mouth. The tangy aroma under my nose of the red wine I'd brought home. The weight of my long bob piled messily on top of my head. The sound of Selena Gomez singing 'Bad Liar', a song whose soft beats always put me in the mood for the sun.

I'd just clicked onto the travel pages of a lifestyle magazine I liked, tempted by the photo before even reading the headline. It showed an archipelago of islands resting in a cobalt sea. Each one atop an almost luminous mint skirt where the shallow water bathed over white sand. The islands looked like diamonds, glowing inside a velvet jewellery box.

Smiling, reaching for another delicious mouthful of mackerel, I then saw the headline:

*When Can You Start? Take the Plunge and Be a Bookseller on Bounty Cove Cay.*

Wow. A resort in the Maldives, on a private island, was looking for somebody to take a temporary position to launch a hotel bookshop, in the hope that it could be part of a push for a new type of clientele.

When could I start? *Right now, please!* I put down my fork and took a swig of wine, chuckling to myself as I read further into the article. Could you imagine? I mean, if I didn't have a shop to run and customers relying on me, and a business partner who wouldn't take kindly to being ditched.

According to the article it was the 'dream job', with accommodation included, and open to international applicants. They were expecting a *lot* of applicants, apparently.

But just *imagine* …

The door opened at that point and I closed my laptop quickly, which probably looked way more suspicious than what I was actually doing. But in walked Evan, who met my eye from across the room, a smile spreading across his face as he regarded me for a hot minute with what I was sure was a warm twinkle in his eye, and I forgot all about the article.

# Chapter 3

# Marianne

Marianne held on to Drew's hand tightly as they walked back through the quiet, lamp-lit streets of Bayside. She was *so* proud of him, and so proud to be with him. He'd shone in their bookshop tonight and then had made such an effort to get to know her brother over drinks in the pub afterwards. Now, Evan had returned to Jenn's home above the shop, and she was taking Drew back to her flat. The storm had retreated and the pavements were left glistening in the dark with pools of resting rain.

'You're a natural in front of people, you know,' Marianne said. 'You had the audience eating up every word. I think you sold every copy of your book.'

Drew tucked her in under his arm and grinned. 'Thanks. Let's hope they're still hungry by the time I've written this second one.'

'They will be,' she said with full confidence. She remembered Jenny's question from earlier in the night. 'You don't get nervous doing this kind of thing, do you?'

'Oh, completely!' he laughed, and she turned to him in surprise.

'You do? But you seem so confident up there.'

'I fake it. I mean, I'm not faking enjoying it or faking my emotions, but I'm faking the confidence. I get nervous, but I do it anyway, because I want to.'

'Huh,' Marianne replied. She'd assumed he was like her and a bit of an extrovert, but she kinda liked that he had a secret sensitive side that only she knew about. At least, she was the only one in Bayside. It was good to have somebody 'new' around, someone she didn't already know everything about. Living in such a small town, it sometimes felt like everyone had already dated/snogged/fancied everyone else. 'Well, you were great, and I loved being right there to cheer you on.'

He glanced at her, a grin on his face, as if to convey that he was pleased she was there too, and she snuggled into him for a moment, radiating in his warmth. They continued walking by closed shopfronts, their wares twinkling out in the dark from behind the glass windows.

Bayside might not be big, but it had everything you could want. Cute shops, nice pubs, tasty eateries, a wide beach and kind people. When she was young, Marianne had imagined herself living in London or moving from country to country in some high-powered, nomadic role. And for a while, she did travel with the cruise ship, but Bayside was so full of memories that even though the breeze took her away on vacations from time to time, she'd moved back because she no longer wanted to be away permanently. She *wanted* to live among those memories now.

So why did she keep feeling as though she had itchy feet these days?

'What are you thinking about?' Drew asked her as they turned the corner and began climbing the hill towards her home, leaving the sleepy town in their wake.

'My mum,' Marianne replied, and he tightened his arm around her. Drew already knew the basics of the story, that Marianne's mother had passed away a little over ten years ago now, back when she was still at school, from the horrible C-word. It had been the worst time in her life, and she still missed her mum every day. With Evan at university and Marianne's dad living in Germany (though both had come back for a while), Jenny's mum had taken in Marianne, who subsequently clung to Jenn like family. As soon as she could, though, she left Bayside to travel the world and leave the memories behind. But she'd changed since then.

There'd not been a single thing Marianne could have done to stop her mum from passing away. The only thing she could do was vow to live her life to the full. It was a vow she was sometimes afraid that she wasn't remembering to stick to.

'She'd be really impressed with you, I bet,' Drew said. 'Owning your own shop. And also impressed with Evan. He was telling me when you went to the loo in the pub that your mum used to go and watch him surfing at the beach all the time. I bet she'd like that he was back and pursuing life-saving.'

'It's true. She wasn't like your average mum who'd probably be worried about the height of the waves and wishing he'd come in closer; she was always cheering him on, encouraging him to join clubs, get his qualifications. She just wanted him to do what he loved. I, on the other hand, would be sat on the beach next to her, usually with Jenn, talking about which of his friends we wanted to snog one day. And then running far away if they came past.' Marianne laughed at the memory.

They reached her house and she led the two of them up the external steps to the entrance to her first-floor flat. She liked that Drew was slowly getting to know more about her, and she about him. They had a lot to learn, but he was the first love interest she'd had that she actually *wanted* to open up to.

But anyway, enough thinking. She held open the door for him. 'Mr Inkbridge, world-renowned author, can I interest you in a nightcap?'

At first light, Marianne's eyes opened to a sight she hadn't seen in days: sunshine! At least, the promise of sunshine to come. It was just past seven and the skies were a pale, cloudless blue, not a hint of rain in any direction. It might still feel like a chilly February outside, but in her heart it was – even if just for a day – a sign of the spring to come.

'Get up, get up,' she said, tapping on Drew's bare torso while he snoozed in her bed.

'Morning,' he rasped. 'Oof, that nightcap finished me off. I have a headache.'

'I know what'll cure it – let's go *swimming*!'

'Pardon?'

'In the sea. Let's go for a dip before I go to work. The storm's passed and you'll feel better in no time. Believe me.' Actually, she couldn't remember if sea swimming had ever cured one of her hangovers, but she felt awake and alive so she was willing to try.

Drew sat up and rubbed his face. 'Any chance I could join you tomorrow instead? I woke up in the middle of the night and realised a massive plot hole in my last three chapters and it took me bloody ages to fall back asleep. I think I need to get on it before my thoughts disappear.'

'Is this just a ruse to get out of plunging into the wintery British sea?' she side-eyed him.

'Only a bit. Next time, though, I promise.'

'OK. Oh, before I forget – Jenn said yesterday we should all go for dinner sometime.'

Drew prised open his drooping eyes. 'That sounds great!'

'It does?'

'Yes, she's your best friend and … well … I was kind of getting the impression she didn't approve of me, so this must be a good thing.'

'She loves you!' Marianne cried, which might have been an exaggeration, but Jenny had no reason *not* to love Drew. 'She's just tightly wound. Seriously, all she does these days is live and breathe that shop so she's probably just been distracted.' Marianne left him in bed (not easy) and changed into her long-sleeved swimsuit, pulling on joggers and a sweatshirt over the top. It was going to be *freeeeeeeezing*, but what the hell. And she knew somebody who'd be up for joining her.

'Morning, sis!' Evan called from the beach, where he was already waxing his board. The sun was now well above the horizon, casting a golden light on the surface of the water.

'Morning, dummy!' she called back good-naturedly, coming to stand beside him. 'Thanks for meeting me. I take it you couldn't coax Jenny to join us for a refreshing dip?'

'Jenny?' Evan laughed, looking a little abashed. 'I haven't even seen her this morning. Did you want me to ask her?'

'No, I'm just kidding. It's nice to have some brother-sister time. Besides, she's busy and you have nothing going on in your life.'

'And how's your famous author boyfriend this morning? Have you convinced him yet to prove his love by naming a character after you?'

'Shut up,' Marianne chuckled, shoving him.

'He seems cool, actually. It was nice to spend time with him last night. I feel like the two of you have a similar vibe, like you're destined for big adventures together.'

'He likes you too.' Marianne watched the rolling waves for a moment. Drew was nice, she was really starting to like him a lot. Which scared her a little; she wasn't one to let people get close, and she was determined not to lose herself in the process. She'd just have to make sure they stayed spontaneous, kept living their lives wild and free. 'I wish Jenn had come along, though. To the pub, I mean.'

'Yeah, I think she was just tired.'

'Of course she was, she's always tired because she's always working. It . . .' She shook her head. She didn't want to bad-mouth Jenny in front of anyone, let alone Evan, who was now living with Jenn.

'What?' he coaxed.

Marianne sighed and glanced behind her to where she could see the bookshop in the distance, partially hidden behind the seafront railing, its lights already on even though it wouldn't be opening up for another hour or so. 'It's just that I think she really needs a break. Ever since she moved into that flat it's like you can't drag her away from work. And it makes me look like an asshole because I'm not there *all the time* and because sometimes I take time off to go on trips or just chill. But that's how it should be, right? We own our own business, so we should have *some* freedom?'

'Have you said this to her? Maybe she needs to be forced into a mandatory holiday or something.'

Marianne went back to facing the sea and with a deep breath peeled off her clothing, the cold morning air kissing the skin not covered by her swimsuit. 'I've said this to her countless times. Countless. But she just says she's fine. So if that's how she wants to be, I can't force her to change. And I'm still going to take every advantage of being my own boss and live my life.' She faced her big brother, getting ready to run into the surf. 'Last one in the sea is a stupid twat called Evan.'

Fresh, invigorated and pretty chilled to the core, Marianne crossed the beach up to the bookshop, with one small pit stop, and, tinkling open the door, trailed sand across the blue carpet.

'Jennyyyy,' she called, and Jenn, as predicted, poked her head out of the stockroom, where she had been working away for a while already.

'Morning,' Jenn replied, coming out with an armful of books, her eyes noticeably flickering to the sand. Marianne ignored her look – sand was something that got walked into the shop daily around here, it was no big deal.

'Thanks for cleaning up everything last night – I did tell you I'd help if you left it until today.' Marianne dumped her backpack on the counter, sending some inventory sheets fluttering to the ground. She really would have helped instead of going swimming, but she'd learned with Jenn that there was no point trying to control a control freak. Instead, she pulled two small packages wrapped in greaseproof paper that she'd picked up during her small detour between the beach and bookshop.

'That's OK,' Jenn said, her back turned to Marianne as she restocked some travel guides. 'I just wanted to get it done.'

Marianne prised open one of the packages and wafted it towards the back of Jenny's head until she straightened, sniffing the air, and turned.

'Bacon sandwiches?' Jenn asked, her voice immediately sounding perkier.

'A thanks for supporting Drew last night. And saying you wanted to get to know him more.'

'Oh, Mari, you didn't have to do that ...' Jenn said, but the words were muffled, her mouth already wrapped around the deliciously buttery bap.

Marianne chomped on her own bacon sandwich, the two friends looking like polar opposites in their tiny shop. Jenny neat and professional in a knitted dress, burgundy tights and grey ankle boots, her make-up minimal and her hair pulled back into a ponytail. Marianne in sweats and flip-flops, her toes and fingers sporting chipped nail polish, her hair wild thanks to the breeze and the sea salt, her face bare but for a slick of hot-pink sunblock down her nose. The only thing they had in common right now was the look of serenity as they enjoyed their bacon sandwiches.

When she had finished hers, Marianne licked her fingers and grabbed her backpack, about to head up to Jenny's flat where she'd grab a shower and get changed. She paused at the door and turned to her friend, saying, 'Do you remember when we had those huge churros for breakfast on the beach in Spain?'

Jenny looked over, swallowing her last bite and nodding enthusiastically. 'Of course, they were incredible.'

'We thought we might come home and open a churro café, we were so convinced they cured our hangovers.'

'To this day, if I have a hangover, I'll find something doughy and sugary.'

Marianne laughed and looked at Jenn for a moment. 'Can't we go somewhere together again this year?'

Jenn's smile faded a little and she shrugged, her mind already made up. 'Who would look after the shop?'

'Then just you go,' Marianne said. 'I'm serious. Go to the beach in Spain, or Greece, or Australia, and eat enough churros for the both of us and then come back and tell me all about it.'

'No, Marianne, we have a business to run.' Jenn shook her head and turned away, and Marianne felt a ripple of hurt. She bit her tongue before they descended into their usual polite disagreement. Couldn't Jenny see she was trying to help?

# Chapter 4

# Jenny

Another week had passed, as had the storm, and the customers were no longer dripping on the books. But despite the sun making the sea glow again, and the promise of spring being just around the corner, I had this unshakeable feeling of *hmph*.

I knew I needed a break, but how could I take one? It felt like every tick on the to-do list created two more tasks. I just wanted everything to be perfect, and that took a lot of effort, especially as the stock turnover, the events, the community involvement, the profits and losses and all that jazz, just seemed to keep growing. Which was great, of course, but …

When I cried at discovering I'd just put out a whole box of new books before their publication days and had to pack them all back up again, I knew I was burned out. I am not a crier. I'm just more of a 'silently fume for three seconds and then find a practical solution' kinda girl. Marianne says my inability to let it all out makes me tightly wound, and it was the reason she bought me a box set of Nicholas Sparks DVDs at university. They didn't make me cry, but did give me an awakening on Liam Hemsworth, and feelings I carried with me for a good couple of years. Or more.

'Are you OK?' Marianne asked when I reappeared on the shop floor, which thankfully was clear of customers for a moment. 'Were you just crying?'

'No,' I rushed to say. I should have just told her, there really wasn't any reason not to be open with my best friend, but I couldn't admit it. As much to myself as to her. She gave me a look and then carried another armful of books towards the windows, where between me leaving to take back the not-yet-released novels and returning post-sob, it looked like someone had pushed over a bookshelf. 'What's going on? Why are all those books on the floor?'

'I thought we could switch up the window display again,' Marianne said, reaching down over the window seat into our wide window sill and scooping up an armful of our Mother's Day picks and dumping them on top of a nearby display table.

I looked at the books she'd dumped, how they'd jogged the neat pile underneath them. 'But we only put these out two weeks ago. Mother's Day hasn't even happened yet.'

'Oh, I know,' Marianne said with her back to me as she plucked more books from the window and chucked them behind her. 'But it's better to keep things fresh, and maybe you could put the Mother's Day picks somewhere near the counter.'

I gritted my teeth. 'What do you want to put in the window now?'

Marianne turned and grinned at me. 'I'm thinking, "Sun's out, get your buns out" – an inspiring collection of travel guides to get everyone in Bayside ready for a vaycay!'

'Wouldn't that be better in a couple of months' time, when it's actually nearly summer?'

'No, because then we'll want to dazzle them with all of our beach reads. This will be great, trust me.'

*Trust her.* I did trust her … to leave me to do all the hard work, as usual.

That probably wasn't fair. She wasn't being vindictive, I was just in a slump, exhausted and fed up. I could do with a few days going by between her 'exciting' ideas.

'Look at this.' Marianne held up a travel guide to Tahiti with a luxurious matt cover depicting a sparkling cyan sea with latte-coloured water villas on stilts. '*Sure* you don't want to get the hell outta Bayside and take a vacation here?'

'No,' I brushed her away. *There's that automatic lie again,* I thought to myself, a memory of the Maldives bookseller job whispering in my mind.

Marianne shrugged and put the book down in the window display, picking up *Lonely Planet's Best of USA* and flicking through, taking her time amid the heap of books all over the floor. In the middle of the workday. 'Suit yourself. I'm ready for a holiday, though. I might suggest to Drew that we go away somewhere, once he's finished his first draft.'

She wasn't exactly asking my permission, but she raised an eyebrow at me. 'Go for it,' I replied, reminding myself internally that other people were allowed to take time off.

*I* was the one who chose not to. I had no right to deny her a long weekend with her new man. 'By the way, did you input the expenses from the first Meet the Author into the accounting software like you were going to?'

'Hmm?' Marianne was perched on the low window sill, reading a page on New Orleans. She didn't look up, but said, 'Oh no, not yet. I will at some point. But you go ahead if you want to.'

It being a Friday night, and the end of a particularly frustrating day, I treated myself to a big salty bag of scampi and chips from the best chippy in town and walked back home along the seafront, scoffing my feast and hiding the chips from the nosy seagulls.

Evan was on a call in his room when I got in, and because our rooms were right next door to each other, I always felt like I was eavesdropping if I went in there when he was on the phone. Instead, I poured the last of my dinner onto a plate, opened some wine and lifted the lid of my laptop, ready for another delicious and much-needed dive into internet travel porn.

I clicked on an article about cheesemaking in France, followed by a list of sustainable safaris in Botswana, but despite the beautiful words and tantalising imagery I soon found myself on the website for Bounty Cove Cay, at the job selling books in their Maldives resort for three months. I just wanted to check the application deadline had passed, that was all, then I could put it out of my mind.

But … it hadn't passed. In fact, the deadline was this weekend. And the more I read, and then reread, and the more I swigged on my wine, the less out-there this whole concept seemed. For me, I mean. I could actually do this job pretty well.

Hang on, let me clarify: the *theory* of me being right for this job was perfectly sensible; I had the qualifications, the drive, the know-how. But the *idea* of me actually applying for a job across the other side of the globe, pitting myself against a world of other hopefuls, of not having Marianne beside me and leaving my own shop for three months … that was as out-there as you could get.

I wouldn't even consider dropping Marianne in it to run the bookshop by herself for a *week*; I was kidding myself if I was entertaining leaving for three months.

I navigated back to my French-cheese article, but much as I love *beaucoup de fromage*, my mind kept dancing back to Bounty Cove Cay.

I felt impulsive and naughty (but in a nice, structured way) as I typed away glowing answers to a series of questions about why I'd be the perfect candidate to pick for a job on a tropical island.

I never meant to start the application form. It was just a bit of fun, nothing serious. Only, by this point I was two glasses and seventy-five per cent of the online submission form in. I was whizzing my way through the questions, hungry to get more deeply lost in this imaginary world where I was as spontaneous as Marianne and as adventurous as the people behind the articles I liked to read inside my safe little flat.

*Detail your experience in a leading retail role, preferably within the book industry.* Oh, OK, let me tell you about MY OWN BOOKSHOP that I opened and have run for three years!

I'd all but forgotten Evan was in the house, so when he suddenly flung open his bedroom door it made me jump. But even the sight of him, casual in PJ trousers and a knitted sweatshirt dragged up his tanned forearms, that grin, that hair, those arms, couldn't distract me for long. 'Wine?' I asked, holding out the bottle and returning my gaze to the screen.

'Sure,' he answered, heading to the kitchen and grabbing himself a glass. I felt him move behind me, leaning down to look at my laptop screen, which I should have shut, but I was too in the zone. I felt his breath close and the weight shift as he leaned against the back of my chair. 'Are you doing it again?' he asked, his ASMR voice in my ear.

'Doing what?' I gulped, trying to defog my brain and remember he was *Marianne's brother.* I mean, Marianne probably wouldn't even care if I got another crush on him, or even if, by some twist of fate, he really did have feelings for me and it wasn't wishful thinking. Her brother was a great guy, we were all grown-ups and she was the most open-minded, 'do what makes you happy' woman I knew. Still, though. He was her brother.

'That thing you do with the wine and the secret travel blogs.'

I gulped. 'They aren't secret. You talk like I'm viewing them on the dark web.'

'*You* keep them secret.' He pointed at my screen, his arm brushing against mine on the way past and nearly causing me to hyperventilate. 'What's this? Are you applying for a job?'

'No, no.' I shooed him away; I really did need to focus. Even though I wasn't going to follow through and submit these answers. 'Well, yes, but I'm not actually going to apply, I'm just having a bit of fun.'

'You do strange things for fun. What is this fun job application, then?'

I explained it to him and couldn't keep the smile forming on my face as I spoke, and he soon sat down beside me, leaning in to take a look, until all of a sudden he turned to me, fixing me with a stare that took me by surprise.

'You *have* to apply for this,' he said.

I searched his eyes in case my answer was somewhere in there, but all I found was a fairly feeble, 'Why?'

'Because you could do this. Because it's the Maldives. Because I think ...' he trailed off and I wanted to catch the rest of that sentence, but he leaned back in his seat and shifted his eyes to his glass of wine. 'Well, why *not*?'

'Because I have a flat, I have the shop, I can't just take off for three months.' *It's not the kind of thing I do.* I continued, 'Because I can't leave Marianne for that long, that would be so unfair of me. Because I've never lived abroad on my own. Because I wouldn't know what I was doing. And because of ...' I looked at him, stopping myself from blurting out that actually one reason would be that me taking off might stop something from happening between the two of us. That it had been a long time since I'd felt even close to this about anyone. Instead, I concluded with, 'Well, there's also the fact that a million people are going to apply and I am not a stand-out-from-the-crowd kinda girl.'

'I think you are,' he answered, his gaze locking with mine for just a moment, and I didn't know if it was the wine, the make-believe Maldives dream or the words he was saying, but I felt a surge of *wanting*. I wanted him. And I wanted to go for this. 'Shooting my shot' was not a very Jenn move. It was way more in Marianne's comfort zone. So maybe it was what I needed to do, for a change.

But then he grinned, breaking the spell, and breaking our eye contact. I found him impossible to read at times. One minute I thought he was trying to send me a signal that he saw me as more than a flatmate, then the next minute I wondered if to him I was just his sister's best friend.

I said, 'That's nice of you, but really, I'm just dreaming. I'm not going anywhere.'

He shrugged and stood up, stretching, and then moved to the sofa, where he flopped down, looking all inviting. 'I'll just say one more thing,' he said, keeping his eyes on his drink. 'Marianne would love you to do something like this, I know it.'

I hesitated, not sure what to say to this. I didn't agree she'd be at all happy about me taking off for a quarter of a year if it meant she wouldn't be able to take any breaks during that time. I gulped some more wine and shook him out of my head. If I couldn't even tell my crush of ten years, finally, that I liked him, there was no way I was going to be able to take a risk like *this*.

'And,' Evan piped up once more, 'don't forget to mention in your "fake" application your passion for marine conservation. And the charity work the Book Nook supported over Christmas. And don't forget to hit that green button at the bottom of the page.'

'That's the submit button,' I said, in case he hadn't realised.

'Exactly.'

I would never actually take the job if I got it. What was the point in torturing myself?

Or would I torture myself more if I never knew what might have happened? I did like to torture myself, one way or another, so perhaps I should just take the door of failed opportunities today, as opposed to the one for missed opportunities. My life was *fun*.

'Should I press it?' I whispered to Evan.

'Yeah, go on,' he whispered back.

I knocked back my wine like I thought I was in a Wild West saloon. *Bugger it. Submit.*

# Chapter 5

# Marianne

'Jenny was being weird in the shop today,' Marianne declared over a bowl of pasta Drew had made for them one evening in March. He was a good cook. She hadn't known that about him until now, but she very much approved, and decided to stay at his rented shepherd's hut more often.

'Weird how?' Drew asked. 'Still snappy?'

Marianne winced at that, feeling bad at having complained about Jenn to her boyfriend. 'No, not snappy. Jumpy, perhaps? Like she had something on her mind but didn't want to talk about it. She kept staring into space and dropping things. Which is usually me, not her.'

Drew laughed. 'She'll tell you when she's ready.'

'Anyway, Mr Author,' Marianne changed the subject, 'how was your day today? Did you get a million marvellous words down on the page?'

'Maybe a couple. Actually, it went well today. I blasted out a few chapters, including one I was dreading because I didn't really know how to deal with a certain character.'

'Ooh, are they based on me?'

'The cantankerous fisherman with a motive to kill? Totally.' He smiled at her. 'Actually, I heard from my editor today. She wanted to know how it was all going, but also wanted to tell me she's going to be doing a fair amount of travelling in May and June. So she said if I can send her the first draft by the middle of next month, she'll try and get notes back to me ASAP but won't need the second draft until later in the summer.'

'Does that mean you'll be able to take some decent time off?' Marianne sat up, her food forgotten for a moment.

'Yes, I should be able to put the brakes on for a little bit, if I want. Which I do. It's been so busy, which is great, but I haven't had a break for probably over a year. So once this draft is in, I'm going to make the most of it, even if I have to do a bit of promotion and next-book plotting in between.'

Marianne put down her fork. 'We have to take a trip.'

'A trip? Where?'

'Anywhere! Everywhere! Drew, this is a rare opportunity – we need to grab life by the balls and take a vacation together.' *Yesss*, this was exactly what she'd been wishing for. In fact ... 'I actually brought home a stack of our travel books this weekend because I wanted to persuade you to come on holiday with me.'

'Are you allowed to take those from work?'

'I mean ...' Marianne hesitated. 'They're part of our stock, so we're just borrowing them ... it's fine, we're just using them for inspiration, I won't bring them near the pasta or anything.' She looked longingly towards the stack, but the pasta was just too delicious, so she went back to her meal. 'So where shall we go? Do you need to do a research trip anywhere for book three?'

'Um ...'

'Wait, is this too soon? Do you want to take a trip with me? Usually I'd go on my own, or in the past I used to go with Jenn, but, you know ...' The last time she'd seriously tried to get Jenn to go away with her had been about a year ago. There had been a festival up in Scotland and Marianne had wanted to close up shop for a few days for some good old-fashioned glamping. But Jenny had acted as though she was being forced to skydive without a parachute and the whole idea had fizzled out rapidly.

Marianne was getting tired of trying to nudge Jenny into relishing the benefits of being your own boss: making brave and creative decisions about your business, working out hours that could suit the schedule you wanted, plus having a great work/life balance because you could take ... well ... not *unrestricted* holidays, but at the bookstore they didn't have strict, apportioned annual leave days like she'd had in previous jobs. She wished Jenn would relax more, but since she wouldn't, Marianne had a habit of overcompensating, hoping it would rub off on her best friend. But the thing was, Marianne didn't want to feel guilty about living her life differently to Jenn, and Jenn got so huffy when Marianne brought up wanting time off that it was easier just to spring it on her unapologetically.

Drew scooted his chair closer to hers and leaned over for a smacking great kiss, before grinning and saying, 'I'd bloody love to go on a trip with you, Marianne!'

'This is so exciting, I haven't been away for *sooo* long,' Marianne exaggerated. At least, not for any real stretch of time. 'Let's make it a decent-length holiday, though, something long haul and adventury.'

'How much of a decent length were you thinking? I wouldn't normally be able to do this, but with no commitments in the calendar, a long deadline from my editor and the fact it's been a while since I've taken time off ... I could probably combine all my leave and stretch to a couple of months. If you didn't mind me keeping on top of a bit of social media and research while I was away.'

'A couple of months!' Marianne shrieked, getting giddier by the second. This would be the perfect way to keep things fresh and exciting between her and Drew. It would be a hard one to run by Jenn, though. 'I'm not sure I could wangle that much time off work, although I'm pretty sure Jenny doesn't really need me around any more anyway, ha ha ha.' She felt a little stab inside her as she made the joke. 'Although two months would be amazing. What would you do with that, ideally?'

Drew thought for a moment. 'Maybe head to Australia and do the west coast? I did the east before uni, but never got around the west. You?'

'I'd take a road trip across the USA.'

'That didn't take a lot of thinking – is that on your bucket list?'

She nodded with enthusiasm. 'I'd love to start at one side and weave all around the mountains and the hot

South and the Plains and then end up at the other side. A swim in both oceans! Have you been?'

'I've been to New York a couple of times. I've always fancied doing a literary road trip through California and Nevada, like I read about a while back. You know, visiting places found in *The Big Sleep*, *Leaving Las Vegas*, etc.'

Marianne paused for a second. She really liked this guy, his wide smile, his infectious laugh, his talent, his kind heart, his tendency to jump in head first, like she did. She wanted to do this with him, *for* him. 'Let's do it.'

'What?' he laughed, but already she could see that excited twinkle in his eye.

Yes, this could work. The timing was great, actually, with his book being in soon, and they'd be back before the school holidays, which was always a busy time in their shop thanks to the influx of tourists in their small town on the coast. In fact, their big summer programme of events would be starting in July, so she'd even be back before all of that kicked off. Jenn would understand. Sure, two months was a long time to leave her in charge of the shop, but they could hire a temp to help, and Marianne could offer to do all weekends for the rest of the year to make up for it. Besides, she hadn't been *entirely* joking about the idea of Jenny preferring to have her out from under her feet. So, she nodded firmly. 'Let's take a road trip. We'll stick to the West Coast, we'll take a couple of months, you'll find loads of inspo for your third big blockbuster, and we'll come back either hating each other or wildly happy and recharged. I think it's worth the gamble. Don't you?'

# Chapter 6
# Jenny

I was acting weird at work. I knew it, but I couldn't stop it, and I thought Marianne had noticed. The thing was, I got an email in the middle of the day about the bookseller job in the Maldives. They wanted me to interview.

By the following morning, which, thankfully, was a Sunday so the shop was closed (though I'd probably scoot down there for a bit, just to do some admin and stocktake), I knew what I had to do.

Sitting in front of my laptop in serene silence, Evan being out with the beach lifeguard crew, I opened the email from Bounty Cove Cay inviting me to the Zoom interview in a couple of days.

OK. There was no easy way to say this, to say I didn't want to proceed with my application, that I was withdrawing from the interview, because if I listened to my heart instead of my head, I'd hear it shouting at me to get away from that keyboard.

I resisted the urge to torture myself with yet another Google Images search of the minty archipelago of Maldivian islands. This wasn't a time for dreaming wild fantasies and playing at other lives. I had my own life, here, and it needed me.

*Dear—*

A commotion near the door of my flat pulled my attention away, and seconds later Marianne burst in without knocking, which was pretty typical of her, but she was beaming more than usual and for a second it felt like maybe all the tension between us had been nothing more than my imagination.

'Jenn, you're home!' As she twirled in and went directly to the fridge to slurp my juice straight from the bottle, I shut the lid of my laptop.

'I've come to tell you something exciting, but also to ask a teeny little favour.' She bounced through my apartment, a vibrant tornado, billowing herself in the cushions on the sofa.

'What is going on?' I asked.

'I have news. Very exciting news, and it involves me, and Drew, and fun in the sun.' She was bursting, absolutely bursting. I didn't think I'd seen her this excited since Justin Timberlake did a UK tour while we were at school and I agreed to bunk off with her to go and see him. I liked seeing her this happy. Whatever it was about, Marianne didn't have it easy, so as much as I begrudged her at times, I did love that happy face.

'Spit it out then.' I was imagining some big new idea to pop out of her about a summer seafront literary festival we would single-handedly be running. I certainly wasn't expecting her to say:

'We – Drew and I – are going to take road trip, a vacation, you know, like we spoke about the other week.'

Oh. It was *that* kind of favour. The 'I'm taking a week off, you'll look after things here, right?' kinda favour. 'Where are you two going?'

'Well, the thing is, Drew's going to finish the first draft of his book in the next few weeks, so he will have a bit of a gap in his schedule. And we're not too busy in the shop for a while, so it makes sense to take this amazing opportunity.'

I don't think I have to tell you what I was thinking. Forcing myself to sound jolly, because although I was happy that she was happy to be taking this step with her boyfriend, it did feel like another one of Marianne's whims, I asked her, 'How big is this road trip?'

'We're going to the USA, a literary book tour or something, Drew called it. And if we're going all that way it has to be done properly.' She waved her hand in the air like that was obvious and only a fool would say otherwise.

We were teetering on an edge here, like we had been for a few months, where I tried to keep the business running and Marianne made me feel like all I was doing was being a massive drag.

Marianne stood up on my sofa twirling an imaginary lasso, which she tried to catch me with, but I asked again, 'For how long?'

'A couple of months.'

'*A couple? Of months?*' I tried to find my words. 'You're taking off for several months to have an extended holiday?

With your latest boyfriend?' I couldn't help but laugh, but I was aware it was coming out a little manically.

Marianne's eyes narrowed a little at 'latest boyfriend'. 'Yes,' she answered me, then took a deep breath. 'I know it's a little out of the blue, but we've spoken before about holidays and I know you don't like to take them any more, but I do, and I don't want to always feel bad for that. I'm excited about this trip, I'm excited about doing this with Drew. Can you be excited for me?'

'Can I be excited that you're just dropping everything and assuming I'll hold down the fort on my own for two months?'

She sat back, a frown cutting through her happy sparkle. 'What difference does it make to you, really?'

'It makes the same difference it always does, Marianne – it's the expectation that you can do whatever you want and I'll always just be there to pick up the pieces.' Was she kidding? I paused, trying to verbalise what I felt. 'You're just ... you're just going for it, aren't you?'

She wouldn't meet my eye. 'I've been feeling weird lately, not myself. Or more ... like I'm losing myself? I think I need to get out of Bayside and have an adventure. I need this, Jenny. Please be OK with it.'

I nearly relented. Of course I wanted to be excited and happy for her, especially if she felt she needed a break. But what about me? What about me?

'What are you annoyed about here, Jenn?' she asked, slicing into the silence. 'Are you annoyed that I made some decisions about my life without running them by you first?'

'It's not about running them by me, it's that you just make these decisions without even *thinking* of me.'

'I'm here, aren't I, how is that not thinking of you?'

'I don't think either of us should pretend you're asking me, though, should we?'

Marianne took a long inhale and I could see she was trying not to get mad. 'I don't have to *ask you*, Jenn, you aren't my boss. As much as you like to act like you are.'

Looking back, that was where it felt as though I took the first punch, a solid thwack in the ribcage. Marianne would probably argue that she'd taken the first punch when I shifted the conversation from this singular decision to 'these decisions'. 'I know that, but I am your partner. You can't just take off whenever you feel like it for months on end.'

'Before now, name one time I've left for months on end.'

'Name one time I've taken longer than three days off in a row since we opened.'

She laughed and wagged her finger in the air. 'Do not blame me for that. I am *always* encouraging you to take time off. Just because you have to be some kind of saint of the bookstore, working all hours even though we both know you could be just as productive in half that time, doesn't mean I have to do the same.'

That wasn't fair. That wasn't fair at all. All my endless hard work reduced to me trying to be a saint? My heart beat loudly and my mouth became dry with all the scratchy words I was catching to stop myself from saying them. I tried to reason with her.

'I'm not being a saint, Marianne, but someone has to keep the business running. There's only two of us, it's all on our shoulders, and you don't seem to care you'd be placing that weight entirely on me. What if I can't manage it and we start to lose business? What if I'm sick and can't open up for weeks? What would you do if I suddenly announced I wanted to take months off to jet around the world?'

'I'd say great, about time, don't forget to remove the stick from your arse before you go.'

'Oh really? You would? Because I could do it, you know.'

'I'd love to see that.'

I reached for my laptop, hesitating for only a moment, the usual, sensible Jenn clawing me back from this place where I was forgetting to just silently fume and take things on the chin. Then I ignored that Jenn and thrust an open web page at Marianne. It showed, in bright turquoise Technicolor, Bounty Cove Cay in the Maldives. 'I've been offered an interview for a job here. For three months. Starting at the beginning of April. So, yes, I could do exactly what you're doing, only I wouldn't leave you to look after the shop on your own like that.'

Marianne looked up from my laptop and into my eyes. 'You've been offered a job?'

'An *interview* for a *temporary* job, yes.' I closed the laptop again. That wasn't how I'd meant to tell her about it – *if* I ever told her about it – but it was out there now.

'Doing what?'

All right, maybe I should have listened to Sensible Jenn's voice. 'Running a bookshop, in a resort.'

'In the Maldives? The actual Maldives?'

I nodded.

'How did they find you?' she asked.

'I applied. Just for fun – I didn't think anything would come of it.'

'But it did.' Marianne looked confused, hurt, and part of me wanted to reach out to my best friend, but I was still kind of mad at her for what she was doing. 'You're applying for jobs now, for fun?'

'No, not jobs plural, just this job, and I wasn't looking for a new job or anything, I was looking at some travel articles online and saw a piece about this.'

'When's the interview?'

This was sounding worse by the minute. 'On Tuesday. It's a video interview. You can imagine how awkward I'd find that.'

But Marianne didn't seem amused. 'Well. Congratulations.'

This was going off track. 'Anyway, I was going to turn it down.'

'So why haven't you?'

'I just haven't yet. But I was going to. I was just starting to email them when you came over.'

She stood up and collected her things. 'I see. You don't trust me. My contribution to our business is, as always, less than yours, and I couldn't possibly manage things without you.'

'I didn't say that.' But I had meant it – as terrible as that made me.

Marianne sighed. 'You know, if you stopped trying to be so perfect you might actually be a bit brave. I've been waiting a long time for you to climb out of your own head and think about what you want, what would actually make you happy. I'm realising now that for you to be happy you need us *both* to just never grow, never change, to never have experiences, just work, all day, every day.'

'That is so unfair, I've never tried to hold you down—'

'This is just how I imagined our future when we opened a business together, Jenn,' she continued, her voice laced with sarcasm that diluted into sadness. 'The world is in our hands. As long as our fists remain tightly closed, right?'

Marianne headed for the door and part of me knew I should stop her, but I was too incensed. How could she be mad at me when she was the one who was always taking advantage of my dependability, always expecting me to put in the hard work and pick up the pieces? I was even going to turn down this once-in-a-lifetime job because I didn't want to put us both in a bad position. And now she was mad at me?

I didn't stop her, because right then I didn't know what to say. I only knew that this wasn't finished, but I let her leave anyway.

The next forty-eight hours were the tensest that Marianne and I had ever been through together. Except, we weren't together, we were avoiding each other at all costs, Marianne busying herself with customers and then leaving at closing time without a goodbye, while I dealt with as much as I could out the back, making myself absent around the end of the day.

By Tuesday morning, it was too late to cancel the interview. I'd meant to, but I'd got caught up in work and in my own head. And, yes, maybe I also didn't one hundred per cent *want* to cancel. Maybe I wanted to interview to see what would happen, to spite Marianne. Maybe I just didn't want to release the fantasy back out into the atmosphere just yet, but keep it mine for just a little longer.

Because of the time difference between here and the Maldives, my interview was scheduled for 7.30 a.m., and Evan – who'd probably been told by Marianne during a rant about yours truly – had made himself scarce on a morning surf.

So here I was, sitting in front of my laptop, neat and tidy, my nails trimmed and that button on Zoom which says 'touch up my appearance' pushed, when the screen came to life and a panel of three ever so slightly pixellated strangers appeared before me.

'Good morning,' smiled the woman in the middle. She introduced herself as Khadeeja, one of the Bounty Cove Cay resort directors, and then introduced her colleagues as Something and Someone, names that of course I immediately forgot because I became fixated on my own thumbnail image. Had a button popped open on my shirt? Risking a quick downwards glance under the guise of paper shuffling, I confirmed all was fine. *Here goes nothing.*

They asked questions, I answered, it was pretty standard interview stuff, but all I could see was me in that thumbnail, tripping over my words, taking too long to think of examples, coming across as the least sunny, luxury-resort type I could imagine. I just couldn't shake the thought of Marianne and the fact I knew I couldn't do this. Even though, when Khadeeja explained more about the role, a part of me felt like I really, really could.

I drank some water as Khadeeja and her colleagues murmured to each other for a moment before facing me again from their office across the world. 'That's about it. Any questions for us?'

I cleared my throat. I knew I'd fluffed it; I wouldn't hire a big bland butty like me. But there was one thing I was curious about. 'What made you open this out to international applicants?'

'It's threefold, really,' answered Khadeeja. 'One, because we already have a new manager lined up for the start of the next high season – she's actually a Maldivian resident, like me – but we'd like to start the ball rolling and test the waters, as it were, before then. This means we need somebody who can start as soon as possible, with experience similar to yours, and opening the job up internationally gives us a bigger pool. Two, we pride ourselves on having a well-treated staff who are as diverse and international as our customers. We like to think we're getting a rich variety of experience, and giving our staff a rich experience back.'

Oh, well that was quite nice to hear.

'And three, because, to be frank, it's good publicity for us to advertise an opportunity like this. You may have seen a similar scheme called the "Barefoot Bookseller", where one of the other resorts here opens a pop-up bookshop on the beach every year and has an international hunt for somebody to run it. For the right person, this could be a great opportunity and adventure, and we want to appeal to someone with that adventurous streak. This means the advert gets exposure beyond the usual job listing, which means we're promoting the resort around the world at the same time.'

An adventurous streak? Now I should definitely just hang up. Why did I think this could be the job for me? Except ... I was on this call, wasn't I? Interviewing for a temp job on a tropical island?

'To sum up what we're looking for, Jenny, and to be very clear,' continued Khadeeja, 'what we're dealing with here is not a business that needs saving – a magic wand waved over it and a new lick of paint. We don't have a bookshop here yet, just a space we'd like to turn into one. We were impressed by your ...' She paused and I saw her look down at her notes '... your Book Nook on the Beach start-up in the UK and the profits you've made opening an independent store in a tourist town.'

She seemed to be looking me straight in the eye, through the camera. 'We want someone self-sufficient and organised, who can start soon, work hard and won't mind that there's no chance of the job continuing after three months, perhaps because they have something else to go back to, and with the experience to launch a bookshop. Does this sound like you?'

I gulped. Because actually … it did.

When the interview had concluded and I ended the call, I sat back. Well, that was that, it was definitely over now. But then, hadn't I always known it wouldn't get to the point of me getting on a plane? I couldn't be sad about something that was never going to happen anyway.

I sighed, my silent flat now feeling too silent, too … flat. Even the waves outside my window didn't give me the familiar feeling of comfort and belonging they always did, because, well, they *always did*.

I guess it would have been nice to look out at different waves for a time.

They wanted me. The Bounty Cove Cay resort wanted *me*. I was being offered a three-month live-in job selling books in the Maldives, the same one I'd seen advertised and merrily applied for only a couple of weeks or so before.

I saw the email when I got home – that they'd made their decision already – but I didn't tell anyone. Not Marianne, not my mum and dad, not Evan; I didn't even say it out loud to myself.

That night, I didn't sleep well. My argument with Marianne had left me with knots in my stomach as big as Chelsea buns, and I was a bag of worries about what to do, teetering between giving in and doing whatever she wanted, and standing my ground. But also because, well …

I wanted to go to the Maldives. Not just because I needed a holiday, or just to spite Marianne. But because something in me ached to open that door and let something *change*, and if I didn't change something, I might suffocate.

*A change is as good as a rest.* That's what they say. Taking a new job, albeit a temporary one, wasn't the break I'd originally craved, but a change of scenery, and some space between me and Marianne, could be just what I needed to restore my passion for the Book Nook, couldn't it? Besides, I already knew exactly how to run a bookstore, so this would be an adventure, not a risk.

I stared at my ceiling for a long time, between 1.23 a.m. and 3.16 a.m. to be precise, rolling through a list of the pros and cons, but all I kept coming back to was this deep-seated feeling in me that I wanted this for myself. I wanted this experience, this adventure. I wanted to feel alive, and not stressed. I wanted to see those internet images come to life. And I was being offered this dream on a plate – a chance to wander, but not get lost.

The next morning, before the Book Nook opened, I found Marianne had come in early and was tweaking her window display. Evan was up a ladder hanging something that, from what I could see around him, looked like paper aeroplanes.

'Hi,' I said, trying to keep my voice relatively neutral.

Marianne didn't say anything.

'Hi,' Evan replied, giving me a smile and throwing an aeroplane down onto his sister. I liked that he was there; it made me feel less alone.

'So, um,' I started, facing Marianne, whether she wanted to face me or not. 'I had my interview yesterday, for the temporary job. In the Maldives.'

'And?' she asked, standing up to face me. She was cold ... I thought ... but she also seemed a little sad, unless I was just projecting.

'And, they offered me the job.' My eyes flicked to Evan, who broke out in a huge grin.

'You bloody legend!' he cried, and Marianne thwacked him, wobbling the ladder.

She turned back to me. 'And?'

'And, I don't know ...'

Marianne sighed. 'Would you just tell them yes and go for it?'

'What about your trip?'

'I still want to go on my trip. More than anything. But I refuse to become someone you spend your life resenting because I made you stay when you were finally about to do something for yourself. I'm not letting you do that to me.' Her tone was steely, which I'd never been on the receiving end of before. I didn't like it much out there in the cold.

'Well, we can't both go,' I shot back.

'We could, if we just got a temp or something,' she grumbled in reply.

'This is our shop, Mari. It's our business. It's our livelihood. Whose hands we would leave it in is not a tiny detail; we have to give it to the right person, because it's too precious not to.'

Evan cleared his throat and stepped off the ladder. 'I have a suggestion.'

'Shut up, Evan, we don't need your mansplaining right now,' Marianne snapped, but he just laughed.

'I wasn't about to mansplain, I wanted to offer my services.' We both turned to him and he shrugged, leaning back against the ladder. 'I'll do it. I'll look after the shop and then you can both go.'

He'd do what now?

Marianne shot him a look. 'You can't run our shop.'

'I could.'

I was about to tell him thank you but no thank you, then hesitated. 'Wait, what do you mean?'

'I mean, I've been keeping an eye out for temporary jobs. Before I can look at working full-time for the RNLI or get involved in training people, I need to retrain as a lifeguard myself for a couple of months over weekends and evenings, since any qualifications I had have lapsed. I'm not saying I'd do it for free – maybe we could cut some deal where I don't pay rent while you're gone or something, but I'm here, I'm available and you can trust me. Win-win.'

He was just like his sister – spontaneous, confident . . . kind.

For a moment, neither Marianne nor I had an answer for this unexpected proposal, and then the phone rang. Usually I'm the first to answer, but not this time, and when Marianne picked up, I took the opportunity to pull Evan closer by his sleeve.

'You don't have to do this,' I said to him, my voice low.

'I know, but it could actually work out pretty well for me, and if it helps you go away ... I mean that in the nicest possible way.'

'But ...' That stung a little. I searched his eyes, trying to see if he really wanted this, trying to see if it meant anything.

'Listen,' he glanced round to his sister, still on the phone, and then grazed the back of his fingers against my hand, leaving them there for a moment, warm against me. 'I think you need this. If you don't give yourself a break, I don't think things will get better between you and Mari, and I don't think you'll magically get happier.' He smiled down at me. Couldn't he see that he was making me more conflicted, more confused, with every look, every touch?

'What are you two whispering about?' Marianne huffed, trying to maintain her temper, although I could see she was musing on the idea.

'Looking for travel guides for the two of you,' Evan said, smooth as a chocolate button, picking one of the books out of the window display.

'Well, neither of us are going to Peru, so that doesn't fill me with confidence for you working here,' she said, grabbing the book from him and putting it back. Not in the same place. *I have to get out of here.* She faced me, her arms crossed in front of her. 'What do you think?'

'About Evan looking after the Book Nook? Um ...'

'I did manage a surf shop back in London, you remember. Plus, Mari, you'll still be around for a fortnight or so after J's gone by the sounds of it, so surely the two of us can't fuck it up that much?'

'Don't call her "J", you weirdo,' Marianne said, but secretly I liked it. 'Well, it's fine with me. I think it's good, actually. And then we can both go our separate ways.'

I nodded, slightly shell-shocked. I knew how close she was with Evan, and that once she'd simmered, she'd have him over for a beer and thank him properly. And even after I was gone, she would make sure he was all up to speed with the shop before she went away too.

I hoped.

'So that settles it then?' I asked. 'Are we both going?'

Marianne nodded and stuck out her hand to shake mine, which seemed formal and cold, but not enough to cool the spark of excitement that was igniting under my skin. 'We're going.'

I looked around my bookshop by the sea. This place was my baby, my second home. I'd never left it before and although I did think it would be safe, I was still afraid. When I'd imagined myself jetting off to the Maldives, back when I was happily filling out that online application form, one thing I'd never expected was to lose a friend over it. I couldn't help but worry if I was going to lose everything.

When the day arrived for me to leave for the airport, I couldn't believe how quickly it had come round. That morning I said goodbye to my parents, who waved at me from their doorstep like I was going off to war instead of to the tropics for three months. It seemed like only yesterday that I had been standing in the shop fighting with Marianne, and now I was leaving to travel up to London to stay there overnight before flying to the Maldives. She and I had barely spoken beyond discussing the logistics, such as how we'd keep both of our salaries going while we were away. Even our final goodbye had been a strained hug and a formal-sounding 'Safe travels.'

I knew she was still mad at me for applying for another job behind her back. And also, probably, for basically telling her I wasn't going to take it because she was too irresponsible to be left alone for three months. I was still mad at her for doing exactly what I'd been so afraid of doing to her, and doing it with barely a second thought, just assuming I'd pick up the pieces while she took off to America.

'You've not lost her,' Evan told me as I checked I had my passport for the fiftieth time. 'Believe me, I've been on the receiving end of her grumps on several occasions and they always come to an end.'

'But you're her brother, she has to like you.' I shook my head. 'I don't know, this just feels so much worse than something you can come back from. We said some pretty mean things. Things that can't be taken back.'

'Maybe they needed to be said,' he said, gently.

I shuffled my bags to the door and turned to face Evan, who was standing close. *What about the things you and I need to say?* I screamed at him silently, because I really didn't know if he wanted to say anything at all.

I wished I was someone who could throw caution to the wind and be brave and say how I felt. Instead, I studied him, my gaze capturing his face, his hair, his jawline, his torso, the line of his arm leaning against the door. I wanted to make sure, just in case this was the last time I could be this close to him, that I would remember every detail.

Evan's eyes were flecked with gold, as if they were always watching the sunset for the perfect waves. But this morning they looked sadder, greyer, like the overcast day outside, and I got so lost in them that it took me a moment to notice his other arm rise, his hand stopping on my upper arm, pulling the two of us a millimetre closer.

'I'll miss you,' he told me.

His touch burned through my sleeve and I nodded, my breathing shallow. Then I managed to take a tiny leap of faith and reply with 'I'll miss you, too.'

And then there were no suitcases, no clouds, no gap between us, just him and me, breathing together, warm against each other, and he held my gaze. It was as though it was the first time we were properly seeing each other, but in the same moment we saw something we'd known was there all along.

Evan kissed me, and it was as if all the years of wanting collided into one moment. His lips were salt water and home, and his fingers grazed the side of my head, loosening a lock of my hair.

But ... I had to go. I had to go and this could be nothing more than the perfect end before my new beginning.

'What was that for?' I asked when he pulled away.

'I don't know. It's just …'

I nodded. He and I felt like a slow, beautiful burn, and I couldn't explain it or what it meant. But I had a plane to catch.

And so our adventures began, with me stumbling on jelly legs away to the Maldives, Marianne due to leave a couple of weeks later for America.

If I was going to lose everything, I had to make the most of this and damn well find myself.

# Chapter 7

# Jenny, in the Maldives

I jolted myself awake. Even in my sleep my stomach had lurched forward when the plane dipped. 'Are we descending?' I croaked to nobody in particular, and strained to look out of the window from my place in the middle aisle.

Seatbelt signs were on, tray tables were up, seat backs were upright and passengers were rubbing sleepy eyes or putting on moisturiser, or scratching through their seat-back pockets for that tiny cellophane-wrapped square of flapjack they'd squirrelled away earlier. It was definitely nearly landing time.

I rolled my neck. After leaving the UK the evening before, a brief layover in Dubai and nearly thirteen hours of flying, I would shortly be arriving in the Maldives. And I still hadn't figured out the meaning of that kiss with Evan. Whether it was just a friendly goodbye, a come-back-to-me plea or a moment in time that meant precisely nothing. I was scrunched and exhausted and dry-skinned, but slowly, like a saline drip, the knowledge that I was nearly at my destination filled me with that vacation buzz I hadn't felt in a long time.

Forgetting Evan for now (because what else could I do?), I pulled my folder out of my seat pocket and checked my careful notes one last time, though I knew them off by heart by now. I was to arrive, go through passport control and baggage claim and all that, then follow the signs to the seaplane terminal and board my flight to Bounty Cove Cay, where I would arrive after about thirty minutes. I had ginger tablets in my handbag in case I felt travel sick in the tiny aircraft, along with a pair of what were basically glorified jelly shoes to change into at the airport, in case I was expected to step straight from the seaplane into the sea. I was organised and ready.

And yet ... The dream I'd just been having kept probing me, fidgeting to be noticed among all the very real and very pleasant thoughts, but what was it? Had I been dreaming about dating Zac Efron again, and him dumping me again? That was always a harsh one, which saddened me for a while after I woke up. No, wait, but it *was* about being dumped ... on a plane?

I didn't know. I tried to shake it off.

Although I couldn't see much of the action from my seat in the centre of the plane, I did spot flashes of turquoise sea advancing towards us as we approached the runway of Velana International Airport. Only then did it begin to sink in that I was really there. That feeling was heightened again as I stepped off the plane and straight into nearly thirty-degree heat, the humidity tickling the edges of my hair as I followed the line of passengers into the terminal. The bright blue sky and the sensation of my skin lapping up the heat, even under the light shirt I had on, were enough to make a wide grin spread over my face despite me plodding along on my lonesome.

After immigration, I watched the string of suitcases weaving their way on the baggage-carousel parade, looking for my own. I'd had it since I was a teenager and it was the colour of sand, with a bright blue strap and a sticker of a starfish so that it wouldn't get confused with anybody else's. Perhaps now I was twenty-eight it might be time to get a new case ... But for now, it was time to head to the seaplane lounge and go to my island.

Flying to my Maldives island on a seaplane made me feel like James Bond. With just a dozen or so passengers seated inside this tiny aircraft-with-skis-attached, it was cosy, cocooned and only mildly terrifying. The hum of the propellers was diminished slightly by the earplugs we were given, but all sound was drowned out when I leaned forward to peer into the open cockpit, only to see the pilot, who'd introduced herself to me as Layla, pull her waist-length black hair into a band and kick off her sandals to fly barefoot.

'Um,' I said out loud and she turned to face me, in the nearest passenger seat to her.

'We like to fly barefoot here in the Maldives,' she explained, with a wide and welcoming grin.

Any worries drifted away as we ascended high enough for me to look down at the view below, the view I'd not managed to see from my plane into the Maldives a couple of hours previously.

I pressed myself against the window but didn't dare breathe in case I fogged my view. The plane arced to the left, a sweeping soar that filled my vision with marbled mints, aquamarines, turquoises, cobalts and cyans. Sandbanks rose through the blues and greens like strings of white pearls, the bigger ones, the islands, dusted with the rich green of palm trees clustered together. White boats dotted the seas around some of the larger islands, a few leaving fading white streaks in their wake as they moved.

The plane cast a shadow upon the surface of the water and I followed it for a moment with my gaze, imagining this was what it would be like to watch a whale or a dolphin from above. I wriggled my toes inside my jelly shoes with anticipation and allowed myself the tiniest of squeals, which, thanks to the earplugs and the noise, was hidden from the other passengers.

We were closing in on an island the shape of a mussel shell, the plane creating a glorious circle in the sky above. Along one edge, the island had a long, wide beach whose sand melted into the ocean seamlessly. In the centre of the beach, a lengthy wooden pier stretched into the sea with coffee-coloured villas neatly positioned along both sides, holding on to the pier by individual walkways.

As the seaplane dipped further still, I noticed cabanas on the beach with light curtains billowing in the breeze, and sunloungers spread far apart for the utmost in uninterrupted comfort. There were people dotting the bay, swimming, sunbathing, strolling. Among the trees I could see glimpses of other buildings shading themselves, and a long boardwalk that seemed to circle the whole island, holding its guests in a protective hug.

Nope. *This* had to be my dream. Not that Zac Efron one – what was happening now. There was no way this island, this place, was my reality for the next three months. There was no way in heck somebody was actually paying me to be here.

'Next stop, Bounty Cove Cay,' Layla spoke over the tannoy.

*Noooooooooo.* I didn't want the seaplane ride to end. But also, yes! This really was happening! And as a bonus, we were about to land and I hadn't even needed my anti-vom ginger tablets, so double yes!

Around me, the other passengers were squeezing each other's arms in delight and gazing out of the window. I must have looked a bit strange being here on my own, but whatever. I watched the water get closer, and closer, and I wondered if Layla realised there wasn't a runway— Then *whooooooosh,* all of a sudden, we, the plane and all of us in it, were skiing on the water.

I realised, of course, it was called a seaplane for a reason, but it still took me by surprise to actually land on the sea. Especially this sea, which appeared so see-through and so like topaz-tinted glass that it barely looked as if it could hold up a manta ray, let alone a whole bloomin' plane.

I wondered if we would be getting out in the water and wading to shore. I also wondered what on earth I was thinking, bringing a suitcase that was basically island camouflaged with its sand-coloured casing, turquoise belt and starfish sticker. I was definitely going to lose it immediately if it got dropped in the ocean during our disembarkation.

Suffice to say, at a luxury island resort guests are not expected to jump in their Jimmy Choos straight into the sea, and we climbed out onto a clean, bright, wooden jetty. I was so busy shielding my eyes from the sun while trying to see everything before me all at once, I almost missed the bright yellow-orange mango juice being thrust under my nose until the sweet scent wafted into my consciousness and a voice said, 'Welcome to the Maldives, and to Bounty Cove Cay, miss. Please, have a drink.'

'Oh, actually, I'm—' I did start to tell the man, who was dressed in crisp white slacks and a short-sleeved shirt trimmed with silver thread. But before I knew it, I'd put the straw in my mouth and had taken a large slurp of the sunshine-sweet liquid, and the next thing I knew I was being handed a cool towel and my suitcase handle was being gently removed from my fingers.

'She's one of us,' Layla told him, appearing behind me and taking the suitcase from him.

'Sorry, I drank your mango juice,' I told him.

He laughed. 'Enjoy it!' He then moved his attention to another of the new arrivals.

'How was your flight?' Layla asked.

'Incredible,' I replied, gulping down the rest of the delicious drink before anyone could take it off me. 'So, do you work here too?'

'Yes, I'm the resort's main pilot for their private seaplane, plus I'm the skipper for their boats. Do you want to take a seat somewhere in the shade? I need to help out with the rest of the new arrivals, then I'll give you a bit of an orientation, walk you over to where you'll be living, and you can let me know if you have any questions.'

'I can just find my own way there, if you like?' I replied. 'You sound pretty busy and I don't want to be in the way.'

'Not at all,' she smiled. 'It's my pleasure. I won't be long. Here's a resort map, just so you can start to figure out your new home.'

Layla handed me the map, printed on colourful matt paper and rolled like a scroll. I almost expected to find a big X marking a spot when I unravelled it. I settled myself and my suitcase under the parasol of a lone sunlounger beside the jetty, avoiding sitting too close to the real guests as they relished the end of the afternoon sunshine, in case it was frowned upon, and opened my map.

Inside was a careful drawing of the whole island and I followed it with my finger, looking up to see these things come alive in front of my eyes, excited to explore, excited to *be*.

I enjoyed the gentle lapping of the tide, the quiet chit-chat of relaxed guests for a while. I didn't even want to guess how much it cost to vacation here. At one point, a woman walked past me on the beach with huge shades on her face, a wide-brimmed hat the colour of the sand and a swimming costume that seemed so perfectly second-skin I wondered if it was custom-made. She was listening to something through her AirPods, and she looked completely at ease. I wondered how long it took to get that island vibe. Because I, on the other hand, probably looked a right mess, having just stepped off a whole lotta plane.

Luckily, here was Layla again.

'Sorry for the wait.' She held out her hand to help me up from the lounger. 'Have you been looking at the map?'

'I have. There's so much here! From the sky it looks like it's all beautiful huts and palm trees, but it says there are three restaurants? Tennis courts? A spa? And do we get to eat at the restaurants?'

She laughed. 'You probably won't want to. They're delicious, but a little expensive when you need to feed yourself every day because you live here. Plus, you'll find that if the guests recognise you, you won't be able to tuck into a tuna taco without being asked for your latest book recommendations. We have just as yummy food in our staff dining room. But, yes, if you have an occasion you want to celebrate or have just had a particularly shitty day and want to treat yourself, you can eat there.'

'Tuna tacos?' I asked, my ears perking up.

'Any kind of fish taco you want,' she laughed. 'There's a lot of fresh fish in the Maldives, and a lot of what you'll eat here will be local. If not caught here or grown on this island, then from others nearby. By the way, did you know you've arrived on the island right at the beginning of Ramadan?'

I nodded. 'Yes.'

'Great. There won't be a change in service for the guests, but just be aware that any of our fellow staff members, or visitors, who observe Ramadan – it's called Ramazan here – will be fasting from sunrise to sunset. And in a month's time, as it comes to an end, there'll be Eid celebrations here on the island, which will be a lot of fun.'

'I can't wait!' I enthused.

'All right, I expect you're keen to see where you'll be living and freshen up, so I won't give you a full tour right now.'

At that, I gave myself a subtle sniff.

Layla continued. 'But follow me and we'll walk some of the boardwalk so I can point out a few things before we head over to your accommodation.'

We began walking alongside the main stretch of beach, the sea on our left, away from the jetty with the seaplane. 'We call it the "jet-setty",' said Layla. 'And this is the main beach, known as Coconut Cove. This is where visitors find the water sports, jet skis, they can book private boat excursions and also relax on the loungers, cabanas and daybeds.'

'"Cocktail Cove"!' I read the sign above an inviting-looking tiki hut that was surrounded by tanned sun-worshippers sipping on tall-stemmed drinks and sitting in front of platters of fruit.

'I love that place, it always has a nice, relaxed vibe, even for somewhere like this, which doesn't do a lot of "casual". From dawn till dusk, Cocktail Cove specialises in Prosecco cocktails and oysters, and the bartenders are just the friendliest. Oh, hey, Rish!' All of a sudden, Layla waved at a guy in the Bounty Cove Cay white shirt and turquoise shorts as he jogged lightly past us on the beach, carrying two snorkel-and-mask sets in individual white netting sacks. She looked again in the direction we were going. 'Further up the beach, you see those villas?'

'The ones on legs?' I pointed to the string of villas we'd flown over, which looked like people holding dress hems out of the water.

'Yep. Those are the Laguna Private Water Villas, and they are as expensive and awesome as they look. The bigger building at the very end is this stunning open-air restaurant called To the Moon.'

'Have you eaten there?' I asked. I didn't mean to be so obsessed by the food, but I couldn't help it.

'No, it's pretty romantic, so not the kind of place you just go to with friends. Or on your own,' she replied. 'On the other side is a private beach for people staying in the villas, along with another bar and BountEco, which is the sustainability centre and turtle sanctuary—'

'Oh, a turtle sanctuary!' I interrupted, as we veered off the beach onto another boardwalk that carved through the greenery, cutting across the small island.

'It's really lovely. And it's not far from the main staff accommodation building, which is right on the tip of the island. That's where you'll get your meals. We'll head over there this evening, so I'll show you it then.'

I wondered why we weren't going there now, since I'd thought this was a quick tour before she showed me my digs, but perhaps I'd misunderstood. 'How long have you worked here?' I asked Layla.

'Oh, for years! I can't even remember. Maybe seven or eight? I moved over here from Tahiti right when they were first opening this place. It's changed a lot, and it's just a beautiful place to work, but the management are always looking for ways to move with the times to try and make it stand out.'

'Wow, Tahiti.' I was impressed.

'That's where I was born and raised,' she said with pride. 'And my mother is originally from Hawaii. You can't keep me away from island life. What's it like where you live? In England, right?'

'Yes. It's by the coast, but the ocean seems a lot choppier than it is here, for a lot of the year! I live in a small town called Bayside, and I own and run a bookshop by the sea.'

'Ah, hence you coming here to kick the bookshop into shape. So, who's running the shop while you're gone?'

I hesitated. 'My business partner's brother. I hope.' I laughed to try and dispel the nervous tinge in my voice.

Layla nodded, and I saw her glance at my face before shifting the conversation. 'Have you ever worked in a hotel like this before?'

'I've never even set foot in a hotel like this before,' I answered, at which Layla let out another tinkle of laughter and we lapsed into companionable silence while the boardwalk narrowed a little and we had to shift into single file.

The wheels of my suitcase rat-a-tat-tat-ing softly on the wooden planks of the boardwalk was the only sound for a few minutes as we navigated through the flora away from the main hum of guests and staff. Sunlight dappled through emerald leaves and I took a deep, serene breath.

'All right.' Layla's voice drifted back in. We'd curved round so that now we were close to the centre of the island, with Coconut Cove beach on our right, back through the trees. I knew from the map that on our left, the whole other side of the island was dedicated to what were called Island Paradise Villas, which seemed to be not on the water like the others, but shaded by palms and facing out towards the sparkling sea. 'This is the Cove Pavilion.'

We came to a large two-storey structure with gleaming wooden pillars, set back from a vast infinity pool. All those images I'd gazed at on my laptop only a few short weeks ago had come to life on this tour. Guests seemed to laze in the water in slow motion, palm trees swayed in the soft breeze, the staff waved and smiled at visitors as they held open the huge glass doors of the Pavilion for them. 'What happens in there?' I asked.

'That's where reception is, the concierge service, two more restaurants, some shops – a gallery, a gift shop, a pharmacy, and the space for your bookshop, too. And it's also where the resort directors have their offices.'

I was keen to wander in and see my shop, but I also knew I could easily explore further in my own time, and it was possible I'd want to stare at it for a while anyway. Plus, I could do with that freshen up Layla had mentioned.

Layla and I continued past the Pavilion, walking between it and the pool, where I tried not to gawp at any of the beautiful sun-worshippers. 'From the Pavilion you can get to nearly everything else just by following the boardwalk trails. The tennis courts, miniature golf, the cinema under the stars, the Divine Ocean Spa and Gymnasium – which, by the way, has cracking sunrise yoga if you ever get the chance to join one day. But for now, let's head to your new home.'

I nodded and turned around on the path, banging my suitcase against my ankles as I went.

'Where are you going?' Layla asked.

'To the staff accommodation. Wasn't it back up that way? Near the turtle sanctuary?'

She shook her head, a smile on her lips.

The Maldives sun was lowering further now as we followed the boardwalk away from the Pavilion and back onto Coconut Cove beach, but this time with the sea on our right, heading towards the opposite tip of the island to where I'd thought we'd be going. Perhaps my map-reading skills were a little off thanks to jet lag.

Layla led me across the beach, the sunset sea lapping in and out, in and out, like fingers trailing through the sand, which was still warm after a day of sunshine. We followed the curves of the island until we came across a crop of tiny white bungalows shaded by wide, palm-thatched roofs.

Layla checked the key in her hand. 'Number six ... this is you!' She stopped in front of one of the bungalows, which was nestled among rich foliage, with a pathway of wooden slats that led round to the main hotel boardwalk, or, in the other direction, off onto the beach. Beside the door, strung between two trees, was a turquoise-coloured hammock, which I was just gagging to take a flying leap into.

'This is me?' I clarified, because she couldn't be serious? Surely the hotel wasn't putting me up in a beach bungalow of my very own. Perhaps I was expected to clean these as part of my duties?

'Yes, this is your home for the next three months.' She grinned, noticing my expression.

If I'd been a cartoon character, I'd have been doing that thing right now of rubbing my eyes and looking again, my eyeballs popping out of their sockets with an *'Awooga!'* 'This can't be staff accommodation.'

'It isn't usually, but management feel these are getting a bit too shabby for guests and they're planning to give them a complete makeover during the middle of the summer, when the number of visitors are down due to the rainy season and they can shut off this side of the island and nobody will be disturbed by building works. Until then, all the staff were recently given the option to move into these for a few months, if we wanted.'

'But there's only, what, ten?' I'd done a quick count. 'There must be more staff than that who live on the island.'

'Twelve, actually. There are, but we have pretty nice staff accommodation on the other side of the island – everybody has their own studio apartment, plus there's a gym, a dining room, a games room, a TV room. Most people didn't want to uproot themselves for such a short amount of time. Which means not all of them were taken, so we thought you'd like one. You can still use all the facilities in our other building, of course. Is this OK?'

'Um, yes, this is OK, this is like a dream.' I reached up and ran my fingers over the tan-toned dried palm fronds that hung like eyelashes above my door. 'I used to spend so long looking at photos of places like this and imagining staying in one of them.'

'I'm glad you like it. I actually prefer it over here. It's quiet and you can get a lot of thinking done.'

'You live in one of these?'

'Yep,' she grinned. 'I'm in number two, just around the pathway on your right.'

'You weren't too worried about dealing with a temporary move?'

She shook her head. 'I like to say yes to as many things as I can, and I'd never had a place right on the beach, despite living on islands my whole life, so here I am. I guess we both like an adventure, right?'

'Oh, I'm not very adventurous.' I waved away her words in that classic British way we do of refusing to accept any kind of compliment. 'My best friend is always trying to get me to jump in with both feet, but I'm usually more of a toe-dip kind of gal.'

I dropped my eyes to the sand, wishing I hadn't brought up Marianne. I wondered what she was doing now. Probably packing, as they were heading off in less than two weeks, I thought. Although, actually, there was no way Marianne would be as organised as to be packing already. And then I wondered if she was thinking of me at all.

Layla stuck the key in the lock, shrugged and said, 'Well, you say you aren't adventurous, but you're here, aren't you?'

On the other side of the door, the bungalow opened up before me: white walls decorated with hand-painted aquamarine brushstrokes that made it look as if the ocean was right there with you, about to lull you to sleep. A chunky wooden double bed sat in the centre with a white mosquito net canopying overhead. Small tables and chairs were dotted around the walls, and a soft mint blanket rested on the foot of the mattress.

I circled the room, my fingers running over the smooth wood, taking in the light scent of sea salt and flowers in the warm air, the sound of unfamiliar birdsong and gentle waves. This was a long way from my flat in Bayside.

'This is "too shabby"?' I asked, incredulously. It looked pristine and as if it would cost a fortune.

Layla gave me a knowing smile. 'Wait until I show you the villas. Then you'll see why management thinks of these as shabby.'

I sat down on my bed. 'So they're doing a total overhaul of the resort, then, right? I know the bookshop is new, but ...'

'Yep, they still want it to be really clean and modern, but with the look and features of a classic Indian Ocean resort. I know they want to elevate the whole Bounty Cove Cay brand. There's only so much they've been able to do during the high season without causing too much disruption, though. Right, shall I leave you to get settled?'

In response, my stomach growled so loudly it made the room echo.

'I'm going to head over to my place,' Layla laughed. 'Take some time to freshen up, get acquainted, maybe follow your path to the beach and back again, to make sure you know your way before it gets dark, and then I'll take you over to the staff dining room and we can eat there tonight. It's really good.'

'Layla, thank you. If you have something you'd rather be doing—'

'That is what I'm doing. See you soon. I'll come and get you.'

When Layla left, I did another slow twirl in my new bungalow, thinking, *I am the luckiest girl in the world.* Seriously, this place was lush.

I wandered to the back door of my bungalow and slid it open, revealing a tiny walled courtyard, partially roofed, with an open-air rainfall shower! Holy moly, I was going to be showering in the buff. Which is what I normally do, but like *really* in the buff. I've never showered without a roof over my head before. Thank God there were walls. Also, thank God the loo was positioned under the roofed part, because that would have felt less Herbal Essences commercial and more the bear from the Charmin advert.

Standing there, I could hear the inhale and exhale of the ocean close by, so soft it was as if I'd been transported to a spa. I liked Layla's idea of navigating myself to the beach before we lost the light, so after relieving myself with an *ahhhhhhh*, splashing my face with water from the sink and changing into a clean pair of shorts and a light jumper, I stepped out of my bungalow and set off down the path.

With the sun sinking below the horizon for the evening, this little tropical island looked as if it had been given a lavender filter, the sky and sea a soft pink and the sand lilac, the distant palm trees becoming silhouettes. Directly in front of my bungalow, once my feet hit the now cool beach, was a low, long-trunked coconut palm reaching out towards the ocean, green leaves big and blissful, some low enough to be tickling the surface of the water. I didn't remember ever seeing a proper palm tree in real life before – one growing out of a beach, I mean. These ones were even more gorgeous than in the photos on the website.

'Hello, gorgeous tree,' I whispered to it, stroking its bark.

'Hello,' the tree replied. 'I'm Rishan. Call me Rish.'

A man poked his head out from the palm leaves, which was shocking – though not as shocking as if the trees here could talk. I was definitely more jet-lagged than I'd realised. The man dropped to the ground from his perch and landed on his feet in the sand with a soft thud.

'You made me jump,' I said.

'I could say the same to you,' he replied, and I realised he was the same guy Layla had greeted earlier, the one running along with the snorkels. Rish was tall, barefooted, with a big smile and eyes that crinkled at the corners even when he wasn't grinning. He was still in his Bounty Cove Cay shirt and shorts, and he was holding three coconuts.

'Did you just pick those?' I asked, which was quite the stupid question because who would climb a coconut palm already holding an armful of coconuts?

'Would you like one?' He held it out. It was big and green and, frankly, not like the ones you find in the supermarket. But that made it all the more exciting, especially since I was sure I could smell its sweet scent.

I took it, giving it a shake and hearing the slosh of the coconut water within. 'So, you work here?'

'Will we always speak in questions to each other?' He chuckled and then said, 'Yes, I do. I'm part of the entertainment team, but also chief coconut collector. Which is a self-appointed role.'

I held my coconut with tenderness. I had a coconut! From a tree outside my house! 'I just started working here – I'm going to be running the bookshop. I'm Jenn.'

'Oh,' he said, nodding. '*You're* Jenn. My manager is, erm, dying to meet you.'

Hmm. That sounded a little ominous. But Rish just crinkled his eyes at me and started scrambling up the tree again.

'Want another one, Bookshop Jenn?' he called from halfway up.

'One's probably enough for now, but thank you,' I replied, and found myself wondering if *I* could climb a palm tree and get my own. Probably not ... But maybe I could try it ... But probably not.

I said goodbye to Rish and took myself inside my bungalow again, making it back just in time to plonk my coconut on the side and shake the sand from my flip-flops before Layla reappeared to take me to dinner.

'I met a guy in a palm tree,' I told her while we walked the boardwalk back past the Cove Pavilion, crossing the length of the island. I craned my neck, trying to see in, hoping I didn't get too sleepy later before I could have a proper nosy around.

'Was it Rishan?' she asked, her eyes seeming to twinkle, but maybe it was the moonlight.

'It was Rishan,' I confirmed.

'Rish is great. It feels like he's worked here for ever, too. His ancestors came from the Maldives so he's passionate about the culture and environment, but he's from Sri Lanka and moved here about the same time I did. He also lives in one of the bungalows at the moment, so if you want him to, he'll probably leave a coconut or two outside your door every day.'

'Oh, I wouldn't want to trouble him. I'm sure I could try to climb up and get my own,' I said.

'All right, be sure to let me know when you give that a go, I'd love to be around for it. Here we are.' We had stopped outside a two-storey building on the far side of the island. Quiet and contained within lush greenery, it was painted the colour of avocados so that it almost blended in. Lights were on inside and when Layla led me through the door, the opposite wall, at least on the lower level, was completely glass, with a magnificent view out to the ocean.

'The boardwalk that circles the island takes guests inland for just a minute to go past the staff accommodation, in the same way it does behind the Island Paradise Villas, so this view of the sea is just for us. Unobstructed and unobserved. This is the dining room in front of us, the TV room is down the corridor to the right, along with the gym and other facilities, and the bedrooms are on the floor above.'

'It's really nice,' I marvelled. 'I always assumed staff accommodation at resorts would be quite basic.'

'I'm sure that is the case sometimes, but not here.'

The staff dining hall was thronging with people chatting, some wearing the white and silver shirts I'd seen earlier, some in casual clothes.

After filling our plates at the counter with *bajiya*, which looked like samosas and were stuffed with onions and locally caught fish, we sat together at a white table near the window as the view grew even darker outside.

'Do you think Rish picked the coconut in this dip?' I asked between mouthfuls.

'Maybe,' Layla shrugged. 'But we serve up a *lot* of coconut dishes here, so the chefs, the staff, even the guests sometimes, all pool their findings.'

The *bajiya* were delish and I could have eaten ten thousand of them, but before long I could feel the yawn monster creeping up, and not wanting to look incredibly rude to Layla, I asked if she'd mind if I took my leave and went back for some Zs.

'Of course, you must have been awake for hours!' she said. 'Want me to walk you back?'

'No, no, you stay. I'm going to head back via the Pavilion and see my bookshop, and then just turn in.'

'All right. If you get lost, just find your way onto the boardwalk – eventually you'll end up at the bungalows, whichever way you go round the island.'

I waved her goodbye and stepped back out into the night. Above me, a million stars had lit themselves in the inky black sky and I had to stand for a minute, just looking up. Wow. The stars over the sea in Bayside were usually pretty impressive, but this was almost heavenly.

I was really here, wasn't I? Little me, a speck in the universe, on a tiny island, very far from home. What was I going to do with this freedom?

# Chapter 8
# Jenny, in the Maldives

I pulled open the heavy glass door of the Pavilion, feeling a whoosh of air con blow into my face. The space opened out to a wide lounge area on my left, its floor-to-ceiling windows facing out over the swimming pool, then the beach, and beyond that, stretching into the ocean, the pier that housed the overwater villas. The lounge, much like the interior of my beach bungalow, was decorated with pale mint and turquoise splashes among the otherwise white decor. Big white candles filled cylindrical storm-lantern jars on all the surfaces. A young couple lay propped together on a pastel green loveseat, staring out at the sea, sipping from shallow coffee cups.

To my right was reception, at this time in the evening with one member of staff behind the desk, accompanied by a concierge nearby, both in smart white and silver shirts and traditional Maldivian sarongs known as *feyli*. Both were dealing with customers in low, soothing voices.

Soft jazz filled the air with gentle music, rising up to the mezzanine level, with its glass bannisters overlooking reception. I realised that the swooshing of the waves could no longer be heard.

I studied a sign beside the sweeping curve of staircase leading to the mezzanine, which pointed guests towards lounges, ice machines and restaurants named 'Palms' and 'Pink', but couldn't see any mention of the bookshop-to-be. So I walked on, my flip-flops making a rather awkward *slap-slap-slap* sound against the polished flooring, but thankfully I didn't pass anyone in the quiet hotel to give me the evil eye.

Shops! Aha! They were closed now, which seemed a bit of a shame as I'd bet the after-dinner crowd would happily walk off their à la carte meals with a browse and a bit of wallet-opening. I did some window-shopping on their behalf.

There was a large resort gift shop displaying fluffy robes, bright white golf caps and beach bags emblazoned with *Bounty Cove Cay*. A designer-swimwear store showcased a rainbow of kaftans and wide-brimmed sunhats with dangling price tags that I imagined had a lot of numbers on them. A jewellery store displayed a window-height image of a woman with rich black skin and sparkling silver hoop earrings from which hung polished sea glass. Next door was a gallery where photo prints and paintings sat side by side, and I guessed they were all of the island, but I'd know more when I could have a proper look. And finally, a small essentials shop with bottled water, snacks and newspapers and magazines from around the world.

I yawned. But where was my bookshop? I had reached the end of the stores and was facing the entrance to the spa, so I helped myself to a chilled cucumber water from the glass dispenser beside the door. There was nowhere to go from here, it seemed. I considered heading all the way back and asking somebody at reception, but my eyes drooped further at the mere suggestion. So, instead, I followed the signage that led me out of the side exit, the warm evening air enveloping me once again as I walked to have my first sleep on my Indian Ocean island.

Lying in my bed in my beach bungalow, listening to the steady sound of the sea only metres away and the soft squeak of a little gecko who appeared to be my roommate, clinging onto the wall with his wide toes, my mind refused to fall straight to sleep. Instead, I thought of Marianne, and that time we'd taken a holiday to Paris and they'd put us up in a romantic honeymoon suite together and we'd gone to town on the minibar. And I wished she was here to see this place.

If Marianne were here, she'd already have been swinging from the palm trees and skinny-dipping in the ocean, or something else wild that my totally non-wild brain couldn't even think of. But I'd make the most of this place too, I knew I would. I had it all planned out ...

'This is it?' I asked in the morning, looking around for the rest of it. 'This is the bookshop?'

Nadim, the concierge who'd kindly brought me over here, nodded with mild discomfort.

'There isn't another bookshop somewhere, like a part two?'

'This is the only bookshop,' he clarified, and I saw relief flash across his face as a woman in a smart suit and great shoes started clacking her way towards us from a distance.

Nadim left me standing agape, looking at the bookstore I was supposed to run for the next three months, my folder of careful planning and spreadsheets and numbers and projections dangling from my hand.

We were in a dark corner of the hotel, not too far from where I'd ended up yesterday at the spa, but so hidden away that unless you knew the shop was there, or were so sloshed on mai tais that you'd stumbled into this corner for a romantic midnight tryst, you would never find it. I mean, *I* hadn't found it.

The bookshop, or rather the store cupboard allocated to be my bookshop, was small and cramped, I could tell even through the locked door. There was no sign above, no welcome to guests. Really, it looked like a supply closet.

'Jenny, good morning. I'm Khadeeja.' The woman reached me and stuck out her hand, which had an immaculate pearl-pink manicure.

'Hi, I'm Jenny,' I replied, stating the obvious. So, this was the big boss, or at least one of them, in person. I remembered her from the video interview panel, though she looked both more intimidating and even more polished in person. I tried to sound bright and sparkly. 'This is my bookshop?'

'It is,' she replied, taking out some keys to open it up. 'The space hasn't been used for a while, though, so apologies if it's a little musty inside.'

'Oh, I'm sure it's – ah, right, well, yes, it is a bit.' I coughed as we stepped in. 'Has there ever been a bookshop here before? In the resort, I mean.'

'No. We're actually doing a lot of behind-the-scenes changes to make sure Bounty remains one of the Maldives' most attractive luxury options for our clientele, and one of the ways I've been spearheading that is through the ecotourism route. We have been making steps in that direction, but it's a big job and we have a long way to go, and frankly I don't have a lot of time. Meanwhile, we've noticed the resort has been getting more synonymous with wealthy partygoers. They're very welcome here, but if it leans too heavily that way, it puts off those who want the very best in idyllic relaxation and rejuvenation. We want to cater to them too, and we thought a bookshop – and everything that comes with the bookshop – could be a nice draw.'

'"Everything that comes with it"?' I asked, for clarification.

'Events and suchlike. By the time the next high season starts, we want this bookshop and whatever magic you can bring to it to be not just a feature but a highlight for the guests. We want to promote the events on our social media, through the press, and wherever else you think would be worthwhile. We have a great manager lined up to start at the beginning of the new season and she'll take all this forward, but we wanted somebody dynamic and experienced to get it off the ground beforehand. Really get the hotel on the map in the literary world, have it become a place to be. And that someone would be *you*.' She smiled.

'Thank you,' I gulped.

'Until then, this is the test run,' Khadeeja said. 'I'm sure you'll make it work. From the activity in your own shop back home, I can see you're not short of creative ideas to bring in the crowds.'

I laughed a forced and slightly shrill laugh, because, of course … they were all Marianne's ideas. Khadeeja sure was giving a lot of weight to the events, more than to the basic profit margins and day-to-day running of the bookshop itself.

I looked around. It wasn't that I'd been expecting an airy pop-up right out there on the sand, but, well, musty was the right word for the bookshop, as it stood. It wasn't quite the shoebox it had appeared from the outside, but it was at most half the size of the Book Nook on the Beach, probably even smaller. There were already dust-covered shelves that reached to the ceiling, which did give an appealing haunted-library aesthetic but didn't really lend themselves to easy customer browsing. A few books, which had perhaps once been on sale in the gift shop, were scattered about, a fluorescent light dangling overhead causing glare from the covers, those that weren't blanketed in a layer of dust. And the books themselves? Well, I'd been in there for several minutes now and nothing was making me scream *You're coming with me to a sunlounger, baby!*

'What's that you have there?' Khadeeja interrupted my thoughts.

'Ah.' I looked down at my folder. 'I just wanted to put in a bit of homework based on the info you gave me – the average number of visitors to the resort throughout the year, projected growth rates, that kind of thing – but, um, I think I'll do a bit of tweaking.'

'You expected bigger?' Khadeeja smiled.

'I expected a shop,' I admitted, 'with foot traffic.'

'Yes, it is a little out of the way from the rest of the hotel, but I have every confidence you'll make it work. After all, you beat a lot of competition from all over the world with your application.'

*Aaaaah ha ha ha, so no pressure then*, I thought. 'You mentioned already having the new manager lined up, for after I leave?'

'Yes, I've worked with her at another resort in the past. She's very experienced in retail, including bookselling, but has never launched a business, which is effectively what this place will need. But she can't start until November because of commitments elsewhere. You'll meet her at some point. I'm sure she'll pay us a visit.'

Khadeeja gave me another smile and stepped back out of the shop into what now seemed like a lovely and bright corner of the hotel, compared to what was inside the shop.

'I'm hoping you can open the doors to the shop as soon as possible, but I know that will be dependent on you acquiring some stock and whatever else you deem necessary. Feel free to price up a proposal for an opening soirée of some kind. Then, when you're up and running, you'll be expected to work six days a week, with the bookshop closed on Fridays. On Fridays, please feel free to use the facilities, but I would also recommend exploring some of the other islands while you're here – there are ferries and the seaplane that you can use, as long as it isn't taking a space from a guest. The time will go quickly and before you know it, you'll be sailing away.' Khadeeja checked her watch, and I found myself thinking that she was who I strived to be – polished, professional, clear, in control and confident. 'Right, I have a meeting to get to. Layla's your buddy, should you need anything. I assume you met her yesterday?'

'Yes, she's great, so helpful,' I enthused.

'Indeed she is. Did she collect you by plane or boat?'

'Plane – it was amazing. She mentioned she drives a boat here as well.' Pretty sure that wasn't the right term.

'Oh, yes, Layla's both our pilot and our skipper. She's quite an asset to our corner of heaven.'

Marianne would like Layla, and vice versa. They both seemed bold and fearless. I found myself looking forward to telling Marianne all about her when I got back home, only to try and shut that thought down because I remembered I was still supposed to be mad at her.

'And how's your bungalow?' asked Khadeeja.

'*So* nice. I feel so lucky. I should be paying you, ha ha!' *Oh, shut up, Jenn.* But Khadeeja just chuckled and left me with a wave. I called after her, 'Should I come to you to run by any plans I have for the store?'

She looked back at me and thought about this. 'If you really need an extra pair of eyes, or approval for a large expense, send it over to me. Otherwise, go wild.'

Go wild. I wasn't quite sure if that meant she had all the faith in the world in me or felt this hidden corner of the hotel was such a wasteland that I couldn't make it any worse. I picked up a book on tall ships of the 1800s and puffed a layer of dust off the cover.

I could do this. I'd done this before. I had a successful business that I'd started from scratch, and it was engaging and the community loved it. I exhaled a deep, nervous breath, trying to quiet the thoughts that shouted at me. *But you did all that when you had Marianne to help you. Now you're on your own!*

Well, although 'wild' was hardly my middle name, 'wild' I would have to go. Not for the last time, it would turn out, a little part of me wished the wildest girl I knew was there to help me: my best friend.

This might be the most perfect job in the world, I thought as I lay on my back in the sea, warm aquamarine water silking around my body, a big cloudless blue sky up above and unadulterated sunshine blasting me. I could feel the nerves and overthinking from my meeting with Khadeeja simply melting away.

After spending the morning having a clean of the shop, I intended to take my findings, and my laptop, somewhere with a bit more daylight to do some serious revised planning. I loved serious planning. But first I'd grabbed a chicken club sandwich from the staff dining hall – saying hello to some new faces, even though it was scary – and then donned my swimmers for a dip in this holiday-brochure ocean.

I idled about in the water, letting it lap against the sides of my body and through my hair like the most relaxing massage ever. My mind was beginning to settle instead of darting through possibilities, the things I could experience, the problems I needed to overcome. '*Shhh*,' I whispered aloud, bringing my mind back to the present.

*Remember, Jenn: I am in a holiday brochure. I am a pixel floating in a widescreen image of the ocean on one of my travel websites. I am here.*

A shadow caught my eye, something under the surface of the water, moving under *me*. I let out a small gasp, but tried to keep my body relatively still, and instead of thrashing about like an extra from *Jaws*, I slowly curled my body into a cannonball, my arms moving to keep me afloat while I looked down through the ripples and into the glass-like sea.

It took me a moment to realise where the shadow had gone, but then I saw it again. An unhurried disc, dark teal against the pale water, like a very large pebble, a couple of feet in diameter.

There was salt water on my cheeks and it took me a moment to realise it was tears. Where'd they come from? I told you, I'm not a crier! But there was a turtle swimming below me, a real live turtle, his little flappers paddling his way through the ocean. I would have given anything in that moment to have a snorkel with me, but even without one, it was mesmerising.

The Maldives were simply epic. Seeing new things with my own eyes, not just in photos, was just great. I paddled my own hands under the water in a happy dance.

The rest of the afternoon I didn't *take off*, as such, but after seeing my friend the turtle I realised I'd actually stayed still and focused and not thought any of those other busy thoughts for a good few minutes. I used to be so good at focusing, being organised, getting the job done, and I still was. Only nowadays it oftentimes felt more as though I was living in an escape room rather than living in the moment, always trying to beat the clock. So I didn't take the afternoon off, but I did let myself stop for a moment and concentrate on here. Now. The island.

Squinting in the brightness of the light reflecting off the brilliant white sand, I stood beside the tiki bar, the Cocktail Cove, and waited to be served by one of the bartenders, who all wore white beach shorts, the resort's white and silver shirt and dazzlingly white smiles. I felt extremely short beside two lofty Americans who might have been models and were almost certainly influencers, judging from the photos they were snapping on their latest iPhones.

'CeCe, lean your ass back a bit,' one was saying to the other. 'And angle it toward me so I can see the branding on the bikini, or they won't want to collab.'

'Like this?' CeCe asked, striking a pose.

'Yeah, but drop your head forward or that palm tree behind you looks like it's growing out of your crown.'

'Good afternoon, miss, welcome to Cocktail Cove. What can I get you?'

I was snapped back to attention by the bartender. 'Just a cucumber lemonade, please. I'm on the job. I'm Jenny.'

'You work here?' he asked. 'Then welcome to the whole island. I'm Dan.'

'Hi, Dan,' I said, amazed he was able to not let his eyes drift to where CeCe was now contorting herself into a sort of Z shape to avoid palm-tree head or hidden-bikini ass. He poured my drink and then wouldn't accept any payment for it.

'Don't tell my boss, but let's say the first one is on the house.'

I thanked him, but was interrupted by a phone screen being shoved in my face by CeCe's friend. 'What do you think? Would you buy this swimsuit?'

I peered at the screen. 'Oh, that looks great!' I meant it – CeCe looked lovely and the bikini branding was very visible. The friend was a good photographer.

'Thank you,' said CeCe's friend, and then to Dan, 'And sorry if we got in the way at all.'

As a couple approached the hut and Dan got back to work, getting out the champagne glasses as if he already knew what they were going to order, I took my lemonade and set myself up on a sunlounger in a quiet corner, completely shaded by palms and out of the hot sun, so I could do a spot of people watching. I sipped at my drink, an audible *mmm* escaping as the delicate, refreshing flavours of cool cucumber, tangy lemon and a sprinkling of sugar, all expertly combined, filled my mouth.

Although it wasn't peak high season here – that was in the early months of the year – I'd been told that the hotel was still 'busy' and would remain like that for a while. The Bounty Cove Cay resort had certainly perfected the art of making itself feel spacious and tranquil for all, the ambient sounds coming only from the sigh of the shore, the tinkle of ice in glasses and the chatting of low voices peppered with happy laughter. If this was 'busy', then this was my kinda place.

Speaking of busy, I wondered how the Book Nook was doing. I didn't want to bother Evan with questions when I'd only been out of the UK for little more than a couple of days, plus he hadn't contacted me yet and I didn't want him to think I was finding an excuse to bring up the kiss. Which I would have been. Instead, I opened Instagram and checked our shop's business page, which Marianne kept bright and colourful and up to date.

Sure enough, two more pictures had appeared. One showing a packed shop, and one showing the morning sunshine on the sea through our windows. Marianne, I believed, would be handing the socials over to Evan while she went her merry way to the USA. I'd tried to check, but she'd shut me down with a withering, 'No time for micromanaging, Jenny, you've got your new business to think about.' Maybe she didn't say it quite so meanly.

I saw a pink ring around the icon of her face for her personal Instagram account, suggesting she'd added to her Stories, but I resisted clicking on it. She was fine. The shop was fine. There was no need to fill my head with matters a million miles away.

'Hello, miss,' a voice interrupted my thoughts. 'Is everything to your satisfaction?'

I put my phone down and shielded my eyes from the sun as I looked up and saw a familiar face, eyes crinkled. 'Rish!'

He plopped down on the sunlounger next to me and lay back, his hands crossed behind his head. 'Taking a day off already? I don't blame you.'

I laughed. 'I'm not quite taking the day off, just taking things in.'

'Did you see your storage cupboard, I mean bookshop, yet?'

'Yes, I saw it,' I admitted. 'It'll be fine. Hey, thanks for the coconut yesterday.'

'You're welcome. Anything else you need? Jet ski? Paddleboard? Game of Monopoly? A lesson in marine biology?'

'Maybe not today, but I'm sure I'll take you up on some of those on my actual days off.'

A man was walking across the beach in front of the pool, his head turned towards us. He wore nearly the same clothes as Rish, though was slightly smarter, in chinos rather than shorts, but still with the Bounty Cove Cay emblem on his shirt, and had the swagger of a high-rolling resort guest, though he couldn't be. He was glaring at us and Rish noticed him and stood up hastily. 'Right, better get back to work. See you around, Bookshop Jenn!'

'I saw a turtle!' I blurted out by accident, having meant to say 'Bye!'

Rish gave me a thumbs up. 'One of our best animals. We must protect the turtles!' And with that he bounced off and I watched him skirt round the pool and stand beside a canoodling honeymoon couple stretched out on a beach daybed. He started chatting to them and they greeted him like an old friend, enthusing about something and showing him photos from the woman's phone.

From what I could see looking around, and considering where I was, which wasn't a very prime location for snooping as I hadn't wanted to invade the guests' space, I'd have said that most of the people relaxing by the pool or on the beach had a book with them. Some had them open, some closed beside them, some resting on stomachs while their owners fell asleep, while some took the unmistakable form of a sleeved Kindle sitting beside a towering, creamy cocktail.

I opened my laptop to make a note. It occurred to me how little time I put aside for reading these days, and I was a bookseller! Perhaps it was the same for some of the Bounty Cove Cay guests. This vacation was finally giving them the headspace to relax and pick up a novel, to sink into its pages like toes into the sand.

Time is precious. I wanted to help them, to be there with the perfect book that would allow them to forget their busy lives back home, the warm sun kissing their skin and the soundtrack of lapping water not far away.

Didn't I used to have that same passion with the Book Nook back home?

I planned to have our opening night in under two weeks' time, the day I knew Marianne would be flying off on her road trip, actually, and the first thing I needed to do was get some sparkling new stock. I imagined it was a niche type of traveller who wanted to lose themselves in a chilled Prosecco cocktail, a gleaming plate of oysters and a hefty textbook on tall ships.

# Chapter 9

# Marianne, in the USA

'How much longer?' Marianne asked Drew, probably for the fortieth time.

He uncrumpled his arm from under his head, where he was using it as a pillow, and checked his watch. 'Just a couple more hours.'

Marianne turned back to the vast, panoramic window of Dallas-Fort Worth airport, where they'd been waiting out an eight-hour layover for a little under six hours now. She looked up at the cloudless, late-afternoon sky of Texas and wished they'd left the airport for a quick exploration when they'd had the chance. Her skin was positively itching to get out under that warm sunshine, but alas, they'd have to hold on until they reached California now.

Because Drew had wanted to be absolutely sure he'd make the deadline for the first draft of his manuscript before booking their flights, they'd ended up paying the price for leaving things till the last minute, and the only affordable option had been a non-direct journey into San Diego. They'd had a vague idea to start their literary tour in San Francisco and then travel south, since they'd both loved the novel *Tales of the City* by Armistead Maupin, which was set there. After exhausting all options, they'd realised it was just too convoluted a trip. But no matter, they could travel up the West Coast instead. They were feeling optimistic about their no-plan plan; they were just going to go with the flow. Just how Marianne liked it.

She wandered back over towards Drew and sat on the edge of the row of seats he was lying on. They were in a quiet corner of the vast airport, with just a few other sleepy passengers waiting for connecting flights like them. They'd eaten a big meal at a place called Dickey's Barbecue Pit, chased it up with some frozen yogurt from a Pinkberry stand, wandered around the shops, tried on a Stetson, purchased some American snacks and magazines, considered trying out the airport yoga studio, but had felt too full, and were now here, with Drew trying to catch a few Zs and Marianne trying to keep on her feet before they boarded the final three-hour flight.

'You OK?' Drew asked her, placing his hand on her back, a gesture that felt perfect.

'Yes. Yes, of course. Just want to get there now, you know. Get to California, jump in a hire car with the windows down and start the road trip of our lives.' She grinned at him.

'Not long now.'

Drew had a lovely, reassuring way about him. He didn't seem phased by her impatience, or even by the delay in getting things going. Outside of her family, Marianne had only taken adventures with Jenn before now, but she sensed Drew was going to make the ideal road-trip partner.

Marianne got up again and went back to the window, where planes were drawing slow circles around each other on the black tarmac outside. She looked up at the big blue of the sky and thought for a moment about Jenny, all those miles away, and wondered what kind of sky she'd be looking at right now. Marianne didn't even know if it was day or night over there. Her interest had not exactly been engaged by Jenny's Maldives trip since their argument, but then neither had Jenn's in hers.

But thanks to the friends app, Find My, she did know Jenny had made it safely. And had stuck it out nearly two weeks. That was all Marianne needed to know, for now. She had her own adventure to enjoy.

Everything felt good in California, even in the evening; there was just magic and warmth in the air when Marianne and Drew stepped out of San Diego International Airport. There were palm trees, wide roads, billboards and a sense of freedom and excitement. Marianne took a huge inhalation, which was interrupted by a yawn midway through.

Beside her, Drew rubbed his eyes. 'We made it!'

'Yay!'

'Are you OK? You sound tired.'

She turned to face him. 'No, no, I'm fine, let's get a car, let's hit the road. Where shall we go, though?'

'Well, it's dark and we're pretty sleepy, so we might as well spend our first night in San Diego.'

'For sure,' she agreed.

'You don't mind? I know you didn't want to book somewhere before we came because you wanted to be able to get on the road straight away.'

Was she imagining it or was there a touch of grouchy passive-aggressiveness in his voice? 'That's what *we* decided, yeah,' she replied. They hadn't lined up a hotel for the first night because they'd agreed to sleep on the plane journeys and in the airport, but even with short kips it hadn't stopped the groggy feeling of just wanting to take a shower and climb into bed. 'Perhaps *we* were being a little short-sighted. Let's just get a car and drive into the city. I'm sure there'll be plenty of great hotels we could spend the night in.'

'You're right.' He put an arm around her. 'Although I suppose we could think about all that in the morning and instead have a night over there.'

Marianne followed his gaze to the façade of a building off to the side of the airport. 'An airport hotel?'

'Just for the night. I'm a little jet-lagged,' Drew confessed.

Ah, that explained his slightly grumpy attitude. Marianne nodded. 'Let's do it. Just for one night, then we'll get going.'

One night turned into two when Marianne and Drew overslept, tangled in a deep slumber of arms and legs in the centre of the huge king bed. Waking up with just minutes to spare before checkout time, Drew called down to extend their stay for an extra night and they vowed to spend the rest of the day getting their shit together, eating a big American brunch and making, perhaps, just a small plan. A tiny plan. Jenny would have mapped out every hotel, every loo stop, every minute of fun, but Marianne was happy with just a baby plan. At least so they knew what direction to turn the car when they collected it from the rental office.

While Drew was on the phone to reception, Marianne pulled on a T-shirt and fiddled with the coffee machine in their room until it chugged and churned a thick, delicious brew into two mugs, which she topped up with half-and-half creamer from individual pots.

'All OK?' she asked when he'd hung up.

'Yep, no problems. And breakfast is available for another hour. So, we don't need to head straight down.'

That grin, she couldn't resist it, and she climbed back into bed next to him, putting her coffee on the side. With all hints of her impatience and his jet lag having drifted into the Californian breeze, Marianne was extremely happy to start their trip. Soon.

A little while later, Drew had drifted into a light, contented doze again, his arm slung across her bare chest. She trailed a finger along the satiny skin of his shoulder, watching his eyelids twitch, his mind sailing away in some kind of a dream. She wondered if his dreams were like his books – detailed, flowing, hard to

Lucy Dickens

leave behind – or whether maybe he dreamed of her sometimes.

In that moment, nothing else mattered. Not plans or spontaneity, not arguments or making up, not adventure or responsibilities, just this moment. With him. Marianne was happy just to be present. She'd even say, she loved it.

However, when he let out the most massive snore the spell was broken, and Marianne picked up the TV remote. She muted it immediately so as not to disturb him because she liked his heavy warmth resting on her, then surfed the American channels.

Sport, news, infomercial, *Friends*, sport, sport, cooking show, news, weather, soap opera, reality TV, a travel show about Las Vegas. She paused on that one, watching images of bright, jewel-toned lights and fountains rising into the night sky fill the screen. She couldn't wait for them to get to Vegas, whenever in their trip that would be. It felt very much like somewhere she and Drew could have a lot of fun. It had been somewhere she'd felt a pull to visit ever since her brother had shown her the movie *Ocean's Eleven* when she was probably, well, roughly eleven.

The show moved to a montage of shots of the polished interior of a luxurious hotel. Wow, it was huge. Long, wide corridors with fancy shops, a vast casino floor, sunlit-twinkled swimming pools, happy guests sipping champagne, massive plates of food, rainbows of flowers spilling from indoor installations, a picture-perfect bride being dipped by her groom in front of some delicate lights, pristine suites with panoramic windows over the Strip, and finally a shot of the exterior: two soaring, curved, copper-coloured towers.

'The Wynn Las Vegas and Encore Resort,' Marianne whispered, reading from the screen. Beside her, Drew stirred and opened his eyes.

'Oops, did I fall asleep again?'

In answer, Marianne's stomach let out a huge growl and she switched off the TV. 'You did, but I liked it.'

'You're comfortable,' he said, kissing the skin above her breast, before closing his eyes again.

'I know, but I'm also hungry,' Marianne laughed, nudging him upright, then stepping from the bed and pulling on her underwear as she walked towards the window. She pointed to the sunny, hazy sky, the palm trees and the sparkle of water in the nearby harbour. 'Come on, let's get breakfast and then get out there and start seeing SoCal!'

At sundown, Marianne and Drew sat on the sea wall in the La Jolla neighbourhood of San Diego, watching the colours of the sky change and the seals and sea lions bask on the still-warm rocks below. In the cove in front of them, a few families remained on the beach, laughter drifting into the sky.

'We packed in a lot this afternoon,' Marianne commented, biting into a zingy, crunchy, grilled fish taco.

'It was a good day. I don't think we could have done that if we hadn't had the big sleep we needed.'

She nodded. 'We made the right call stumbling into a hotel five minutes away rather than joining a long hire-car queue and then driving around the city. How's your taco?'

Drew made a *yummy* sound, his mouth full of delicious ahi tuna.

They'd spent the afternoon navigating San Diego's public transport to explore as much as they could. To start, they'd joined a foodie tour of the Gaslamp Quarter area, which left them swaying a little like palm trees in the breeze thanks to the samples of margaritas and craft beers. They'd then taken a ferry over to Coronado Island and walked on the beaches, and finally they'd made their way to La Jolla, stopping in at the University of California, San Diego to look up at the jagged concrete and glass Geisel Library, named after La Jolla residents Audrey and Theodor Seuss Geisel. Outside sat a bronze statue of Dr Seuss himself, overlooked by his Cat in the Hat.

Now they were here, chomping away and soaking up the fading Cali sunshine, the sky a million perfect shades of pink.

'So. Where do you want to go first?' asked Drew, breaking into Marianne's memories.

'I don't know. I guess our guide should be what books or authors are connected to this corner of the state.' She pulled from her bag a glossy fold-out map of California that had been provided in their hotel room and studied the names of the highlighted destinations not too far from San Diego, before they started travelling more northwards. 'We could stay around here for a while, or go down to

Tijuana in Mexico, up to Palm Springs, Joshua Tree National Park ...' She trailed off and picked up her phone. 'Wait a minute.'

'This taco is delicious. I'm happy to head off from San Diego, if you are. It's amazing, but we have a lot to explore—'

Marianne gasped. 'Coachella!'

'What about it?' Drew swallowed the last of his meal and turned to look at Marianne, who thrust her phone in his face.

'Coachella is this weekend! Well, the first weekend of it. I've always wanted to go to Coachella.' Marianne was on Instagram now, scrolling through hundreds of peach-toned pics featuring Ferris wheels, Beyoncé, desert selfies, festival OOTDs, Beyoncé, mirrored sunglasses, Beyoncé.

'Where is it? Around here?'

'Indio, near Palm Springs.' She tapped the destination into her maps app. 'Which is, like, two and a half hours' drive from here. What day is it?'

Drew thought for a moment. 'Thursday, I think.'

'So if we headed over tomorrow we could go? It's not literary, I know, but surely there are some books set in Palm Springs?' It had been her pipe dream to attend the Coachella Valley Music and Arts Festival, which was always so packed full of celebrities, sunshine, amazing music and just as amazing outfits and body paint. She couldn't believe she hadn't put two and two together until now and that the stars would align so perfectly. Drew *had* to say yes, because frankly, she wouldn't take no for an answer.

'Sure,' he replied, easy as pie, and she leaned over and kissed him hard on the mouth.

One of the sea lions from below lifted his head towards them and let out a long, loud bark, causing them both to break from each other and laugh. Marianne felt happy, and excited, and full of sunshine. She grinned at Drew. 'We're a good match, you know.'

# Chapter 10
# Jenny, in the Maldives

Opening night. It had been more than three years since I'd had an opening night, and I'd tried to remember everything about it in order to plan for this moment.

I'd spent a while creeping about the pool and lounge area, sitting on the beach, watching people come and go from the ferry and the seaplane, and had placed an order for a selection of novels, all rather serious looking, with beautiful, expensive-looking cover designs, all modern, all 'must-reads'. Rather than keep the mishmash of floor-to-ceiling shelves the bookshop contained, I chose light-framed racks no taller than head height. From the gallery, I purchased a couple of prints depicting the island and placed them above the new shelving, which helped it feel more in flow with the rest of the hotel, at least by a small amount, rather than like the bookshop that time forgot.

I wasn't loving my finished window display. Looking at it, I could tell I'd played it safe. I was reluctant to admit it, but even though it always irked me when Marianne bowled in at the last minute to change or update one of my displays, they had always looked better. No matter – these could improve with time if I could think of some fun things to do with them. Things Marianne would have thought of. In fact, without Marianne around, maybe my own ideas might start to blossom ... Maybe.

So. Opening night. I thought back to over three years ago, to that stormy night in Bayside when Marianne and I had been so nervous that nobody would come. But they had, even that reporter from the local paper had made the drive over. We'd done it then, we could do it again, now. Well, I could do it now.

I checked my watch and then clicked the button on my docked iPhone and soft background music began to play. I'd picked a generic piano moods playlist, because who doesn't like a bit of piano moods, even though it did sound a bit like an elevator, now I was hearing it in situ. Never mind. It was 8 p.m. Showtime.

I wondered who my first guest would be. Khadeeja had said staff could come along as well, after the designated guest slot, but that ultimately I should aim it at the clientele. I'd seen a group of women in the jewellery store earlier that day and I could swear at least one of them was a Real Housewife. Maybe, since they must like shopping, they'd turn up? A nervous ripple of excitement babbled in my tummy. I'd heard about celebrities coming here, but wasn't sure it was the kind of thing I could ask about.

'Do you think the name of the event is OK?' I asked one of the servers, Sadeera, who was helping me that evening, on loan from Cocktail Cove to help with the drinks and the appetisers, which had been provided by Pink restaurant and were, in fact, all pink. Like there was anything I could do about the name now anyway. Maybe I should have texted Marianne for help after all, but it had been two weeks since we'd spoken and I didn't really want to call in a favour already. Plus, she was flying to the States right about now, taking off on her own adventure, and we'd both made it pretty clear we could handle things without each other.

"'A Night in the Bookstore",' Sadeera read from the neatly printed placard I'd had made, which was propped on a stand beside my table of complimentary wine and champagne. 'Yes, it's nice.'

There were several of these signs, all encased in stand-up gold frames that led the way from reception to the shop. I'd also advertised the opening night in the island newsletter, which appeared on the guests' in-room TVs and tablets every morning at five. I'd even asked if reminder cards could be delivered along with the sunrise bottles of water to the rooms today.

By eight fifteen, I was getting a little nervous.

It was fine. People would show up. I strolled back through my shop (which didn't take long) and ran my hands over the books. The books I'd chosen for them, the guests, were ready to be placed in their hands. Through all my organising and planning, that was the heart of what I was good at, what I loved. Picking the perfect read for someone. Curating themed groups of books. Talking books. Breathing books. Only, I hadn't breathed a lot lately. I didn't much feel like picking up a novel when I finally returned home after the end of a long day. It was beginning to dawn on me that I'd let myself lose a little of the love. I hoped I'd find it again.

By eight thirty I'd started to wish the champagne and white wine hadn't been pre-poured. At eight forty I nearly cried with relief because an older couple rounded the corner, but then they backtracked and it became clear they'd been looking for the bathrooms.

'Don't worry,' said Sadeera. 'I'm sure they'll all come after dinner. Guests take their time here, nothing is rushed, so they'll probably make their way over when they're done.'

Eventually, as Sadeera had anticipated, a few guests dawdled over after the clock had passed nine. There was some mild perusing of books, glasses of wine accepted, one or two purchases made, but, overall, I was painfully aware of the lack of a buzzy launch-party feel to the evening, and it was beyond deflating. I just kept thinking back to the warm, busy, happy, wind-blown winter's night that had opened the Book Nook, and how even though I was in a tropical paradise now, I felt so much colder.

A little later, some of the staff, including Layla and Rish, turned up and kindly made a bit of a show of looking at the books and *mmm*-ing at the remaining nibbles. I noticed Khadeeja arrive and sweep her eyes over the scene with a poker face.

'You must be Jenny.' A voice loomed behind me and I turned to see a man in his late thirties, perhaps early forties, it was hard to tell through all that slightly too even tan. He was thickly built, with cropped brown hair and grey eyes.

He was smiling at me, though not with the crinkle-eyed warmth of Rish, or the breezy smile of Layla, but in that way that people smile at you when they want to make it really, really obvious they aren't really smiling at you. Here was a guy who'd never got the memo about smizing.

'Hello,' I replied. 'Have we met?'

'Not yet.' He pushed his hands in his pockets and kept his eyes focused on mine. 'Blane Priestly. Director of Entertainment.'

My eyes flicked across the hallway to Rish, who raised his brows at me. So, this was Rish's manager. This was the guy who had apparently been 'dying' to meet me. Well, Blane didn't exactly look like he was enjoying himself right now.

'Nice to meet you, Blane. Thanks for coming,' I pushed on, not really sure what else I could do at this point. I tried to steady the nervous wobble in my voice that I always had trouble hiding if I had to play host. 'Can I interest you in a book?'

*Snort.* At least I think that was the derisive noise that emitted from him. 'I'm good, thanks. A bit busy to read.'

'I know that feeling,' I said, because I did, but I wasn't sure I'd ever snorted it in such a condescending manner. 'Wine, then?'

'We've never needed a bookshop on the island before. What makes you think that all of a sudden it'll be good business now?'

'Actually, Blake, it's management who think it'll make good business. I'm just here to steer it that way.'

'Blane. Not planning a bunch of boring book events, are you? People come here for a vacation, not a lecture.'

This guy was charming. How the hell anyone had ever promoted him to be in charge of entertainment was something I hoped to figure out over the coming weeks. 'No boring events, Shane, I promise. Just great ones.'

'*Blane.*'

*I know, you ding-dong.*

Blane ran a cursory eye over the nearest rack of books and then made quite the show of turning away.

'Good luck to you, Jenn,' he said, without looking back at me. 'You're going to need it.'

Well, that wasn't a nice end to the evening. I didn't know what his problem was, and if Marianne were here, she probably would have found something deliciously cutting to hurl back at him. But before I could dwell on it, Khadeeja approached and Layla and Rish did an about-turn, having also been about to head over.

'Good evening, Jenny,' she said, her smile stiff. 'How was opening night?'

'Erm,' I started. 'Good ... ?'

Khadeeja stared at me. 'Good?'

'Well, goodish. Not great. Not sure I quite got the right vibe, unfortunately, or maybe it's just because the bookshop is a little hard to find—'

'Let's not make excuses,' Khadeeja cut me off. Gulp. I'd all but forgotten how nice it was to have nobody to answer to except Marianne.

Khadeeja continued, looking around at my sad little attempt at a party. 'I must admit, I'd forgotten it was this evening. I think you got a little lost in the sea of things on offer here.'

'You're right,' I concurred. 'I thought the temptation of free drinks and nibbles might stick in people's minds; that was always a sure-fire way to get customers through the door at home.'

Khadeeja observed me for a moment, and I assumed she was thinking of something encouraging and motivating to say. But what she actually said was, 'You need to remember, and quickly, that you aren't at home any more. This is a very different setting and a whole different set of customers. I'm not surprised our guests weren't lured here by lukewarm drinks and a couple of snacks – it's an all-inclusive resort with a very refined clientele, and the event was during their dinner time. Let's try and think things through a bit more clearly before the next event, all right?'

My heart pulsed so loudly in my chest as she walked away that I thought it might burst out. I'd never been accused of not thinking things through before, because I always thought things through, and through, and through again. But she was right. She'd asked me to use my imagination – 'go wild' was what she'd said – and here I was trying to use my tried-and-tested formulas when the variables had changed, a lot.

When I walked back towards my bungalow late that night with a heavy, lonely heart, I barely even noticed that someone had turned all my opening-night signs to face the wall. All I noticed was the voice in my head whispering to me, *'This is why you don't take risks.'*

*Uggghhhh.* For the first time since arriving in the Maldives, I didn't sleep well. Usually, the smell of the salty water, the lapping of the waves just steps away, the little flying foxes flapping through the branches, the delicate squeaks of my gecko friends, all acted like white noise to me inside my bungalow and let me drift away like a paper boat on the tide. But not that night, not after my disaster of an opening night.

That night, I was staring up at my canopy mosquito net into the early hours. Imposter syndrome was making itself comfy among the folds of my brain and I twisted myself into spirals of imagined failure, picturing how nobody was going to visit my store today, nobody was going to buy my books, I couldn't do this on my own, I was out of my depth, who did I think I was, trying to recommend books to this wealthier, more worldly-wise clientele?

When I did doze, I had scratchy shards of a dream that I was somewhere in the California desert, waiting for Marianne's plane to arrive. It never showed up and I was too hot and I was angry, but I couldn't reach her. She'd left me there and I'd been furious rather than worried about where she was. In the dark of my bungalow after jolting awake yet again, I remembered that *this* was the dream I'd had on the plane on my way to the Maldives almost two weeks ago. *This* was what had left me feeling a bit puzzled and off-centre. And now all I wanted to do was check that Marianne had arrived safely. Even if I wasn't with her, even if I was still mad at her, even if I was ashamed at the words I'd retaliated with, I wanted to know she was OK.

I reached for my phone in the dark and went to the Find My app. I'd half expected her to have removed me, but there was her face in its little circular icon. I waited what felt like an excruciating amount of time for the app to find her and then, finally, with all the breath I'd been holding in my body, I exhaled as the last location popped her on the map somewhere unexpected. Dallas, Texas? Probably just another spontaneous decision by the happy couple.

I was reassured now I knew Marianne was safe, but I needed to forget her again. Climbing out of bed, I pulled on a sweater and stepped out of my bungalow into the night, walking a few steps onto the beach and looking up at the starry sky. Wow, it was still pretty warm, even at this time, and I rolled up the sleeves of my sweater. I was barefoot, and I let the cool sand envelop my toes, my soles, and ground me while I gazed upwards. The world, my world, was still and quiet but for the rhythmic swoosh of the tide, and with a few deep breaths I could feel my mind beginning to still, too.

# Chapter 11

# Jenny, in the Maldives

In the morning, basically as soon as the sun came up at six, I gave up on sleep and wrestled my way out of the canopy. I had four hours before I'd be opening my doors, which meant three hours before I'd like to show up and get everything spick and span and ready. I needed to be in a better mood by then. I was in the Maldives, for Christ's sake.

*Hi, Evan,* I texted.

I waited a moment for a sign he was replying before realising like a thicko that if it was just after 6 a.m. here, it was just after 2 a.m. back home. Rather than leaving it sounding like a desperate booty call (do people say booty call any more?), I followed with *How is everything going with the shop?*

Jeez. Could I sound more like I thought of him as an employee?

*And you? How are you?*

Did that sound too much like an afterthought? So I added, *The Maldives are beautiful, sea less choppy than in Bayside, ha ha. I saw a turtle! Wish you were here.*

But then I deleted the 'wish you were here' bit. It was too cheesy. And did I wish he was there? I needed him running the shop, and I had a different shop to run. And with the distance between us, at least I wouldn't be constantly thinking about kissing him again.

It seemed odd to leave it at 'turtle', though.

My fingers hovered over the buttons, wanting to type 'Have you heard from your sister?' but that just made me feel sad again and then resentful because my lack of sleep was making my brain worry too much for someone who had been given the opportunity of a lifetime.

*I officially launched the shop here yesterday evening, and it's the first day of being open today. Scary stuff.*

*Anyway. Hope you're well. Miss you.*

~~*Miss you.*~~

*J xx*

Seven consecutive messages. *Playing it really cool there, Jenny.*

I went off to brush my teeth in my semi-alfresco bathroom, and returned to see my phone screen glowing with an incoming message.

*OK, I'm awake!* It was from Evan, and just seeing his name made me feel less alone.

*Did I wake you up?* I typed.

*Yes, but that's fine. How are you, J? Congrats on the launch! I bet you're nailing it.*

Hmm. It didn't feel like it at the moment. *Yes, it's going well. How's home?*

*All good, nothing to worry about here. Your customers miss you though, and now M's gone as well I reckon they'll think I've locked you both away in a basement.*

I paused, wondering what to write. I wanted to tell him everything, details about the island, the warmth of the water, the shape of the seashells, the taste of the food, the way I was feeling, and how I did, in fact, wish he was there because I could sure do with his kind, familiar face and a second one of those kisses right now.

As I stood there wishing I could tell him all this, he wrote again. *How's the island? Send pics!*

I dutifully sent a photo of the sunrise from a few days ago, the sky in pinks and yellows and the palm tree that Rish had leapt out of in the foreground. *It's completely beautiful here. Just like on the website. How's the flat?*

*Completely beautiful,* he joked in reply. *Weird without you here, though!*

Was that an opening? Of course it was, now would be the perfect time to confess that I couldn't get him out of my mind, but in the few seconds that passed, a thousand worries zoomed through my mind, all of which centred on me ruining things between us. So I ended with *Great, thank you again!* and felt like a coward for waking him up for what was basically a business update.

Putting my phone down, I cursed my cowardly self out loud, and nearly choked on my own scratchy voice. Although I was thirsty, I didn't want to face the dining hall in the staff accommodation quite yet, but on opening my mini fridge the last remaining liquid was my cucumber face toner, which I thought about slugging for a moment until something caught my eye.

'Aha! Come here, you!' I rasped aloud to my coconut, the one Rish had given me on my first night here. He was a nice guy; it was kind of him to come to the opening night. Whenever we crossed paths, it felt like he was flirting, just a little, but I was sure that was just his manner – he was obviously just a really genuinely charming guy with everyone from co-workers to guests.

The coconut had sat like a decoration on my table for nearly a fortnight now and I'd kept wandering past it, thinking, *Oooh, must crack into that bad boy*, but never doing so. Well, today was the day.

Picking up the green orb, I gave it a shake, and yep, the liquid was still in there. I grabbed my penknife and sat on the edge of the bed with the coconut between my knees.

Stabbing at it at rates accelerating from instant-coffee-lid to full-on-slasher-flick left me with zero access to the coconut water and a sweaty brow. Changing tack, I threw it on the floor, which as soon as I'd done it seemed stupid as the sweet liquid could have sloshed out across my bungalow, but I needn't have worried because the damned thing didn't even crack.

Blowing a chunk of escaped reddish-blonde hair out of my face, I decided to get out of there.

The sea is my happy place. It was why I wanted to stay in Bayside, it's why I've always favoured boat trips over any other form of travel, and it's why those images of a string of islands making up the archipelago of the Maldives wouldn't leave my mind even when I'd tried to make them. But now I was there in person, well, this ocean was a whole different kettle of fish, pardon the pun. I'd never lived anywhere before where stepping outside could make me instantly drop a couple of notches on the worry scale. My flat back home was lovely, and it was mine, and I was only a short walk from the beach, but coming out of my bungalow here and instantly facing palm trees, feeling the press of the cool morning sand under my feet, the subtle scent of the native pink roses in the air, was just blissful.

I wondered if having a break from Bayside would, in actual fact, make me feel that way about my hometown again ...

This morning, the sky and sea were blended with shades of lemon and mango, the ocean still and reflective like a mirror to the heavens. Clutching my coconut, I began my walk around the curve of the island.

When I reached the main stretch of beach, where one or two people were having an early dip in the sea and resort staff were straightening towels on loungers, combing the sand, lining up boards with paddles, I spotted the coconut aficionado I was after.

'Rish?' I called.

He looked up from where he was polishing a jet ski. 'Good morning, sunshine!'

Rish's smile was infectious, despite my mood. 'Good morning to you. Thank you for coming to the launch last night.'

'Of course, of course. It was successful, huh?' he said kindly.

'Well, I don't know about that. I didn't make a lot of sales.'

But he just waved a hand. 'You will. You don't need to sell everything on the first day. Just relax into it. Now, have you been picking my coconuts?'

I looked down at the thing in my arms. 'Actually, you're just the man I wanted to find this morning. I wondered if you could help me?'

'Sure.' He put down his cloth and walked across the sand towards me, lifting his shirt for a fraction of a second to mop his brow and flashing me a beautiful six-pack, which made me drop my coconut.

Scooping it back up, I handed it to him and he inspected it for a second, running his fingers over the stab wounds my penknife had created. 'Did you two get in a fight?'

'I just wanted to finally break into it and try the coconut water, but it's just ... stupid.'

'It's very stupid,' he agreed. 'Is this the one I gave you a couple of weeks ago?'

I nodded. 'Sorry.'

'Nothing to apologise for, you're part of the family now, so do whatever you want, whenever you want.'

'I'm not sure our bosses would agree with that. Especially yours. Is he always a bit of ...' I trailed off, looking around. I didn't know anybody here well enough to start bad-mouthing people; it wasn't my place, and I was just a grump from lack of sleep.

'An asshole? Yes.' Rish looked around too and put a hand on my arm, leading me a little closer to the edge of the water, a little further away from his colleagues. His touch was pleasantly warm. 'He wasn't always quite this bad. He's pretty influential within particular party crowds and they bring a lot of money, and friends, and every time they do his ego grows just a little bit more.'

'I got the feeling Khadeeja didn't want the island going that way too much,' I said. 'Maybe that's why he was so sniffy with me. If management wants to move away from what he's bringing in, does he consider me and my shop a threat?'

'That's what I think too. Don't get me wrong, we've never had a problem with those guests, they're just as welcome as anyone else. It's more that it feels like Blane wants this to be a cash-splashing party island, and I don't know, I think it would be a totally different vibe if it went too far that way.' With that, Rish reached behind a podium, pulled out a machete and in about ten seconds had crouched on the ground, *hack-hack-hacked* one end of the coconut into a point, and then, with a final slice, when I was sure his hand was about to go flying, he cracked the top off and handed it to me. And there it was! My big green coconut was open, and inside was the nut, the thick snow-white of the flesh and a pool of silky water. It had been in there all along.

'One second,' Rish said, scooping up the remnants of the shell and swapping them and the machete behind the podium for a silver metal straw that he popped in the top. 'Go ahead, try it.'

I sipped it and … *mmmmmm*. I'm not a big fan of photos of myself, usually, but sipping on a fresh coconut on an island in the Maldives at dawn begged to be 'grammed. 'Sorry to be a big tourist,' I said to Rish, getting out my phone. 'But would you mind taking a photo of me?'

'Of course, my pleasure, and I love working with tourists because they're the happiest people on earth.' He took my phone and held it up, taking a couple of pictures and then scrutinising me for a moment. Reaching back behind the podium again, he pulled out a paper umbrella and popped that in the coconut too. I struck my pose, again, but he still wasn't quite satisfied. Coming close to me, he removed the tiny umbrella, asked, 'May I?' and then pushed my hair aside a little to stick it behind my ear.

There was a moment, just a microsecond, there on that beach, when I met Rish's eyes as he touched the side of my face. It was as if the human contact, pretty much the first I'd had since Evan and I had said goodbye, pulled me like a magnet into the present. I felt myself brightening again under his gaze. I liked it.

Rish stepped back, easy-breezy, and took the photo, then looked at my phone before handing it back. 'That's beautiful,' he murmured. 'Have you ever been paddleboarding?'

'Um, no,' I said, putting my phone back in my pocket, resisting the overwhelming urge to counter his compliment with a self-deprecating comment and wondering if I'd dreamed the whole thing.

'How long do you have before work this morning?'

'We open at ten, but I want to be there for nine.'

'So a couple of hours. Why don't you take one of the boards out? The sea is perfection this morning.'

I looked to where he was gesturing at one of the absolutely bloody massive boards lying on the beach, a paddle ten times my height lying beside it. Ten times is an exaggeration, but the point was it was ginormous. 'I've never been paddleboarding,' I said, instead of giving an actual answer.

'It's easy, especially on calm water like this. There's not even a breath in the air. I'll show you.'

'I don't have my swimsuit on.'

'You won't fall in.'

'Are you kidding? I will absolutely fall in.'

'No, you won't, and if you do, is that the worst thing in the world? You'll be staying shallow and I'll keep an eye on you, the water is clear, the sharks are just babies and it's not a bad way to wake up. Wash off those cobwebs?'

'Sharks?'

'Babies,' he repeated.

Hmm. He had a good point about washing off the cobwebs. My moment of hesitation was enough to spur Rish into action and he held a basket in front of me. 'Here, leave everything you don't want to take in there, including your coconut, and let's go.'

I unloaded my phone, my nut and my flip-flops into the basket and followed him to the board, which he lifted easily with one hand.

'Isn't that heavy?' I asked.

'Nope, it's inflatable.'

'It is?' This didn't look like your cheap pool inflatable with stretched, crinkled edges and squeaky plastic. It looked solid and hard-wearing and reliable. And big. Like a cross between a big surfboard and that door Rose lies on in *Titanic*.

Rish moved it down to the shoreline, dragging it through the sand with one hand and holding the paddle in the other. Putting the board down, he stood the paddle beside me, scrutinised the two of us and then fiddled with a lever until he'd adjusted the length to a little less than a foot taller than me.

'All right, when you're on the board, you need to hold the paddle with your arms far apart, like this.' He held the paddle in the air with one hand on the very end and the other about an arm's length away. 'Well, not exactly like this, you want the paddle in the water, ha ha. When it's in the water, keep the paddle this way around, close to you, and keep calm.'

'Keep calm? Who can ever keep calm when they're told to keep calm?'

'*You* can,' he grinned. 'Now, let me show you how to stand up.'

'*Noooo*,' I said. 'I can't stand up – I'll just sit on the board.'

'Yes, you can. Now look.' He wasn't taking my concerns very seriously, but then neither was I. It was as if I'd been programmed to first say no to anything challenging these days.

I put that thought back in its box and focused on Rish instead, ready to prove myself wrong.

'Kneel on the board first to get you out into the water, then just put your hands down, with the paddle resting on the board in front of you, and stand up one foot at a time. Try not to look down. Or have your feet too far forwards – you should stay central.'

That was a lot of things to remember, but I kept my mouth shut, attached the leash to my ankle and took a couple of steps into the water, the coolness waking up my ankles in a not unpleasant way. I put my hand on the board, and it felt solid and safe.

Rish briefed me on some more safety need-to-knows, including how to come back in, thank God, and then stood back on the beach to watch me, an encouraging smile on his lips.

I looked at him. 'Aren't you coming in?'

'I'm working.'

'I'm going in alone?'

'Yep, you'll be fine.'

I felt him watching me as I climbed on the board, wet trickles tickling my shins as I knelt. It swayed under my weight, but not in a haphazard way that made me scared I was going to fall, more in the way that for something to change, you need to rock a boat. I used the paddle to slide the water alongside the board and push myself out above the seabed.

Then, when I was feeling suitably relaxed and serene and in charge, I stood up, legs shaking, board tilting, core muscles wondering what in fresh hell was going on, my head and shoulders desperate to tip themselves forward and stare down into the water below me. And while all this was happening, I was standing, I was paddling and I was afraid, but I was doing it.

'This is *soooo* weird,' I called back to Rish, who was now standing at the edge of the water, his thumbs up in the air.

'You're doing great,' he called back.

'You are,' I retorted, for no real reason.

I wouldn't say it was easy, and I had the big advantage of being on water that was as flat as a pane of glass, but it wasn't as hard as I'd always imagined paddleboarding to be. I sometimes saw them out in the sea off the beach back at home, people who'd taken advantage of a rare calm morning and hurtled down to the esplanade with their equipment. I always imagined it took the kind of person who was good at surfing, owned an array of high-tech swimsuits and could pull off that sea-salty mermaid-hair look. But, actually, I could do it too. I didn't have to just watch it or look at pictures any more.

'Where should I go?' I called back to Rish.

'Where do you want to go?'

I looked back at this wonderfully new view of my island, turning my head left and right. To my left, from this spot, was the long jetty with the overwater villas. To my right was the shorter jetty and seaplane, and the longer stretch of sunlounger-sprinkled beach, which, if you followed it all the way along as it curved round the very tip of the island, took you to the beach bungalows.

'Can I go and see my bungalow?'

'Sure. Don't go too far out – you don't want your paddle damaging the reefs. And stay close enough on this side of the island that I can still see you, since this is your first time, and enjoy!'

I tried to give him a wave, but removing my palm from the top of the paddle had me wobbling in panic, so I quickly clamped it back on again and set sail, as it were.

The island drifted past on my left as my gaze drifted with it, taking in the tall, lush trees, the stark, double-cream-coloured sand and the coffee-hued boardwalk I could just see trailing between the beach and the vegetation. I soon forgot my wobbles, physical and emotional, and sank into the flow of migrating forwards, eyes open. The water below me was crystal clear and the colour of an opal, but I didn't need to look down to see it because it was all around me, and I felt like that turtle I'd met when I first arrived, just enjoying the moment.

From my spot in the sea, I could see other neighbouring islands dotted around my horizons, those little diamonds I'd seen from the seaplane on my way here. I breathed out. I was so, so lucky. I had to remember that. A month ago, I had been looking at images like this on a computer screen, and now they were in front of my own eyes, and I was living *my* life and not somebody else's. Today was a new day, my store was opening and it would be very un-Jenny-like to give up at the first hurdle, so I wasn't about to.

There it was: my home. The bungalows sneaked into view, partially hidden behind the coconut palms like ladies behind paper fans, and I could just see mine tucked a little way back, the flash of the turquoise hammock strung in front of it visible against the white walls and green leaves.

I angled the paddle into the water so that the board relaxed to a pause, and sat down, dangling my legs over the sides and letting the cool water stroke my calves. I could smell my eco-friendly sun lotion mixing with the salt water on my skin, and felt the early heat from the sun settling on my upper back and warming my hair.

It was easy to see why people started their day like this. Maybe, though I didn't want to think about it right now, even when I wasn't in my holiday-brochure paradise, I could create my own pockets of paradise at home.

# Chapter 12

# Marianne, in the USA

If Drew made one more comment about the fact this girl hadn't turned up yet, Marianne was going to tie him to the railings and leave him there. She was already nervously shifting from foot to foot, trying to look casual, like they were just waiting to meet a friend somewhere in this huge crowd of festival fanatics. There was a lot of security milling around the entrance, and although Marianne didn't *think* they were doing anything illegal, she also wasn't sure exactly how 'OK' it was for them to buy second-hand Coachella tickets from someone who had to leave early.

They'd picked up their hire car that morning, Marianne practically itching to get out on the open road.

'We've got to get a Mustang,' she'd said upon arriving at the car-rental garage back in the airport. 'Come on, Drew, we're going to be driving across the desert – is there anything more *Thelma and Louise*?'

'A Thunderbird?' he answered.

'Well, I don't see a Thunderbird here, just a bunch of boring cars and this.' She draped herself over the red convertible until she noticed the rental man in his hut starting to blush.

'Let's do it!' Drew had enthused, and they'd driven straight to Palm Springs, a town so inundated with visitors that they finally settled on staying at a colourful motel a decent stretch from the rest of the town, after being turned away from five other establishments with no vacancies.

No sooner had they checked in, they jumped on the shuttle bus straight to Indio and to the Coachella festival entrance. Marianne had pulled together all her biggest jewellery and smallest denim. She had also purposefully snapped a cheap necklace and, using eyelash glue, had stuck the diamanté stones around her eyes, finally adding a leather shoelace from one of Drew's shoes to a braid in her hair. She looked perfect. Now she just needed to damn well get in there.

'She said three p.m., Drew, and it's only twenty past. And it's a long walk from the shuttle buses so she probably got caught up.'

'I didn't say anything,' Drew said in return.

Marianne patted her pocket, where she'd put the eye-watering amount of cash she'd drawn out to hand over to the wristband seller she'd connected with on social media. It turned out there wasn't a chance in hell they would have been able to buy new tickets at this point in the game.

Around her, it was as if Instagram had come to life before her eyes. Flower-haired beauties strolled about with neon paint on their faces. Art installations rose up from the street, ready for that perfect backdrop pose. Loud, lively music could be heard atop the still desert air.

'Do you want some water?' Marianne asked Drew, handing him the dregs of the large bottle. It was hot hot hot out here.

'Better make it last.' He waved it away, and in doing so not so subtly checked his watch.

'Do you have somewhere better to be?' Marianne asked. She'd meant it to be teasing and cute, but she came out sounding frustrated and, thanks to her dry mouth, like a scratchy nag.

Before Drew could answer, two women approached, walking fast in cut-off T-shirts, shorts and high-top trainers. They both wore mirrored aviators and spoke quickly.

'Hey-are-you-Mary-Anne?' one asked.

'Yes, that's me!' Close enough. 'Are you—'

'We've-got-your-wristbands,' the other woman said, and the two of them huddled in front of Marianne and Drew, their backs to security. After a little tugging, they slipped the bands off their arms and held them out. 'We-have-to-leave-early, thanks-so-much-for-buying-these.'

'Family-emergency. Thanks-again-you're-a-total-babe.'

'So these will just work at the security counter?' Drew clarified, his voice utterly unconvinced.

'Yes, we-just-came-from-inside, they're-totally-legit.'

Drew faced Marianne. 'I don't know about this,' he said in a quiet voice.

Marianne hesitated. It didn't seem *quite* right to her either, but she looked at the wristbands again and they did seem to match those flashing past on the wrists of other attendees. This was their only chance, really, so surely it was worth the gamble?

'Look,' the first woman said, pulling out her phone and holding it up for her to see. 'Here are photos from us inside. We'll even knock a hundred off the price. We just want to make back as much of what we've lost as we can and then we need to get going.'

'Drew, let's do this,' Marianne said, and he shrugged. Drawing the cash from her pocket, she asked the women, 'Did you see any celebrities inside?'

'Oh yeah, loads. We hung out near Nicki Minaj.'

'No way!'

With the cash in their hands, the women leaned in and gave them both a quick squeeze and then ran off towards the shuttle buses while Marianne and Drew made their way to the entrance.

Marianne couldn't believe she was really about to be here! This was beyond exciting; it was a dream—

'Excuse me, miss.' The security guard's hand on her arm caused her blood to run cold.

'Yes?'

'Can I see that wristband?'

With a thudding heart, and Drew's hand on her back, she raised her arm to him. He took her wrist and squinted, tapping the plastic digital reader on the top, then moved her arm to the electronic scanner again.

There was no bleep. Nothing. Marianne even pushed her arm flat against the scanner.

The security officer asked her to step aside. 'Where did you get that wristband?'

'I ...' Marianne looked back to Drew's eyes and then past him in the direction the two women had disappeared.

The security officer placed a hand behind her and another did the same to Drew and started guiding them away from the festival, away from the lights and colours and music and fun.

'You two are going to need to come with me.'


As time ticked by and Marianne and Drew sat side by side on hard plastic chairs inside a mercifully air-conned but sparsely furnished room, surrounded by other miserable faces and flanked by security personnel, she just kept thinking: *All that money.* Marianne felt awful, and she was sure Drew was going to be mad at her – *she* was certainly mad at her.

'Sons of bitches,' she muttered, looking at Instagram on her phone. 'Nicki Minaj isn't even at Coachella this weekend.' She looked up at Drew to apologise, again, but he was laughing.

'What?' she asked, nudging him, but that made him laugh louder. She glanced at the security officer, who raised her eyebrows in the direction of Drew. 'Shush, they'll think you're high and then we'll be in even more trouble.'

Trying to quieten himself, Drew ended up letting out a loud snort, which set Marianne off into giggles. 'What are you *laughing at*?' she hissed, trying desperately to control herself with deep breathing.

He gulped, and then looked down at her with sparkling eyes. 'Just this whole situation. We've found ourselves in the equivalent of Coachella jail, for God's sake.'

Marianne felt her shoulders shaking. 'It's not funny. You're supposed to be pissed at me. I just blew a chunk of our cash and wasted a day of our trip here … in Coachella jail.'

Their wristbands – the fakes – had been snipped off and thrown away, along with a little of their pride and a lot of their money. Outside, the sky had turned dusky and whenever the door would open to let out, or in, another jailbird, the bass of another hit song would briefly flood the room.

'I'm sorry you didn't get to go to Coachella. I know you wanted to.' Drew smiled and reached his hand up to her face to boop her nose, which made her laugh again.

'I'm sorry. I guess maybe – in *some* situations – advance planning can pay off.' She rolled her eyes theatrically.

Drew shrugged. 'So be it. We had an adventure today, didn't we? That's what this whole trip is about.'

'Maybe you could put this in a book one day. Only can you not make it me that falls for the scammers?'

Then, they were allowed to leave, and with a last, mournful gaze at the neon lit-from-beneath palm trees and twirling colours, they left to ride the bus back to their motel.

'Are you sad?' Drew asked her on the way back as she rested her head on his shoulder.

'A little. But we still went to Coachella. We just didn't go *into* Coachella. That's better than nothing.'

When they reached the motel, they changed into their swimmers for an evening dip. As Marianne sunk into the motel pool to the distant sound of an A-list headliner belting out beats into the desert sky, she found herself thinking about how she could have been in there right now. Coulda, woulda, shoulda. Oh well. A weekend in baking Palm Springs, staying well under the shade of these tall palms, wasn't something she was ever going to complain about.

# Chapter 13

# Jenny, in the Maldives

I was closing up the shop when I heard a drumbeat in the distance. Wondering if it was an incoming headache, I ignored it for a moment and went back to my thoughts. I'd noticed a pattern since opening the shop a few days ago. The people who came in, who were fairly few and far between, tended to pick up a couple of books with beautiful covers, read the backs, put them down and move on. Occasionally somebody would purchase one, but more often than not interest would wane before they'd even done a full circle of the shop.

At home I was used to seeing people mull and muse and walk back and forth between the shelves, almost as if there was too much choice and they were having to really decide what to spend their money on. But I didn't think a tight budget was the problem here, so what was it?

Making my way back towards the entrance of the Cove Pavilion, waving at my fellow sales assistants and managers as they closed up their own stores for the night, I could still hear that faint drumming. It seemed more incessant now, more rhythmic, and less like the doom of an incoming migraine.

I followed the staircase that led from reception up to the mezzanine, which I realised I hadn't explored before, and I noticed two things at once.

One, the space was big and airy. Sparse shelves dotted with magazines lined one wall, while comfortable lounge chairs and low tables invited guests to relax in the peace and quiet, and the air con. The huge windows stretched all the way from the ground floor to the roof of this level, giving a gorgeous view down across the pool, the beach and the ocean. I imagined the colours must be ever-changing. What a retreat this area was. And yet it was completely empty.

And two, that outside the windows, on the beach, there seemed to be some kind of performance happening. I could see a large group of men dressed in matching *feyli* and T-shirts, beating drums and swaying and moving as the sun was setting behind them. Guests were lounging in the cabanas and on beanbags, and flickering flame torches had been poked into the sand.

Whipping out my phone to take a photo, I realised I hadn't checked on Marianne that day. Most mornings since she'd left the UK, I'd got into a habit I hadn't intended of checking on her Instagram, both her feed and her Stories, searching for clues as to what she and Drew had been up to while I was asleep.

Anyway, I'd forgotten this morning for the first time, so I checked now. Just a few snaps of her looking happy and of bright sunshine, just like in the Maldives, but instead of my turquoises and greens, Marianne was against a backdrop of dusty khaki.

There was a pink ring around her profile photo, indicating a new Story, and with trepidation I pressed it and watched my phone fill with a laughing video of her face. Her pretty, familiar face. That big laugh. That big energy. She was covered in flouro face paint and had flowers in her hair, while music played in the background. A sticker had been applied to the Story that read, in wavy lettering, 'COACHELLA'.

And just as quickly as it had appeared, her face vanished, and I was back on her grid. She looked like she was living her best life, like she didn't need me to be there or missed me at all.

And after the things I'd said to her? Who could blame her?

Those drums sounded again, pulling me back to the present. I scuttled back down the steps and outside, where the temperature was still balmy and in the late twenties, rounded the pool and hovered in the back, watching what was taking place.

It was magical. The men were singing, dancing and banging, and the whole crowd was mesmerised, the drumbeat reverberating through them. The fiery torches and papaya-coloured sunset added to the atmosphere, and I noticed a sign had been erected that said: *Boduberu: Traditional Maldivian Performance, 6 p.m.*

When I looked back up, I noticed Layla also standing at the back, under one of the trees, so I made my way over.

'Hi,' I whispered.

'Oh, hi, Jenn!' She tore her eyes away and grinned at me.

At that moment the drums flourished and with an almighty coordinated *bang* the performers came to a stop and the beach was filled with the sound of clapping.

'Are they finished?' I asked.

'No, they'll have a break for about five minutes now and then do another couple of songs until the sun disappears completely.'

'Oh, brilliant. Are we allowed to be out here?'

Layla laughed. 'Yes, of course. Have you not seen one of these yet?'

'A bod ... bodyberry performance?'

'*Boduberu*. The resort puts them on every week.'

'Ah,' I nodded. 'Most evenings I've been staying in the shop pretty late after closing. You don't hear a lot of the hotel atmosphere back there.'

'I'm glad you made it this evening. Did you see Rish?'

'Where?' I looked around, and then up into the nearest coconut palm.

'Over there.' She pointed towards the crowd of performers, and all of a sudden one of them shifted his weight and Rish's face came into view, followed by his body, dressed in one of the matching T-shirts and sarongs.

'Rish is one of the performers?'

'Yep, he's a drummer,' she said with a hint of pride. I side-eyed her face for a moment as she beamed towards him, the sunset golden in her irises. Was there something between those two? Or were they just good friends? I wasn't sure. It was also possible he really was just a bit of a flirt, and that was fine. My hand reached for my phone in my pocket, thinking of Evan and how he was only a call or a text away.

'He's very talented,' I commented about Rish.

'Mm-hmm,' she nodded. 'And a really nice guy, too, you know? Not like Blane, who has to hold court in every room he enters.' She met my eye. 'Rish told me Blane was being a pain to you. I'm sorry. I don't know what it is, but he has some kind of delusion of grandeur about his position in this place. One day he'll cross the line and Khadeeja will fire his ass. Anyway, Rish will have your back.'

'Thanks. Rish did tell me a few things about Blane and his ideas for the island which might explain a couple of things. The guy got my back up the other night, but really, how often are the paths of the entertainment director and the bookshop manager going to cross?' I hoped that was true. 'Rish was really kind, though. He showed me how to paddleboard and that dosed me with sunshine again.'

I glanced back at her again, looking for signs, just in case me hanging out with Rish was stepping on any sandy toes, but to my surprise her grin grew even wider. 'That's awesome. You know, I've been friends with Rish for *suuuuch* a long time and I would love to see him find a nice girl. And you seem like a nice girl. Do you have anyone special at home?'

Now that was a loaded question. I had an Evan at home, did that count? Because he certainly wasn't *mine*. 'No, not really,' I answered.

'Not really?'

'I mean, no. There was a guy I liked before I came away and I thought it might develop into something, but we've been friends for a long time, so I don't think either of us wants to risk ruining that, to be honest.'

Layla nodded, as if she understood. 'Well,' she drew lines in the sand with her toes, 'Rish keeps mentioning your name. And it's not against the rules for colleagues to have a relationship, only against getting frisky with the guests. I'm just saying.'

*Boom, ba-da-boom, ba-da-boom.* The drummers started up again and with that I had to stop the conversation, but I looked to where Rish was standing in formation. I watched the final golden drips of the sun wash over his exposed arms, highlighting his muscles, his feet digging into the sand and the heavy-looking drum strapped around his waist. He was quite sexy, I had to admit, though that could have been the fire and the beat and the sunset talking. No matter what he was doing, he never seemed to lose that happy and free look about him.

Beside me, Layla was tapping her feet, swaying her long hair, lost in the music, while I wondered what it would be like to have a new beginning, and to get lost in Rish.

# Chapter 14

# Marianne, in the USA

'*Wild*, by Cheryl Strayed. That journey started in the Mojave Desert.' Marianne glanced at Drew in the passenger seat, a lock of her curly hair blowing across her face in the warm wind. The Mustang's top was down, they were on the open road, the radio was playing and her man had his eyes closed, the sun on his face and the breeze lifting tendrils of his own dark hair. This was the road trip she'd imagined.

Now they were on the road and heading away from the pastels and neons of Palm Springs, they were naming books to each other that were set in this warm, dusty region of California that stretched as far as Nevada, Arizona and Utah.

Drew opened his eyes for a moment, pulling up his sunglasses and meeting her glance, and offered a slow, chilled smile. '*The Valkyries*, Paulo Coelho.'

'You look hot,' Marianne commented.

'No, I'm good, I'm just enjoying the weather.'

'No, I mean, you look *hot*. It suits you, riding in my car.'

He laughed. 'It suits you, driving a convertible.'

'My dad had one, you know.' She hadn't meant to bring up her dad, not at this moment.

Drew shifted in his seat. 'I didn't know that.'

'I don't talk about him a lot.'

'I'd noticed. Is he still around?'

'No.' She shook her head, her eyes fixed on the long, straight road ahead and the ripples of heat haze in the air before her. 'It's OK. We weren't close, not like I was with Mum, and that goes for Evan, too. Dad moved to Germany after he and my mum split, when I was still in primary school, and I barely saw him again. He was a good guy, flawed, but fine, like us all, I guess. And during those short years we did all live as a family, I remember he had an open-top car. Which seemed ridiculous at the time because it was hardly ever good enough weather to have the top down, but now I get it. It's kind of freeing.'

'I'm sorry,' Drew said, moving a hand onto her shoulder.

'No, it's really fine. I'm fine. I can't wallow, all I can do is enjoy the shit out of my life.' She threw him a grin, letting any melancholy get whipped away in the breeze. '*The Other Americans*.'

'The who?'

'That book from a couple of years ago by Laila Lalami. *The Other Americans*.'

'Of course, that was about a family living near Joshua Tree National Park,' he nodded.

'Are we in Joshua Tree now?' Marianne asked.

Drew leaned over to zoom out on the satnav. 'We're nearby. You'll see when we hit the park boundary, I think.'

They'd left Palm Springs about an hour ago, at first light the day *after* the day after Coachella. Even without wristbands to get them into the festival, they'd found the town still fizzing with cool pool parties and non-stop vaycay vibes and they'd had a blast. Wanting to avoid crawling out behind reams of other traffic, they'd spent Monday relaxing with bed, books (*Interview with the Vampire*, after Drew had read an article about Anne Rice having a home nearby at one point), and shopping in the outlet mall, and had woken up that morning having had their first full night's sleep since the long slumber in the San Diego airport hotel.

Marianne and Drew had jumped in the car with iced coffees and no real plan other than to let the roads ribbon them in whatever direction they felt like. Then, when they were done for the day with views and sun and photo ops, they'd find a hostel or motel, or maybe even a glamping pod, to rest up in and shower off the sweat.

'When we enter the park, do you just want to drive around and see some viewpoints?' Marianne asked Drew, her right hand on the wheel and her left hand tapping to the music on the hot metal of the car door. She'd always liked cars, and driving on the other side of the road, with all the controls on the other side of the car, felt like an adventure in itself.

'Yep,' Drew agreed, lowering his shades again and settling back to let the reflective glass shine bright blue from the cloudless sky above. 'Though we should take it easy, maybe not go down any dirt roads. This isn't a four-by-four.'

Marianne nodded. But inside she thought, *We'll see about that.*

'Well, it's fucked.' Marianne slammed down the hood of the Mustang and stamped back round to the driver's seat, hot dust puffing out from under her trainers with every step. She leaned in and glared at Drew. 'We're fucked.'

As he pulled out the rental car's instruction manual from the glovebox, his mouth clamped shut, she stood up and shielded her eyes from the sun. To her left was one long, winding strip of dirt road that cut through the barren landscape until it disappeared in a shimmer of heat haze on the horizon. To her right, the exact same vista. Mountain peaks watched them from a far distance and rocks, both vast and small, jutted between the tenderstem-broccoli-like Joshua trees sprouting from the earth.

They'd been driving a while in the park on quiet, tarmacked roads, enjoying the scenery, when Marianne had pushed for them to head off on one of the sand-toned tracks. Surely that would have the best viewpoints, the quietest moments of zen. Maybe a little spot for some outdoor excitement away from the public eye? But then, after crawling along for a while, the car, now coated with a thin layer of dust, had started emitting a slightly odd aroma.

At first, Marianne had fiddled with the air con, then she had moved their massive, half-eaten bag of Cheetos out of the drinks holder in case that had something to do with it, and then the engine warning light had begun flashing.

'Um, just going to pull over!' she said to Drew.

'Where?'

'Literally anywhere, there's nothing out here,' she'd snapped, more out of embarrassment than frustration at him.

This wasn't Marianne's first experience with car trouble, being quite a frequent 'It'll be fine'-er when it came to engine warning lights and the like, so she jumped out of the car to take a look under the hood.

She saw it immediately: a radiator leak.

Shitting, fucking shit.

Jesus, it was hot out here. A prickling heat, unrelenting. She stood with her hands on her hips, looking for signs of life coming from either direction.

She pulled her phone out of her shorts pocket and cursed, again, under her breath when she saw she had no signal.

'Mari, what's up?' Drew called from the passenger seat.

'Nothing,' she said back, from behind the open hood.

He appeared beside her, his hands on his hips, and together they looked at the inside of the car. 'Hmm.'

'It's fine,' she said.

'Can we fix it?' He mopped his brow with his T-shirt, but even the glimpse of his toned stomach couldn't quite distract her from the problem at hand.

'Can I borrow your phone?' Marianne asked. 'The torch on yours is brighter than mine and I just need to see something.' That was rubbish, she could see fine, but she wanted to see if he had any signal before she admitted anything to him. He handed it over and … no. No service. 'Bollocking shitballs. Shitting, shitting cocks.'

'Something wrong?' Drew asked, his voice light in a way she found irritating.

'We'll need someone to come out and help us. And … we don't have any phone signal out here.'

Drew was quiet for so long, shading himself under the open hood, that eventually Marianne snapped. 'Just say it. I know this is all my fault and we shouldn't have driven this car down here.'

'I wasn't going to say that! Jesus.'

'You know what, though, we were doing fine. This car should have been *fine*. This is just an unfortunate incident that could have happened to anyone. So stop being like that.'

'Like what?'

'Like a disappointed teacher.'

He threw his hands up in the air. 'I'm so sorry for standing here quietly.' He walked back round to the car and reached into the glovebox, pulling out the emergency contact number. 'You stay here and somehow shelter away from the sun. I'm going to take a walk and try and get a signal.'

'No way!' Marianne slammed down the hood of the car and reached in to grab her bag and bottle of water. 'One of us will absolutely die if we split up. We'll go together.' She didn't love the idea of them leaving their car full of their belongings, but if anyone came over to steal it, perhaps they'd also let the two of them borrow their phone?

She and Drew began their ascent up the nearest slope, her trainers slipping on the loose rocks. It was all just bad luck, but a gnawing part of her felt like Drew was being very *Jenn* about the situation. Silently judging, biting his tongue, not blaming her with words but with silence. 'Just yell at me, if you want to,' she muttered after a while.

Drew sighed. 'I don't want to yell at you. I'm not pissed off – that's *you*. I'm just trying to conserve a bit of energy in case we're stuck in the middle of nowhere for the rest of the day and night.'

'That's not going to happen,' she dismissed him. She hoped. 'I am sorry.'

'It's fine.'

'Just so you know,' she needled, like the needles in the Joshua trees, 'I hate the "It's fine" end to arguments.'

Drew kept walking, but glanced back at her, the look in his eyes masked by his shades. 'Why are you doing this?'

'What?'

'Pushing for this to be an argument?'

'I'm not.' Was she? They'd never had a proper argument before; she didn't know what he was like when he was angry, and he didn't know what she was like when she was vindictive. Maybe they needed to learn that about each other.

'Do you always get like this when things go wrong?' he asked, and picked up his stride, ascending the rocks fast, one eye on his phone.

'Like what? I'm being perfectly normal.'

'Well, for someone who likes spontaneity, you don't seem to cope very well when it doesn't work out how you want it to.'

'That is not true, I am fine with things turning out however they want to turn out. I just don't want to have to always apologise for making decisions we both agreed to.'

'Literally nobody is asking you to apologise. Shit happens.'

There was a humming sound in the air for a moment and she stopped to check the road behind her, her eyes searching for signs of an incoming car.

Ahead of her, Drew took another big step upwards, his phone held high, his face turned towards the sun and the screen, but as Marianne swivelled to tell him to shush a moment and stand still, he let out a loud yelp, and stumbled backwards.

Marianne caught the brunt of him, her own trainers skidding in the dry stones underfoot. 'What the hell?'

'Ow, bloody hell, *ow*,' he was muttering, his breathing fast, as he grabbed her hand and, limping, pulled her further back down the slope.

'What's wrong, where are we going?' Marianne was worried now and gripped his hand in hers, their tiff forgotten. 'Drew? Are you OK? *Stop.*'

He halted and checked the ground around him before collapsing into the dirt and gripping his ankle. 'Up there, there was ...' He tried to catch his breath. 'A snake.'

Marianne felt her skin grow cold, despite the heat. She had nothing against snakes in general, but she'd heard that humming sound. That rattle. 'What kind of snake?'

'I don't know, I didn't see it properly, that's probably why it attacked me.'

'Did you step on it?'

'No, but I put my foot down right beside it. I only noticed when I saw something move, something long and mottled brown. Oh man, this is really painful.' He went to touch the skin of his ankle and Marianne batted his hand away.

'Did you hear a noise, just before?'

Drew looked up at her, pushing his sunnies onto his head. 'Yeah. Do you think it was a rattlesnake?'

They were silent for a moment, looking into each other's eyes, the only sound coming from the wind.

'Do *you* think it was a rattlesnake?' Marianne asked him in return.

'I don't know. It's painful, though.'

She stood up tall and looked around. If Drew had been bitten by a rattlesnake, then the venom was poisonous. And they were out in the desert, with no phone service, alone.

'I'm going back up,' Marianne stated, shielding her eyes from the sunshine. It was midday now, and though she felt as if she could see for miles in all directions, there was still no sign of any other cars.

'What do you mean?' Drew asked, gripping her hand to stop her from leaving. 'You're not going up there only to get bitten yourself.'

'Of course not. I'll look with every footstep. But one of us needs to get to the top of those rocks and get a bloody phone signal, and it's not going to be you.' She bent down to him, taking his face in her hands. 'I didn't mean that horribly, I meant that you have to stay here and rest and not panic and not walk on it.'

He nodded, his face pale. 'If it was a rattlesnake, it could be …'

'But it could not be,' she countered, and smiled at him, even though inside she was screaming. Yes, it could be fatal. A particularly gruesome scene of a thriller she'd read a few years back, in which the lead character had died out in the desert, crossed her mind. But it might *not* be fatal. There was no use thinking about that right now because time was ticking down and they needed to get to an emergency room, to some antivenom.

Marianne ran down the remainder of the slope to the car, where she unzipped her case and pulled out a pair of skinny jeans from near the top. It might be baking, they might be impractical for a tough climb, but she wasn't about to go back past that snake, or any of its friends, without at least a modicum of leg covering. Quickly switching her shorts for them, she grabbed the sunblock and ran all the way back up to Drew, panting.

'Put on some more sun lotion and stay here,' she instructed, and then stood, ready to trek back up.

Drew grabbed her hands and pulled her back down. 'I'm sorry for our argument. I really wasn't angry at you. I don't care about car troubles.'

'It's OK, I know.' She had to go, and she tried to extricate herself.

'I love you.'

'I *know*. Wait – what?' She stopped and looked down at him, her heart pounding, the dust settling. 'You what?'

He sat up taller, wincing in pain. 'I love you.'

'Are you just saying that because you think you're going to die?'

'No, I'm saying it because these past few months together have been incredible, and exciting, and fun, and only a little bit death-defying. And I've been wanting to tell you since San Diego. But I guess I'm saying it now.'

Marianne stood rooted to the spot for a moment, taking it in. Nobody had told her they loved her since her mum had died. No boyfriends, no girlfriends; she and her brother didn't say it to each other, though they obviously did. She and Jenn would sometimes say goodbye after a big event with a 'Love you', which of course was just as powerful and real, but nobody had looked her in the eye and said the words *I love you*.

'Mari,' Drew broke into her thoughts, 'I love you, but I'd also love some antivenom right now.'

She snapped back to the present. 'Of course. I'm going. Thank you. I mean ...' She stooped down and touched his forehead, allowing herself one more short moment to look into his eyes. 'I love you, too. So ... don't bloody die.'

With that, Marianne leapt up and ran, looking down the whole time, forcing their exchange, wonderful as it was, to the back of her mind. She checked every step and slowed as much as she dared when she neared the spot where Drew had been bitten. She listened, waiting for the vibration, for the rattle, but heard nothing.

And then she saw it: the snake, basking in the sunshine as if nothing had happened. It was big, maybe four foot long, with brown scales and a slim head. Marianne checked her phone, which still had no signal, and looked up. The top of the rocks wasn't far, she could make it, but first ...

'What are you doing? Don't get near it!' she heard Drew's voice call out from below as she leaned forward to take a photo of the snake from a distance. This wasn't for Instagram, but something told her it might be useful to plan ahead for going to a hospital. They might want to see the snake, to know for sure what kind it was. She took three quick photos and then backed up, leaving the snake in peace and finding another route to scramble over the hot stone.

Marianne reached the top, her hands filthy and sore from pulling herself over the gritty terrain. Her thoughts running at a million miles an hour. Her lips parched and her head beginning to thump.

She checked her phone. She could have easily, so easily, sat down and cried because she still didn't have any signal. She checked Drew's phone, which she'd taken as well, just in case, and nothing.

Turning on the spot, she scanned the horizon, wondering how long it would take to make it up the next crag of rocks. And that's when she saw it, a plume of dust drifting into the air, following a white vehicle far in the distance.

'*Hey!*' Marianne shouted and started waving her arms. '*Hey!*' She whipped off her top, a flouro-pink T-shirt, and held it high over her head, waving it until her arms ached, yelling the whole time. The person had to see her, they just had to. She glanced down to Drew, who was also on his feet, waving his arms, which she could have killed him for, if she hadn't been worried that it would kill him first.

At the end of their dirt road, the vehicle slowed, and for a long second Marianne thought they were going to drive on. When they turned and started heading towards them, she scrambled down from the rocks, *almost* forgetting to check her footing, and made her way back to Drew.

The Joshua Tree National Park ranger had been sent from heaven. He was kind, with a soft-looking moustache, and Marianne had told him, oh, about a thousand times how she couldn't believe their luck that it was a ranger who'd been passing by and had seen them. Now he was studying the snake photo on her phone, while she sat in the door of his cool van.

'Yep, that's what I thought. That's a gopher snake, not a rattle. They're harmless.'

'I beg to differ,' Drew said, with a half-smile.

The ranger laughed. 'They bite if they feel threatened, and I know it can hurt like hell, but they don't have any venom. She would have just been giving you a nip and telling you to get your great foot away from her sunlounger. She climbed high for that view.'

'So he's not going to die?' Marianne asked.

'No, he won't die. I have a first-aid kit in my car, so we'll get it all cleaned up and it'll heal soon enough. Even if it had been a rattle, it doesn't mean it would have been fatal, but it could have been, so you did the right thing trying to get help.'

'We couldn't get any phone signal. I didn't know what I was going to do if you hadn't shown up,' she explained.

'Always try and call 911 even if you have no service. If there's another network service nearby the call should pick up.'

'Good tip. So do gopher snakes rattle? I thought I heard the rattle.'

'We both did,' Drew interjected, and reached for her hand.

'Gophers like to mimic rattlesnakes because it makes them seem more threatening. They don't have the rattle so instead they shake their tails against dry grass – that'll be what you heard. See in this photo?' The ranger passed Marianne's phone back to her. 'Her head is small, about the width of her body. Rattlesnakes have bigger, more triangular heads. You're going to be just fine, sir.'

As the ranger cleaned Drew up, helped them contact the rental company's car service and moved their bags into his van with him, Marianne watched Drew.

*He loves me.* She'd known it anyway; they'd become so close and they gelled in a way she hadn't felt before. But usually it ended before the I love yous. Usually, that was fine with her. Marianne liked to think of herself as a lone wolf, or at least able to operate as one, and it scared her that she was falling in love. That she'd already fallen, to be more accurate.

But also, she'd never been one to lean away from a new adventure if it felt right …

# Chapter 15

# Jenny, in the Maldives

'*Hiiiii!*' I said when the faces of my parents filled my phone screen. It was my lunch break, which was the start of the day back in the UK, and I'd arranged to FaceTime with my folks for only the second time since arriving in the Maldives three weeks ago. The first call had mostly been me giving them a video tour of every palm tree, every grain of sand and every lap of the ocean.

I took a seat on a quiet bench tucked behind BountEco, the island's conservation building, which was where I was meeting Layla for lunch when I got off the call. This part of the boardwalk was usually guest-free, since if you kept following it the only other thing it led to was the staff accommodation, unless you were doing a full lap. It meant I could sit undisturbed, other than by the soft squawks of the Asian koel birds hanging out in the trees overhead.

'Hello, darling,' my mum said as she and Dad adjusted the laptop to fit them both in the frame. Behind them I saw the familiar living room I'd grown up in, the family portraits on the wall, the painting Marianne had made for them as a thank-you present for letting her live there whilst we finished school. I loved that picture. Painting had been a passing passion of Marianne's at the time and she'd been very into abstract art, so this particular canvas was a square-metre celebration of pink and yellow and blue brushstrokes. It was just happy-looking, you know?

'There we go,' my dad said, shuffling in towards my mum and slinging an arm around her shoulder. 'How are you doing, love? How's life on a tropical island today?'

'Pretty spectacular,' I smiled. 'I went paddleboarding and didn't fall in once.'

'Well done!' Mum said. 'I'd like to try that one day. One very calm day. Is it all sunshine and sandy toes and sexy men?'

'Mum!' I cried. Even Dad looked at her with surprise.

'What? I remember being your age before your dad and I got together. There's nothing better than a holiday romance.'

'Nothing?' checked Dad, amused.

Mum laughed. 'I'm just saying. You're in the Maldives, Jenny. The *Maldives*. It's just so exciting.'

'It is exciting,' I agreed. 'And, yes, the sun is shining and I can confirm that I currently have sandy toes.' I always seemed to have sandy toes these days. I liked it.

· Mum changed the subject, thankfully, instead of starting off again about sexy suitors. 'And how's the bookshop? In your email it sounded like your big opening night didn't go quite as planned?'

'Yeah, it could have been better,' I shrugged, trying to keep the concern out of my voice, but of course my parents saw right through it.

Dad leaned towards the laptop screen. 'It's going to be brilliant. I bet you've already got customers lining up.'

'Not quite,' I admitted. 'The shop is fairly lacklustre at the moment, but I'm not sure what I can do about that. I need to think of a way of pushing it into people's line of vision more. The management want it to have loads of fun events and I can't think of any yet because the space is so different from the shop at home.' I liked that Khadeeja was so hands off – I had total freedom and control – but actually it would have been nice to bounce ideas off someone.

'Speaking of the Book Nook, I popped in the other day to see how Evan was doing,' Mum said.

'Oh yeah?' I asked, super casually.

'It was bustling in there! Lots more young ladies coming in for a browse. I think the new surf-dude salesman is proving quite the attraction.'

'Who do you mean?' Dad asked, mildly affronted.

'Evan, of course,' Mum said.

'Oh.' He turned back to me. 'Is he good-looking to you young 'uns?'

'I don't know,' I spluttered and saw Mum smirking because I was pretty sure she'd always been aware of my crush, and I was really trying to push Evan to the back of my mind. 'Anyway, I'm glad to hear the shop's OK.'

Mum shuffled in her seat, and I knew that meant she was about to broach something. 'Have you spoken to Marianne yet?'

There it was. 'No. But I know she's made it to America, so she's fine. She's in Joshua Tree National Park, according to Instagram.'

'I bet she'd love a video tour of the island, like you gave us?'

'Mum, we're just taking a breather from each other at the moment, don't worry about it.' Mum loved Marianne like a second daughter, and I knew she hated that we were fighting. 'What are you two doing today?' I asked.

'Oh, the usual,' Dad said. 'You?'

'I'm working, but I'm on my lunch break at the moment. My friend Layla is going to show me the conservation centre here at the resort before we have lunch. Then after work I'll probably do more brainstorming for events.'

'What was it Marianne always used to say about organising community events and things?' Mum said, tapping her chin with her index finger. 'Something about giving people access to things they wouldn't normally think of wanting. Like ... here's an evening of book readings beside your hammocks so you don't even have to get up. Or whatever.'

She had a point, and I was quiet for a moment, thinking about it. We chattered a little more until I saw Layla approaching with smoothies in both hands, so after holding up the phone and introducing them all I rang off, feeling happy and grounded for having spoken to them, way back in Bayside.

'How's your day going?' I asked Layla as we made our way towards the door of BountEco.

'It's good. Two seaplane journeys done and I'm spending the rest of the day out on the boat, which suits me just fine. We should take the boat out together sometime.'

'That would be great!' I enthused.

'Peace and quiet mean island perfection to me, and taking a boat out can feel *very* island perfection.'

At that exact moment we heard the roar of a jet ski in the distance as somebody whizzed round the perimeter of the island. Layla rolled her eyes and opened the door.

BountEco was wide and dimly lit and pristine. There was a quiet echo from the dark walls, but one side opened out, with a short walkway leading to an enclosed bit of beach. Layla showed me the turtle sanctuary first, a peaceful series of tanks where the little guys were fed and monitored until they were strong and healthy enough to head back into their ocean, and then the research and work being done on local coral regeneration.

'Rish is the best person to ask about all this, if you want more details – he's all about trying to make Bounty Cove Cay more eco-friendly. Has he told you his pitch yet?'

'No.' I shook my head, watching over a tank of baby turtles as they peacefully swam about in the turquoise water.

'Ask him about it. He has big ideas for this place, but he won't speak up. I think they're worth listening to, though. Perhaps he could tell you over a date,' she teased.

'Shut up,' I laughed. We left BountEco to grab a quick bite from the staff canteen before we both needed to head back to work, but Layla's words were on my mind. Was she serious about Rish liking me? I didn't think so; if anything, I was probably just a shiny new addition to the island, and he was just being nice. Besides, it never took long for my thoughts to return to Evan, and the possibility of what we might be. Or could have been. Or were. *Argh.*

I needed to know where I stood with Evan. I'd tried not to care, tried to focus on the beautiful present moment in time and all the experiences I was having. But that kiss was a hell of a thing to have happened right before I left, and it meant I was in a state of limbo, wondering what he was doing back at home and what I should be doing here.

It was also exactly what I'd wanted to happen. But still, the timing was awful.

Late that evening, I plucked up the courage to call him.

'Hi, J,' he said, his voice friendly and familiar, and just the sound of his voice as he spoke made my heart bounce. Like it always did.

'Hi, Evan.' I took a deep breath, my hands shaking. *We need to talk about what happened.* 'How's, um, life?'

'Life is good,' he answered, then chuckled. 'Probably doesn't compare to life where you are, though. That photo you put up of you with the coconut and the pink umbrella behind your ear made me pretty jealous.'

His laugh was my favourite song. I hesitated, wanting to find a subtle way of asking him, *'Jealous, how?'* But before I could think of anything, he continued. 'So what's been happening in paradise today?'

'I, uh ... Well, I spoke to Mum and Dad today. And I was working.' *We need to talk about what happened. Just say it.* 'So, I was thinking ...'

'Just a second.' I listened to what sounded like him moving some paperwork and then taking a seat, maybe on my sofa. 'OK, what's up?'

I inhaled. 'We need to talk about what happened.'

He was silent for a moment, and I wondered with a cringe if he didn't know what I was talking about. And then he said, 'You're right. I'm sorry. I shouldn't have done that to you right when you were walking out the door. I think I just got caught up in the moment.'

I sank down on my bed. I hadn't known what I wanted him to say, but hearing a pretty conclusive 'It was a mistake' wasn't it. 'Yeah, no, me too,' I said, my voice so quiet it was nearly carried away on the breeze from my open window.

'I want you to enjoy this freedom and experience and I didn't mean to put anything complicated in the way of that.'

'No, I mean, you didn't, we didn't.' *We did.* 'So, are you saying ... ?'

'I guess I'm saying sorry.'

I could picture him in my flat, if that was even where he was right now. I could picture the freckles on his nose, his hair probably salty like it always was, his skin smelling of sun lotion. Maybe he had his fingers curled around a beer because it was the end of his workday. Maybe his tanned, toned chest was bare, because he was always warm and walked around as though he might take off running into the ocean at any moment. 'You have nothing to be sorry for.'

He was right, though. We'd been caught in the moment and now had to let each other be free from weird feelings. I was here to have a change of scenery, after all, wasn't I? Maybe that included needing a change for my heart. I had to untangle my heartstrings from him, let us slip away from each other's grip, even though we'd been bound for longer than he realised.

It came to me in the middle of the night, probably thanks to that phone call with my parents and possibly also because my mind was finally on its way to releasing itself from thoughts of Evan. At least, somewhat. I was having a dream where I was drinking pink cocktails at the To the Moon restaurant and trying to look at the pink sky and Selena Gomez kept asking me what book I wanted to pair with my drink.

After waking up disappointed that I wasn't, in fact, friends with Selena Gomez, I sat up in my bed and got my hair full of mosquito net.

'A book-pairing event,' I said aloud. That would be fun; it would have a good vacation vibe. If I could ask the mixologists at Cocktail Cove to come up with some bespoke cocktails with bookish names and combo them with a curated set of high-quality reads, that would be fun, right?

I lay back down, thinking it through a little more and feeling a sense of relief, tinged with excitement. Guests like cocktails on holiday. And they do like reading on their sunloungers. This would be a different type of drink, one the all-inclusive set wouldn't usually get, plus a way for people to try new novels and authors.

What a good idea. *This must be how Marianne feels every day.*

I went back to sleep, sparkles of excitement for my job waltzing in my mind with bookish cocktail names, like Les Margaritas and Sense & Singapore Slings.

Against the backdrop of another week of barely any beach bookworms visiting the bookshop, and even fewer sales, I worked my butt off to try and turn things around, pinning everything on the event I was planning. I used all my spare time organising, setting a date for a couple of weeks time, and thinking through every possible problem to make sure it didn't happen. I estimated profit and loss, I ordered extra books, I managed to get two mixologists on board – with the approval of Khadeeja, of course. I was excited. This was going to prove to everybody, including myself, that I could make this bookshop the roaring success it deserved to be. I reckoned that if it worked, this could be a regular event each week … We wouldn't even need to switch up the books-and-cocktails list that often, because the guests were always changing. Maybe just alternate two sets, so there were fresh books and drinks for anybody staying for a fortnight?

I was getting ahead of myself.

Occasionally, I let myself be pulled away for a drink in the staff accommodation, a cooling swim in the ocean, or a shared lunch with Layla, or Rish, or both, but mostly I kept to myself, doing what I do best: planning everything down to a T. Planning, organising and using my experience from home would all mean I couldn't fail, because at home I was in control. At home, I never let things come crashing down.

# Chapter 16

# Marianne, in the USA

The evening that followed the big snake adventure, Marianne and Drew found a cute glamping spot near Joshua Tree and spent the twilight hours sharing a delicious and filling steak dinner in a town on the outskirts of the park. The car company offered them an SUV as a replacement, or the Mustang again if they were willing to wait for repairs or for one to be brought in from further afield. They took the SUV, though they'd loved their Mustang, because both of them fancied staying around the national park and exploring some of the hiking trails. Slowly. Watching out for the wildlife.

Over the following week, the couple picnicked, backpacked and hiked. They did dramatic readings to each other from location-appropriate books downloaded on their Kindles. Sometimes they slept in and sometimes they rose early. Sometimes they stayed up late to stargaze and other days they crashed at twilight. Each morning, they'd called reception to ask if they could tag on 'just one more night'. Joshua Tree was a dream, but the adventure wasn't ending there. They could have stayed for ever, happy and basking in sunshine and new love, if it wasn't for the lure of Los Angeles.

Detouring away from the desert and back to the coast, with a vague idea that they'd then head back in to Las Vegas before making their way up to Northern California, Marianne and Drew spent busy days and nights exploring the sprawling City of Angels. From their base in a cute hostel with free breakfast in the Hills, they walked the Sunset Strip in the footsteps of *Daisy Jones & the Six*, visited Hollywood Boulevard and transported themselves back to *The Big Sleep*, strolled through Downtown's Central Library, where Octavia Butler had sometimes written, read and volunteered, and drove past the Beverly Hills estate Jackie Collins had for years called home. They also squeezed in a Warner Bros. studio tour, a Santa Monica beach day and a trip to Universal Studios, but there was one thing both of them desperately wanted to do before moving on to Las Vegas.

Now, Marianne reached for Drew's hand, the cool breeze kissing her cheeks. Above them was an unusually cloudy morning, but it felt all the more magical to be up here, behind the huge white letters rising from the mist.

They'd woken early and so far seemed to be the first ones that day to have completed the hike. The winding path had offered increasingly spectacular glimpses the closer they got, until they'd reached the summit, where they now stood, directly behind the Hollywood Sign.

'We made it!' said Marianne, a swell of pride inside her.

'Living the Hollywood dream,' grinned Drew.

'You were really keen to see the sign up close. Do you think you'd ever want to write a movie or anything?' she asked, suddenly realising she didn't know as much about his future dreams as she'd like to, beyond the one of being a successful author.

'I've thought about it – maybe. But the thing I'd really like would be for one of my books to be made into a film.' Drew gave Marianne a bashful smile. 'I know it's so unlikely to happen, but that would be my wish, if I could have one.'

'That's why you wanted to come up here?'

'Yep. There's something about the Hollywood Sign that just makes me feel like I could manifest my dream, one day. Does that sound silly?'

'Not at all. I like it. I like big dreams.'

'So now we're here, what was your reason for wanting to do this, above anything else in LA?'

She took a moment. 'It's because my mum always wanted to come to California, and she never got the chance. She used to be an actress and singer when I was really little. She was so brave and colourful, and though I don't think she ever wanted to come to Hollywood and make it big, she wanted to ... I don't know ...'

Drew stroked her hand with his thumb. 'Enjoy having a big dream?'

'Yeah. I remember her playing this game with me where we'd stand on the sofa and pretend it was the Hollywood Sign and shout "I'm a star!" to our adoring fans below.' Marianne laughed at the memory. Not least because if you did try to climb on the actual letters themselves, you'd promptly be arrested, and you'd have to scale a large fence anyway.

The breeze whipped through the gap between them and Drew raised Marianne's hand in the air.

'What are you doing?' she laughed.

'We're going to shout things to our adoring fans.'

'We don't have adoring fans. And what should we shout?' Marianne wasn't about to turn down the chance to be a bit loud.

'You should say "I'm a star", for your mum, and I'll shout … I don't know, I'll make it up on the spot.' Drew planted his feet firmly on the ground. 'Ready? One … two …'

Marianne watched his face for a second, feeling so present and at the same time warmed by the hug of a nice memory.

'… three!'

They both sucked in a deep breath, and then Marianne shouted, *'I'm a star! And so is my mum!'* And in a way, she was.

Drew yelled, *'I'm going to have a book turned into a movie and it'll be huge and all the celebrities will want to be in it and it'll become a franchise and I'll have theme-park rides named after it!'*

And just like a moment in a movie, Drew dipped Marianne back, her leg kicking out in the air, and they kissed.

# Chapter 17

# Jenny, in the Maldives

In the centre of Bounty Cove Cay, behind the Pavilion and nestled in a clearing among the trees, was the cinema under the stars. Complete with its own bar, it had daybeds and beanbags peppering the sandy ground, candles that flickered in the breeze from holders sunk into the sand, and soft lo-fi beats pumping into the night before the movie started. One night a week, this treat was reserved for off-duty staff, and it was always popular.

I arrived to see Rish standing at the bar on his own, dressed in a casual turquoise shirt and shorts, his feet bare. He was laughing with the barman, his face animated, and when he saw me approach, he waved with enthusiasm.

'What can I get you, Bookshop Jenn?' he asked.

'I'll have a mojito, please,' I said.

'Coming right up,' said the barman.

Rish held up his fingers. 'Make that two.'

'Shall we get one for Layla?' I asked, looking round to see if she was coming.

'Miss Layla has stood us up,' Rish answered.

'What do you mean?'

'Check your phone – she sent a group message five minutes ago to you and me saying she's *sooo* sorry, but she has to work and are we OK just hanging out the two of us?'

I raised my eyebrows at Rish and we both laughed, because we both knew when we were being set up.

With our mojitos, we sat next to each other inside a large wicker daybed.

'Layla was showing me the inside of BountEco, and she mentioned that you have ideas for how the resort could be more eco-friendly?' I asked him, acutely aware of his proximity as we sipped from our delicately garnished cut-crystal glasses, the rum and lime swirling in my mouth, and the scent of mint between us.

'Not just more eco-friendly, totally eco-friendly,' he said, sitting up straighter. 'You remember I was telling you that management are trying to keep this place as the real jewel of the Maldives? They want it to be in every luxury-resort shortlist, to be every glossy magazine's go-to?'

'Yep,' I said, gulping at the pressure that meant for me, having been brought in to help steer it that way.

'Well, Khadeeja is right, I think, and travellers are becoming more climate-conscious. I hear it from the guests, I see it from what other hotels are doing. But mostly I see that it needs to happen. The reefs have been hit by bleaching, sea levels are rising and we need to reduce waste. For the Maldives to survive and biodiversity to thrive, we all need to make changes.'

'But that's what Bounty Cove Cay is doing, isn't it? With the conservation centre?'

'Yes, absolutely. In fact, most resorts are doing their bit – everyone here in the Maldives wants to preserve it. But other resorts are the front runners. Zero waste. Carbon neutral.'

I studied him as his expression of excitement dimmed like the candle in front of us when the breeze blew past. 'I feel like there's a "but" coming ...'

'Blane thinks if we move in that direction we won't attract the big bucks any more.'

'He doesn't care about the environment?'

'I wouldn't say that ... but he thinks the super-rich, the elite guests, want their luxuries no matter what. They don't want to feel lectured. I see what he means, but I just think the world is changing. For example, if we were to no longer deliver plastic bottles of water to the rooms each night and give guests reusable bottles instead, is that such a big deal?'

'It doesn't sound like it.'

'That's just one idea. Layla thinks I should speak to Khadeeja about it.'

I nodded. 'You should. She seems a busy woman, but we know this is a direction she wants to go in, so I'm sure she'd appreciate your input.'

He shook his head. 'Blane is my manager; I'd be crazy to go over his head.'

I shrugged. 'I think you should.'

'You're just saying that because you don't like Blane, and you do like me.'

He caught my eye and laughed, giving me a playful nudge and causing me to laugh back.

I settled against the seat, not knowing how to handle a flirty conversation. I was awful at flirting. 'I can't believe how beautiful it is here,' I said, my eyes drifting up to the stars. 'I live by the coast at home, but it's been so long since I sat on the beach looking at the night sky.'

'It doesn't get old,' Rish nodded, and lay back beside me.

Would I ever live in the Maldives again, or was this my one shot? A twinkle of a shooting star threaded across the darkness and sparked something inside me. 'I think I just had an idea,' I said aloud, turning my face to Rish.

He looked at me, his gaze soft. 'What's that?'

'It's about the event I'm planning.'

'Your perfect-pairings event?'

'Yes. I just realised – there's a chance people will only be holidaying here in the Maldives once in their lifetime. So why would they want to spend even a second of it in the darkest corner of a hotel, in a bookstore that could be anywhere in the world?'

He waited for me to continue, clearly not sure if it was a trick question and not wanting to offend me. 'Because your bookstore is nice?' he ventured. 'And it has air con? And a friendly manager?'

'But it doesn't have *this*.' Stretching my arms in front of me, I gestured at the palms, the sand. 'The bookstore doesn't have the Maldives. It has some pictures of the Maldives, but if I was staying in an amazing resort on a tropical island, I don't know if I'd want to hole myself away inside for any length of time.'

'I don't know, I often hear guests saying it's time to get in from the sun. They don't necessarily like to be outside for the entire day.'

I nodded. 'But then they probably have a siesta in their beautiful villa. Or head to the spa for a tropical beauty treatment. Or relax in a *lounge*.'

'Why did you say lounge like that?' he asked.

'I'm leading to something, I promise. What if I moved the event to one of the lounges, like the big one right by reception with the huge glass windows overlooking the pool and beach, under the mezzanine? Wouldn't that be more appealing?' I could see it now. The bright space filled with the natural Maldives light, against the picturesque backdrop of the ocean and the island so attendees didn't feel they were missing a second of their tropical vacation. A break from the daytime heat, but still a chance to try a bespoke cocktail under cool air conditioning, and mere steps from where they had been relaxing anyway. In fact, I could even offer to deliver their purchases straight back to their sunloungers as soon as the event was over.

Rish was nodding. 'You'd also be advertising your shop to the new arrivals, since you'd be right there by the check-in desk. And for anybody using the concierge service, too.'

'So you like it?' I asked. 'Do you think it would be allowed?'

Rish grinned. 'I'm certain it would. As part of the entertainment team, we hold stuff all over the hotel. Check with Khadeeja, and your mixologists, but I can't see that it would be a problem.'

Check me out, thinking outside the box. Maybe when I got back, I could take a look at whether any of the Book Nook on the Beach events could work offsite. Although maybe I should wait and see if this one was a success first, I supposed.

'I hope this works,' I said to him, and in the dark he reached for my hand, squeezed it for a second, and let it go.

'It will.'

The skin of my palm tingled from his touch. My mouth dry, I reached for my mojito.

'Back in the UK, my friend – my business partner – was always better at event planning than me.'

'Oh yeah? Have they given you any tips?'

'No, we had a bit of a fight before I left for the Maldives . . .' I hadn't meant to get into this now, but something about Rish made it easy to open up to him.

'What about?'

'She was kind of angry I applied for this job without telling her.'

Rish chuckled, which was unexpected. 'Why didn't you tell her?'

'I was never really going to take it – I was just dreaming. Don't tell Khadeeja,' I said, and couldn't help smiling back.

'So where is she now? Back in your bookshop at home, throwing darts at photos of islands?'

'No, she's gone on her own trip with her boyfriend. They're in America. That was also part of the fight.'

'Who's looking after your shop?'

'Oh, her brother, he's just doing us a favour.' I didn't want to talk to Rish about Evan, especially not right now when I was having a nice evening. 'Anyway, it'll all blow over.' At that point, the big screen came alive and the opening credits of La La Land appeared, the bright blue sky and LA traffic. I loved this movie. One day maybe I'd visit LA. For now, any chatter stopped, and I leaned closer into Rish, and he into me. Our eyes locked for a small moment and I wondered: was he the romantic change I'd been searching for?

A couple of sleeps later, on an island in the middle of the Indian Ocean, I found myself dancing in a way I hadn't in years. Bounty Cove Cay had opened up the whole of Coconut Cove beach to become an Eid al-Fitr celebration to mark the end of Ramazan. Drumbeats whirled in the air along with fire from the dancers, and cushions and candles were propped in the orange-glowing sunset sand. A belly dancer shimmered through the attendees, encouraging those willing to jump up and join her.

For one night I forgot about pining over Evan, about flirting with Rish, about bookshops near and far, and just danced. Marianne wasn't wrong when she said that unexpected plans can make incredible memories. One day I hoped to be able to give more yeses to my best friend.

# Chapter 18

# Marianne, in the USA

'Marianne, wake up, look.'

In the dark, Marianne became aware of Drew tapping lightly on her leg, but when she opened her eyes, a strange sight disoriented her. Through the car windscreen a pyramid was coming into view, black against the night sky but with its sharp edges illuminated and a giant beam of light protruding from the point, up into the atmosphere.

'What's that? Where are we?' she asked in a groggy voice, and reached for a Cheeto.

'I think that's the Luxor, the Egyptian-themed hotel. I think we've reached the Strip.'

'We're in Vegas?' Marianne sat up straight. 'Finally?'

'Finally,' he agreed, and shot her a grin.

She wiped her palms across her eyes and when she opened them again her vision filled with a million lights as Drew turned the SUV onto the Strip and joined a heavy stream of slow-moving traffic.

The two of them had left Los Angeles late that morning, taking a crawling route to Las Vegas via the beaches of the OC, the Mojave National Preserve and a handful of interesting photo-op stops Marianne had plucked from the internet. What an unexpectedly wonderful fortnight they'd had in Joshua Tree and then LA, all fuelled by their newly admitted love for each other.

The night before, as Marianne had been checking her fun new-freckles situation in the mirror and Drew was flicking the channels of the TV, a familiar TV travel show had come on and had caught her attention.

'Doesn't that place look amazing?' she commented, watching the smooth images of the Wynn Las Vegas flood the screen again.

'Very,' Drew agreed. 'Still keen to do Vegas next?'

'Oh, definitely,' Marianne said, though they hadn't actually made a commitment to anywhere in particular.

'Are you ready to leave here, though?' He stood and came over to her, wrapping his arms around her from behind and watching her in the mirror.

'You know, I think I am. Las Vegas will feel quite different from the chill of Los Angeles, but that's all part of the excitement, I guess.'

It sure did feel different, Marianne thought with a big smile as they crawled along the Las Vegas Strip at a snail's pace. She dropped the window beside the passenger seat, and a warm breeze, like opening an oven door, settled over them.

'We're a long way from home,' she murmured to Drew.

'There aren't a lot of people dressed like that in Bayside, are there?' He gestured to a couple of women in bejewelled bikinis and vast feathered headdresses standing among the crowds on the pavement.

Bayside certainly couldn't be further away from here if it tried. A memory danced through Marianne's mind of her and Jenny as early teens talking about moving to Las Vegas and becoming showgirls. Or, thanks to Marianne's new obsession with *Ocean's Eleven* at the time, thieves. They barely knew what Las Vegas was, or what showgirls were, but that hadn't stopped them sticking sequins all over themselves and making up a full, high-kicking dance routine to the tune of 'Crazy in Love'. Bayside hadn't been ready for her uh-oh dance then; she wondered if Vegas would be ready for it now?

They stop-started their way down the Strip, passing crowds of people strolling, some holding up cameras, some holding up long plastic drinking vessels, some holding up each other. On either side, the hotels were big and extravagant with every footprint, often taking up a whole block or more. They passed a medieval-themed castle, a New York City complete with replica Statue of Liberty, some towering glass skyscrapers whose construction looked straight out of a Batman movie, an Eiffel Tower-fronted Parisian hotel …

'Look, the Bellagio! And the fountains!' Marianne knelt up in her seat for a better look and some partygoers gave her a passing *whoop*.

She'd never seen anything like it. The number of lights alone should have been enough to blind you, but being here in Las Vegas was like plugging yourself into the circuit board, and instead you fizzed along with them. She could feel her car crumples melt away in the warmth of the evening, and with a glance at Drew she felt full of happiness about her decision to come away with him.

Even if her best friend wasn't here to stand in the lights with her.

Drew rolled the car into the Encore parking garage sometime later, having eventually made it through the traffic.

Taking out their desert-dust-covered suitcases from the boot, they rolled them into the hotel's rear entrance, through soaring double doors and into a wide, air-conditioned concourse where the tinkling of slot machines and ice cubes in glasses could be heard.

Marianne had read somewhere that Las Vegas had something close to a hundred and fifty thousand hotel rooms, so although they'd gone straight to the Wynn Las Vegas and Encore Resort, if they didn't have space she was sure it wouldn't take them long to find somewhere else. She really hoped they had space, though …

'This place looks incredible. Views over the Las Vegas Strip, pools, a spa, a big buffet restaurant, a casino, a night-time beach club, SoulCycle *here in the hotel*.' Not that she'd ever done SoulCycle, the A-lister spinning classes where an instructor boomed motivational pep talks to you and your legs, but if she could crawl straight from there to the breakfast buffet, she was more than willing to give it a go.

When Marianne had suggested going straight to this hotel Drew had asked, 'Can we afford it?'

'Yes, they have a deal on.' The price wasn't cheap, but they had an offer that wasn't completely out of their budget. 'I think it's fine to go a little wild during our time in Vegas, since we're going to be going to motels and hostelling for the remainder.'

They stood in the lobby, taking in their surroundings, waiting to check in. Behind them, somebody cheered, and Marianne turned to see a group of women sitting around a nearby blackjack table, jewel-coloured cocktails in their hands, a croupier laughing as the women hugged each other.

'Have you ever gambled?' she asked Drew.

'I remember my uni having a casino night once, so I gambled there, but I'm pretty sure there was a five-pound maximum bet. Have you?'

'Not really. But we should do a little while we're here, don't you think?' Marianne wondered if he could see the dollar signs in her eyes. Imagine if they won big, then there'd be no motelling and hostelling for them.

She was just wondering how much it would cost to have an Elvis impersonator follow them around, when they were called up to reception.

'Good evening and welcome to the Wynn Las Vegas and Encore Resort,' the receptionist said in a smooth American voice like a commercial for coffee. 'My name is Daniella. Do you have a reservation with us tonight?'

'No,' Drew answered. 'We're just hoping you have some rooms available? We saw this place advertised and we knew we wanted to stay here.'

'All righty, let's see what we have.' Daniella started tapping on her computer. 'Are you two lovebirds in Las Vegas for a special occasion?'

'Yes!' Marianne said, rather loudly. 'We've eloped!'

Whoops, where had that come from? She felt Drew turn a fixed smile towards her, much like a ventriloquist's dummy, but she refused to look at him. It was only a white lie, but it might just get them a free upgrade so it was worth a go.

Daniella smiled, all red lipstick and perfect teeth, though she didn't seem as surprised as Marianne expected. Maybe they weren't the first guests to show up and announce they'd eloped to Las Vegas. Maybe not even the first that week. Or even that day.

'That's wonderful,' Daniella said. 'Do you have a plan for where you'll get married?'

Well, obviously not. Marianne and Drew hadn't actually discussed marriage, let alone where it would happen. Or when. They'd only been together about five months, after all.

As Marianne and Drew hesitated, Daniella continued. 'We have a range of ceremony options here in the Wynn, if they would be of interest to you?'

Remembering the Wynn bride in the TV being dipped before the fairy lights, Marianne asked, 'Do you have any information on them?' Drew was still doing his static grin at her, not so much in a groomly way, but more of a *What the hell are you doing?* way. But what harm did it do to get some info? It just added weight to the claim they were here to get married, nothing more.

'Certainly.' Daniella retrieved a brochure and handed it to them. 'Just speak to your concierge if you'd like any more details and they can set you up with one of our wedding planners. Now then ...'

She went back to tapping and Marianne took the brochure, flicking through pages of beautiful cream roses and candlelit aisles. It was stunning. She held on to the brochure tightly, feeling very bridal and important.

'How many nights are you hoping to be with us?'

'About a week?' Marianne answered. 'Maybe longer. We're not sure.'

'All righty,' Daniella said in her liquid voice. 'We'll start with a week. I can put you here in the Encore side, in one of our Panoramic Suites on a beautiful high floor for seven nights, does that sound good to you?'

'That sounds amazing!' Marianne turned to Drew. 'Doesn't it?'

'Yes, let's do it.' He was gawping as a couple, decked out in full designer swimwear and huge shades and trailed by an entourage, waltzed through reception and out to one of the pools.

'Wonderful.' Daniella printed out a Wynn-headed piece of paper and handed it to them, using her gold pen to point to the numbers. 'This will be your daily rate, these are your taxes, and this is the daily resort fee. And this number here will be your total, should you choose to check out after your seven nights.'

Marianne blinked at the numbers. They couldn't be right. That had to be the area code, or the door code, or something. She shook Drew's arm, bringing him back to the present. 'Drew, um ...'

He looked at the paper. 'Whoa, Mama.'

Marianne kept her voice low, not wanting to highlight the fact that they suddenly felt very out of place. 'Erm, I thought I saw that you had an offer on at the moment?'

'This actually incorporates our latest offer. Perhaps you were looking at midweek arrivals?' Daniella asked.

'What day is it today?'

'Friday.'

'And maybe the taxes weren't included ...'

'It's quite common for taxes to be included afterwards for hotels in the US,' she explained.

Drew softened his hand around Marianne's and turned back to Daniella. 'May I ask what the price would be for five nights in maybe,' he lowered his voice even further, 'in maybe a cheaper room?'

'Of course, not a problem.' Unflappable Daniella went back to tapping on her computer. 'I could put you in an Encore Resort King for five nights, and here ... would be your total.' She slid another piece of paper towards them.

It was still steep for what they could afford, and a lot more than they'd budgeted for, but more struggle-up-a-hill steep than scale-Everest steep. Though who were they kidding, their 'budget' was little more than a pooled holiday-fund account with an idea to not spend it all in the first four weeks so they could afford a second and have enough to take them around for the rest of the trip. And though Marianne knew it would have left Jenny screaming into a whirlpool of spreadsheets and formulas and daily allowances, what was the point of coming all this way to Vegas if they weren't going to enjoy themselves?

'I think we should just go for it,' she told Drew. 'I'm sure there are cheaper rooms in other hotels, but we don't know that for sure unless we start shopping around now. Let's just book into here for five nights and if we're not done with Vegas by the end, we'll move somewhere else then.'

Drew looked around him. 'It is nice here.'

'And it is our wedding week,' she reminded him, a teasing look in her eyes. But she wondered what it would be like to spend her life with this vibrant, interesting, funny guy.

Drew turned back to Daniella. 'Let's go for it. Five nights, but let's go for the Panoramic Suite.'

'What?' Marianne said.

'Since we're getting married and all,' Drew winked, a playful smile on his face.

'Wonderful,' Daniella replied. 'You're going to have an amazing time here. May I see your passports for a moment?'

If Marianne was being sensible, she'd have stopped Drew and insisted on the cheaper room. But that wasn't really her style. Whatever, you had to live a little wildly when in Vegas, right? And they had still dropped from seven to five nights, so they were still making a saving.

After a few more taps, Daniella handed them their keys. 'All righty, you're on the thirty-ninth floor.'

Marianne shrieked as quietly as she could, but it was still a shriek. With thank-yous bestowed upon Daniella, and after telling her they were fine with their own cases, they rolled their bags towards the private gold elevators.

'So, we're getting married in Vegas, are we?' asked Drew, once they were ascending.

Marianne chuckled. 'I thought it might get us a free upgrade. Are you mad? We could get married for real if you feel like it was too deceitful?' Seeing his look of surprise, she added, 'I'm just kidding, relax.'

'Hmm,' he said in response, and took her face in his hands to kiss her all the way to the fortieth floor.

Moments later, they stepped into their suite, where they faced floor-to-ceiling windows with a view over the night lights of the north end of the Strip. They had a wide sofa with a chaise longue to lie back on and look out of the window. They had a bed as big as a cloud. A TV that displayed a message saying 'Welcome to the bride and groom'. A bathroom with a bathtub, separate shower, two sinks and heavy, super-soft waffle robes.

See now, if they'd planned and organised and done all those things Jenn was always berating her for not doing, if they hadn't just jumped in and gone for it, she would never have been in this place. They'd be in some budget hotel that was still probably very cool and enormous, but this felt special and once-in-a-lifetime. Sometimes you just had to grab hold of life.

*Oh, Jenny.* In a wash of fondness, Marianne excused herself to visit the ginormous bathroom, and while she was in there, she pulled out her phone to call her. She couldn't help it. She knew they were still fighting, but she wanted to tell Jenn she'd made it to Vegas. Still, she hesitated, instead navigating to Jenn's Instagram, where the last few photos showed her looking beautiful and smiley while holding a coconut, picture-perfect seas, and a moonlit outdoor cinema with some delicious-looking mojitos in the foreground.

Maybe she wouldn't call her. Jenn was clearly doing just fine; of course she was. That girl would have planned for every eventuality, every transfer, every time-zone change, every possible problem throughout her journey, but perhaps she wouldn't be planning on Marianne calling and reminding her of their argument.

On the Find My app, Jenny's face appeared inside a little circular icon, plopped down in what looked like the middle of the hugest expanse of ocean. Her best friend seemed very, very far away.

# Chapter 19

# Marianne, in the USA

'Drew? Are you awake?' Marianne whispered into the dark of their hotel room. It was past midnight and they'd decided to have an early night and catch up on sleep before enjoying Las Vegas for all it was worth tomorrow. It had been a great and sensible idea in theory, if only Marianne hadn't found that iced espresso in the minibar and thought it was too tempting not to drink. 'Drew?'

'Hmm?' he said, coming to.

'Are you asleep?'

'Um ...'

'Don't you think it's amazing how quiet the hotel room is, when all *that* is happening right out there?'

'How quiet it is?' he said, rolling over to face her, his skin barely visible in the dark. 'In here? Right now?'

She took his point and when she heard his soft snores return, Marianne climbed out of bed and wrapped herself in one of those yummy robes. She padded across the soft carpet and pulled back the curtains at the large window. The bed area was behind a partition, so she was pretty sure this wouldn't disturb her 'fiancé', but she was a little hopped up on caffeine so didn't give it quite the level of care she'd normally like to think she would.

Climbing onto the sofa and stretching out her legs, she looked at fabulous Las Vegas living its best life below her. From here she could see neon billboards flashing in an endless rotation of sky-high Cirque de Soleil trailers, close-ups of roulette wheels and the names of the world's biggest DJs. She could see cars and limos trailing up and down the Strip. She could see hotels stretching into the distance, lit from all angles, some with fountains and fire catching the eyes of passers-by. The left-hand side of the window offered a view over the Wynn building, which was copper and curved just like the Encore, and was a sleek addition to the skyline.

The endless movement was mesmerising, and Marianne didn't even realise she'd fallen asleep until a bright yellow morning light fell upon her.

She sat up, adjusting her robe around her, and gasped at the changed view. There was still the other tower of the Wynn, and the Strip, but now she could see mountains framing the miles of flat desert that Vegas sat in. A brilliant blue sky filled with wispy clouds was overhead, and the hotels she'd seen in the night were now bathed in golden sunlight. The Treasure Island, the Mirage, Caesars Palace, behind them the Rio – all of them stood tall and proud, ready to start another day. Or, more likely, still wide awake from the night before, if the tales about this town were to be believed.

That sunshine, though, it looked so big and incredible and warm that she couldn't wait to get out there and shake out her slightly achy limbs, thanks to her impromptu sofa slumber.

There was a snort from the bed and Drew sat up, calling, 'Marianne?'

'In here,' she said, and in he padded, all naked, even though there was a whopping window, because nobody could see in! Hoorah!

'Good morning, sunshine.' He greeted her with a kiss that tasted of toothpaste. 'What do you want to do today?'

'I want to see everything. Do everything.'

'All right. We'd better get ourselves a big breakfast, then.'

Two hours later and Marianne held her stomach tenderly, her cheeks pink. Drew looked exhausted as he flopped against the back of his seat, his head lolling.

'I think I ate too much,' she whispered.

'No, I think you ate the exact amount you're supposed to eat at these things. It's Vegas that's too much, not you.' Drew held a hand over his own swollen tummy.

The Wynn's breakfast buffet was unlike anything Marianne had ever come across in the world, and she'd worked on a cruise ship. And by the time they'd walked through the hotel from the Encore elevators to the opulent buffet restaurant, stood in the queue and been seated in the atrium, surrounded by cascading flowers and colourful fruit-decorated pillars, they were starved and ready to go.

You know when you go to a supermarket hungry and you accidentally buy one of everything in the store? This buffet was like a supermarket, where all the food was already paid for, and prepared for you, and you could go around as many times as you liked. And everyone was having the time of their lives so nobody judged you if you walked past their table for the seventh time holding a plate containing bacon, sushi, breakfast pizza and a chocolate chip cookie all together.

'I'm so full we could probably save money by not eating for the rest of the week,' Drew joked.

'Mmm,' Marianne agreed, eyeing up a yogurt parfait somebody was scuttling past with; she'd have to remember to try it tomorrow. 'Do you think you could live in a place like this?'

'A place like Vegas?' he asked.

'Yeah. But more specifically, a place where you could get a buffet breakfast every single morning. Do you think you'd enjoy it or get sick of it?'

Drew laughed. 'I'd get sick of it. I like living in cities and having the option to have whatever breakfast you want, whenever, you know, budget allowing, but I couldn't handle a buffet every day. Could you?'

'Yeah, for sure, this was the breakfast of my dreams,' Marianne answered without hesitation. Then she looked at him. 'Do you prefer living in a city to living in Bayside?'

'There's a question.' He shifted uncomfortably, but whether it was due to the answer he was concocting or to his overfilled stomach, she wasn't sure. 'I'm a city-dweller at heart. I love London. I want to live in New York one day. The thought of having an apartment in a brownstone and writing through the night, then taking the subway to my favourite diner for coffee in the morning appeals.'

'I never realised you were such a Carrie Bradshaw.'

'I like the noise and the people watching and the twenty-four/seven-ness of it all. I like the anonymity, but also the potential for dreams to come true.'

Marianne nodded. It all sounded great. Only, what did that mean for them? She asked him, 'Do you think you'll leave Bayside once the book is finished?'

Drew looked into her eyes for a moment. 'I have no plans yet.'

'I like no plans,' she nodded. Was that still strictly true, though, or just something she liked to constantly tell herself? Because Drew was the first man she'd loved and the thought of him just disappearing one day made her heart ache.

'I know,' he replied.

They were quiet for a moment while Marianne thought about their conversation. She didn't want him to leave. But he hadn't said he *would*, and he'd only finished the first draft of his book; there was plenty of time and surely lots of edits and rewrites to go before they had to make any kind of decision. So she shook the thought from her head for now to focus on the present.

'Do you still want to explore today?' he asked, his voice soft.

'Yes … How about we walk off some of this with a wander down and back up the Strip? Then see how we feel. Do you need anything from the room before we set off?' Marianne asked.

'No, I'm good. You?'

'Nope.'

The two of them walked through the hotel until they reached the exit and stepped outside, away from the air conditioning and apparently straight into a firepit.

'Holy *heatwave*, it's boiling out here!' Marianne commented as they made their way onto the Strip. There were people everywhere, strolling in the sunshine, sipping from drinks, cooling themselves with handheld electric fans, but it didn't feel too busy, at least not on this part of the boulevard, thanks to the wide pavements and even wider road.

'Left first?' Drew checked, and Marianne peered down the street in both directions. Left certainly seemed to be where most of the action was, so that was where they started. The pavements were sunbaked and clean and before long they hit a set of escalators that, if they wanted, could take them up and over the road to the opposite side, where a shopping mall called Fashion Show sat, its shade enticing them inside.

It was tempting, but Marianne thought that might be giving up too soon, and they'd be back up this end of the Strip again in no time. 'Shall we go right down the length of this side, cross, then come back up on the other side?'

After about another five minutes of walking, they reached one corner of The Venetian, which, like the other hotels in Vegas, rose high into the air above them. 'Do you think we're allowed to walk through the hotels?' Marianne asked.

'I think part of the thing here *is* to walk through the hotels.'

And so they did just that. They walked, and they walked, and they walked. They saw gondolas gliding through the calm indoor waterways of The Venetian. They strolled past Parisian patisseries in Paris Las Vegas. They gawped at an indoor rainstorm in Planet Hollywood. They also people-watched, window-shopped and eyeballed the high rollers. And that was just one side of the street.

Marianne had had no idea the Strip took this long to explore. Without stopping, it might have taken them under an hour to walk from the Encore down to the MGM Grand, and then the same back, whereas she'd thought, *Hey, it's just a handful of hotels on each side, maybe twenty minutes each way?* With stopping, it was early afternoon by the time they'd crossed to the other side of the road and were outside Excalibur, the big medieval-castle hotel.

As they paused at a crossing, Marianne leaned her weight on Drew to give her hot, blistering feet a moment of light relief.

'Those sandals are killing you, huh?' he asked.

'A little bit,' she admitted. 'I'd never worn them before today, and I don't think I comprehended quite how long a walk this was, and quite how hot and sweaty and slidey my feet would get ... *Pleasestillloveme.*' She glanced up at him and noticed a pink glow coming from the top of his forehead. 'Are you getting sunburned?'

'Oh no, am I?' Drew reached up and dragged a nail over his hairline and then winced as presumably it began to sting. 'Yep, I think I am.'

'Do you want more lotion?'

'I think we're past lotion.' They walked a little further, until Drew pointed towards a big store called CVS across the street. 'That's a drugstore. Mind if we pop in and I'll see if they have any sunblock?'

'Sure. Maybe they'll have some socks I can wear with my sandals. Again, please still love me.'

They entered the cool of the store with a joint sigh of relief.

'Wow, this isn't like your average pharmacy,' Marianne commented as they wandered the aisles. This had walls of drinks, soft and hard, racks of food and snacks, candles, clothing, accessories, magazines, toys and, of course, pharmaceutical goods aplenty. It was amazing. She picked up a bottle of refreshing-looking coconut water on her way past, which in this heat she would chug in five seconds flat, as soon as they'd paid.

She'd lost Drew some time ago to a rack of books, when she found the most perfect thing in the whole world. 'Drew?' she called, peering up and down the aisles.

'Marianne?' she heard from somewhere behind her.

Turning, she still couldn't see him. 'Drew?'

'Marianne?'

'Drew?'

'Marianne?'

By following each other's voices, they finally came face to face, both looking pleased as punch. Marianne gasped in delight at what Drew was holding in his hands, and he laughed joyfully at her find.

'You have got to get this,' Marianne said, holding up a stonewashed denim baseball cap with the word *Vegas* in large red diamantés stuck across the visor. On the front panel were two large, sparkling golden dice.

'It's perfect to cut out the sun!' he exclaimed. 'And you have to get these.' He held up a bright white pair of women's trainers completely bedazzled with silver rhinestones and with a 3D *Welcome to Fabulous Las Vegas* sign poking out of the tongues. They had squishy bubble soles and Marianne was in love with them straight away.

'These are so much better for walking in than my bloody sandals,' she cried, holding them close.

Did they step back out of that pharmacy and onto the street looking more like tourists than ever? Sure. Did they also feel on top of the world and like total ballers? Absolutely. Anything goes in Vegas, after all.

Marianne and Drew arrived back at their hotel early evening, pretty shattered. With happier feet and heads, but still shattered.

'All I want to do is sink into that hotel pool,' Drew commented when they reached their room, plonking down the shopping bags and his bright red daiquiri yard drink. He yawned and rolled his shoulders.

Marianne flopped face down on the bed, imprinting the sticky remains of her make-up onto the sheets. A few moments later, she looked up at him. 'Yes, agreed. That sounds perfect.'

Finding two yellow-and-white towel-covered loungers side by side at the nearest pool, Marianne and Drew dropped off their things and slid in, lying back in the cool water with unison *ahhhh*s, the tower of the Encore above them.

'Did you speak to Jenny at all yet?' he asked after a while and for a moment Marianne pretended her ears were underwater and she couldn't hear him. He asked again.

'No, I haven't spoken to her.'

'Why not?'

Why was he bringing this up now? They were having such a nice time. 'She hasn't spoken to me either.'

'But ...' He was quiet for a moment.

Marianne waited, twirling retorts around in her mind but trying not to jump ahead and mind-read what he was going to say. When she couldn't bear the silence any longer, she said, 'I've seen her Instagram and she's having the time of her life, finally.'

'Social media isn't always quite a true reflection of real life, though. Maybe she's alone out there and needs a friend.'

That was a sucker punch to the gut. Marianne stood up in the water. 'She's the one who applied for the job.'

'And you told her to go for it.'

'And she told me she wasn't going to because I couldn't possibly cope without her. Here I am, coping without her.'

'I don't think she meant coping on holiday ...'

'I know what she meant. Just drop it, Drew. We're just having some time apart, it's nothing for you to get involved in.'

He stood with her and put a wet hand to her face, dripping chilly droplets onto her shoulders. 'I'm sorry. It's just that it's been over a month now since you two last saw each other, and that seems like a lot for you both. She's been a good friend to you in the past, from what you've told me.' He paused. 'But it's none of my business.'

No, it wasn't. Marianne's feelings were valid; her feelings mattered. Jenn had made her feel as though what she brought to the table wasn't important and it sucked, and they'd probably get over it. But not yet.

# Chapter 20

# Jenny, in the Maldives

'The stars have aligned!' Layla declared, in a dramatic entrance to the bookstore.

I looked up from my laptop. 'They have?'

'They have.' She sauntered in and perched on my one small book table, shifting a novel about time travel with her bottom, the ends of her hair tickling the covers of the other books. 'Guess who has a day off tomorrow.'

Well, I knew I couldn't afford to take my day off tomorrow, so ... 'You?'

'And you!' Layla cried in return. 'We have a day off together. But that's not all.'

I stopped her there. '*Noooo*, no, I have to work tomorrow. I'm sorry.'

'No, you don't,' Layla said. 'Tomorrow is Friday. This place will be c-l-o-s-e-d. *And* ...' She paused before teasingly pointing her finger at me. 'Rish also has the day off tomorrow. But that's still not all!'

'Oh, I'd love to hang out with you both, but—'

She held up her hand. 'I know for a fact that you haven't taken any of your days off since you opened.'

'But I can't. I have the new event next week and there's still so much to do.'

'Like what?'

'Like ...' I faltered. In reality, I was totally organised and ready, books ordered, cocktails devised. But that didn't mean I didn't want to go over it all tenfold beforehand, and I'd been hoping to spend my day off tomorrow over in the space, making sure I knew how it was all going to look and work. 'I can't list it all. I just know I'm too busy.'

'Do you know what your problem is?' Layla asked, hands on hips.

'What?'

'You're one of those people who can fill every single hour of a day and you still don't feel like you've done enough. There will never be enough hours in the day for you. But the crazy thing? You would have the same result if you only had one hour. Because you can't just do something and then let it go. Has anyone ever told you that?'

*Well, yes, actually.* I was trying to think of an answer when Layla picked up a book from my shelf.

'Now, about tomorrow,' she said, and tossed her super-long hair behind her shoulder, her eyes sparkling. 'Do you know what this is?'

I looked at the cover of a book called *Marine Life in the Maldives*. 'That's a fish.'

Layla rolled her eyes. 'This is a whale shark. It's one of the highlights of our oceans here.'

Taking the book from her hands, I studied the creature, who was a deep blue with a large rounded head and gaping mouth. His body was speckled with white dots. 'I like him. Have you ever seen one?'

'I have. Do you want to see one?'

I nodded. 'Mmm, yeah, that would be cool. Wait, *do I*? Like, do you know where I could see one?'

'I might do. But you have to give yourself a day off and come with me tomorrow.'

'But—'

'Live a little,' she said. 'Because you're only going to live in the Maldives once.'

That was how I found myself taking a not-as-rejuvenating-as-I-imagined outdoor shower before the sun rose the following morning. It was actually quite chilly standing out there in the dark, the sounds of the fruit bats gently squabbling in the trees above. It was tempting to climb straight back in under my duvet, but Layla had told me I needed to be outside my bungalow, swimsuit on, beach bag packed, at 5.30 a.m.

Was I falling into my bad habits again? I pondered as I waited on the step of my home. Layla was right, I did have a tendency to get sucked into my own whirlpool of attempted perfection. And I wanted to do a good job here, a great job, a perfect job even, but if it were my best friend burning out in front of me, wouldn't I tell her to take a break, and that she would be more capable afterwards?

Or would I tell her to stop abandoning me, like I had with Marianne ...

Layla appeared through the shadows together with Rish, and we waved a silent hello to each other so as not to wake anyone in the other bungalows. It wasn't until we were on the main stretch of Coconut Cove beach that I said to them, 'Can I know where we're going yet? Whereabouts on the island do the whale sharks come to?'

All of a sudden, Layla and Rish took a sharp left onto the jetty. The sun was rising now, though it wasn't over the horizon yet, which gave the sky and the sea a lilac dawn tone. We stopped before we reached the seaplane, which was sleeping on the ocean at the jetty's end, and there below us, gently thunking against the wood, was a boat, smaller than the ferry, about the size of the speedboats used to take guests on private tours.

'Are we going on a boat trip?' I asked, which might have been the silliest question possible, since both Layla and Rish were already reaching their things down and climbing in.

Rish looked back up at me and held out his hand. 'All aboard, me hearty,' he sang.

I didn't really need to hold someone's hand to get into a boat on sea as calm as this, but the kind gesture was appreciated. Our fingertips touched, his warm palm gripping my cooler one, and it sent a tiny sparkle of excitement and adventure through me.

'Where are we going?' I asked, as Layla started the boat and pulled us away from the jetty and into open water.

'We're going to a Marine Protected Area in the South Ari Atoll,' she told me, which didn't mean a lot to me, but I nodded anyway. 'We're going to – hopefully – swim with some whale sharks this morning.'

'Swim with them?' I cried loudly, and then repeated, more quietly, 'Swim with them?'

Layla turned her head to me and laughed, her hair whipping in the breeze and the purple morning clouds behind her, the smell and taste of salt water in the sea spray that misted us. 'Yes, swim with them. Don't worry, they're completely safe.'

'They only eat plankton,' Rish added, passing me a Bounty Cove Cay-branded fleece blanket from under one of the seats, which I wrapped around my shoulders. 'And sometimes a fish or two. Very rarely a person.'

I laughed. 'I'm not worried, I'm excited. I've never done anything like this!'

'Even though you live near the sea at home?' Rish asked.

'I go in the sea a fair amount, and I have swum near a couple of seals once, but never anything like these things. Do they only come out first thing in the morning?'

'Huh?' Rish leaned closer, struggling to hear me over the wind in our ears and the hum of the speedboat.

'Do the whale sharks only show themselves in the morning?'

'No, they're around all day.'

'Pardon?' I shuffled closer to him and caught Layla raising an eyebrow.

'We're heading over there early,' she interjected, 'not because the whale sharks will be going anywhere, but because the later we leave it the more tourists there'll be in the waters. It's a popular thing for people to do.'

'Do the sharks mind the people?' I asked them both, and Rish took this one.

'No, they don't mind. But still, the less busy we can make it for them, the nicer they're bound to find it. Did you remember to not put on any deodorant?'

I tried to sniff my armpit, embarrassment washing over me. 'I didn't put any on, just like Layla told me – do I smell?'

'Not at all, just checking. And no perfume or sun lotion?'

'Nope, I remembered.'

'That's good. The chemicals in them can hurt the environment the whale sharks live in. We have eco-friendly sunscreen here on the boat, so you can put some of that on if you want.'

'Oh, that's actually the brand I brought with me!' I exclaimed, helping myself, and caught Rish flashing a happy smile to himself.

Layla turned back to us once again. 'We're past the reef so I'm going to speed up now, and it'll get a bit noisier, OK?'

Rish and I nodded from our huddle. As the boat revved satisfyingly, I was very aware of how close he and I were. I watched our island shrink as we pulled away from it, and felt myself and my sense of adventure grow.

*

We had been moored for about half an hour before the first fin poked up out of the water. We'd been enjoying the quiet and the early morning sunshine, munching on mango and papaya that Rish had brought with him, and chatting about our lives away from Bounty Cove Cay.

'Do you ever travel home to Tahiti?' I asked Layla.

'Whenever I can,' she said. 'But I do consider the Maldives my second home now. What I can't imagine is ever living in a city.'

'I lived in a city for a while,' Rish added. 'First in Colombo in Sri Lanka, then Manila in the Philippines. But I agree with Layla, I am all about the reef and the sunrays now.'

'Did Rish tell you he's hoping to be a resident marine biologist for Bounty Cove Cay?' Layla asked as he leaned over the side of the boat, deep concentration and a snorkel mask on his face.

'Yes, he did. What with that and the pitch, he's really into all the biodiversity of the islands, isn't he?'

She nodded. 'He's in training at the moment, and he spends a lot of his spare time working on the new coral regeneration project on the island, which is where broken coral is saved while it's still alive and tied onto frames placed on the seabed. In a couple of years, a new load of coral has grown.'

Layla and I continued chatting, idly watching Rish study the sea while we talked more about conservation in the Maldives, which she, too, was passionate about. Behind us were a smattering of islands so like our own, of varying sizes and shapes, but each with its own sense of individuality.

'Hello, you,' Rish said all of a sudden, bringing his head up and pointing at the advancing fin.

We whipped our heads round and Layla's smile lit up. 'There she is,' she whispered, and then said to me, 'Ready? Let's go.'

I scrambled to follow the two of them as they threw off their cover-ups and slipped on their snorkels in record time, lowering themselves into the water and waiting for me to stumble, trip and army-roll my way to the swim platform at the stern.

Dropping into the water in the Maldives, even at such an early hour, felt like climbing into a warm bath. Well, *ish*. It still shocked me how unshocking it felt, unlike at home, when an involuntary *'Yowwwwzer'* would escape my lips every time I entered the icy-feeling ocean, despite having lived there my whole life. I treaded water for a moment while I defogged and then adjusted my snorkel, and then, on feeling Layla's hand tap my arm below the surface, I dunked my head under.

I found Layla's hand and tried not to grip it too hard, and tried not to kick my legs too much, or breathe water in through my salt-tingling lips, because there, swimming past me, at least seven metres long, was the big, beautiful, dotted creature I'd been promised. She (I went with 'she' as Layla had called her a she) glided past us without so much as a glance, much like somebody passes a stack of iceberg lettuces when they're on their way to the bakery counter. I watched the whale shark, every inch of her, as she swayed her body, her big mouth hanging open, her dark blue skin covered in markings like stars in the night sky. Her tail propelled her along, and just as I thought we weren't going to see her again, Layla tipped herself forwards and started a slow swim behind her, holding my hand so that I did the same.

We met three whale sharks that morning. We swam next to them, we gazed at them, we pointed them out to each other, we watched them eat, and even after we'd climbed back onto the boat I kept looking and looking in case any of them came back.

I removed my snorkel and mask and sat back, wiping my face with my towel and staring open-mouthed at Rish and Layla, probably looking much like a whale shark myself.

Rish was telling us all about the lives of the fish, his face animated yet calm, the way someone looks when they're talking about somebody they love deeply, and it made me want to hang on to every word.

When he paused, and I'd recovered my conversation skills, I said to him, 'I can see why you're training to be a marine biologist. You're great to listen to.'

'*Nooo*,' he demurred, but I saw a smile on his lips when he looked back out at the water.

Layla returned to her position at the front of the boat and started the engine. 'Shall we go to our next stop?'

'There's a next stop?' I asked. 'Where are we going?'

'My favourite island,' she replied.

I wrapped my towel around my shoulders, though the sun was high in the sky and keeping us all toastier now.

I didn't really mean to, but I found myself leaning back against Rish, enjoying the touch of another person's body against my own. My mind began to drift to Evan, but then I forced myself to stay in the present and enjoy what was happening around me right now. I was in an island paradise, just like I'd dreamed, and God was I happy right now.

I stole a sideways look at Rish, his open shirt flapping in the breeze, beams glinting off his shades. He was solid sunshine, and he had a way of making those around him feel lighter and brighter too. Or maybe it was just me.

'Welcome to Dhigurah,' declared Layla, as she pulled the boat in to dock.

There were less markers of luxury resorts here, such as coordinating parasols stretching down the long beach, uniformed staff waiting with a tray of juice and a stack of cold towels, neatly lined-up jet skis. What I saw was a peaceful paradise. The same lush green forest, aqua seas with telltale dark patches under the surface where the coral was living and white sand that seemed to go on for miles, even after the main island had finished, but without the big hotel vibes I'd become so familiar with over the past month.

'What is this place?' I asked. 'Is it a resort?'

Layla shook her head. 'Nope, this is a local island, where people live. There's a small population, and a few guest houses, but it's a fishing village mainly, with homes, shops, places to eat. This is where we're having lunch. Did you pack that long dress?'

I nodded and took my maxi dress from my bag – a lightweight fabric in bright orange, with billowy sleeves that grazed my elbows – and pulled it over my swimwear. We stepped from the boat onto the sand, warm under our feet, and I couldn't get over how quiet it was. 'Does nobody know about this island or something?'

'This is the beauty of the Maldives,' Rish said, standing beside me and stretching his arms into the air, uncrumpling from the morning of swimming. 'It's easy to feel like you're the only people in the world here.'

We walked a little way up the beach, ducking under low palms, past the blue-painted *Welcome to Dhigurah* sign, which was topped with bright Maldivian flags that were fluttering in the barely-there breeze, and found ourselves following a long, sandy pathway between low buildings painted in bright pinks and greens and blues. In fact, there were colours everywhere. Tropical flowers spilled out of the greenery on all sides, and bicycles of bright yellow were propped against walls. I stopped to look in the window of a shop selling wooden crafts and then my stomach made a huge growl that could probably be heard across the whole island.

'Hungry?' Rish laughed.

'Swimming always makes me peckish,' I admitted.

We followed Layla as she wove through the streets, heading to an eatery she knew of that served great local food. I liked it from the moment we crossed under the wooden archway propped up by two surfboards. Inside, the air was cool, but the owner greeted us with all the warmth of the Maldivian sun.

'Could I have the *mas huni*, please?' I asked.

'*Mas huni* is usually for breakfast,' Layla explained, but just as I was about to change my mind the owner grinned at me.

'If you've not had *mas huni*, you must have *mas huni*, no matter what time of day it is.'

Rish nodded. 'It is delicious.'

It sounded it. Flaky coconut and fish served with flatbread? I'll have forty, please, thank you. While we waited, we sat at one of the tables with our toes tickling the sand and sipped papaya-flavoured fizzy drinks straight from the can.

After we'd finished eating, Layla stood up. 'Shall we take a walk down to the end of the sandbank?'

I rubbed my tummy. 'That sounds perfect, I could do with walking this off.'

'I'll catch up with you,' Rish said. 'I'm just going to stop in and say hi to a friend who lives near here.'

'Will he know where to find us?' I checked with Layla as we began our walk down the length of the island.

'There'll be no missing us,' she replied. 'Once we hit the sandbank the island tapers to being literally a few metres wide. You'll see.'

We strolled at a slow pace, quietly letting the island of Dhigurah shade us. And you know when you just *know* somebody wants to say something? Sure enough, Layla asked, 'How are things going with Rish?'

'I think he's great,' I answered, honestly. 'He's kind and funny and he cares about the planet. What's not to like?'

'Do you think he's hot?'

'Hot? Yes, I suppose so,' I laughed. I mean, obviously I did, because he was delicious and he walked about looking like a *Love Island* contestant. 'Why do you ask?'

'He told me how your date went.'

I cast a sideways look at Layla. 'It wasn't meant to be a date; you were supposed to be there too. I'm not usually ...'

'What?'

'Someone who dates a lot. I don't want to do the wrong thing.' I didn't quite know how to put it into words. I didn't want to string Rish along, but I did want to see where it led? I didn't want to fall for him and then have to leave. I didn't want to give him my heart because part of it was still holding out for Evan.

'Just take it at your own pace. He won't push you.'

'He told you about us?'

'He mentions you from time to time,' she chuckled. 'I don't know ... he seems happier since you arrived.' We continued to the end of the island, or what appeared to be the end until I noticed the long stretch of sandbank trailing out to sea, like a manta ray tail. We kept going, following the sand, the lagoon water lapping just feet from our feet on either side. 'Anyway, I just wanted to say that Rish is great. He really is kind, like you said, and he's real. He's not falling in love with every new guest that comes to the resort or anything. And he's smart. And fun. And he likes adventure – like you.'

I nodded along to all of this, like a voter listening to a live debate. At that moment we heard footsteps jogging up behind us and turned to see the man himself approaching. I saw Layla's smile light up, and she nudged me towards him.

'Rish, Jenn was just saying how interesting she thinks you are.'

*Thanks, friend.* Rish looked at me, surprised but pleased, so I added, 'I just think the marine biology stuff you're doing is great. I'm very impressed with the conservation work that is occurring, you know, in all of the Maldives.'

Why, oh why can I not talk like a normal human being sometimes? For years I've watched Marianne and envied her easy patter with people. Customers, future lovers, friends, they're all drawn to her honesty and openness, while I often feel as if I'm trying to follow a set of unwritten rules for conversation and can never remember to be natural along with it. *I'm very impressed with the conservation work that is occurring.* I was being more formal than I was in my job interview.

'See, I told you,' Layla nudged Rish. 'Everyone thinks you should pitch your ideas to the resort directors. Don't you agree, Jenny?'

'Absolutely, what have you got to lose?'

Rish laughed. 'My job?'

'As if,' Layla said. 'I'll stand with you – we can pitch together.'

'Yeah?'

'Yeah. Khadeeja and I get coffee together from time to time and we talk,' she said, with a smile. 'I have some ideas of my own.'

Rish seemed genuinely pleased. 'In that case, I'll think about it.'

As I walked the sandbank, and it got thinner and thinner, it was as if I was out in the middle of the ocean. I felt unrestricted and free, because out here, in this moment, there weren't any rules, really. You just had to be. Breathe in the sea air, notice the sparkling dart of a fish under the surface of the shallow water, feel the warm water coming close to stroke your feet as you stood on the powdery-soft, icing-sugar sand.

A *dhoni*, one of the traditional Maldivian fishing boats with a long, curved bow, sailed slowly past, painted in bright red and blue, and I waved, like saying hello to strangers was something I'd never even been scared to do. My heart sang when the passenger waved back.

We turned then, and headed back towards the main blob of Dhigurah, the sand sinking beneath our bare feet with every step, my toes luxuriating in the soft grains hugging each of them individually.

'Did you say people have picnics out on sandbanks?' I asked Layla. 'Like, they bring some sandwiches and just sit down? Isn't that annoying for anyone else trying to walk past them?'

'Some of the sandbanks are much wider than this, or they curve into loops at the end. The picnics I was referring to are usually run by the resorts and they have a proper table and chairs, and candles in glass jars, and you eat fresh local delicacies and watch the sun go down. They're very romantic,' she nudged Rish.

'Have you ever been on one?' I asked her.

'No.' She kicked at the sand, and I let it drop because moments later she looked up, grinned and changed the subject. 'Ready for your final stop of the day?'

'There's *more*?' I checked my watch. It was already mid-afternoon.

'We have about one thousand two hundred islands here. There's always more in the Maldives.'

My friends promised more, and they delivered. Another boat ride, a few sweet cocktails and one sunset later, and I had sunk into a beanbag on yet another beach while fire dancers twirled around me and Rish's beanbag toppled in towards mine, meaning his weight was against me. We were on another island, this time, a large resort that I recognised from an article I'd read a while back about some models vacationing there. It was very beautiful and trendy, with endless facilities and endless attractive people, and very not my usual scene, but it was new and out of my comfort zone, and for that reason alone I was going with the flow. *See, Marianne, I can be fun and spontaneous … when someone else has done the organising.*

We were at one of the resort's fancy moonlight parties, which was *wonderrrrrrful* and I didn't *think* it was the flower-topped cocktails that were talking.

'There are mermaids in the pool,' I said to Rish, over the beat of the music. I pointed at the betailed women dipping under the surface of the water and up again.

He leaned closer, causing his beanbag to tip him further into me. 'What did you say?'

I brought my lips towards his ear, aware of how this was the closest he and I had been since I'd arrived on the island. I looked at him for a moment, straightening my gaze, taking him in. Was what Layla said true? Did he like me like *that*? I'd never had a holiday romance, but maybe it would be just the thing I needed to stop me thinking about my Evan entanglement. So I needed to ask myself ... did I like Rish, like *that*?

I took a beat and then repeated, 'I said, there are mermaids, in the pool.'

'Yeah,' he said, not taking his eyes off me.

The music pulsed around us. I recognised it – 'Waves' by Mr. Probz – and the lyrics, the beat, the melody, caught my heart and lifted it towards Rish. I moved closer to him. It would be so easy to kiss him right now.

I wanted to forget about that certain someone else back in Bayside. My lips wanted to press against Rish's, I wanted to lift my hand to the skin of his cheek.

He had a hand behind me, and the fingers of that hand moved to the back of my neck, exploring, testing, and I let them send a tingle down my spine.

Rish leaned forwards, pausing millimetres from me, checking for permission, which I gave with the tiniest nod.

His kiss was warm, that sunshine in him pooling from him to me, and we sank into it, probably for no more than a few seconds but enough for me to forget everything and everyone other than him and the music.

He pulled back, his smile catching in the soft lights of the party, and I smiled. I did like him, and he liked me, and we clearly both enjoyed *that*. Only … neither of us leaned in again. Perhaps the setting, as amazing as it was, didn't feel right.

My alcohol-loosened mind cleared a little and with a tiny sigh I realised: perhaps he and I just didn't feel right.

# Chapter 21

# Marianne, in the USA

The day after their epic Strip walk, Marianne and Drew spent most of the daylight hours by the pool.

'Is there anything you actually want to do while we're in Las Vegas?' Marianne asked him late in the afternoon over a poolside snack of chips and guacamole, with a side of Belinda Jones's book *Divas Las Vegas*. She was over their mini argument from the day before, and actually she had found herself on Jenny's Instagram again while he was taking a shower back in their room, just to reassure herself that Jenn was, in fact, absolutely fine. Which she was. She seemed to be having a great time, actually. In fact, she'd only just posted a series of photos from a snorkelling trip with a hunky guy and a smiling girl. Jenn and the girl were laughing, arm in arm, like best friends.

'I want to check out some locations from *Fear and Loathing in Las Vegas*, and also there's a really great independent bookstore downtown I'd love to visit called The Writer's Block, if you'd be keen and it wouldn't be too much like going back to work?'

Marianne snapped her attention back to the present. 'Yeah, sure. Because we only have two days left, unless we do extend our stay here, should we plan anything?' Though Vegas seemed like a pretty live-in-the-moment kind of place.

He thought about it for a moment. 'I've heard they have good pool parties, but I think that's an all-day thing. I'd be happy to see a show. Or try some bars. How about you?'

'I want to see the Bellagio fountains, and have a go in a casino.'

'All right then.'

'But not right now,' she grinned, and leaned over to give him a bite of her tortilla chip.

'All right then,' he laughed, before the two of them abandoned their food to slide their bodies back into the water yet again. She loved his skin against hers, it was so hard to resist.

That evening they took a walk back down the Strip to see the Bellagio fountains, even enjoying some complimentary cocktails – extra strong – en route, thanks to a walk through a casino floor at the right place and time. At the fountains, Marianne watched, mesmerised, as the water danced and jumped up into the dark sky, perfectly in time with the music being pumped out across the street. She stood beside crowds of people oohing and aahing at the show, Drew behind her, his arms wrapped around her shoulders.

She was happy. Not just from the liquor, or the music, but from him, them, the whole situation. And she could tell he felt it too.

They were in love. *She*, Marianne, was in love, something she'd never thought was on the cards for her. And she didn't want it to end.

Behind her, Drew leaned close, a tendril of his hair tickling her cheek as he whispered something into her ear.

'What?' she asked, turning her head slightly.

Drew rested his forehead against hers, looking down at her lips, and she studied him in close-up, her breathing slowing. He looked serious all of a sudden, but the corners of his mouth were ever so slightly rising up towards the sky.

There was a long moment where Marianne tried to read his eyes, wondering if he'd really said what she thought he'd said, wondering if her heart could start beating again. She watched Drew's lips carefully as he spoke again, quietly, confidently. 'I want to marry you.'

'No, you don't.' Marianne nudged him with her elbow, a small chuckle escaping, but she didn't take her eyes off him.

'I do,' Drew whispered.

'Are you serious?' The dancing fountains were behind her, the crowd forgotten, the music fading apart from the bass that was beating against her heart.

'I can't stop thinking about it,' he admitted. 'Ever since you mentioned it at check-in, it hit me, like it was the obvious answer I'd been waiting for, even though I didn't know I was asking. Literally.'

'This is just Vegas talking,' Marianne laughed, but every part of her, the spontaneous part, the wild part, the vulnerable part, the *in-love* part, was leaning in, fast. Her fingers shook as they reached for his face, touched his stubble, felt his jawline.

'It's not. I've maybe even been thinking it since Joshua Tree – who knows, maybe before. It's just that now I know, I want to marry you now. Today. Yesterday. Every day.'

Gulping, Marianne stepped back, looked straight on at him and asked him in a clear voice, 'Are you actually asking me to marry you, Drew Inkbridge, or is this a joke?'

Around them, a few other tourists tore their eyes from the fountains and stared at them. One turned their phone around to capture this moment instead.

Drew swept his hair back off his face, his eyes bright, sparkling, reflecting all of Las Vegas's lights. 'Marianne ...' He knelt down on the concrete pavement, and the nearby tourists gasped. 'Will you marry me?'

This was ... Marianne was lost for words. This was ... perfect. This was incredible. Just the adventure she'd been looking for. 'Yes,' she answered.

Drew's eyebrows shot up nearly as quickly as he did. 'Did you say yes?'

She nodded, then laughed. 'Yes! Sure! Yes.'

# Chapter 22

# Jenny, in the Maldives

With one more sleep until my big event, I closed the shop early again (as in, on time) and went back up to the mezzanine level of the Pavilion to finish my day with the spectacular view from there. As I did a deep, satisfying stretch, my thoughts ran away with me about the next day. I was scared, I couldn't deny it, because Marianne wasn't going to be there to take charge. I'd have to do all the talking, all the schmoozing, myself. But I told myself I could do it. I could do it.

I spotted something I hadn't noticed before – a selection of books arranged on a neat white-and-gold bookshelf on wheels. Like a bar cart, almost. A smart printed card declared the books were available to borrow and enjoy at will.

'A book exchange,' I muttered, picking a well-read copy of *The Kite Runner* off the shelf. 'So, you're my competition.' The cart was tucked away behind an armchair, but must have been used a lot by those who found it, judging by the state of the books. Books that had been read and borrowed and spine-cracked and thumbed through, again and again.

It was just surprising to see them in a resort like this, where everything else was so pristine.

And the broken spines and thumbed pages were across the board; I couldn't see that one particular genre, like literary fiction or classic mysteries, was getting the most reads. Clearly the bonkbusters, the historicals, the romcoms and the slasher novels were getting just as much playtime down on the sunloungers as the others. It dawned on me that I'd pigeonholed and judged the guests too early. What a rookie mistake. I knew better than that ...

With this on my mind, I headed down the staircase, running into Khadeeja en route.

'Hi, Jenny,' she said, looking up from her phone.

'Evening, Khadeeja. How are you?'

'Very well, thanks. All set for tomorrow?'

'I think so.' I chuckled with nerves, but Khadeeja raised her eyebrows so I super subtly turned my laugh into a cough and added, 'Yes, yes I am.'

'Good. Let's make sure this is the first successful event of many, all right?'

'Yes, ma'am,' I did a sort of curtsy, which was very cringe, so I shuffled off down the stairs post-haste. Tomorrow *was* going to be a success. I was definitely *not* going to overthink things all night long.

With no other plans that evening, I took myself for a walk somewhere I'd been meaning to meander ever since the seaplane had swooped over the island on my arrival. Joining the boardwalk outside the main building, I followed it down until it veered off as if going towards the beach and then swept straight ahead, out over the sea. I walked the pier, where the overwater villas, or the Laguna Private Water Villas as I should call them, sat in quiet serenity on either side. Feeling a bit like a clicky-clacky disturber of the peace, I removed my flip-flops and padded my bare feet along the warm wooden boards, silently passing the backs of the villas, one by one. Or were they the fronts? I assumed 'front' would refer to the big windowed other side of the villas, where guests could dip straight into the ocean from their porch.

As I passed one, it had its doors wide open, and I sneaked a sidelong glance and nearly fell off the jetty. Inside, the room opened out into a huge suite, complete with a massive bed, mood lighting, tranquil furnishings, waterfall shower, soaking tub, long white sofas and even a section of glass flooring showing a circle of turquoise ocean. OK, *now* I could see why my beach bungalow was considered, *cough*, 'shabby'.

Call me Captain Obvious, but it was very relaxing here, and I felt my anxious thoughts slide away. When I used to stare at images of tropical islands on my laptop, I would think how nice it would be to stay in a place where you were forced to slow down your mind. I knew working in the resort meant I wasn't quite having the same experiences as the guests, but there was just a different pace of life here. An opportunity to take things a little slower, enjoy the colours more, breathe in the air. Or maybe it was me, maybe I was simply giving myself a greater allowance to experience those things here.

I watched a school of little clownfish shimmy their way from one side of the pier and pop out the other to carry on their way, and I kept walking to the end. As there was a restaurant at the tip, I figured it was probably all right for me to be nosing about.

Sure enough, at the end of the pier the long sweep of boardwalk curved back around, so that To the Moon was pointing towards the setting sun. The restaurant had open walls, allowing diners to have a full view of the ocean while they enjoyed their meal. Tonight, the sky was turning a bright, brilliant pink, with candyfloss clouds separating it from the teal ocean, and I took a moment, leaning against the wooden railing, to let the colours imprint on my brain. I knew a photo wouldn't do it justice, but I took a few anyway, because one day I wanted to look back on this very moment and remember the stillness. I couldn't believe I nearly hadn't come to the Maldives.

The water lapped rhythmically, holding my attention, instilling calm in me that I usually didn't feel the night before an occasion. My mind drifted back to Marianne as I remembered the first event she'd ever put on, which had been a fundraiser for cancer research back in Bayside when we were in our late teens. Her mum had been gone for close to a year, and she'd wanted something to keep her busy on the anniversary. She'd held a sponsored swimathon off the beach, Evan coming home to help lifeguard, and it felt like the whole town had come to join in, contribute, bring blankets and hot chocolate, cheer them all on. I'd helped with the organising, but it was

Marianne and her bravery and light that brought in the donations.

I don't know if it was the sunset or the romantic restaurant or the stirring I'd felt when I'd gone on my date with Rish that was still playing on my mind, but I was overcome with fondness for my best friend, despite everything, and for Evan, too. Even if he and I could only ever be friends, he was still part of home, part of my heart.

On my way back towards my bungalow, I stopped and climbed into a hanging seat, a big wicker teardrop dangling from the trunk of a palm that curved diagonally into the sky. I got out my phone, opened Instagram and added a snap of my pink-skied Maldives sunset. I hoped Marianne would see it. I wanted her to have a reason to think of me.

Navigating first to the Book Nook's page, I secretly hoped, as always, to see a selfie from Evan, but there wasn't one. (In fact, Evan – like me – didn't seem to excel at social media and our accounts felt lacklustre without Marianne.) I then moved to Marianne's personal feed again, saw she'd added to her Stories, and pressed on the little icon of her face.

My eyebrows furrowed.

I turned up the volume.

On the screen, Marianne and Drew were pressing their heads together, grinning at the camera, the noise of slot machines and people and music almost drowning out what they were saying. But while Marianne held the phone in her right hand, she held the left one up in front of her face, wiggling her fingers for the camera.

Glinting under the lights, positively dazzling, thanks to a glittery sparkle-effect filter that Marianne had added, was a very unmistakable engagement ring.

I sucked in my breath, a tumble of emotions clattering through me as though somebody had released a bag of tennis balls inside my chest. I was happy for her, if she was happy, but this was so *soon*, and wasn't this taking spontaneity a little too far? She and Drew barely knew each other. But how lovely for her that this had happened on a trip, somewhere exciting – that was exactly the kind of engagement Marianne would have wanted. But what would it mean for the future? Would Drew be moving to Bayside? Would Marianne move with him to wherever his next book would be set?

The thoughts churned around in my mind and I couldn't suppress the ominous feeling that I'd pushed her away. That this wild, adventurous woman was tired of our responsibility-filled life together and tired of me holding her back. But ... did she have to put it on Instagram before she'd told anyone? Before she'd told me? Did I mean that little to her now?

My fingers hovered over my phone, unsure whether to call Marianne or not. Eventually, I decided to call Evan, because awkward or not, I needed to know what was going on.

When he didn't answer, rocking myself back and forth in the seat while I waited, back and forth, back and forth, waves in and out, in and out, I realised he was probably working. I resolved to call him before I went to bed that night, which would be around about the time he was shutting up the Book Nook. It would also give Marianne time to wake up from what looked like a big night, as it would be around ten in the morning in Las Vegas. I could then, finally, call her, too.

# Chapter 23

# Marianne, in the USA

In the morning, Marianne woke up early again, and got out of bed to go straight to the window. Another glorious day in Las Vegas. In the sunlight that flooded in, she held up her left hand and smiled at the large, twinkling diamond.

Well, large, twinkling diamanté. Drew and she had run into the nearest gift shop on the Strip and purchased an inexpensive costume jewellery ring to make it 'official', and though he'd promised he'd replace it with something more thought-out sometime, she wasn't sure she needed anything else.

They'd then stayed out late celebrating, accepting glasses of champagne and warm congrats from anyone who offered. They'd talked about the when and the where, but it was all very surface level, no decisions, no plans were made. Then this morning, Marianne had woken with a smile, and a flutter in her heart that kept saying, *Why not here?*

Drew was fast asleep and Marianne was itching to burn off some of this excited energy, so she decided to try something she'd never done before. Pulling on her gym gear, she wrote Drew a note and slipped out of the room, making her way down in the elevators, through the lobby, past the hard-core few in last night's outfits still hunched over the card tables, and walked the long, wide corridors of the Wynn.

When she thought there couldn't possibly be any more of the hotel and she was about to fall out of an exit, Marianne reached a sign pointing her up a level, and that's where she found SoulCycle.

The studio was vast and gleaming, with a huge neon sign at the entrance that read *Unapologetically Addicted to Soul*. Inside was a bright white reception area, where a super-friendly lady took her details and didn't make fun of her, despite Marianne feeling awkward and as if she clearly had no idea what she was doing there and should maybe have stayed in bed. Marianne was given special clunky shoes that clipped into the bike's pedals, and a locker, and was then asked which bike she would like from a little map on an iPad.

'I don't know, one of those?' Marianne asked, pointing at one in front of the instructor. In her experience, as cringe as it sometimes felt, it was better to be able to see the instructor if you were in a new class than to be at the very back, not really able to see what was happening.

'Have you ridden with us before?' the SoulCycle lady asked.

'No.'

'Maybe try one of these, a little further back and off to the side. You'll still have a great view of your instructor, but you won't have riders behind you using you for pacing.'

No, that didn't sound good; Marianne definitely didn't want to be the one to set a rhythm for the class. She nodded along to the suggestion, and was then directed to a door into another room.

The other room was nearly pitch-black, save for a few glowing candles positioned around a bicycle at the front, which everyone was supposed to face. Marianne squinted to find her bike number among the hundred or so there seemed to be in there, and then climbed on nonchalantly and tapped her feet against the peddles. Shouldn't they click together or something?

In walked the nice lady from reception, who came straight over to Marianne and said in a confident voice within this hushed room, 'All right, you're new, right? Ready to get set up? I can help you with that.'

Marianne got back off the bike so the woman could give her body a once-over and then adjust the position of the seat and handlebars accordingly, and then she was instructed to jump back on.

'Place the front half of your feet down on the peddle – that's right, right there – and now push down like you're good to go.'

*Snap.* 'Oh, like that?' Marianne asked.

'Exactly like that. You good with the other side?'

'Yep.'

'And the height of the seat, all good?'

'Yes.'

'Enjoy,' she said, and held her hand up in the air until Marianne gave her a high five.

Because the others who were filtering in were doing it, Marianne gently peddled to the music (but secretly without any resistance) while they waited for the instructor, who walked in a few minutes before the start, electric-blue hair cascading from them in a long ponytail. 'Las Vegas, good morning, you got up, you came out, you are in control of you today.'

Marianne sat up straighter. You know, she *was* in control of her.

The instructor took their seat. 'Anybody here not Souled before?'

Raising her hand, Marianne said, 'Me.'

'All right, are you visiting?'

'Yes, from England.'

'Awesome, all the love to you for bringing yourself to this class and sharing your time with us while you're on vacation. What fun have you been getting up to in Vegas?'

'I'm … I just got engaged, actually,' Marianne said.

'You're getting married?' the instructor confirmed. 'When?'

'I don't know,' laughed Marianne in reply. 'Maybe today?'

'"Maybe today", she says! Yes, girl, maybe today. We all need your energy this morning, am I right, Las Vegas? Say it with me: *Maybe today.*'

The class shouted, 'Maybe today!' and Marianne looked around, surprised. *Yeah, maybe today …*

\*

That was *hard*. Marianne wasn't sure she'd ever sweated or pushed that hard in her life. Even on move-in day for the bookstore, when she and Jenny had had to haul box after box after box of books in from their delivery van and she'd almost gone right off the idea.

But even with a moment of very real nausea at one point, she'd loved every second of SoulCycle. Something about the dark room, the kind words from the instructor, the motivational soundtrack, the feeling of all those toxins she'd consumed from breakfast pizzas to yard-long daiquiris sweating out of her body, had made her feel amazing by the end. It had been, as promised, good for her soul.

She skipped back to their room with a lighter bounce to her, and when she walked in to find Drew still snoozing happily in a marshmallow duvet wrapped diagonally around him, she flopped down next to him without even showering and said, 'I want to marry you today.'

Drew opened his eyes. 'That's a nice thing to wake up to. OK then.' He sniffed. 'Will you shower first?'

Marianne laughed and jumped off the bed. 'I will indeed.'

'Where have you been?' he asked as she turned on the shower.

'SoulCycle.'

'Well done, you!'

Marianne showered slowly and happily, and when she came out of the room, she had a missed call on her phone from Evan, and a message from Drew saying he'd gone downstairs to get them some takeaway coffees.

She called Evan back, mentally working out that it must be late afternoon in the UK. 'Hi, bro!' she said, as soon as Evan picked up.

'Are you and Drew engaged?' he asked down the phone, before adding, but presumably not to her, 'That'll be six fifty, please.'

'Are you in the shop?'

'Yes, are you in your right mind?'

'Hey, what's that supposed to mean?' She felt herself deflate a little.

'Thanks so much, have a great evening,' Evan said, before speaking to her again more clearly. 'I mean, are you just being impulsive, drunk, wild Marianne in Vegas, or are you actually, happily engaged?'

'Can't I be both?'

'So you are engaged?'

'Yes,' Marianne laughed.

'Happily?'

'Yes, ecstatically!'

There was a pause at the end of the line, and then Evan let out a whoop. 'Then, congratulations, little sis, I'm happy for you. And you know I really like Drew.'

Marianne sank down onto the floor, her back against the panoramic window, Vegas spread out behind her. Her brother was her only real family, and she hadn't meant to share this with Instagram before him, but that must have been how he'd found out. She remembered adding a shrieking, camera-wobbling video to her Stories late last night while Drew gave her a piggyback along the pavement outside Caesars Palace. Or maybe it was inside. But anyway, Evan knew, and he was happy for her. Thank God.

'Have you spoken to Jenny yet?' Evan asked. 'What did she say?'

'I haven't told her yet,' Marianne admitted, but wondered if maybe she would have seen her Instagram Story too. A little bubble of guilt popped in her heart.

'You're not still arguing, are you?'

'No, we're not arguing, we're just ... not in contact. We're taking space from each other. It's fine.'

Evan sighed and she heard the tinkle of the shop door opening in the background. 'Call her and tell her. She'll be thrilled.'

Would she, though? Or would Jenny find a way to make this just another of Marianne's impulsive whims?

'I will,' Marianne replied, *just maybe not yet.*

Evan added, 'I'll be right with you. Wait, Mari, are you going to get married in Vegas, in one of those chapels?'

'Yeah ... I think we might do. What do you think about that?'

Evan laughed. 'I think it's very you, and you two should do whatever you want to do. Just let me throw you a massive party when you get home.'

He was so understanding. Marianne was lucky to have him as a brother. Hanging up, she wished she could magic him there, but it would be too much of an ask, and besides, she loved the idea of this just being about her and Drew. Speaking of ...

'What are you doing down there, bride-to-be?' Her groom walked in the room, dressed in a casual pale blue shirt, shorts and flip-flops. His hair was dishevelled and he had stubble, and she jumped straight up to lure him back to bed before he changed one bit.

Dressed in those wonderful hotel robes, Marianne and Drew sat side by side on the suite's sofa, looking at the internet on their phones.

'I don't get it,' Drew was saying. 'Can you get a marriage licence just there and then from the venue, or not?'

'I'm sure you can – people make impromptu decisions all the time in Vegas. Nobody sends them away because they don't have the right paperwork ...' Marianne huffed, confused. 'At least, that's what happens in the movies and on TV.' She put down her phone. 'Do you think if we spoke to the concierge here they could clear it up for us, or would they only help if we were booking one of the Wynn packages?'

'Would you like to get married here in the Wynn?' he asked.

Marianne scoffed a little. 'It would be *amazing*, but I don't think our budget would allow it. Besides, if I'm honest, there's a place I'd rather tie the knot with you.' Ever since she'd seen a tabloid story about an actress getting married at the Lovely Dovely Chapel of Luck and Love here in Las Vegas a few years back, she'd adored the kitschy cuteness of the place. She adored the idea of getting married in *any* of the chapels in Las Vegas, but this particular one screamed 'We got wild and wasted in Vegas and now we're hitched!' and that appealed to her massively. 'Check out the Lovely Dovely Chapel of Luck and Love,' she said, navigating to the search on her phone and flicking past more recent news stories until she spotted the one about that actress's ceremony there. Within the article were pictures of the chapel in all its frothy blue and pink wonderfulness. 'I know it's a lot, but I figure, if we're marrying in Vegas, we might as well go all in, right? And if we show up and they can't fit us in, I think they even do no-appointment, drive-through weddings.'

Drew looked up at her, a smile on his face. 'It looks great. I feel a little like I should have brought a bright blue ruffled suit to wear, but I love it. And I love that you love it.'

'Are you sure? If you'd rather go for the chapel here, we can – it looks beautiful.'

'Let's go with the Lovely Dovely Chapel of Luck and Love. As soon as possible.'

After a conversation with the concierge, and a buffet breakfast later, they had their answer: yes, they needed a marriage licence. It was easy enough, as they soon found out – a drive to the Clark County Marriage License Bureau, a wait in line, a few forms filled out, and they were set – but it did slightly remove the romantic skip in their step and by early afternoon they'd decided instead to make tomorrow, their last day in Las Vegas, their wedding day.

Marianne was acutely aware that she hadn't touched base with Jenny, and now it would be the middle of the night in the Maldives. But why hadn't her best friend called *her*? Marianne could see she'd viewed her Instagram Stories, so by now she knew – why wouldn't she want to call and congratulate her?

Sadness touched a nerve deep within Marianne. She always knew it was going to be hard getting married without her mum. Did she want to get married without her best friend too?

'What's going on in there?' Drew asked her as the two of them settled into seats at one of the hotel's Cirque de Soleil shows. 'You'll let me know if you change your mind about getting married, won't you?'

'I'm not changing my mind, not at all,' Marianne declared. She really wasn't. She was all in for getting married, but she did wish one or two things could be different. That would surely always be the way, with any wedding. You get everyone you want there, and then it rains all day. Or you get perfect weather but your cake doesn't show up. Or you find the perfect venue but it's too expensive, so you go with your second choice. Whatever, that was life. The important thing was that she and Drew were never going to be each other's second choice. They were choosing each other, and choosing now.

Next to Marianne, an elderly woman leaned forward in her chair to see them both. 'Did he say you two are getting married?' she squawked.

'That's right!' Marianne answered, waving her ring finger in the air.

'But you're babies!'

Another woman, the other side of the first, leaned round her, batting her grey hair out of her face. 'You leave them be, Leenie, we were babies when we got together too.'

'It was a long time before we got married, though,' Leenie said, taking a sip of her drink.

'Ah, not for lack of trying,' the second woman tutted.

Drew smiled at them. 'But you've been together all this time? Well, that's a good sign.'

'I wouldn't have let Bette go if she'd been trying to claw her way out of it,' Leenie laughed.

'Any secrets to success you can share?' Marianne asked, admiring their matching T-shirts that said *Vegas, Baby*.

'No, nothing like that,' answered Leenie. 'As long as you know a hundred per cent about each other and you like over fifty per cent of it, then you're on the right track, as far as I'm concerned.'

The lights dimmed and everyone sat back in their seats. But as trapeze artists twirled and colours swirled in front of her eyes, Marianne found herself wondering, *If I had to put as a percentage how much Drew and I know about each other, what would it be?* It certainly didn't feel like they knew each other a hundred per cent. But what she did know, she liked a lot. She *loved*.

But how deep did it go beneath surface level?

# Chapter 24

## Jenny, in the Maldives

Bedtime came, and I must have watched Marianne's video a hundred times.

'Hello, J,' came the familiar voice down the phone, as warm as the island breeze on my skin and just as enveloping.

'Hey, you.' It was good to hear Evan's voice, and it brought up a swell of emotions that I needed to push aside for now.

'Everyone's missing you here,' he said, and I heard keys so I knew he was locking up the bookshop.

'I miss everyone, too.'

'So ...' he said, his words drifting off.

I needed to stay focused. I had my big event tomorrow and I didn't have the headspace for both best-friend and boy issues. 'Have you spoken to Marianne?'

'Have you?' he answered with caution.

'I've seen her latest Instagram Story.' I didn't mean it to come out so huffy, but it was too late to catch.

Evan was silent for a moment. 'Jenn, just give her a call.'

'Did she call you and tell you about the engagement, or did you see it on there first too?'

'I saw it on there and just called her. And I really think you should.'

I shook my head, though he couldn't see it. 'She doesn't want my congratulations. If she's happy, that's great. I don't want to ruin that by getting involved when she clearly doesn't want me to. I'll congratulate her when she's back and this has all blown over.'

'She would want to hear from you,' he said. He sounded a little frustrated at me.

'Did she say that to you?'

'No, but I could tell, especially—' He stopped short.

'Especially why?' When he didn't answer, I pressed again. 'Evan, *why*?'

'Because she and Drew are planning to do it in Las Vegas.'

'Do what?'

'Get married.'

I had to sit on the bed to let his words sink in for a minute. 'You mean another time, or this time?'

'This time, like, in the next few days, I guess.'

My best friend was getting married, without me. Worse, she didn't want me around. Did she even want me to know? After a while of leaving Evan in silence, I said, 'Would you have told me, if I hadn't called you?'

'It isn't really my place to be telling you these things.'

'Evan,' I felt my voice rise a touch, 'you can't pretend we haven't got closer than this. You can't shut me out too.'

'I can't be your messenger service. It's already a bit … you know … That we've … you know.'

I knew. Evan's loyalty was to his sister, and anything that conflicted with that felt like betrayal. I got it; I really did.

When he spoke again, his voice was softer. 'Listen, J, I better go, but don't lose touch while you're out there, OK? Keep letting me know you're OK. And call my sister.'

'Back atcha,' I said, and I let him go.

I wasn't ready to speak to Marianne yet. I wished her well and hoped she was OK out there, but I needed time to gather my thoughts. Marianne, as usual, was doing exactly what she wanted to do, when she wanted to do it, and I wasn't there to stop her. Perhaps that was the point.

# Chapter 25

# Jenny, in the Maldives

It was here, the day of my event, which I'd named 'Drink In the Pages', and although I wished Marianne – the old Marianne – was there by my side, I was also feeling pretty confident in myself. For today, I was pushing aside the gnawing question of what had become of my friendship with Marianne; I'd come back to what happened last night once the event was behind me. I wasn't surprised by the eloping, not really – it was very on-brand for Marianne, and actually how I'd always imagined her getting married. But why the rush?

Anyway, today was going to be a sure-fire hit, I could feel it, and it wasn't just a *feeling* – because how could anything go wrong when I'd made it so risk-free?

I arrived in the lounge beside the lobby early, having closed the shop for the afternoon. I spent a happy half-hour setting my books out on elegant tables, stacking them artfully beside pot plants, shifting the furniture so it was open and welcoming, with plenty of room for guests to pick up a book and sit and sample it while sipping their cocktails, before deciding to buy a crisp new copy of their very own.

One of the receptionists walked over with a mango juice for me right before the start. 'Just in case you need something to sip that isn't a cocktail,' she smiled.

'Thank you so much,' I said gratefully.

The clock ticked round to 2 p.m., our start time, and I looked at the doors. Well, nobody would be here at the very start. I didn't really expect them to be banging the doors down, did I?

While I waited for the first arrivals, I snapped some photos. These could go on the resort website, perhaps, or in the social media accounts? And even better, I could use them for the future weekly events that would definitely be happening.

A male couple I'd seen earlier in the week taking a cursory browse of my bookshop came down the stairs and strode through reception in matching deck shoes, moving fast, as if they were afraid the sun's rays were about to leave the island.

'Hello,' I called to them. 'Would you like a complimentary cocktail?'

They skidded to an almost halt, glancing at each other and then back at the doors.

'They're all book-themed. This is our wonderful new event at Bounty Cove Cay, where we offer you a bespoke cocktail and pair it, and you, with a really perfect read to relax with during your vacation.' I was selling it well, using my big-girl outside voice and everything. I didn't even think it was too obvious that my legs were shaking like the cocktail shakers themselves.

'Um, it's just that we need to get to ...' the taller of the two men said, pointing outside.

'Maybe later,' added the other, and dragged on his husband's arm with determination.

'All right, we'll be here until *fooooour* ...' I called after them. They sure were in a rush.

Two more sets of guests arrived and skittered off just as quickly in the direction of the beach, and that's when I heard it.

Somewhere in the distance, my ears picked up a sound that it took a moment for me to recognise. A cheer. From a crowd.

I straightened like a meerkat and listened. All was silent for a moment, and then I heard it again, louder this time. An unmistakable cheer.

Moving to the window, I looked out. That was strange. The pool area was nearly deserted. For the middle of a sunshiny day here in paradise, that was very odd. Was everyone off having a late lunch?

'What's going on?' I asked Dan, one of the mixologists and the first bartender I'd met here on Bounty Cove Cay. He was also the one who'd come up with my favourite bespoke cocktail for the event, the I Capture the Cosmopolitan.

'I have no idea.'

I walked to the door of the Pavilion, a sense of foreboding creeping over me that this couldn't be happening again, my second event couldn't be flunking as much as the first. I heaved the door open, stepping out into the heat just as Rish came skirting round the edge of the pool and pulled me to the side, under the shade of a palm and out of the view of both reception and the beach.

'Rish, what's going on?' I asked him. His body was pressed against me and his head close, conspiratorial, and despite the look of urgency on his face I couldn't help the flutter my heart gave at the possibilities of this rendezvous. For a second, I thought he was going to kiss me again, and looking at his lips, my breath caught. I thought, *Well, I wouldn't say no to trying it out, just one more time ...*

'It's Blane,' he said, and that snapped me out of it. I stepped back a fraction.

'What's Blane?'

'He's throwing a jet-ski competition on the beach. Now.'

'Now? At the same time as my event?'

Rish nodded. 'I have to get back to work, but I slipped out as soon as I could to come and tell you. In case you didn't have—'

'Didn't have the attendees I was hoping for?' I snarled, though not at him, of course. Why would Blane do this? 'What's his problem? Did he have this planned?'

'I'd guess he did, but he didn't tell us about it. Just picked up a megaphone about thirty minutes ago and announced an impromptu jet-ski relay race, open to all, in teams, big prizes.'

'A jet-ski race, though? What is this, *Baywatch*?'

'It's pretty popular,' he admitted.

Well, of course it was, it sounded a hoot. And if I knew Blane, he'd turned the charm on tenfold, to the point that any guests would feel as though they were becoming best friends with him if they joined him for the *best time ever* on the beach.

'He's also got Manny from Cocktail Cove to whip up a huge batch of what he's calling "Jet-Ski Jet Fuel" to pass out to everyone who's had a turn in the competition.'

'So, a bespoke cocktail,' I stated, my nostrils flaring.

'Yep. I'm sorry, Jenn.'

'Me too. But thanks for letting me know.'

Rish put a hand on my arm and though his touch comforted me, I was too furious to say as much. He turned to leave and at the last minute I called out, 'Really, Rish, thank you.'

Returning to the Cove Pavilion, I explained what was going on to the mixologists. It was OK, this wasn't the end of the world. There were bound to be some guests who had no interest in a boozy jet-ski competition; this wasn't a Club 18–30 holiday after all. In fact, I couldn't see Khadeeja and the upper management team being too keen on this idea. But then ... it looked as though a lot of bottles of champagne were being carted down there, so clearly guests were opening their wallets and having a good time ...

With every minute that ticked by, the more my frustration with Blane grew. I wasn't one for confrontation usually, but this man was deliberately trying to sabotage me, I was sure of it. But why? For his own ego? What had I ever done to him?

The doors to the Pavilion opened and a couple came in, followed by a bellhop with their suitcases. New arrivals.

The couple gazed in awe at their surroundings, and when their eyes fell on us in the lounge, I made sure to give them a wave. The woman waved back, and I saw her eyes flicker to the table of cocktails. As they checked in, I tried to get a sense of what book-and-cocktail combo would suit them both. *Come on, Jenn, you're good at this. Forget that idiot outside with his jet-powered penis extenders.*

She was in a loose sundress with nautical stripes and a sandy-coloured panama hat perched on the back of her head. Her outfit was pristine, perhaps bought for the occasion, and the way they wouldn't let go of each other's hands made me guess they were honeymooners. I thought she might like a novel I'd chosen for the store that was a *New York Times* bestseller with a blue-and-white-striped cover with gold accents. I didn't think she'd fancy a dysfunctional-marriage book right now, or a gritty thriller, but this was a coming-of-age book involving travel and sailing, and it would make a great Insta pic along with her Taming of the Blue Lagoon cocktail.

After they'd finished their check-in, I could tell the woman was keen to come over, but just as I was about to wave again, the bellhop said something and gestured towards the Pavilion door, and I lost them to the lure of checking out their overwater villa.

Twenty minutes later, I spotted the couple again, but not returning to my event. Instead, I watched through the windows as they hotfooted it across the sand, now dressed in sparkling new bathing suits, towards the jet-ski competition. I sighed.

'Where is everyone?' a familiar voice said from behind me.

'On the beach,' I replied, too ashamed to turn round.

Khadeeja joined me at the window, and out of the corner of my eye I saw that her mouth was set in a straight line. She didn't have to say any more; I knew a look of disappointment when I saw one.

'It's Blane, he's organised a … a … Sorry.' I spluttered to a stop because throwing blame never looks very professional, and he was an institution there while I was a nobody.

I couldn't believe I'd flopped again. I'd worked so hard on this event, poured so much planning into it. I'd checked there were no conflicting events occurring in the resort and timed it so that guests would be done with lunch but not ready for dinner. I'd moved the event to be less of a walk and closer to the most beautiful views of the island. I'd found a way to make the drinks more appealing than 'free wine' in a place where you could get complimentary wine at nearly any time of the day or night.

This sort of thing would never have happened to Marianne.

Marianne. I was failing at my job, and I was failing her as a friend. I just had to think carefully, make a plan, get myself out of this mess.

Khadeeja walked away without another word, and for the remainder of the afternoon we did have a few people show up, mostly those who came in chuckling from the jet-ski competition and exclaimed, 'Oh, look! I forgot this was happening too!' I sold a modest number of books – *extremely* modest – and the cocktails were a hit among the few who hovered. And it was interesting watching the new arrivals at the check-in desk (I was hoping to glimpse an elusive A-lister, but no such luck while I was there). But there was no doubt in my mind: nobody was heading into dinner tonight thinking of my Drink In the Pages event as being one of the highlights of their day here in the Maldives. Which ultimately meant that the bookstore felt no closer to being a highlight of the island. In fact, it felt an awful lot as though it had taken another gigantic step back.

After I'd carried the last of my excess book stock back along the winding route to the store and dumped it onto the table, ready to sort the next morning, I left the main building through one of the side exits and stood in the late-afternoon heat for a moment, letting it prickle my skin. I took some deep breaths, closing my eyes, wanting to calm down, until I realised: maybe I didn't want to calm down. Maybe being too calm and trying to keep the peace was what made me explode when it was too far down the line, so I said things I regretted. Maybe I needed to say what was on my damn mind. Maybe I needed to let my skin prickle, since I was burning anyway.

I strode round the side of the complex and didn't stop until I hit the beach. I saw Blane further down, leaning against a tiki hut and smiling at people as they walked past, soaking in their compliments. Elsewhere on the beach, his staff were polishing the jet skis and putting them in order again, combing the sand in front of them. He looked incredibly smug.

He angled his red reflective aviators at me as I approached. 'Hello, *Jackie*,' he said.

*Yeah, good one, idiot, using my own shade tactic against me.*

'Can I talk to you for a moment?' I said through a pleasant, gritted-teeth smile.

'Of course,' he sang, and reached for my arm to lead me towards the shoreline and out of earshot. I flinched and moved my arm away. He was not a leader I would follow.

'Did you get a chance to watch my jet-ski race earlier? It was quite a hit.'

'No, Blane, funnily enough I didn't, because I was throwing my own event just through those doors.' I jabbed my finger back towards the Pavilion.

'Oh, that's right.' He unleashed a villainous chuckle. 'Your "Books and Booze" event was on today, how could I forget?'

'You clearly didn't forget, did you, or was it just one massive coincidence that your impromptu water-sports Olympics had to be thrown at exactly the same time?'

'Water-sports Olympics … interesting idea … Let me know if you need a job, won't you, Jackie?'

At that point, a group of guests walked past, so Blane and I smoothed our faces into polite smiles.

'Lovely evening,' I said.

'Indeed,' he replied. 'Have you seen how the seaplane looks out there— *Now listen here*,' he hissed as soon as they'd gone. 'I'm sorry if your event was a disaster, but guess what? This isn't your little local village and nobody here cares about a bookshop.'

How. Dare. He. *Nobody cares about a bookshop?* I was going to kill him. 'What is your problem?' I asked, cutting to the chase, once and for all.

Blane glared at me. 'My problem is you. I want guests out here. On my beach. Spending their cash at my events and with my team. I don't want them in there. I don't want them buried in a book. Do you think anyone writes a good review for a resort because they spent the whole time reading a book? Do you think anyone recommends a resort to their wealthy friends because there was a cute event to build book forts or whatever? No, people spend money on fun.'

'Well, how about, for just a minute, you climb out of your own asshole and think about what *they* might want?' Whoa! Where had I heard that before? Before it came out of my mouth, at least? I was sure Marianne had said something similar to me during our fight …

He stood up taller, his eyes darkening. 'Excuse me? You've been here two minutes and you're trying to tell *me* what the guests want?'

My automatic reaction was to apologise and backtrack – 'Oh no, I just meant …' – but I felt a little as though I had Marianne by my side in that moment, and I stopped myself.

'I'm not saying the guests here don't want *that*,' I said, keeping my voice calm and gesturing to the jet skis. 'What I'm saying is they should be given the option to also have *that.'* This time I pointed back towards the main building, i.e. my bookstore. 'They're on vacation. They shouldn't have to pick sides.'

'I don't have to take this from you,' he snorted. 'You've been here five weeks and sold, what, fifty books? People don't even know you and your bookshop exist. And by the end of next month, it won't. This is my island, my clients, my rules.' He went to walk away, but I blocked him.

'And I don't have to take this from you. You are not my manager. You are not *the* manager at this resort. You think you can use this place like your playground, but it won't last. Besides, you are nothing to me but a fly in the ointment. And I will not be intimidated by a nothing.'

And then I turned and left, without looking back, on the way passing Rish, who treated me to a subtle 'down low' high five. The touch of his fingers felt reassuring against my skin, which would probably still be prickling in this heat for some time.

# Chapter 26

# Marianne, in the USA

Marianne woke up the next morning, the day of their wedding, having slept the whole night with her back pressed against Drew's in a wonderful, warm slumber.

The words of the old couple rang in her ears.

'Drew,' she whispered. 'Drew.'

'Hmm?' He rolled over and kissed her nose.

'Do you want to have children?'

That woke him up. He blinked his eyes fully open and edged a little further away from her. 'What? Now?'

'No, just in general. Do you want kids?'

'Er, sure. Maybe. Do you? What time is it?'

'Do you or don't you, Drew?' Marianne sat up.

Drew followed suit and rubbed at his face. 'OK. No, not at the moment, but I might one day. How about you?'

'Sometimes I think I do, but mostly I think I don't.'

Drew nodded. 'Is this about what those old people said to us at the theatre?'

'They were right, there's a lot we don't know about each other – we don't even know where you're going to live after you've finished your book. I have a business in Bayside and you want to live in New York. You're going to get me pregnant and leave me looking after the baby while you make it big in the Big Apple. And I didn't even know if I wanted children, Drew.'

'All right, let's put the brakes on a minute,' he said.

'I'm serious, though.' They blinked at each other, and Marianne added, 'I am excited, and I do want us to get married here, it's just … Are we rushing into this?'

They had a lighter than usual breakfast of only three trips up to the buffet, followed by a gentle swim in one of the quiet-at-this-time-in-the-morning hotel pools. They walked hand in hand through the casino, where early-morning, or very late-night, gamblers were still deep into their games. They bought takeout coffees and strolled past the shops and the artwork and the theatre that were all housed in this one complex.

'Hey, I'm sorry,' Marianne said to Drew, quietly.

'What for?'

They stopped under the colourful foliage of the hotel's atrium, an extravagant indoor garden where vibrant flowers and delicate lights dripped from the branches of trees, and Marianne took his hands. 'For being subdued on our wedding day. I'm overthinking. Which is not like me – and I *don't* like it.'

'I do,' Drew said, pulling her in close.

Marianne smiled softly, liking the sound of him saying those two words. 'I do,' she whispered back, and they pressed their foreheads together. 'Where should we go from here? I do want to marry you, but ...'

'But today's not the day,' he nodded.

'Today's our last chance, we leave tomorrow.'

'We don't have to,' he said, wiping a tear off her cheek with his thumb.

She sniffed. 'What do you mean?'

Drew paused, pulling back so he could look her in the eyes. Even though they were surrounded by other holidaymakers – new arrivals wheeling their suitcases in awe; departing guests with heavy hearts but maybe not so heavy wallets – and cocktail waitresses expertly balancing trays of expensive drinks, it felt as if it was just them. Being real.

'Mari, can I make a suggestion?' he asked.

'What is it?'

'Why don't we just relax for a few days, enjoy Vegas, spend some time getting to know all the things about each other we think we don't already know. We don't really have anywhere else we need to be, we have no plan, we haven't even figured out where we want to go next on this road trip. Maybe we just slow things down.'

'Slow things down? Is that a euphemism for not wanting to get married yet?'

'Not at all,' he laughed, gently. 'I would marry you in a second, right here, right now, if I could. But I just think that the beauty of having no schedule is we can stop where we are for as long as we want. Why not just take a few more days, enjoy it, relax into it, and then we can set a day and get everything ready and, if we're still keen, go for it. Tomorrow, the next day, the day after that, we'll know when it's the right time. The Lovie Luck Duck Chapel will still be there.'

'You mean … do some advance planning?' Marianne said, with a half-smile.

'Steady on, not too advanced,' he laughed. 'Just like a couple of days so we can check we have all the paperwork. So we don't accidentally eat too much and feel sick during the ceremony. We can go to a pool party and all that, like we wanted, and then we'll have the best, most perfect day. You and me.'

*What if we go off each other after all this 'getting to know' each other?* Marianne worried, silently.

As if reading her mind, Drew said, 'I can tell you're still worrying. We've been pretty solid for five months now. Let's not think about it as learning more about each other so much as just experiencing more together for a few days.'

'I like the sound of that.' Marianne stepped back from Drew, breathing in the scent of the flowers surrounding them. 'But I think we should have a no-kissing, and no-sex, rule until then. We need to not be all "honeymoon phase" the whole time so we know if we want to get to the honeymoon phase.'

'No kissing at all?' he laughed.

'Nope. Well …' She leaned forward and gave him a long, final smooch. 'From now on. Unless we really want to.'

'You're such a pillar of strength, ha ha.'

Marianne slapped her hand to her head. 'But wait, if we do stay, we can't stay here. Drew, I love this hotel, but we can't afford it for any longer.' She was deliberately not checking their travel fund on the banking app on her phone, but she was pretty sure they'd dipped into it quite substantially already.

But Drew just shrugged. 'So, let's move hotels. No big deal. It's been an amazing experience staying here, but let's give something else a go.'

Marianne nodded. 'If we find something a little more in our budget, we could spend the money on some of the things we want to do here instead.' They were both well aware that this was slightly flawed logic, as they didn't really have money 'going spare'. 'Do you have a hotel in mind?'

Drew gave her a slow, wide smile. 'Fancy something completely different?'


Marianne left Drew at the bar getting them booked into a new hotel from tomorrow, for seven nights this time, while she went back up to their room to wash her face. She didn't want to know where he was picking; she wanted to be surprised.

As she packed away some of the belongings she knew she wouldn't be using that day in preparation for moving hotels tomorrow, she picked up the Wynn's wedding brochure and smiled. It wasn't the kitschy, cute chapel she imagined for her and Drew, but it sure looked lovely. She reached forward to throw it in the bin and then hesitated. Well, maybe she should take it with her, just in case it gave her any ideas for their wedding day, now that they were giving themselves a little extra time to plan the thing.

When she got back downstairs it took her a moment to find Drew, until she spotted him standing by a roulette table watching the action. 'We should play this sometime,' he said when she approached. 'It looks fun. And more importantly, it looks easy.'

Marianne laughed. 'Isn't part of the problem here that it all *looks* easy?'

'You might be right.'

'Did you book the hotel?'

'Yep,' he beamed, clearly pleased with himself.

'For a whole week?'

'Indeed. Get ready to slow things down a little and enjoy Sin City!'

'But without any "sinning",' she reminded him. 'Well, maybe a little. Is the new hotel still on the Strip?'

'Sure is!'

'And we can afford it?'

'Yep.'

'Well, then,' Marianne pulled a twenty-dollar bill from her bag, 'let's play roulette!'

'Actually,' Drew led her a little away from the table, 'that table has a hundred-dollar minimum bet. How about we save the roulette for tomorrow at our new hotel?'

That night, they stayed up later, sitting on their big, comfortable Encore bed, just talking (no touching). Drew told Marianne about his childhood, about his favourite holidays, his career fears and how he felt about planning for the future. Marianne shared memories of her schooldays, her times on the cruise ship, even including anecdotes about Jenny. At one point, when he went to get more ice, she considered calling her friend and putting it all behind them, but stopped herself. This evening was about her and her husband-to-be, and she was pretty sure, she thought, with her heart bubbling, that after all this she was going to like him way more than the recommended fifty per cent.

'We're staying in the *castle*?'

After checking out of the Encore and saying a fond farewell to the beautiful Wynn complex, Drew had driven their car back down the Strip. Marianne had watched the looming hotels get nearer and then pass by, until Drew started indicating outside the Excalibur.

'Is that all right?' Drew asked, flicking his eyes to her and grinning at her reaction.

She loved to watch him drive, his forearms strong, his face concentrating. It was like watching him write. 'Of course,' she grinned back.

'I know it might seem an odd choice, considering we're from the UK, to pick the medieval-Europe-themed hotel, but it's fun, it's big, it's so Vegas, and it's about as far down the Strip from the Wynn as you can get.' He paused, turning into the parking garage. 'And I mean that in a good way, because now we can explore this end.'

'It's like a two-centre holiday,' Marianne agreed. 'Up there it was all sleek buildings, shopping malls and Venetian canals, and down here we've got knights and round tables, plus New York and Egypt just a stone's throw away!'

'That's my girl.' Drew parked up and sped to her side of the car to hold out his hand. 'M'lady.'

'Are you going to be like that the whole time we're here?' she laughed, accepting his help.

'Absolutely.'

'Whoa,' Marianne commented as they passed a giant billboard by the entrance featuring a row of shirtless men, all rippled abs and tanned pecs. '"Thunder from Down Under". Is my bachelorette here too?'

The lobby opened out into a vast space complete with faux-stone walls and turrets. It was like being in Disneyland, Marianne mused, only ... not. Chandeliers hung above the lobby, the low lighting adding to the medieval feel, and in stark contrast to the bright Vegas daytime happening outside.

'Now, if you don't like the room, we can swap,' Drew cautioned. 'It's not got the view of the Strip like the Encore did, but we did want to keep the cost down ...'

'Would you stop with the disclaimers?' Marianne laughed. 'I love this hotel, it's awesome. You did great.'

Their room had a view of the castle's turrets, which was cool. Plus it had a big jacuzzi tub *in the bedroom*. Not in the bathroom, but in the corner of the bedroom, so you couldn't go wrong with that.

As intended, Marianne and Drew let themselves enjoy Las Vegas for a few days, planning to have the wedding in four days' time. With seven more nights to play with, play they did. In fact, not a whole lot of slowing down happened at all.

They went across the road to the MGM Grand and joined the fun at a Wet Republic pool party, they danced at the Coyote Ugly bar in the New York-New York. They made the most of happy hours and bottomless brunches. They had late nights and later days, because there was always another new experience, another dose of hedonism to not miss out on.

Only once did they take a look at their bank balance – which was dropping at a speedy rate. They had a brief conversation about how they might need to camp in their car some days, or stay in dorms in hostels, but this was during the open bar on the High Roller so they raised glasses to the idea, went back to gazing at the view of the sun going down over the Strip, and forgot all about it.

# Chapter 27

# Jenny, in the Maldives

I'd been so furious after the event finished, I hadn't got around to contacting Marianne, or even deciding if I should. In fact, I hadn't thought about her at all until I woke up, sweating, in the middle of the night and reached for my phone. I clicked on Marianne's Stories and went to her feed, searching for clues as to what she and Drew had been up to while I'd been asleep. I was torturing myself really, because the thing I was looking for was the thing I was hoping not to see. I didn't want to see my best friend getting married, because it would mean she'd really done it without me.

She hadn't done it yet, or if she had, then she hadn't posted about it. There were hints of her and Drew still being in Las Vegas, though. Either that or they had somehow visited an extremely lush indoor garden in the middle of the desert. But it was probably still somewhere in Las Vegas. And it was probably only a matter of time.

Once upon a time, when we were young, Marianne and I played dress-up, imagining a life for ourselves in glittering Las Vegas. The dream was to become showgirls, from what I could remember, but we definitely used to take it in turns acting out Elvis-led Vegas weddings. It didn't matter who we were marrying that day – we were always each other's bridesmaids.

I didn't want to think about it, so instead I started thinking about the bookshop, and that left me in even more of a brain fizz, so I ended up pulling over my laptop and working away until daybreak.

I couldn't fail. Failure wasn't an option for me; it would be too embarrassing, too excruciating to know I'd let people down. I was the one who made things happen, so there had to be a way for the bookshop to thrive under my watch. Even without Marianne holding my hand.

At the first sign of dawn, I stepped from my bungalow and breathed in the Maldivian morning. Then, for the next twenty-four hours, I started really listening. I listened when somebody came in the shop and laughed, commenting that it was like a hidden treasure trove. I listened when guests answered my questions about their favourite books to read on vacation. I listened to what was being said when people walked through the main door of the Pavilion and into the cool indoors. I listened to the low chatter in the lounges and watched what was being picked up from the bookshelf on the mezzanine. I listened when Layla and Rish, and the other members of staff, spoke with experience about what they'd found the guests to be most interested in.

While I listened, ideas began to form, swimming in my mind like fish in the aqua seas. And once I'd gathered all these outside contributions, I shut myself away in my bungalow to create, as quickly as possible, a new plan for the bookshop. Sometimes I came out for air, giving my soles and my soul a moment of soft sand and sea air.

If Layla and Rish could be brave, like I knew they were, and put themselves forward to work with Khadeeja on the bigger picture, I could at least try and save my tiny bookshop. Eventually, I was ready to put my thoughts into action.

Forty-eight hours after my failed cocktail event, I caught a moment with Khadeeja beside the entrance to the Divine Ocean Spa, where she was grabbing a cucumber water. I told her of my plans.

She raised her eyebrows after I'd finished babbling at her. 'You want to change the name of the bookshop?'

I nodded. 'I do. I understand that we're not pulling in the profit to justify asking you to *move* the bookshop, so this way I want to make the most of its location. Use it to its advantage.'

She thought for a moment, and then said, 'OK.'

'OK?'

'OK, you have my approval. Go ahead with everything you've proposed, and we'll keep an eye on how it's all working. Just make sure this does work, all right?' she said. 'It was my idea to try and launch the bookshop. Is there anything you need from me?'

'Yes,' I answered, and asked for something that had been my bugbear since I first arrived. 'I need a sign in reception.'

*

I had to be doing the right thing, surely? It didn't get me any closer to having a full calendar of events, which I knew I needed to keep Khadeeja happy, but I hoped this new plan would really put the shop on the map. The Bounty Cove Cay map, at least.

'What's the worst that could happen?' I asked myself in the mirror before sunrise the following morning, my reflection lit up from the moon outside my bungalow window. I grabbed my bag, slipped my sandals between my fingers so my flip-flopping didn't wake my neighbours, and set off for work.

The boardwalk was cool underfoot but the sky above was clear, the stars still out, peeping their last look at the island before they went to sleep for the day. My friendly fruit bats chirruped overhead as I walked, but there was no other sound except the lapping tide on my left, a pool of moonshine on its surface.

I had been up late into the night ordering a whole new stock of books from the mainland, in multiple languages because of the international clientele, hoping they'd make it soon. I'd already asked as many staff members as I could find what their favourite books were in their native languages – that way, everyone could play a part in recommending books to the guests. And while I waited for the books to arrive, there were plenty of other things for me to be getting on with.

The Pavilion was still quiet, save for a few early rising guests heading towards the gym, or to the spa for sunrise yoga. I turned the corners until I reached my shop, and for the first time I didn't look at its hidden-away location as a hindrance: I saw opportunity.

My plan had a lot of moving parts, but one of the first things I needed to spend some time on – and fast – was the interior of the store itself. Could I fix the impossible and make it bigger and more prominent and right off the lobby, with huge windows letting in natural light? No. It was small, darkly lit and tucked away. I accepted that now, and it was time to work with it.

From behind the counter, I pulled the big bag of merchandise I'd bought from the gift shops with the approval of Khadeeja. I had billowing scarves the colours of the sea, replica shells and coral and faux pearls. A scattering of props – not too many to make the place kitsch or like some kind of rip-off *Pirates of the Caribbean* ride, but enough to add a subtle theme to the place. I added firefly-like fairy lights and natural candles in glass lanterns. I arranged the books by colour and theme, filling nooks and crannies and making twinkling displays in the window. I'd swap out some of them as soon as my new stock arrived, and the real pièce de résistance would be when my new shop sign got here. Plus my sign in reception, of course, together with a tiny wooden carving of the new logo: a book tied to an anchor.

Shortly before my opening time ticked around, I stood back and admired my handiwork over the past three hours. It was a start; well done, me.

Welcome to the new, improved Secret Bounty Bookshop Hideaway.

My shop sign, commissioned from a woodcarver on Dhigurah, arrived in record time, thanks to a favour called in by Rish, and on the same day as my first shipment of new novels. Layla and Rish swung by the shop to help me hang it, and we sat on the floor outside the doors after closing time, unpacking.

'"The Secret Bounty Bookshop Hideaway".' Layla read the sign aloud, holding it out in front of her. 'I like it! Great concept.'

'Thanks.' I grinned at her, pleased with myself. 'I just started thinking, maybe I should work *with* the space, rather than try and hide what it is. And people who do find the bookshop have commented that it's like a hidden treasure trove. Like a secret pirates' cave filled with treasures. I added the bit about treasures. But that's what I'm going for. I want it to look, and feel, special, like the guests have found a cave full of wonders hidden in the depths of the hotel.'

'I like it,' Rish echoed Layla, unpacking a box of books. He and I hadn't spent any time alone since the moment outside the cocktail event, which felt kind of like the elephant in the room. Nevertheless, he continued chatting in his usual sunny manner. 'It definitely feels like there's more of a draw to come and find this place now. I can imagine a lot of guests wanting to explore when it gets too hot outside.'

'Let's hope so,' I replied, thinking of today's temperature, which was sidling up towards thirty-one degrees. 'And when they come in, let's hope they buy something.'

Rish nodded, checking out the cover of a novel he'd pulled out, then flipping to the back. 'They will, for sure. Hey, I think I know this author – is he local?'

'Yep,' I smiled. 'Most guests I spoke with just want to escape when they're on holiday. They want a wide variety of genres, from the most fabulous bonkbusters to the "If not now, when?" classics. I've got a bigger range of books now, but also, people said they wanted to escape *here*. The amount of people who mentioned how they love reading books set in places they're currently on holiday, or have been on holiday, or are by people from the places they've vacationed, made me want to have a whole, big section dedicated to Maldivian and South Asian authors. And who knows,' I shrugged, 'maybe the new manager will be able to get some of them to the island for talks or readings or whatever.'

'Don't talk about the new manager, you leaving makes me too sad,' Layla pouted.

'Same,' said Rish, and our eyes linked for a dazzling moment. 'By the way,' he said, 'Layla and I set a date to talk to the resort directors about our ideas. In just over two weeks.'

'That's amazing! Congratulations!'

'Thanks. Layla talked me into it in the end—'

'He had this great idea,' Layla interrupted, 'but I told him he had to get in there quickly if he was to have any chance of making it work. He thinks the beach bungalows should be turned into individual eco-retreats, all fully sustainable.'

'But still completely luxurious. All made using recycled material, reclaimed wood, solar energy,' Rish chipped in.

'Since they're going to be redone anyway,' added Layla.

They were so excited, they were talking over each other. It was nice to see. Rish smiled before carrying one of the boxes inside the store.

Layla leaned in the minute he was out of earshot. 'He's a little nervous. Also, he's going to miss you a lot when you leave, you know.'

I rolled my eyes at her. 'I'm sure he's not. I don't think we have that special spark.'

'The way he looks at you …' she sighed. 'What?'

I just shrugged. 'Layla, I think you need your eyes checked.'

# Chapter 28

# Marianne, in the USA

It was strange. Weren't people supposed to get wedding-day jitters? Impulsive urges to run in the other direction? At the least a stomach flip-flop and a thought butterfly asking yourself if you were doing the right thing? But Marianne felt none of those. She trusted herself, she always had; second-guessing and delaying grabbing hold of her life weren't things she allowed herself to do any more. Minus the blip thanks to that old couple. But she and Drew had just come out stronger, more determined to celebrate their love, all in.

Their time in Vegas was, again, coming to an end. And they'd chosen today to be the big day. That would then give them two full, final days in the hotel before continuing with their road trip. Or should she say, their honeymoon?

Also, she hadn't been physical with Drew for nearly a week now; she was definitely ready to accept they knew each other, weren't just lusted-to-the-eyeballs, and could have themselves a wedding night.

After breakfast, as they were strolling back through the hotel, Drew faced Marianne, taking her in his arms as if there was no one in Las Vegas but the two of them. 'Are you ready, future wife?'

'Hell yeah, I'm ready,' she answered, unable to keep the beam off her face. 'Are you? Are you sure?'

'I'm so sure. I'm so ready. Before you, I was always in my head, and now I can do what I love to do, but also be alive, living this vibrant life, not just in the pages of my books. *You* did that. Yes, I'm ready.'

'OK then.' She let slip a giddy giggle. 'Let's do this. Let me get my dress!'

Drew, already dressed in his smart trousers and sky-blue Oxford shirt, stopped her. 'Wait.'

'What?'

'I shouldn't see you getting into the dress. Shall I meet you downstairs?'

That was a good point. Marianne thought quickly. 'Meet me in the Lobby Bar.'

'All right, see you there, take your time,' he said, and gave her a quick kiss. 'Don't take *too* much time.'

Marianne laughed and pushed him away. 'Cheat!' she said, but she didn't mind one bit. This was her wedding day! Running up to the room, she opened a miniature of whisky she'd saved from the plane to steady her nerves and then turned this way and that, a frantic desire to do everything at once.

She plugged in her curling wand and slapped on some foundation, which she had to wipe off and redo after she blotched some liquid eyeliner beyond all repair halfway across her face. In the end, she settled for no eyeliner but plenty of shimmering eyeshadow; it would probably all melt off in the heat anyway. She pulled her nicest underwear out of her suitcase, where she'd kept it hidden from Drew for a special occasion, and what occasion on this trip would be more special? It was nothing fancy, but it was new and it was pretty. And it was matching.

Checking her reflection in the mirror, Marianne took a deep, steadying breath and slid her feet into her silver heels. Time for her wedding dress.

She opened the wardrobe and touched the garment bag for a moment, closing her eyes. *Mum. I wish you were here to help me into this.*

As soon as they'd made the decision to get married on this trip, she knew the dress she wanted to wear. A pale, almost silvery blue sheath dress in soft satin. It had been her mum's, a gown she'd taken on every holiday and worn with love under summer sunshine, for special meals or pretty excursions. Marianne herself hadn't worn it outside the house until now, but when she'd been packing for this trip she'd felt as though her mum would have wanted it to come with her.

She didn't want to cry right now, she didn't want anything else to delay this moment, so, sending a silent bubble of love for her darling mum into the atmosphere, she grabbed for the zip.

Her fingers were still shaking and she laughed out loud to herself. 'Come on, Marianne, pull yourself together,' she murmured, pushing back the thoughts that floated in of how she also wished the other woman she cared most about in the world, Jenny, was here with her.

Reaching again for the zip, she tugged. Then tutted. The zip was caught on itself, so she gave it another yank down and—

*Rrrrrippppp.*

Marianne stood frozen to the spot, no longer shaking, no longer breathing, just frozen in a moment she wished she could reverse. Eventually, she reached for the garment bag and lifted it carefully from the wardrobe, taking it to the bed and laying it down. She pulled it gently back over the dress, revealing the delicate fabric, praying the rip had been no more than a layer of detailing, something that could be altered. But the long gash right down the centre was irretrievable. She ran her fingers over the tear, wishing she could turn back time, willing to settle for either going back to five minutes ago, or back to their arrival in Las Vegas, when she should have taken the dress out of the bag there and then; that way, even if this had happened, she would have had time to get it repaired.

The tears that had wanted to come earlier welled inside her, burning at her throat and stinging her eyes. She needed to speak to Drew.

Throwing on a navy romper decorated with pelicans, she turned from the dress and left the room without looking back. She spotted Drew in the bar sipping on a martini, and went directly to him, sitting down on the booth chair beside him.

'You look beautiful,' he said, it not even occurring to him that this outfit wasn't what she'd planned to wear for their wedding.

'Drew,' she said, her voice quiet, and he saw then that something was wrong. 'I ripped my wedding dress.'

'On purpose?' he asked.

'Of course not. Accidentally. When I was taking it out of the bag.' Her eyes filled with tears again and he pushed away his martini to drag himself to her side.

'Hey, it's OK.'

'I shouldn't be this upset about a stupid dress, it's just a dress, but I thought of my mum just before I was going to put it on, because it was once hers, and then it ripped and I just felt—' She sniffled and took a minute. 'I know it's been a really, really long time since I lost my mum, but sometimes I just wish she was here for certain things, you know?'

Breaking their pact, Drew took her in his arms and kissed her, holding her tight, vowing to be there for her always.

Marianne slipped a hand into Drew's and they headed back up the Strip and into the huge Fashion Show mall. But after a long time shopping around, nothing jumped out at her. There were some wedding dresses, and some white dresses, but some of the clothing was pretty pricey in there, and she just didn't fancy spending a small fortune on a dress she probably wouldn't wear again. Especially not a hot, heavy, spun-sugar taffeta one.

'Nope,' she said, coming out of a branch of Forever 21, just in case they'd had something, and seeing Drew munching his way through a bucket of Auntie Anne's Mini Pretzel Dogs.

'Check these out,' he said, handing her one. 'Hot dogs in pretzels – genius! These are going in my next book. No luck with the dress?'

Marianne shook her head. 'It's crazy, I usually know exactly what I want, all the time, but it's like my mojo is off. I don't know if I want to replicate the dress I had, if I want something completely different, if I even want it to look like a wedding dress ...' She trailed off and helped herself to a few more pretzel dogs.

'Shall we hit the outlet mall? You never know ...'

Las Vegas North Premium Outlets was, much like most things in Vegas, vast. Terracotta rows of sunshine-soaked shops stretched in all directions once they entered the complex, and tiny spritzes of air mist were pumped onto hot bargain-hunters below. A few oops purchases – but no wedding attire – later, Marianne and Drew found themselves in a store which seemed to sell a mixture of inexpensive Vegas-themed clothing and showgirl props.

Marianne was admiring a rack of white feather headdresses and wondering if she could fashion one of them into a top if she found a white skirt, when Drew appeared, looking pleased as punch with himself.

'Listen, I don't ever want to be the type of husband who picks all your clothes for you, but I've found you the perfect dress.'

'You have?' Marianne asked, one eyebrow raised.

'Look.' He held up a thing. She wasn't sure if it was a dress. It might have been a nightie? Or a beach cover-up? It was a bright white satin slip, no shape, though it looked like it finished a little above the knee, with spaghetti straps. Covering the vast majority of the fabric were silver sequins. 'Don't you think this will go great with the shoes?'

'My silver heels? I guess so.'

'No, the trainers. The Vegas trainers from CVS.'

'You think I should wear the Vegas trainers for our wedding day?' Marianne chuckled.

'Sure.'

'And that thing?'

'Why not? It's loose, it's comfortable, it's so Vegas. Try it on.'

Humouring him, she took it into the fitting room and slid it over her head. She looked, as expected, quite like a glitter ball. Although ... he was right about it being comfortable. Despite the sequins, the fabric felt cool and baggy and as if air could flow right through it. And sure, it didn't look a lot like a 'traditional' wedding dress, but what about their wedding did look 'traditional' at this point, and wasn't that why she was doing it this way?

She threw open the curtain and struck a pose, and Drew gave her wild applause. 'She's going to be my wife,' he called to the sales assistant, who joined in the clapping, through lack of knowing quite what else to do.

Marianne had never imagined herself getting married in a sequinned dress and diamanté trainers, but she'd never imagined a lot of things in her life before they happened, and she'd never lived by a rule book.

# Chapter 29

# Jenny, in the Maldives

After revamping my Bookshop Hideaway, I was feeling pretty confident, especially as I started to notice one customer per hour turn into two, one sale become more. I'd done all I could, for now, and I had to let the bookshop settle into itself. Every five minutes, I wanted to check stock levels and social media tags and TripAdvisor reviews that might mention us, but I restrained myself. *Let it be,* I repeated, over and over again.

And then, I got a real confidence boost that I'd done the right thing. The Hideaway was quiet and I was checking up on Marianne's trip online again, on what she was sharing, wondering why she still hadn't wanted to call and tell me her news and wondering if I should call her. Hearing the sound of a lone pair of heels clacking across the floor, I stowed my phone and stood up straight, expecting Khadeeja, as most customers weren't in stilettos at that time of day.

When an actual celebrity walked through the door of the shop, I almost lost my cool, and knocked into a pile of romcoms on my way to get her an iced tea.

It was unmistakably her, even hidden by a wide-brimmed hat and expensive sunglasses. Loriella de la Day, current queen of the silver screen and one of Hollywood's most in-demand young actresses. Her ash-blonde hair was woven into a chic side fishtail braid and she wore a white sundress and white skyscraper heels. She greeted me with a wide smile.

'How are you?' she asked in her cool, raspy American accent, removing her sunglasses.

'I'm, um, yep, lovely, how are you?' I replied, if you could call it that.

'I am a huge bookworm and I left my last book on set and didn't think to pack any others. I am clearly ready for a break,' she laughed, and it was so surreal because I'd watched her move around and laugh and pick stuff up in movies and now she was here, doing that in *my shop*.

Marianne would have been straight in there, confidently leading her around the shelves, chatting like old friends within minutes. I, on the other hand, overpoured the iced tea, handed it to her without a word, and then knocked into that pile of books again.

*Pull it together, you idiot,* I scolded myself, and took a deep breath.

'What kind of books do you like? I'd be happy to give you some recommendations?'

'I'd love that,' Loriella nodded. 'I'm in the mood for feel-good. I'm an actress and I was just working on something *suuuuper* bloodbathy, so I need a pick-me-up!'

I liked that she didn't assume I knew who she was. As we walked through the shop, she kindly picked up a copy of every single one of my recommendations, and refused to let me carry them for her, instead running back and forth to the counter herself as she piled them up.

'How long are you staying for?' I asked, with a chuckle.

'Only a few days, but I like choice and I have space in my suitcases. Oh, God.'

I looked up towards the window at her change in tone, to see Blane opening my door and striding in.

'Lori, there you are.'

'Loriella,' she corrected him, her smile in place, then turned her back, continuing to browse.

'I've got the perfect thing lined up for you. How about a private catamaran cruise out to the far reef? Unlimited champagne?' he schmoozed, gesturing to the door to try and coax her out of the shop.

'No, thank you,' she answered and turned back to me, only for Blane to edge around into her line of vision.

'I know I can interest you in some wakeboarding?' He reached his arm between us, trying to guide her like cattle.

'Excuse me—' I interjected.

'No, thank you,' Loriella said, firmly, directly facing Blane. 'Please stop bothering me, I'm here to relax. Thank you.'

The way she stared him down was tremendous, and he left the shop with his tail between his legs.

'I'm so sorry about that,' I stuttered, embarrassed on behalf of the hotel.

'Oh, don't worry about it, I'm used to it,' she said, and I breathed a sigh of relief that she was OK about the whole thing, even if I wasn't. Blane was really pushing boundaries, I felt. 'You just got to be firm with people like that, hang the consequences. Though you know what, I need to work on this compulsion to say thank you to guys when they're pushy. Now, what were you saying about Jane Austen?'

# Chapter 30

# Marianne, in the USA

Their wedding day had arrived. Again. For what, the fourth time now? Marianne slipped on her dress and her trainers, not even sending Drew out of the room this time. They were in this together, completely.

She'd wondered over the past couple of days if she should do the thing she'd heard chapels did nowadays – dialling guests in to watch via a video stream. But would Evan really want to do that? He probably wasn't bothered. Drew's family had told him to just go and have fun and that they'd throw the two of them a party on their return in the summer. And Jenn ... well, Jenn was in a completely different time zone now. In fact, it was pretty much the middle of the night there already.

Again, a little pinprick floated into her consciousness, nagging at her that she should have called Jenny and told her about the engagement, about the wedding, about everything that was happening, rather than announcing it on Instagram. But on the other hand, Jenny had seen it, and she hadn't got in touch. That hurt.

Marianne would be doing this without her. And that was OK.

Nothing was going to go wrong today. She had her dress, her shoes, her groom, her wedding licence. The chapel's website had been down, but that wasn't a big deal, she just grabbed the address from Google. They'd eaten breakfast – not too heavy, not too light. They'd made reservations for the Camelot Steakhouse tonight and a pool cabana for tomorrow, so they could spend their final day in Vegas in relaxed, wedded bliss, planning the rest of their honeymoon.

Leaving their room, Marianne felt as though the sequins were inside her, not just on her dress. She was about to get married. She stole a peep at Drew. At that lovely, funny, risk-taking, talented, ride-or-die man.

'M'lady!' A man dressed in a full knight's costume appeared in front of Marianne as they reached the lobby. 'That dress, those sequins,' he bellowed. 'You must be a queen?'

She laughed. 'Just for today – we're getting married!'

'A wedding! Joyful day! Thou hast your marriage licence, yes?'

'Yes, this time. We've been trying to get married since we got here!'

The knight bent down on one knee. 'May all the luck be bestowed upon you both. Will you be returning to us to dine this evening?'

'We shall,' answered Drew.

'A gift for you,' the knight said, pulling from his pocket a voucher with a medieval-style font declaring that it could be exchanged for a ten-dollar slot-machine card.

'Thank you so much,' Marianne laughed, and gave it to Drew to pop into his suit jacket.

'To the chapel!' the knight declared, and wandered off to take a photo with another family.

Outside the hotel, Drew called them an Uber and they held hands in the back seat as they gave the name of the chapel.

'Of course.' The Uber driver peered at the two of them in his mirror. 'A lot of people are heading over there today. You're the first two I've seen who've dressed for the occasion, though.'

'We are?' Marianne looked down, wondering if her dress was a bit much after all.

'Yeah,' he replied. 'I'm sure there'll be others like you there too, though. People have memories here and they like to mark the occasion.'

'Yeah ...' Marianne said, not really quite following what he was saying. After about twenty minutes of driving, traffic, driving, traffic, Marianne sat up, peering out of her window. 'There it is! The Lovely Dovely Chapel of Luck and Love! It looks just like how I imagined.' She could only see the top half of it from where they were, plus there seemed to be a steel chicken-wire fence blocking their view, but they'd be past that soon.

The chapel was just as she'd remembered from the article, with a tiny steeple and all painted a faded baby blue, plus a giant mural of a garter around a big pink heart on one side. This was really happening.

The car pulled in on the opposite side of the road, the chapel still a little way in the distance. 'OK if I drop you here?' the driver asked.

'Can you not get closer?' Marianne asked. Surely he could just pull in out the front, rather than make them walk along the side of the highway and then find a place to cross?

'That right there is where you're going to want to stand – with those people.' He pointed towards a small crowd standing facing the fence.

What was going on? Marianne stepped out of the car, her dress flapping in the breeze of the vehicles that whizzed by. The sun beat down on her sequins, which caused stars to dance on the sidewalk as she moved. She walked towards the crowd, watching them, wondering why they were staring at the chapel.

She reached the throng and was about to tap on the shoulder of a woman wearing a Lovely Dovely Chapel of Luck and Love sweater and ask her what they were all looking at, when Drew caught up with her.

'Mari,' he said, panting. 'The driver just told me—'

'Ten … nine …' A voice came over a megaphone, tinny and excited.

'Who's that?' Marianne asked, standing on tiptoes to see the front.

'… eight … seven …' It was a man in an orange hi-vis vest.

Drew put his arm around her, trying to turn her to him. 'Mari, it's OK—'

'… six … five …'

'What are they doing?' she asked nobody in particular.

'… four … three …'

Marianne looked at the chapel, at the spire, at the mural.

'… two … one!'

There was a moment of silence, before a series of pops echoed across the street, followed by a rumble of thunder. And just like that, from right to left, the little blue Lovely Dovely Chapel of Luck and Love tumbled out of sight.

'No!' Marianne yelled. Then she was speechless for a moment, staring at that point in the air where the steeple had been only moments before. They'd imploded it? 'They *imploded* our wedding venue?'

The woman in front of her turned around, grinning, and on seeing Marianne's shocked face, said, 'Honey, this hasn't been used as a wedding venue for years. Did you not know?'

'For *years*?' Marianne spun round to Drew. 'I didn't know. I didn't realise. But it was right there.'

Drew was just as surprised as she was, and he stared at the face of his future bride with the look of a man who didn't have an answer. But zero point five of a second later, he did. The answer, at least right now, was to stop her from going under.

'Hey, it's OK,' he said, putting an arm around her and pulling her back from the crowd. 'We didn't know – we couldn't have known or planned for that.'

'Of course we could have,' Marianne said. 'I should have just taken the pissing time to look into it properly, rather than going off a four-year-old news story. How could I have been so underprepared for this whole thing, and so stupid?' She faced the rubble that was left of the chapel again, dust still hovering in the air.

'Don't blame yourself. We'll just pick another chapel – there are so many here.'

Marianne felt her knees wobbling and she didn't want to give into them. This wasn't the time to get upset, this time she was angry. Why couldn't this one thing just go right? Why did it have to be this hard? They'd spent so much money and time and energy chasing this so-called 'impromptu' wedding that her best friend, her brother, *her mum* weren't even going to be at, and for what? Dead end, dead end, dead end. Why did life have to keep kicking her like this when all she was trying to do was live it?

# Chapter 31

# Marianne, in the USA

Marianne wasn't one to overthink things; she prided herself, in fact, in being more in the moment than that. But after the chapel explosion, walking back towards the hotel, she stewed under the oppressively hot desert heat, as if she had Jenny with her, processing and thinking and trying to come up with solutions, though nothing was coming to her. Yes, they could find another chapel, yes, they could try *again* for another day, but, yes, she was tired.

And so, they walked. Marianne felt the need to think and struggle and punish herself, and Drew was beside her, a quiet rock, wishing he'd brought the hire car, but they'd assumed they would be drinking a glass of champagne inside the chapel at this point.

It was long, hot walk, the heat of the sun broken only ever so briefly by the sporadic shade of tall, dry palm trees. They stopped in a dollar store at a strip mall for two bottles of water, and some sunglasses for both of them. With his suit jacket slung over his shoulder, Drew held her hand the whole way back, even though their palms were slick with sweat.

When they finally reached the Excalibur, Marianne led them straight to the Dick's Last Resort bar, just off the casino floor, and ordered them two giant Big Dick Super Margaritas.

'What's going on in there?' Drew asked, as they sipped from their huge glasses, the bright liquid sloshing dangerously close to the edge.

'In where?' she asked. The sticky drink coated her teeth and lips, her senses were filled with the sounds of nearby revelry and the smell of sweet drinks, and she'd been really trying to focus on all of those things instead.

'In your head. I feel like you're silently fuming, which you don't normally do, but all I'm getting is the silent part, so I'm not sure.'

'I'm sorry, Drew,' Marianne sighed. 'I'm just mad at myself. I really thought that at this point, nothing more could go wrong. I thought today was the day.'

'Today could still be the day,' he said, and then looked at the margaritas. 'Or tomorrow. Shall I take a look at some other chapels? Maybe they even have one here in the hotel?'

'What's the point?' she sighed into her drink.

'The point is, I asked you to marry me, and you said yes, and it's OK if you've changed your mind or you need more time, but you have to just let me know. Don't make me guess.'

'I'm not trying to make you guess. I've not changed my mind and I don't need more time, it's just that everything keeps going wrong.' She caught herself, not meaning to snap at him.

He gazed down into his drink, and then said, his voice tense, 'I thought this was going to be a fun, impulsive thing borne out of very real feelings. But every day I'm having to reassure you and it makes me feel ... it makes me wonder if this wasn't a mistake.'

'What?' Marianne could feel her hands beginning to shake. 'Now you think it's a mistake?'

'Not us.' He rubbed his face. 'Just this. Trying to get married in Las Vegas. It was supposed to be easy, and now you're saying "What's the point?" which just sucks.'

Seeing his hurt face, Marianne said, 'I didn't mean that. I mean ... is this a sign or something? Is it worth us even trying to get married at this point, since everything seems to be against us? Or are we just going to end up with a bunch of failed memories?'

Drew seemed to simmer down as well, taking a long sip of his margarita. 'That's not like you, you know how strong you are. Let's just take it out of the equation for today.'

'Again.'

'Yes, again.'

'Fine.' With that, Marianne gulped down the rest of her drink and ordered them two more. If this wasn't going to be her wedding night, or even her wedding trip, she was going to leave Las Vegas in style.

'I've got an idea,' Marianne said, leaning against Drew, the alcohol making her speech just a tiny bit slurred. They were now a few drinks, and a few hours, in, and Marianne was feeling the classic mix of fifty per cent down in the dumps and fifty per cent not giving a flying fuck, which was about to prove to be a less than winning combination.

Her wedding dress strap kept slipping off her shoulder, but thanks to her trainers, at least she wasn't trying to totter around in massive heels. 'Why don't we just blow the rest of our money tonight?'

'That's not a good idea,' Drew said, and then stopped himself. 'Is it?'

'This is what we should do.' She pulled out a stool for herself and then sat Drew down on it. 'We should bet all our money on roulette. You said so yourself – it's *easy*.'

Drew tried to focus on a nearby roulette table, the wheel spinning away. 'I don't know. Doesn't the house always win? It can't be that easy.'

'Yes, it's so easy, you just put your money on … something and the wheel decides.'

'We don't have all that much money left.'

'But think what we could have. Let's go over there and bet our money. If we win, we get married tomorrow. Back at the Wynn. Win-Wynn, *ha ha ha*. And then continue the trip and go on our honeymoon.'

He looked at her and she tried to focus on him.

'And if we lose?' Drew asked.

She paused, and then said, looking him directly in the eye, 'We go home early.'

Drew whistled. 'That's quite a gamble.'

'This is who I am, I take risks. I'm no *Jenn*.'

'Not every risk is worth taking. You don't always need to prove something.'

Marianne ignored him, disliking his tone. 'Don't you want to say you risked it all in Las Vegas? Isn't that some kind of thing that could go in a book? And anyway,' she took another drink, 'what's the worst that could happen?'

'I guess we'd lose our money and have to go home a month early,' he reasoned.

But Marianne just shook her head. 'That's not going to happen. I have a good feeling about this. We're going to do just fine. Because how much fucking bad luck can one trip have, huh? We already broke down and got scammed at Coachella and you got bitten by a snake and I ripped my dress and we blew up the chapel. If I know anything about maths, and gambling, I know that means the odds of another bad thing happening are pretty low.'

Drew couldn't argue with that logic. Literally. Because he was already slurping the dregs of his drink.

'Let's do it. Let's put it all on red. And black.'

It wasn't so much that Marianne and Drew thought this was a *good* idea, it was more that it seemed like not a bad idea. Like it could help, and if it didn't, well the whole plan was going down the sinkhole anyway. And let's remember, they were pretty drunk.

Returning from the ATM to the cashier counter and exchanging a hefty chunk of their travel cash (which wasn't that hefty at all, really, considering how much pricier everything had been than they'd anticipated) for casino chips, the two of them made a beeline for the roulette table.

'Look,' Marianne said. 'If you bet on red and I bet on black, then the ball is bound to fall on one of them, so one of us will win.'

'But one of us will lose.'

'Well … yeah. And it might fall on the two green zero slots, and then we both lose.'

They toyed for a while about the best strategy for a sure-fire win, only neither of them knew about roulette strategy, so really they were just naming numbers and colours to each other.

Marianne watched the croupier spin the wheel and call last bets, and in a flash she slapped down four chips onto red, and waited with baited breath as the ball bounced and shuffled its way to a stop. On red.

On red!

Marianne looked at Drew in shock. They'd just won.

'Congratulations,' said the croupier, sliding her four chips back to her along with four matching ones.

'I think I just made us …' She counted the chips, her hands shaking, the dollar signs beginning to sear into her eyes, the image of her walking down the aisle at the Wynn filling her up. 'A hundred dollars! I fucking told you roulette was easy!'

Drew went next, betting a hundred-dollar chip on black, and won again.

'We're up by two hundred dollars,' he cried to Marianne. 'Shall we stop there?'

'No,' she said. 'This won't buy us a wedding at the Wynn. It wouldn't even buy our plane ticket home. We should bet more.'

It didn't take them long to lose track of the exact point they started losing money again. Marianne would argue it was when they'd lost all their winnings and were chipping away at their original chips. Drew would argue the winnings were theirs, and so they were losing money anytime they lost anything. The result remained the same, though. They were losing. And they kept losing, until, all of a sudden, they'd lost it all.

'What happened?' Marianne whispered, clutching their final chip. 'Should we bet this one? We could break the cycle, we could make it all back.'

Drew had sobered up fast. They'd lost most of their money. It was over. He pulled Marianne away from the table. 'Let's cash that one out and call it a night.'

'I'm sorry, Drew. I think I can get it back, though.'

'Let's spend some of this on a coffee instead, OK?'

Marianne's head was swimming, as if she'd just come out of a haze of lights and sounds and flashes and money, which, actually, she had. What had just happened? What had she done? 'Do we have to go home?' she asked him, stumbling away from the table.

He took her hand and they left the casino floor. 'I don't know.'

*

Marianne ran the tap on the soaking tub in the corner of the bedroom, wondering if she was going to throw up again, and if she did, whether she'd make it back to the bathroom in time. She watched the water fill up, steam rising, her head thumping. What the hell had they been thinking last night?

Drew appeared behind her, his phone in his hand, and sat on the side of the bath. He looked about as good as she felt, with his five o'clock shadow, unkempt hair and bleary eyes. She'd only seen him like this once before, in the final hours of attempted perfectionism before handing in his latest draft.

'I have a proposal for you,' he said, his voice scratchy.

'Another one?'

'A third option might be a better way of putting it, but we don't have long to decide.'

'A spur-of-the-moment decision?' she said, rubbing her weary eyes and dragging last night's mascara down her face, then turning off the tap. 'Those are my favourite, and they're working out *sooo* well for me at the moment.'

'This one can't fail. But that doesn't mean you need to take it. It's just an option, not an ultimatum.'

She dropped her robe and climbed into the bath. 'I'm listening.'

He cleared his throat. He must be feeling rough if he wasn't even trying to have a sneaky eyeball at her naked bod. And she must be feeling comfortable if she wasn't even trying to suck in her stomach.

'There is a way we could stay out here and not go home tomorrow.'

'I'm not becoming a showgirl, if that's what you're suggesting. I don't have the poise.' The bathwater was warm and it enveloped her into a hug. Her feet were blistered from yesterday's long walk and she wriggled her toes in relief. Her hip, which she'd banged on a slot machine during her drunken rampage, softened in the warmth.

'That's not what I'm suggesting. At least not yet,' he smiled.

'D, we're nearly broke. We can't stay out here in the States any longer.'

'"Nearly" being the operative word. Listen. We didn't blow *all* our money last night. Most of it, granted, but not all of it. What if we stayed in Las Vegas for another, I don't know, two weeks or so?' He held up his hand as she was about to protest, and added, 'We'd have to just chill, not partake in every buffet and burlesque show we come across. But I've had the edits back on my book, and although it doesn't need to be done for a while, if I *do* get it turned around quickly and my editor likes it enough, I could potentially get the next chunk of my advance sent through. Then we'd have some more money, and we could still have the last couple of weeks of road-tripping before heading back to the UK.'

'But you don't want to spend your vacation time doing work,' Marianne stated.

Drew shrugged. 'I'd do it if it still meant marrying you.'

'What do you mean?'

'I mean that I called the Wynn while you were, um, puking. They have several available slots for a small ceremony in their chapel in a little over two weeks.'

'In the Wynn chapel?' Marianne clarified, sitting up, the hangover showing the first signs of shifting since she woke up that morning.

'Yep. If we aren't too picky about the time of day.'

'I wouldn't want to pay a deposit, though,' Marianne said. 'I couldn't risk us losing more money if anything went wrong.' Wow, that was a very un-Marianne-like thing to say.

'We can secure the exact date a little closer to the time, once I've figured out exactly how good I can make this book. The only thing I need you to be OK with is that you'd have to hang out on your own, pretty much, in Las Vegas for a while. I know I wasn't planning on doing any work while we were out here, but I can if it means we don't need to cut the trip short. If that doesn't sound fun, we can forget it and go home. Or I guess we could leave Vegas and then come back again, but the point is, I won't really be able to sightsee, wherever we go, as I'll need to knuckle down.'

Marianne shook her head. 'I can't let you do this. I lost our money. I messed up the wedding plans. I can't let you sit in a hotel room and work just to pay for another "maybe" marriage while I lie by a pool.'

He thought about this. 'You'll be getting your salary from the shop in another week or so, right? So that can go towards it all too.'

'I guess ... Only ...'

Drew took her hand under the surface of the water. 'What?'

The temperature in Las Vegas was getting more oppressive with every day that passed. Everything seemed still, and Marianne longed for a breeze, some air. She'd been thinking a lot about Jenn this morning, wondering how she was doing and how she was coping in the heat of a tropical island. How she was coping without her. How Jenny was out there, alone, and Marianne hadn't checked on her once.

'Babe, what's up?' Drew said, pulling her back to the now.

'It's this heat,' she said, her brain swimming.

'The bathwater? Come on, get out, it's OK.' He wrapped his arms around her and helped her move to the bed.

'Not just the bath. I feel stifled, and it feels never-ending.' The desert, the city, she'd fallen in love with both, but right now she needed a break before she spiralled. She lay for a while, staring at the ceiling while her stomach churned and her sore head thumped. Eventually, she turned to look at Drew.

'I want to do something for you,' she said. How had they been in the US for over a month already? The first three weeks had been such a blur of San Diego, Palm Springs, Joshua Tree and LA, and then it had ground to a halt in Vegas, trying to have a 'quick' wedding. 'I don't think we're going to make it all the way up to San Francisco.'

'Maybe a little forward planning would have been a good idea after all,' Drew chuckled. 'Oops.'

Marianne let out a laugh and then had to lie very still for a few more minutes, before saying, 'You're going to be working so hard, for us, why don't we get out of Las Vegas and head to a national park – find a nice, quiet place to hole up? We'll see a little more of the area, and it's bound to cost less than staying in the city. We had such a nice time together in Joshua Tree.'

'You want to go back there?'

'Or somewhere new. I think Bryce is nearby, or Zion. I'll research it today.'

'What, and then come back here?'

Marianne reached for her phone, and a few minutes later held it out in front of Drew's face. 'Look at this: Zion National Park.' She showed him a photo of a vast canyon, towering red rock on either side of a green valley, a stream running below. 'It's in Utah, just over two hours' drive away. Maybe three. We can stretch our legs, see a bit of nature, breathe for a bit, then come back. What do you think? Around your writing schedule, of course.'

'I think I'm in.'

'Always?'

'Always.'

They drove to Zion the following day, leaving Vegas behind, for now. Two hours of red deserts and winding mountain roads later, and they pulled into the town of

Springdale, Utah. Paprika-hued mountains rose around them as they drove down the tree-lined boulevard, passing low-sitting hotels, restaurants and souvenir shops that looked like they'd been painted to fit in with the scenery.

After being in Las Vegas for close to two weeks, where part of the charm was the excess of man-made structures reaching high into the sky in the middle of the desert, it felt nice to be in a place where two storeys seemed to be the maximum, and the only things that reached higher were the mountains.

They reached Cable Mountain Lodge, a large Stars and Stripes flying in its courtyard, turned the engine off in a parking space in front of a river, and for just a moment after they stepped out, Marianne closed her eyes.

'Do you hear that?' she asked Drew.

He stretched beside her. 'The sound of the river?'

'The sound of pretty much *nothing*. *Ahhhh.*' She sighed in contentment at not rushing through life for five minutes, and they went to check in.

Warm cookies on the reception desk showed them what a gorgeous place this was going to be to stay, and their room didn't disappoint. It was serene and rustic, with a view over the canyons of Zion, and it was utterly silent.

For nine solid days, and some nights, Drew worked hard editing, correcting, rewriting and improving his second novel. It was the fastest turnaround he'd done since becoming a writer, but he knew he was giving it his all, and that it was good. He secretly thought it might be really good.

He just had to hope his editor agreed – enough to release the next chunk of his advance money.

Along the way, Marianne would read chapters for him and give him comments. It boosted him when he was tired to hear her little gasps or laughs, showing that she was enjoying it. When he looked like he was drowning, Marianne would coax him outside for a short trail walk, a dip in the pool, or to refresh himself with iced tea and delicious chips and salsa from one of the friendly restaurants. And sometimes she'd take herself off on her own, with her journal or a book, to enjoy the nature and the scenery and the alone time, or, on occasion, to write letters to her mum that she would never be able to send, but at least she could tell her about Drew.

Finally, one afternoon, while Marianne was engrossed in a book all about the Wild West history of Utah that she had picked up in the reception area, her feet dangling in the cool swimming pool, Drew appeared at her side, stretched and said, 'It's done.'

'It's *done*?' she repeated, leaping up and creating wet footprints on the sun-bleached concrete. 'Have you sent it off?'

'Yep,' he yawned. 'Now we just have to wait for the money to roll in.'

She was so proud of him, and so grateful. Her own monthly salary had entered her bank account a couple of days ago, and she'd drawn out what she could to add to their travel fund, but now, with his money on the way too – hopefully – she was feeling a lot more back on track. 'What do you want to do tomorrow?' she asked, joining him as he sat down on the edge of the pool, letting the refreshing water envelop his feet, his shins. 'Do you want to sleep or explore, or—'

'I'd love to do a big hike,' he answered with a wide smile. 'Get out of the room for the whole day, stretch my legs, see America, be with you.'

'Well, if you're sure, I have quite the plan up my sleeve.' Marianne pulled him up and led him out of the hotel grounds and across to the nearby visitor centre, feeling pretty pleased with herself.

'A plan?' Drew asked with raised eyebrows.

'I know! There's this thing called The Narrows, which is a full day's hike where you walk through the river – like, actually in the river, in a gorge, with the canyons rising a thousand feet into the air either side of you.'

'You walk *in* the river?' Drew looked down at his flip-flops.

'It's OK, we'll go into the town after this and we can hire waterproof shoes and walking poles.'

'You have done your research!'

'I have indeed. It's supposed to be so amazing, and don't you think it would be nice for our feet to walk through cool water for the day?'

'Absolutely. I'm excited.'

'We just need to get our hiking permit, from what I've read.'

Of course, it was too good to be true. As soon as they stepped into the visitor centre, a huge message was taped on a board explaining that due to snow melt (*snow* melt?),

The Narrows were inaccessible. Marianne felt what was now becoming the all too familiar stab of annoyance at herself for not being thorough enough with her research. She'd really tried this time.

They reached the front of the queue, and Marianne put her pamphlet onto the counter.

'Hi. We were planning to hike The Narrows tomorrow, but am I right that they're closed?' She showed the park ranger the map of The Narrows, just in case it helped.

'I'm afraid that's right, it's out of bounds at this time.'

'Will it be open tomorrow?'

'No, ma'am, not for at least another week and it may well be longer.'

Marianne swallowed her frustration. So what she'd planned wasn't available. *No big deal. No need to lose your shit.* 'Can you recommend any other walks – long ones? We've done the smaller hikes.'

'How active are you?'

'Pretty active?' Marianne answered, and Drew nodded, thinking of all the walking they'd done in Las Vegas, and not thinking about all the buffets they'd eaten.

'Well, a really popular walk is the Angels Landing Trail – it's spectacular, but it is strenuous. Are you afraid of heights?'

'No,' they both answered.

'Good.'

*Good? That was never … good.*

The ranger continued. 'Angels Landing is really challenging, and not for people afraid of heights. It's a rock formation that gets very steep, and very narrow, with long drop-offs and chains to hold on to near the top, at an elevation change of nearly fifteen hundred feet. It takes about four hours. Now, you don't need to do that last half-mile to the summit if you don't want to – that's the scary bit.'

Marianne and Drew flashed each other a grin. That sounded fun, actually. 'Why is it called Angels Landing?' Marianne asked.

'Because in the past some said that only angels would be able to get to the top. We showed them, huh?' The ranger grinned and then pulled out a more detailed map inside a park newspaper for them. 'Familiarise yourself with the trail details and if you decide to do it, you'll want to catch the park shuttle from here, then jump off here and follow signs for the West Rim Trail. I'd suggest going early in the morning, like being on the first bus – here's your bus schedule – because you avoid the heat and too much of a crowd. When you get near the top, you'll see why that's preferable.'

'All right,' Marianne and Drew dutifully nodded.

After applying for their permit, they left the visitor centre and Marianne faced her fiancé. 'Does that sound OK to you? Sorry it's not The Narrows.'

'It sounds exciting! Just being here, with you, is exciting. I feel like we'd kind of forgotten the road-trip side of our time here, but this makes me look forward to what's to come.'

'On the road trip? But we're barely going to get one now.'

'For future road trips, then. We have plenty of time.'

That evening, over beef burritos and fresh lemonade, Marianne felt as though they were finally breathing again. The air out here was clean, the sky seemed open, Drew had finished his book and she was very happy indeed to have a couple more days of the sound of babbling brooks before they returned a final time to the music of the slot machines.

# Chapter 32

# Jenny, in the Maldives

I was feeling pretty pleased with the success of the bookshop, especially since my celebrity visitor had been such a joy. Over the next week or two, I kept a close watch on everything, and though I wouldn't go as far as to say that business was booming, to say it was softly singing would probably be acceptable.

On more than one occasion I heard guests round the final corner to the shop and reach the doors to exclaim, 'Oh, here it is!' which was a nice improvement from 'Oh. That's it.'

I did spot one chap squinting as he tried to read the back of a book cover, so I swiftly upped the lighting from Hollister-dark to hygge-light with a few more soft bulbs and warm lamps. And though he didn't know I saw him, one afternoon I even noticed Blane hanging around in the shadows outside the shop, a look of grump on his face, until he spotted something in the window that he clearly fancied reading and scuttled off quickly, only for one of Rish's colleagues, one of the entertainment crew, to appear an hour later to buy that exact book.

I felt as if the shop was really making a little name for itself, and that was the thought I kept repeating to myself when I got a call to come up to Khadeeja's office as soon as I'd closed for the day.

She wouldn't be too angry about the lack of events, would she? It took a while to get this kind of thing off the ground, and in two months I'd gone from nothing to a fully-stocked and well-running bookshop that people liked. And I did have some other things I planned to do over my final month, some of them already in place. In fact, as soon as Rish and Layla gave their pitch about turning Bounty Cove Cay into the Maldives' premier eco-chic resort, I was stocked and ready to host a local-author reading from Rish's friend, also a conservationist, who had published a beautifully written and illustrated book about island life and how it was vital we didn't lose it.

So, she wasn't going to be too mad at me, was she?

Because she'd sounded a little mad on the phone ...

No, no, I was sure everything was fine. I took the long way round from the bookshop to Khadeeja's office, exiting out of the side door and strolling along the boardwalk back around to the front of the Pavilion. There were a few clouds wisping across the sky, and the heat had cooled just a little. I inhaled the fresh air, its scent being so familiar to me now, much like every building, tree and curve of the island. I was part of the family. Things were working out.

When I entered again through the main doors and took the stairs to the second level to Khadeeja's office, I realised it was the first time I'd been in there. Knocking, I pushed open the door. Wow, it was nice. Natural sunlight streamed through big windows onto white walls. It was on the second level of the Cove Pavilion, in the corner, overlooking the beaches and the water villas, which pretty much looked like the most beautiful office artwork in the world.

But with a face like thunder, Khadeeja said to me, without greeting, 'You hosted Loriella de la Day in the Hideaway the other week, is that right?'

'I did!' I was surprised, not expecting this meeting to be focused on her.

'And was there anyone else in the shop with you both at the time?'

'N-no,' I said. 'Was that wrong? Are we supposed to have someone else with us at all times if a VIP comes in?'

'No, I'm just trying to establish if it was just you and Loriella, or whether there were other guests around at the time?'

Blinking, I wondered what she was actually asking me. 'Um, it was just us, there were no other customers for a bit beforehand, and then none for a bit after. I remember because I, um, sent an email to my mum straight away with the selfie she took with me attached. I'm really sorry, I realise now that sounds really bad and was a horrible breach of confidentiality, I just didn't think. My mum really liked her in this BBC adaptation last year. Oh, erm, the BBC is—'

'Jenny, if it was just you and Loriella in the bookshop, I can reasonably assume this was your doing, then? Correct?' Khadeeja spun her laptop round to show me. It was open on a garish celeb-gossip site. The headline read: *Diva Loriella Demands Every Book to Be Hers in Maldives Mega-Hotel.*

'What?' I said. 'She wasn't a diva, and she didn't buy every book, just a nice, healthy amount. Wait—' I looked up, realisation dawning. 'Are you saying you think I sent in this story?'

'"Sources at the resort say Miss de la Day displayed outrageously diva-ish behaviour, forcing the shop to close to the other guests and berating the frazzled shopkeeper,"' Khadeeja read aloud.

'I was not frazzled! I'm not the source – why would I refer to myself as frazzled?' I cried, my heart pounding. 'Khadeeja, Loriella was charming, she was so nice, not a diva at all. I didn't do this.'

'I asked for you to put the bookshop on the map. I did *not* mean using this type of promotion. Our guests expect privacy and discretion, and this is completely unacceptable.'

'I know, I agree.' Who could have done this? Maybe another guest walked past the window and thought they'd make a quick buck from selling a fake story? My mum wouldn't have done this, would she? And then suddenly … 'Blane! Blane came into the shop while Loriella was in there. He was trying to get her to stop shopping and come with him, something about a champagne catamaran cruise.' It all made sense now, though I still felt sick to my stomach that he would do this.

Khadeeja merely raised her eyebrows, waiting for me to go on.

I tried to remember what Loriella had said to him. 'She told him to stop bothering her, rather firmly. I was quite pleased she'd stood up to him, actually, because I thought he was being a dick.' I clamped my hand in front of my mouth. 'Sorry, I know I shouldn't say that about a director. But, well, he was.'

'He's not a director,' Khadeeja interrupted. 'Is he still telling people that?'

'Um, I think he told me that. Anyway, he left, but I'm pretty sure he felt a bit humiliated. I imagine it irked him that it happened in front of me, too, since he's never been exactly my biggest fan.'

Khadeeja sighed. 'I'll have to get him up here to talk to as well, then. One moment.'

'Yes, ask him,' I said, watching her dial, nervous, but confident that he was the one behind the article.

We sat in silence for a minute until Blane came crashing in. He denied the whole thing, said he had no reason to make fifty bucks selling celebrity gossip, 'and even if I did, I know much juicier stuff than that some actress likes reading.' Throughout the confrontation his eyes shot daggers at me.

'Well, I'm getting nowhere, so let this be a warning to you both for now that if this happens again and I think one of you is behind it, I'll be doing a much deeper investigation.'

As Blane and I nodded and stood, he deliberately squashed my fingers between our two chairs.

'Jenny, can you stay a little longer, please,' Khadeeja said, and I lowered myself back down.

When Blane shut the door, I said, 'It truly wasn't me, but I am sorry this happened. Please know that in celebrity-gossip land this is nothing interesting and I'm sure it'll blow over and be forgotten.'

'We'll see. Now, I also need to talk to you about the bookshop.'

Oh, great. A double whammy.

Khadeeja shut the lid of her laptop and sat back. 'I'm feeling heavy-hearted,' she began, and I knew this was going to be every bit as bad as I imagined. I gulped, and she continued. 'Do you remember me telling you that I wanted the bookshop to be a highlight of the resort, something we could promote and build programmes, maybe even styles of holiday, around?'

'I remember,' I said, my voice quiet. Is there anything worse than someone telling you they're disappointed in you? And like a punch in the stomach, in my mind appeared a picture of Marianne's face after I'd told her I'd applied for another job, on the other side of the world from her. She hadn't said so, though it was unlike her to hold back her feelings, but I'd caused her heart to grow heavy too.

Khadeeja turned to gesture at the window, where the weather was turning and rain clouds rolled in across the sea. 'Look at this weather. Guests *want* other things to do. This would have been the perfect time to have a host of events and workshops and ideas to run away with.'

I had no comeback and no excuse; I was just not good enough at this. I nodded.

'The new bookshop manager is due to fly over for a visit soon. I've put her off for now because of the weather,' Khadeeja said. She paused, her eyes running over my face, as if searching for the light she'd seen in me in that video interview. 'I'm afraid if I don't see any improvement, I will tell her there's no job for her here at Bounty Cove Cay. The bookstore will close.'

My heart stopped. 'You'd close the bookshop? Completely?'

'It's just not financially viable in the state it's in.'

'But the new manager, couldn't she try and make a go of it?'

'No, Jenny, I can't ask her to leave her current role for a sunken ship, when she has no experience in launching a business. That's why we brought you in.'

The way she said it was pointed, and I knew what she was saying. Who could blame her? I thought of the manager, of somebody losing a job because of me, and it twisted my tummy to the point I felt I could have cried. I'd failed, and I'd have to admit it to Layla, Rish, my parents, *me*.

She stood up, and I knew I was excused. I left the office completely dejected. I was sinking, along with the ship, and I only had one type of bucket to scoop out the water and that had holes in it.

I left the Pavilion and walked the full perimeter of the island, lost in my thoughts, hoping for inspiration, but all that happened was that I spun myself into sorrowful circles.

I thought about the time our bookshop back in Bayside had been suffering to the point of nearly closing, until Marianne had come zooming in after barging her way into a county-council forum and declared all the seemingly irrelevant things the townspeople needed in their lives. She had a way of hearing something and knowing exactly what to do with that information.

I remembered further back to the time at university when I was too scared to switch courses because I didn't know if English Literature would be better or worse for running a bookshop, which was my dream, than continuing with Business Management, which seemed the sensible option. It was Marianne who told me to take a risk and do what made me happy.

I had failed, despite all my planning. I always thought that if I kept things risk-free, stable and predictable, nothing could come crashing down. But now this dream I'd had for what I realised was actually quite a long time – running a successful bookshop abroad – was falling from my grasp. And in the process, I'd let everybody down, from my manager, to my best friend to myself.

# Chapter 33

# Jenny, in the Maldives

The rain came shortly after I left Khadeeja's office. The blue sky turned away and hid behind thick, dark clouds. It was now late May, and I'd seen nothing but sunshine since arriving in the Maldives at the start of April, though I knew the wet season was overdue. Nobody was worried; they saw it every year, though I could sense the disappointment on the faces of some holidaymakers when they came inside to avoid the downpour.

I knew I had to plan more, do more. As yet, this bookshop I'd been brought in to get off the ground was looking worryingly like it would do better boarded up.

I was so embarrassed. I liked to be in control, and anxious thoughts were spiralling me far away from that.

The rains continued to gush from the clouds above as if they'd scooped up everything from the sea all in one go. It was twilight now, the sun having set shortly before, though the sky was darker than usual thanks to the storm that was now in force.

As a distraction from myself, I hurried along the boardwalk, careful not to slip, to meet Rish where he was sheltering at the main staff accommodation building.

We greeted each other with a kiss on the cheek, and I knew it wasn't just the damp weather that was dulling any sensation of a spark between us. Sitting under the canopy on a bench in front of the building, we drank from beer bottles and played cards as the rain poured down, slapping on the canvas above us as loud as an aeroplane flying low overhead.

'What's Layla doing this evening?' I asked him, not having had a response to a text I'd sent her.

'She's working, though I'm hoping she's come back in now.'

I looked up at him just as the rain started beating harder against the canopy. 'Working, in this weather? Boat or plane?'

'Boat. She'll be OK, she's sailed in worse before.' He didn't look as confident as he sounded, though.

I studied my cards and sighed. 'What are we playing again?'

Rish's hand reached across the table and rested on mine, pushing my cards down. He met my eye. 'Are you still upset about Blane?'

'Not really,' I answered, and took a sip of my beer, watching the rainwater run down the sides of the canopy as if it would never stop. 'Though he's a force of nature, to say the least. But I'm more upset by the fact that he wasn't exactly wrong about the bookshop. I haven't done a very good job.'

'It's not over yet,' he replied. 'You have, what, four or five weeks left?'

'But time is running out. I want to prove myself and I don't want to waste this opportunity, but I just feel a bit ... rubbish. Like I'm waiting for lightning to strike but am losing faith that it's going to.' An almighty boom and the heavens really opened up, raining even more than before, if that was possible. 'Metaphorically speaking. It's getting dark so quickly this evening.' I squinted to see my cards in the gloom.

'It is,' he answered, and looked back out towards the waves of the ocean again, which were now obscured by the sea spray dragging off it and being pulled sideways. Lit up by the soft, pooling floodlights, the palm leaves were all whipping towards the west like toupees in the wind, and the noise of the howling and the pelting had tripled.

'This isn't a passing shower, is it?' I called, and in answer the rainwater piling on top of the canopy took an almighty leap for freedom, landing with a huge splash a couple of metres away from us. 'Shall we go inside?'

He nodded, and I made my way in through the doors. I was shaking the raindrops from my hair when I turned and realised he wasn't with me.

'Rish?' I called, but although the familiar faces of a few members of staff turned to look at me, none of them were him.

'I think he just went down to the beach,' said Sadeera, walking past, pointing back outside.

'What? Is he bananas?' I raced up the stairs to the second level and into the gym, where the windows looked back towards the beach, and sure enough there he was, in the near dark, standing in the sand, his T-shirt billowing in the wind, shielding his face from the onslaught of water. What was he doing?

I watched him for a moment, unsure what else to do, but when a gust blew him backwards and he stumbled, the instinct to go and drag him back inside kicked in. When I reached the door to the staff building, I looked up at the sky, but nothing had changed; there was to be no relenting out there any time soon. Without time to plan a rescue mission, I dashed down towards the shoreline, calling his name, but he couldn't hear me over the downpour.

Rain soaked my face and caught in my eyelashes, the wind making my nose run. It wasn't cold, in fact it was a little like standing under a powerful, warm shower, but the noise of the rain on the surface of the sea, and of the palm fronds clapping in the wind, was deafening. When I reached him, I grabbed his arm. 'Hey, come on, did you not notice the rain?'

But Rish's eyes wouldn't leave the horizon, his eyelashes blinking away the raindrops nearly as fast as they slapped at his face.

'Rish?'

For the first time, he seemed to hear me, and he dragged his eyes to my face. And for the first time, they weren't the happy, crinkled eyes I knew.

323

'What's wrong?' I asked him, over the thunderous sound of the rain hitting the sea.

'Layla's not back,' he shouted in reply.

'She's not back?' I looked at the choppy sea, the mint-coloured waves no longer transparent but opaque with the sand churning under the surface. 'Layla is still on a boat, out there?'

He nodded. 'Her boat isn't docked, she's still at sea.'

No, she couldn't be. Layla was experienced, and tough, and she would have known not to be out sailing in this. But then … the weather had turned quickly, from a series of tropical showers supplemented by bright bursts of sunshine to a full-on storm. What if she *was* out there?

I didn't know what to say. What do you say to someone when they're worried about the life of the person they love?

Because there was no doubt about it, and I couldn't believe it had taken me so long to realise, now that I watched the pain and worry wash over his features. I could feel it radiating from him, the sense of him wishing she was here, wishing he could hold her, vowing he'd tell her how he felt if she could just be brought back to him.

He was looking for Layla the way I would look for Evan. And we'd all been so scared about rocking our deep friendships that we'd chosen to sail beside the ones we'd fallen for instead of with them.

'We'll bring her back to you,' I called out to him, but my words were whipped away. Although I knew he wouldn't hear me, I shouted, 'I'll go and see if anyone's heard anything.' And then I took off, back to the boardwalk, and raced towards the Pavilion.

The boardwalk was slippery, the rain coming down so fast it didn't have time to drain between the slats, but I'd nearly reached the doors when I slipped and crashed down on my hip, knowing I'd find a whopper of a bruise on my bum in the morning.

Nevertheless, I hauled myself to standing just as one of the bellhops lingering inside spotted me and began to race out to help me up. 'Don't come out!' I shrieked. 'Save yourself.' I didn't mean to be so dramatic, but even so I gratefully accepted the towel he was holding out for me as I stumbled in.

'Thank you so much,' I said between breaths. 'Rish is on the beach … he said … Layla is still out there … at sea … sailing.'

One of the receptionists handed me a juice, which I gulped down and then added, 'Do you know anything about Layla being out with the ferry, or one of the speedboats? Is she with guests?'

'Let me find out for you,' the receptionist said and rushed back behind her desk to grab her phone.

Moments later, she returned. 'I spoke to the boat crew. They don't know where she is.'

*

It was an agonising wait, but I couldn't go back to Rish with no news. As I watched the storm outside the Pavilion, I prayed to any god listening that Layla was OK out there. I didn't want to lose my new friend.

I didn't want to lose my old friend, either. Petty arguments about days off and who should sweep the sand out of the store were nothing compared to the lifetime of love I had for Marianne. I didn't know how long I'd be waiting for news on Layla, but a deep feeling compelled me to make a call I should have made weeks ago.

I pulled my phone from my pocket, wiping the slick screen with my equally damp sleeve, and pressed on her name like I'd done a million times in the past, but not at all over the previous two months. It would be morning where Marianne was, quite early if my quick time-zone calculation was correct.

The phone rang, and rang, and eventually clicked through to voicemail. I nearly hung up, when a bubble of tears spilled out over not being able to reach her.

*'Please leave your message after the tone.'*

'Mari,' I snuffled down the line, unable to keep the shaking out of my voice, and unable to play it cool any more. 'I was just thinking about … you. I want to know if you're OK. And I want to tell you how much I miss you, and how sorry I am, and how I can't do this without you, and I don't just mean this, here, in the Maldives, I mean at home, at our bookstore, and in life. You're invaluable to me. I'm sorry if I ever made you feel like you weren't. The truth is, without you, I fall apart.' I paused, gulping in some air.

Had I lost her? Was she still mad at me? Had I lost everything?

I continued. 'I just wanted you to know. I hope you're smiling and safe and I bet you're having the most wonderful time and you deserve it, and I hope that your new husband is making you happy and that one day you'll forgive me so I can get to know all the things you love about him.

'If you want to give me a call back when you have a minute that would be great, but you don't have to, of course.' I tried to find the words to end my rambling call before the message cut out, but I had no brain power left. 'Anyway, if we don't speak, I guess I'll see you when we both get home.'

I hung up the phone. I missed my best friend. And on top of that, my heart missed Evan badly, and I should have told them both more often because I had a horrible feeling of foreboding that it was all too late.

# Chapter 34

# Marianne, in the USA

In the morning, as instructed, they were up before the sun had even risen. Marianne climbed out of the high wooden bed and crossed to the window, opening the curtains to that view of the canyons, still and silent, waiting in the dark for dawn to arrive.

She and Drew packed up his small backpack with snacks (a lot of them), water, the newspaper with the map that had the shuttle stops marked on it, and a hat each, including Drew's ridiculous bedazzled Vegas cap, which he insisted on wearing everywhere now. They tied their laces, had final loo breaks, applied sun lotion and were ready to go like a couple of eager beavers.

They got on the first bus, trundled through the park, seeing the reds and greens come to life as the sun rose behind the mountains, then they hopped off at the start of the trail, and off they went.

It was an easy walk – at first. A pleasant stroll along the flats, a river the colour of spearmint gum gliding along next to them. A little elevation here and there. Some people ahead, others behind. After a while, the trail started making its way up the canyon wall with some switchbacks, a little steeper, and Marianne felt her leg muscles working, but not in an unpleasant way. The only sounds that cut through the silence of the canyon were from their repetitive footsteps on the dusty path and the panting of their breath. With every step in the still-cool canyon, the view of the valley below became more impressive. Every time she'd turn back to look at Drew, he'd throw a grin at her. They were on an adventure.

'Mari, look,' Drew suddenly hissed into her ear, and his arm appeared from behind her, pointing at something to the side of the path. A small animal, like a mouse, peeped up at her from his perch on a jutting piece of rock, before whizzing away.

'Was that a chipmunk?' Marianne asked. 'I don't think I've ever seen one of those in real life before!'

That's when they both looked up, and Drew whispered, 'Whoa.'

In front of them, the path got steep, quickly, in a series of much tighter switchbacks that made it look as though the hikers already up there were on some kind of never-ending escalator system.

Marianne faced Drew. 'Let's just go for it, no stopping, and we'll reward ourselves with one of the peanut butter chocolate bars when we reach the top of this bit.'

'Do you think this was the tough bit the lady yesterday was talking about?'

'No ... unless we've done the walk really quickly ...'

They reached the top of the switchbacks with puffing chests and sweating brows, having power-walked up the whole thing.

Drew pulled a bottle of water out of the backpack. 'I'm so glad that was in the shade!'

'I'm so glad all those cheerleader chipmunks were there to egg us on,' Marianne replied.

The walk continued for a short time before opening out to a dusty clearing where people were sitting on their backpacks, taking a drink, contemplating what came next . . .

Marianne didn't really stop and look at the signs that reminded visitors of what they were to face on the last bit of this hike. Neither of them did. They strode on, energised by the vistas opening out all around them the higher they got, until Marianne laughed and said, 'Oh, wow, look at this bit.'

In front of her, the path became one with the cliff face, a ridge of sloping rock the colour of cinnamon, with rough carved steps where your feet could go. Chains were bolted into the stone to hold on to.

'Wait a minute,' Marianne said, stepping closer to the first chain. 'What if you let go of the chain and slide down this bit of the mountain? Don't you just . . . fall off?'

Drew peered down at the sharp drop into the valley. 'I guess so. Don't let go, will you?'

Huh. Don't let go. Just don't let go. That was easy enough . . . right?

Marianne and Drew stepped forward, following the other hikers, the ledge they were walking on narrowing and becoming steeper before them. Marianne gripped the hard, cold chain with both hands, carefully moving her feet over the uneven rock.

'Are you OK?' Drew called to her from behind.

'Yep,' she said, through slightly gritted teeth. 'You're holding the chain, right?'

'I am.'

'You promise, Drew?'

'I promise.'

To her right, the valley swooped deep below them, beautiful, mammoth and far away. American national parks were something she'd seen in movies but never experienced, and this was truly breathtaking. And maybe that was why she couldn't quite breathe.

Marianne's heart was beating a little faster than usual as she kept going onwards, upwards. The sun was on her now and she felt exposed. Her legs were shaking with every step that had to pull her body weight up with her. The drop on either side of her seemed almost sheer and all she could think was, *I am going to fall*.

How could she not fall? She didn't know about climbing. She had one chain to hold and who was to say that if she lost her footing for a second she'd be able to hold her whole weight by hanging on to the chain? When was the last time she'd done anything to test her upper-body strength?

Tears started filling her eyes and she blinked them away, furious that they'd come now when she needed her wits about her, not blurred vision. Her throat tightened and she attempted to take deep breaths, but she choked before they could be released.

*I am going to fall.*

A hardy granola-type came towards her from the other direction, a man who must have scampered like a mountain goat up to the summit before they'd barely even woken up, and Marianne realised with a shock of panic that this wasn't a one-way street.

*I am going to fall.*

'Drew?' she said, trying to keep her voice level, not wanting to worry him. 'Someone's coming towards us.'

'That's OK, he's going to go around us. You all right, Mari?'

She nodded, though she was pretty sure he must be able to see her ankles shaking from where he was.

The granola man got closer, his fingertips seeming to barely graze the chain she clutched so tightly, and she squeezed her eyes closed, leaning into the cliff. Before she knew it, he'd passed by, and she was just facing the uphill climb again.

But one more step forward and she could feel her breathing getting more rapid.

*I will faint if I don't stop breathing like this. And then I am going to fall.*

'Hey, Mari,' came Drew's kind voice behind her, soft and sing-song. 'Shall we call that it?'

'What?' she said.

'We've seen amazing views; we don't need to go any further. Let's just go down.'

The tears were spilling onto her cheeks now, she hadn't been able to stop them, but through her short breaths she said, 'No, you want to see the top.'

'No, I don't. Let's go back down.'

Marianne wanted to be strong and tough and she wanted to prove to herself that she could do it.

Why did she *always* have to prove to herself she could live on the edge? Was it really so bad to say, '*I tried, and that was enough*'?

She turned her head a little so she could see Drew, and he coaxed her until her feet were facing him instead, then her body was facing him too, and she was able to think, *I might not fall.*

'We're just going to go down a little bit, OK, just to that bit right there where it's a little flatter, that's all you need to get to,' Drew explained, cool as a cucumber. They slowly descended, Marianne gripping the chain and commanding him to as well, and anybody they passed kindly found a way to give them space. After what seemed like a long time but was probably no more than a couple of minutes, they reached a point where the chain stopped because the stone flattened out somewhat, and Drew pulled her further away from the edge to sit there with him for a moment, the breeze tickling her tears.

He let her lean on him, and the tears came in full force. It didn't matter that there were other people around. It didn't matter that he was seeing her ugly-cry. She leaned on him, her future husband, and let herself feel what she was feeling.

'I should have prepared more,' she eventually sobbed. 'The lady said what this was like, but I didn't think I'd find it anywhere near this terrifying. And why is nobody else as terrified? All these other people can manage it, but I don't know why I can't. Why am I suddenly so afraid of heights? What's going on?'

Drew didn't have all the answers, so instead he just said, 'It's OK, it's OK, we're safe, we're fine.'

Marianne sat there for a long time, letting her feelings wash in and out like waves.

Drew's voice eventually broke through her thoughts. 'Mari, is there something else that's bothering you? It seems like you're holding up the weight of the whole mountain.'

Sighing, Marianne opened up. 'I pushed her away.'

'Jenn?' he asked, his voice quiet and careful.

Marianne nodded. 'She was right, I was taking advantage of her. All this time I thought I was just living my own best life, but I never helped her live hers, and when she finally did go for something, I was selfish and made her feel bad, and I pushed her away.

'Since Mum died, it feels like I'm just always wanting to prove I'm OK, I'm living life, doing what I want. And I like being spontaneous, I don't want to change that about myself.'

'I don't think Jenn would want you to. I certainly don't. We love that about you. She just wants you to remember she's there as well.'

'I'm just so scared of becoming complacent and stuck, and then people leaving and life passing me by, that I don't think I let people get close – usually,' she said a few moments later, her face in her hands, blocking out the rocks, the sun, the views, Drew. 'I could see Jenn and me drifting, could feel my feet itching, so I cut loose before we could sink.'

Drew said nothing, but she felt his hand on her back, rubbing her skin, rhythmic and relaxing.

'It feels different now I've met you, though.' Marianne lifted her head and looked at him with pink eyes. 'Or at least, through being on this trip with you. I've still felt free and a bit wild, and I know I don't want to push you away. I want to enjoy all of it and all our dreams and not just race to the finish line and miss the journey en route.'

'I get all of that,' Drew said. 'Do you feel we rushed through this trip?'

'A little,' she admitted. 'I wish we'd taken our time a bit more at the beginning, rather than getting caught up in trying to be as spontaneous as possible. But even with a few difficulties, I've still had an amazing time. And ...'

He waited a little while before prompting her with a 'Yes?'

'And I don't want you to leave. After your book is done. I want to make plans with you. That sounds like an adventure I want to take. Do you?'

He smiled a confident yes, and held her in his arms. 'I love your spontaneity. But I'm most excited about what you just described – the adventure of our lives together.' She knew then that they would figure out where to live, what to do. They didn't need to decide any time soon, but it would be OK. It would be fun figuring it out.

After a little while, Marianne took a deep breath and then nodded. 'I think I'm good. Phew. Kinda weird behaviour from me, having a meltdown on a mountain.'

'Not weird at all,' Drew said. 'Nothing seems out of the ordinary with you.'

Marianne laughed.

'Come on,' he said. 'Shall we head down?'

'Yes, please.'

Marianne felt at peace, standing beside the river behind the hotel. The only sound was the babbling of the water rolling over the stones, and she closed her eyes, drinking in the melody. It was amazing, really, that Angels Landing and all of *that* had been only this morning. But as stressful and overwhelming as it had been at the time, she now felt sort of cleansed. As if crying her eyes out at the top of a rock formation had been cathartic, somehow.

She'd been glad for the slow-paced walk back down the canyon, and glad for the gentle, familiar trails they'd revisited during the afternoon. The glittering sprinkles of waterfalls at the Emerald Pools would always be her favourite. And more than anything, she felt glad to have

Drew. Not because to have him meant she had someone to 'save' her, but it meant she had someone who cared. That meant a lot.

While Drew fetched them some much-needed bottles of chilled beer from the nearby store, Marianne checked her phone for the first time that day, and her eyebrows shot up at what she saw. A missed call from this morning, which had come from the other side of the world, as if the caller knew she needed help. A missed call from Jenn.

# Chapter 35

# Jenny, in the Maldives

I woke up to my phone ringing. It had not been a good night's sleep here in the Maldives, even after the storm had finished ripping through the island, leaving as quickly as it had arrived. Even when slivers of stars cracked through the clouds, causing the wet palms to sparkle. Even after the vociferous, pounding rain had dulled and we could all hear ourselves think again.

News had come through that evening that Layla was on one of the neighbouring islands with the group of guests. She was all right.

With my hip still sore, I'd jogged as fast as I could manage back to the shoreline, where Rish had sunk into the sand, never taking his eyes off the sea.

I fell down beside him, thump into the wet sand, and touched his arm. 'Rish, hey, she's OK. She's OK.'

He turned his eyes towards me with such relief that when he pulled me into a hug and our lips crushed together it felt like a wonderful goodbye to something that was naturally ending. We kissed, short and so sweet, and when we pulled apart, our knees in the sand, he held me for a moment longer, moving the hair from my face.

'Oh, Bookshop Jenn—' he said, and I stopped him.

'I know. It's always been Layla, right?'

'I didn't mean to lead you on.'

'You didn't. I'm in a similar position, honestly. I think we just needed each other for a little while there, but now you need to get your girl. Don't leave it seven more years.' I was one to talk.

He nodded and we sat back on the sand, our fingers touching until the end. 'You've seen her?' he asked.

'No, but she's on one of the next-door islands, with guests. They checked. She knew a storm was approaching, she could see it in the clouds, apparently, so she didn't take the risk. They'll be back over when it's safe. But for now, she's good.'

'She's good,' he repeated to himself.

'She's *fine*. They said she's been helping teach the guests from our resort and the neighbouring one how to *Bandiyaa* dance, though I'm not sure what that is.'

Rish smiled. 'It's a traditional dance of the islands. She does it well.'

I just nodded, no doubt in my mind. 'You want to head back to the bungalows and dry off?'

He laughed, and my heart soared to see the crinkles back around his eyes. Looking down at his damp clothing, he said, 'This is nothing. In the Maldives climate, I'll be dry before I get back.'

We did make our way back towards our bungalows, though, and when we reached my door he pulled me into an unexpected hug, pressing me against his toned chest. He was right; he was almost perfectly dry.

'Thank you, Bookstore Jenn,' he murmured into my hair.

'Of course,' I answered.

He held on to me for a while longer, and I wasn't sure whether it was because he was exhausted, overjoyed or sorry, or just because he knew he would be letting me go.

After climbing into my bed that night, I hadn't fallen asleep for a long time, even though my whole mind and body were teetering on the edge. I worried about Marianne, about Khadeeja and her ultimatum, about Evan and how I wished I'd just taken a leap of faith and told him how I felt.

So when my phone started ringing in the morning, it took a minute for the sound to penetrate my brain, and when it did I leapt upright, afraid of missing the caller, and tangled myself in the mosquito net.

'Hi,' I rasped down the phone.

'Hi,' her voice replied. *Oh, Mari, I've missed hearing your voice.*

'You called back,' I stated the obvious to her.

'Of course. Are you OK?'

'Yes, are you?'

'Yes.'

'Good.' I hesitated, trying to gauge how mad at me she still was, but before I could launch into a million sorries, she beat me to it.

'Jenn, I'm sorry I was so selfish and always just left you to pick up the pieces of everything. I do appreciate you. Believe me, I've seen first-hand over the past two months what life with me is like when I don't have a Jenn to sort me out.'

I was dumbstruck for a moment. 'No,' I said, firmly.

'No?'

'No. I was calling to apologise to *you*. How could I not support you on your big trip? Or call you after your engagement? I am the worst. And I was so belittling to you about what you do in the shop just because I didn't understand it, but now I do, because I am utter rubbish without you.'

'No, I am utter rubbish without *you*.'

'No, you're so clever and talented and brave and loving, and Drew is so lucky.'

'Well that's true,' Marianne agreed. 'And I have missed having you out here. You're my family, and I won't forget that again.'

I couldn't not ask, though I shamefully didn't have any right to. 'Are you a married woman now?'

Marianne sighed, softly, but I could still hear it down the line. 'No, not yet. Though not through lack of trying. It's a whole thing that I'll tell you about when we get back. Right now we're having a bit of a relaxing break in a national park. Well, relaxing-ish. I nearly fell off a mountain.'

'You *what*?'

'Never mind, I'm sure it'll be funny to look back on.'

'I should have said this so long ago,' I said. 'But, Marianne: congratulations. On your engagement, on your wedding when it happens, on falling in love with a lovely guy.'

'Thanks, Jenny.' I heard her sigh, the happiness in her voice. 'So what's going on with you? You sounded really upset in your message?'

I didn't want to burden her, and I really didn't want her to think I'd only called her for advice, because that wasn't true at all, so I just said, 'That was nothing, just a bad sales day.'

'Bullshit.'

'Pardon me?'

'Leave the Oscar-winning acting to those of us who sparkle at it, Jennifer. I've known you for a hundred years and I can tell instantly when something's up, even from the other side of the globe.'

'Well . . .' I gave a brief recount of what a giant screw-up I was and how the shop was going to close and I was doing someone out of a job and none of what I was trying was working for the business, for one reason or another, until Marianne interrupted me.

'Jenny, this is so you,' she said with tenderness.

'What do you mean?'

'I know you don't like failing; I get that. And there's nothing wrong with feeling like that, but really, there's also nothing wrong with failing, you know. As long as you're out there, trying your best and picking yourself up when you fall and then trying a different way. And it sounds like that's what you're doing. But you don't need to do everything all on your own.'

'But it's my job,' I replied.

'Yes, it's your job and your responsibility, but part of that is listening to what your guests, or your customers, or your management want. Not to make their minds up for them just because you're in charge. Do you think I installed the coffee machine at the Book Nook because I fancied a cup myself? No, I listened to people browsing and paid attention to the competition and realised it would give customers a nicer experience and extra browsing time. Do you think our Halloween and Christmas parties were just whimsies from inside my head? No, I spoke to parents when they came in with their kids and realised they wanted somewhere in our village to celebrate holidays with their little bookworms.'

'But my forecast—'

'You have all the skills to make that bookshop fly; we both know it. But forget this idea of having to prove you can do everything without anybody's input. You need to be a solution to a problem.'

I thought about this for a moment. 'I really thought I'd listened to the customers. I'd tried. What else would you do in this situation?'

She thought for a moment. 'The resort directors hired you to start a bookshop, right? So I guess I'd be thinking, what's going to make it shine? I've been on the website and that island doesn't need to make petty cash from selling a few books, so what *does* it need at the moment? How can you be a solution to *their* problem?'

'All right,' I said, quietly. She was right. Her words were causing a few cogs to turn inside my mind, but I made myself stay present. 'Thank you.'

'Of course.'

She was a good friend. The best. 'I'll never forgive myself, you know, for choosing this moment – what turned out to be your wedding – to pull back from you.'

'Hey, you did something for yourself for once. I'm not angry about it, at least not any more, so don't beat yourself up. You need to throw out this imaginary rule book you've been living your life by. Believe me, hiding inside it won't make you feel any better.'

We hung up, promising to stay in touch for the remainder of the trip, which for me was a little over a month, and I thought meant about a fortnight for Marianne.

I felt better for having spoken to my best friend – much better. But as I looked at a photo of her on my phone, a snap taken on the opening night of our bookshop when we were more besties than business partners, I thought, *You're still a million miles away, though.* Would we ever be as close as we once were?

Layla had stayed the night on the other island, and I joined Rish on the jetty to wait for her to sail in the next morning.

I watched with a smile, a genuine smile, as the two of them embraced and I saw in both of them what I'd seen in Rish the night before. They were meant to be together. I hoped they would realise it soon.

In the meantime, after hugging Layla a hundred times myself and hearing all about her adventures on the other island, I had a question for them.

'When are you presenting your pitch to the directors?' I asked, referring to Rish's eco-chic upgrade idea.

'In a couple of days,' he answered. 'Why?'

'Can I run something by you, and if you like it, perhaps I could join you for just five minutes of the pitch?'

Marianne was right. Not me, Marianne. I had one shot, and if it all came tumbling down, if I failed, it sure as hell wasn't going to be because I gave up trying. I was going to go down with this ship.

Waiting outside Khadeeja's office with my binder held to my chest, the same binder I'd held the first time I met her, only now filled with far different data, I felt a confidence I knew had been melting away under the Maldives sun. I was nervous, this was a risk, but that was OK.

Inside, I could hear the faint sound of Rish's animated voice along with Layla's, as they went through their proposal. I was pleased to hear sounds of laughter, and agreement. The directors must be in a good mood, which was great for my two friends.

Khadeeja swung open her office door, and beckoned me in. 'Jenny, I hear you have something you want to contribute at this point? Regarding the bookshop?'

I went and stood beside Layla, who nodded at me encouragingly, and I looked between her glorious smile and Rish's kind, crinkled eyes, and took a deep breath.

'Hello, everyone, thank you for seeing me, and thank you, Rish and Layla, for letting me slip this small, but related proposal into your impressive plans.' They nodded at me and I turned back to the directors, specifically to Khadeeja. 'I've been doing some thinking about how I can be part of the solution for you. You want to build the resort's reputation back to being the cream of the archipelago, and I truly think you've hit the nail on the head regarding the direction you should take to do that. I think Rish's suggestions will have impact, and would be a big, brave and *right* solution. I hope you agree with me. And with that said ...' I paused. 'I think we should close the bookshop.'

Khadeeja frowned and the directors all looked perplexed, so I rushed on. 'That was a little dramatic – I should say, *transform* the bookshop. Because although I think it can do fine, it's never going to do well where it is. Perhaps it could move locations, perhaps it could even go out to the beach, like the Barefoot Bookseller shop. But I think what we should do, here at Bounty Cove Cay, is open a library.'

'A library?' Khadeeja clarified.

'A library. I know we wouldn't make money, but I don't think money is really what you need from this. I think you need the events, which' – I held up my hands – 'I know isn't something I've excelled at. But I think you need events, choice and a lovely place for guests to browse, relax, pick up, put down, learn.

'I run a successful shop back in England. Bookshops are wonderful, and I wish there were more in the world, but here I think a library would work better. For you, for the authors, and for the guests. Fundamentally, what I've been missing here is that I was trying to match what I knew was a successful model from my shop at home to here.' I took a deep breath, handed her my binder and declared, 'I know how to change that.'

She took my binder and opened it. 'This looks very detailed.'

'It is. I like details. I like being organised and planning carefully, and I wouldn't change that about myself, but what you'll see here is the same level of detail I've always applied, but with the creativity it needs so that it can come to life and be seen.'

'And what caused this creative side to suddenly make an appearance?'

'My business partner,' I answered with honesty. 'We work extremely well together, so when we're working apart, I need to teach myself how to use the best bits of her personality alongside mine.'

Khadeeja flicked the pages briefly, the other directors looking over her shoulders.

I continued, aware of wanting to fill my time well. 'I found that guests use the bookshelf on the mezzanine all the time, those that find it, anyway. And they stay there, in that space. That's where I think we should have the library. Why have people walk so far from their sunlounger? This way they can come in from the heat, browse, borrow and enjoy. Not a lot of guests have the suitcase range and capacity of Loriella de la Day, so they generally buy one or two books at the most. But the books currently on the shelf in the mezzanine lounge have seen better days. I suggest we sell all of these from right here in the library, using an honesty box, and all donations can go straight towards the conservation project Rish's been working on with the turtle sanctuary.

'I also want to stock a copy of each of our new collection of local authors in the library, and I want to appeal to people's need to relax on their vacation. To do this, we'd suggest that they take their time with a library book and know that anything they borrow can be *purchased* from the gift shop to take home if they haven't finished it.'

They looked pleased, so I rambled on. 'Kindles, preloaded with the books of local authors, that guests could rent out? That fee could go to conservation too. And we would make all of this sustainable and eco-friendly, just like you want. Plus, the shops here are all closed in the evening. With a full library, guests can browse during the evening, working off their dinners and curling up with a book right there. I know the library wouldn't be staffed after hours, so not all services would be available, but more than there are now.'

After finishing my pitch, I was excused so Layla and Rish could continue theirs. As I reached back to close the door behind me, my heart racing and fingers shaking, I knew I saw a hint of a smile on Khadeeja's lips. I just knew it.

# Chapter 36

# Marianne, in the USA

The following day, when Marianne caught a moment beside the pool while no other guests were around (probably because they were all being brave and scaling Angels Landing), she called her brother.

'Hello, sis,' his friendly, familiar voice came down the line. 'I'm just locking up the store for the night after another day of roaring trade. Are you back in Vegas? Are you finally hitched yet? Or are you just planning to move there permanently now?'

'Ha, ha,' she answered, her feet dangling in the cool swimming pool while the sun stroked her back, warmly. She'd been keeping Evan filled in on their various delays and setbacks since arriving in the US. 'Actually, Drew's finished the rewrites and we're still in Zion National Park, hoping the advance will come through.'

'That's what you've been waiting for?' he asked, sounding concerned. 'I thought you were just hanging out for a while because he'd been given a tight deadline. You're waiting for money?'

OK, maybe she hadn't been completely upfront with him about *why* they'd had the delays and setbacks.

'Yeah, we had … *I* had … a little oops moment in Vegas and might have lost most of our money on the roulette table.'

Evan just laughed. 'Of course you did. So what have you been living off?'

'I didn't lose all of it, just most of it. I've been paid now, so that's a bit more and I held back the usual rent and bills and blah blah blah money. And we figured that if Drew could finish the book and get his next payment, we'd have enough again to get married, in a ceremony we actually want, and then could maybe salvage a couple of weeks' worth of road trip. And now here we are, having a breather, and keeping our fingers crossed that the money comes through.'

Evan paused before saying, 'I think you should use some money from your inheritance from Mum.'

'What? No way. That's our shared money for houses or life or something. That's our safety net. Hanging on to that money is the only sensible thing I've ever done. Mum wouldn't want me blowing it on a wedding.'

'You don't think Mum would have wanted to help pay for her daughter's wedding day? Does that not count as "life"?'

'I mean …' Marianne had never used a penny from their inheritance, and neither had Evan. She couldn't start now.

'Marianne,' her brother said softly. 'Let me contact the bank and get some sent over to you. Have the wedding you deserve, and the wedding you want. I know you're sure about Drew, and I know Mum would have liked him too.'

'I can't, Evan, I don't want to use that money.'

'Let Mum be a part of this, please.' His voice cracked.

Marianne swallowed, lifting her face to the sky, listening to the sound of the river behind the pool, and hoping that her mum would have been happy for her. 'Then I want you to be a part of it, too.'

They drove with the windows down, the breeze beautifully cool against their cheeks and in their hair, for what seemed the first time in forever. They'd stayed an extra couple of nights around Zion National Park, enjoying the tranquillity, both reading Jack Kerouac's *On the Road* on their respective Kindles beside the pool, fingers entwined, letting themselves be still. And finally, Drew received the news he'd been waiting for that his editor loved the new draft and, apart from a few tweaks that could be dealt with when he returned, she was happy to sign off on it and release his delivery advance.

On a stop about halfway back to Las Vegas, they perched on the hood of their SUV and sipped from bottles of water, America's Wild West stretching before them.

Marianne had told Evan she'd get back to him about the money, but the more she'd thought about it, the more she thought that maybe, in fact, she *would* like to contribute some funds from her mum's inheritance towards their big, or not so big, day. It felt right. Just enough to do what they wanted. Only ... what she wanted had changed.

'What do you think?' Drew said, slinging an arm over her shoulder while they gazed at the view. 'What do we do now? We're going to have enough money to do a little road-tripping, and if you want it, we have enough money to get married.'

'You know what,' Marianne answered, choosing her words carefully. 'I was so looking forward to this US road trip. We might have a little extra in the travel fund again now, but what we don't have a lot more of on this trip is *time*. However, we do have our whole lifetimes. Being able to experience the places we've been to – San Diego, Palm Springs, not-Coachella, Joshua Tree, LA, Las Vegas and Zion – has been a wild enough ride for me this time around. Let's come back one day and do the rest of the road trip properly. Ride the streetcars in San Francisco like Maya Angelou did.'

'And visit the Steinbeck house.'

'We could even go further north, to the Portland Book Festival.'

'I like the sound of all of that,' Drew smiled. 'So, two options left. Do we fly straight home? Or do we get married first?'

'What do you want to do?'

Drew rubbed his face. 'I know I want to marry you. And this is what we've been waiting for. But it doesn't quite feel like your heart is in it any more. And that's OK, by the way.'

'My heart is *all in*, Drew, but you're right, in a way. I've not been myself, entirely, on this trip. I mean, I have – in many ways I've felt freer and more open with you than I ever have in any other relationship, but I've also been often in a strange headspace, and indecisive, and getting upset over things that would usually just slide off me. But I know what I want now. For sure.'

# Chapter 37

# Marianne, in the USA

'Shall we head back to the Strip? One last time?'

'One last spin of the wheel?' Marianne smiled at Drew. 'Maybe not literally.'

They'd been back in Las Vegas for a little under a week now, staying in a budget motel off the Strip, wrapping things up, making arrangements, gathering their funds, making *plans*. Plans that involved a beautiful island, and a lost best friend.

When Marianne had suggested to Drew that they fly not home, but to the Maldives, she'd expected him to roll his eyes, tell her that was virtually impossible, get annoyed about abandoning what little of their plans they had left. But, of course, because Drew was Drew, he had just laughed and said, 'Great! I've always wanted to go there!'

And while they were there, they would get married. Finally. In fact, she'd even researched it all during their final days in Las Vegas, to make sure there were no surprises, and it turned out they would have to pop to a registry office when they made it back to the UK to make it legal, but that was fine, they could still exchange their vows and have a symbolic ceremony on a beautiful, breezy beach. As long as the reunion with Jenny went well, that was, and she didn't want to book the ceremony until she knew that, but she'd called the resort and queried availability at short notice, and had been told they were sure they could accommodate something small if she was willing to forego the usual full wedding package.

Walking down South Las Vegas Boulevard again, the section known as the Strip, felt a little like coming home, and that feeling made her sizzle like sunshine. Las Vegas might not be where she and Drew had ended up getting married, but it was where they had truly fallen in love, falling into one another completely.

Thanks to their breather in Zion National Park, the neon lights felt magical again, twinkling and buzzing like fireflies now they walked under the early evening desert sky. The air was warm, but no longer felt stifling. The partygoers were wild and everywhere, but it didn't bother her one bit as they were just having fun. Marianne and Drew walked hand in hand, quietly drinking it all in one last time. She really would have loved a Las Vegas wedding, she had no doubt about it, so maybe she and Drew would create a little plan to come back here in five, ten, fifteen years to renew their vows instead.

It was OK that she'd grown from the person she once was. She was still herself, but she didn't need to prove it every five seconds. Owning a business, falling in love, they were risks and adventures in themselves, and shutting the door on those things wasn't going to make her live her life to the full, it would only be closing opportunities for her own happiness.

They crossed the bridge over the vast road, from New York-New York to their enchanting Excalibur, following the call of its red and blue turrets, and Marianne had to laugh when they reached the inside. 'Hey, remember when I had a meltdown and lost all our money in this casino?'

Drew chuckled. 'I'm sure losing all your money in Vegas is some kind of rite of passage.' She was about to apologise again when he saw it coming and stopped her. 'Want to lose ten more dollars?'

Pulling out his wallet, Drew reached in and took out a piece of paper, folded, with medieval print on it.

'Is that the voucher the knight gave us on one of our not quite wedding days?' Marianne asked. 'I can't believe you still have that; I'd forgotten all about it!'

'Well, despite everything, I still have fond memories of that day. At least, looking back. You looked beautiful, we were ready to get married, we took a hefty gamble, but it all worked out, we're OK now.'

They fed their voucher into the nearest slot machine – a glittering thing with flashing lights, a mural of a medieval woman, and sounds emitting from it that reminded Marianne of nineties video games.

'Here goes nothing,' she grinned at her fiancé, and they pulled the lever together.

*Rattle rattle rattle rattle bling ... bling ... bling ...* Marianne didn't know a lot about slot machines but three unmatched symbols didn't exactly scream *Jackpot!* Ah well. It was time to leave.

As they turned to walk away, Marianne heard that melody that had become so ingrained in them since they'd arrived in Las Vegas she almost didn't notice it any more. The *ding-ding-ding-ding-ding* of a payout, heightened by bells and music, only this time, it wasn't followed by the usual whoop or cheer further down the row.

She stopped, pulling Drew to a stop also, and they spun back to face their machine, which was spitting out a little slip of Excalibur paper, like a piñata.

'Was that us? Did we just win?'

'I think we did,' Drew replied.

'Did we just beat the house, like some kind of Brad Pitt and George Clooney?' she whooped, and they dived forward, grabbing for the slip and studying it. 'We won,' she whispered.

'How much?'

Marianne looked up at him, a smile spreading across her face. 'We won big, baby, don't let it go to your head.'

'*How much?*'

'Fifty dollars.'

Drew's eyes widened. 'We won fifty whole dollars? What are we going to spend it on?'

Later that night, they drove away from where they'd spent their final evening in Las Vegas. In Marianne's hands was a little piece of paper, something for which they'd exchanged their fifty dollars, plus a photo in a cardboard sleeve. Marianne kept glancing at Drew, who kept glancing at her, until she laughed and said, 'Stop it, we agreed not to talk about it!'

'I know, it's just funny that finally—'

'Shh,' she held her finger up. 'This was not it. This was just the formality.'

She wiggled her toes inside her sparkling white trainers.

# Chapter 38

# Jenny, in the Maldives

The resort directors loved Rish's ideas, and welcomed help moving Bounty Cove Cay to the forefront of high-end ecotourism. It was the clear direction they'd been leaning towards, and Khadeeja gave Rish permission to get to work immediately on increasing the island's coral-regeneration project by three hundred per cent, working with any local experts and groups he saw fit. They also loved his idea of encouraging guests to get involved, and suggested that once he was fully trained as a marine biologist, he be the one to lead the initiative.

The directors would take his other ideas forward – including the eco-retreat bungalows, and Layla's request for on-site organic produce gardens and water recycling – to the relevant stakeholders to pin down the logistics, and ask the branding and marketing departments to get to work on the new vision. And how could it not work? Khadeeja's organisation, vision and clear-headedness, combined with Rish's love for the Maldives and Layla's passion for island life, made them a perfect team.

Rish and Layla were beside themselves. Not just because of the win, but because of the real difference they would be making to the environment, and island, they both loved.

As for my library idea … I'm happy to report that Khadeeja had greenlit that too. I still had to work hard on the transformation, in not much time, to prove it was the right move, but I now felt I was halfway up the mountain again, not slipping further back to the bottom.

I was lit up like an electric eel; I was being given another chance. I sent a silent thank you to Marianne for the push I'd needed, but also because she'd rubbed off on me over all these years, and because of her I had the confidence that I could pull this off.

I worked hard, possibly harder than I ever had before, but this time I didn't doubt myself, I didn't triple-check everything; if something didn't work or didn't fit or didn't look right in my new mezzanine library, I let it go and moved on. None of that was easy, but it was what I had to do. And slowly but surely, in less than a week since I'd been given the green light, my library was open.

My custom-made Bookshop Hideaway sign was now in my bungalow, and I was going to take it home with me and hang it in my flat, even if it would cost an arm and a leg in excess baggage. The library was simply named 'Look', a play on the 'book', with an 'L' for library. It was a bit lame; the new manager could always change it if she wanted.

Tomorrow, Look was officially holding its first joint event with BountEco. Rish's author friend was coming to the island to read from his book and give a talk to guests on conservation in the Maldives. We were selling tickets, a copy of the book included in the price, with all sales going towards the author's preferred whale-shark charity. As it would take place over in the BountEco building, I was planning to spend the evening getting the area all set up and ready. But first, I had something to do.

At dusk, the sky over our island was beautiful. The sunsets were never bad here, at least in my limited experience. Even on the rainy days, the clouds seemed to crack apart as the sun went down to create great paint streaks of colour across the sky for all to see.

I walked between the overwater villas, following the snake of the pier, my shoes tapping softly beneath me. The breeze fluttered around the light fabric of my long dress, softly billowing it behind me like a train. I'd put on a little make-up, made my hair look a little more seaside chic than Shipwreck Sharlene. I felt pretty.

When I reached the To the Moon restaurant I stood for a moment, enjoying this sensation of standing at the edge of the world with only sunsets and possibility in front of me, until I heard steps approaching.

I turned around and there he was. He'd come.

'Bookshop Jenn, you look beautiful,' he smiled and it reached all the way to those eye crinkles.

'Hi, Rish.' I leaned over and kissed his cheek, happy to have found a closeness with this lovely man. Thanks to his natural sunshine, I'd found my own glow again, and felt as though I could angle my heart, and this brighter part of myself, towards the person I really wanted. Evan. I missed him.

'I'm surprised you got us reservations here,' he said. 'Sometimes even the guests struggle.'

'I didn't know if I'd get us in, I've been on a waitlist,' I explained. I glanced at him, and he seemed a little nervous, as if part of him wished he wasn't there with me. Hee hee.

This was a risk, but it felt like a risk worth taking. A risk Marianne would have taken, if it could lead to other people's happiness. Didn't she always dive in for me, too, because she knew I was too scared to?

I looked past his shoulder. One down ... and there was my one to go.

'Hi,' I grinned, stepping past Rish and pulling Layla into a hug, whispering, *'Don't kill me.'*

She narrowed her eyes at me and then said, 'Rish, hey, are you having dinner with us too?' I saw her eyes run over the smart shirt that fitted him just right, his loose tie, and then she awkwardly covered her own body with her arm, hiding the twinkling cocktail dress that made her skin glow.

I put my hand on her shoulder. 'Actually, bad news, I have to go.' I shrugged.

'But I thought we were having a fancy girls' night?' Layla asked me through gritted teeth.

I gently pushed the two of them together, putting Layla's hand against Rish's, and then nudged them towards the restaurant. 'Would you two just go and enjoy this evening together?'

'But—' Layla started, though I saw her hand staying close to Rish's, and I saw his fingers twitch towards her, making contact.

'Bye!' I called, already making my way back down the pier.

I hoped that it wasn't an unforgivably intrusive move, but they so clearly just needed to take a leap of faith and go after what they wanted. I was familiar with *that*. Besides, hadn't Layla done the same to me the night of the cinema under the stars?

Before heading over to BountEco, I decided to take a little 'me' time. I'd dolled myself up – never for Rish, this was just for me – and I got myself a takeout red-snapper taco to eat on the beach beside my bungalow. I let the lime juice and the coconut flakes drip out onto my hands and down onto my knees, happy to be alone in this moment, with only the moon for company. Then I climbed into my big turquoise hammock, in my big beautiful dress, with a really good book. It took me away in gentle sways, just like I knew it would.

A while later, I hauled my relaxed self out of the hammock and made my way back along the boardwalk, stopping in at the Pavilion to pick up the last of my boxes of books to take over, and then went on to BountEco to get everything set up.

'Hi, guys,' I whispered into the turtle tanks on my way past. 'I think things are going to get even more magical around here.'

I worked quietly, packing up the gift bags for attendees, straightening the chairs, testing the equipment. Just like I'd done for every event back at the Book Nook. I *was* good at my job, I told myself. Even when I wasn't perfect.

A noise lifted my attention, a roar and some laughter, and I went to the open back of BountEco and peered into the darkness. At first, I could see nothing, save for the glow of the overwater villas and the lights of To the Moon off to my left. The sea rippled, though, starlight dancing over the surface as if something had disturbed it.

I heard it again, and then saw them. Three jet skis vrooming into the curve of the bay, their backsides slicing through the water as one by one they'd swing to a stop before shooting off again.

What the hell were they playing at? I got that jet skis were super fun, but these were too close to the reef.

'Hey!' I shouted into the darkness. I glanced at the villas, afraid of causing a disturbance to the guests with my voice, but when the jet-ski drivers circled back around again, I knew this was too important. 'Stop! Go further out, you'll hit the reef!'

Although the riders' laughter reached me on the shore, they didn't seem to hear me over the noise of the machines. And one laugh I recognised, and it left me cold: Blane.

The coral-regeneration frames were out there, the ones that Rish and the team had been working on so carefully and had just begun to increase.

I tried to wave my arms, I dashed into the shallow water, soaking the end of my dress, in an attempt to get their attention, but it wasn't until after a *crrrunch* echoed in the air that there was silence.

'No,' I whispered.

With the engines now off, I could hear talking out on the water. I could hear Blane telling the one who'd crashed not to worry about it, that he should just hop on over to his ski and Blane would escort them both back around to the main beach, then he'd come back to sort it out.

I was waiting for him when he did.

'What have you done?' I demanded when he strolled back onto the beach behind BountEco, no more than a few minutes later.

'What the hell are you doing here? Are you spying on me?' he demanded, pulling up short, puffing out his chest and standing in a way that was meant to intimidate.

'What was that? A jet-ski joyride? You wanted to show those guests you're the big man?'

'*Pfft.*' Blane started to walk away towards the water.

'That jet ski has damaged the reef.'

'The reef here is dead anyway,' he argued.

'It's *dying*, it's not gone, and Rish and the BountEco team are working hard on restoring it. Because of you, one of our guests just killed their hard work, and part of the ecosystem itself.'

Blane paused, his hands on his hips, seemingly lost for words for a moment. I thought he was about to show some humility and admit he'd messed up, but instead he just turned and came closer to me. His face, illuminated by the moon and the soft lighting of BountEco, seemed to soften.

He flashed me a grin, the one that lacked a certain smize, that didn't really seem like a friendly grin at all.

'Jenny, you won't mention this, will you?'

'Won't I?'

'Come on, we're all on the same team here. Nobody "tells on" each other here, that would just be a really shitty thing to do.'

*What?* I was flustered, trying to make sense of this, feeling as though I was at school again with this line of argument.

'Let's call it our little secret,' he winked at me in the dark, widening his grin. 'I'll stop bugging you? I'll even promise to be extra nice to the new manager.'

Actual *ew*. I took a moment to compose myself. I didn't like to speak up, but I was braver now. It didn't matter if Blane didn't like me. 'I'm sorry – how low do you think my bar is that I'd be so grateful and give you my silence just because you say you'll stop being an asshole?'

'Come on—'

'Blane, no. This isn't about me tattling on you, it's about you just not being good for this island. Of course I'm going to say something. You're toxic, when the island wants to thrive.'

I could see the fury in his eyes. But he clearly had one more trick up his sleeve, and he strode towards me. 'Jenny, I've always admired your strength ...' He put his hands up to my cheeks and brought his face towards mine.

'Oh my fucking God, get off me!' I cried and shoved him back so hard he fell on his bottom on the sand.

As he started to rise, Layla arrived in a flash of long hair and long limbs and gave him a shove, face-planting him back in the sand.

'Layla! What are you doing here – what about your dinner?'

Rish appeared beside me, his face like thunder as he stared down at Blane, sitting mournfully in the sand, trying to spit grains out of his mouth while Layla stood over him like the Captain Marvel that she was. 'We were just finishing up and saw the jet skis bending in towards the reef, so we made our way over as soon as we could.'

'And I received a flurry of noise complaints from the guests in our Laguna Private Water Villas,' came Khadeeja's voice, and we all turned to face her where she stood, arms folded. 'I *never* want to receive complaints, let alone because of something a member of our staff has done.'

Blane sprang up. 'Khad, I told Jenny to stop shouting—'

'It's Khadeeja,' she corrected him. 'And I heard your whole exchange, so stop wasting my time. This happened on your watch, because of your arrogance. Your recklessness has damaged our ecosystem, and the worst thing is that you knew it could happen when you came over here with the jet skis, but your pride and ego were more important. Jenny is right, you don't fit here any more, Blane. Consider yourself fired.'

# Chapter 39

# The Maldives

The event at BountEco with Rish's author friend went extremely well, despite the drama of the night before. It was popular with the resort's guests, and many of them stayed behind long after to explore the centre and chat more to him, and to Rish and the other conservationists.

Blane left the island later that day, Layla having the pleasure of flying him away herself, and Rish was promoted to Head of Ecological Activities and Entertainment.

The part of the reef the jet ski had hit was damaged, badly, and we were all sad about that, and about losing the work Rish and the team had put in with their regeneration kits. But they moved straight into restoring what they could, and it didn't bring them down. Pretty inspiring.

By the following morning, I was desperate to meet up with Layla to find out how she and Rish's date had gone, but the library was proving popular, so it would have to wait until after my work was done for the day.

It was nearly lunchtime when my paradise pieced itself together in a way that made me beyond happy and full of gratitude. I was behind the counter in Look, sipping on some of the delicious new mango iced tea brewed by one of the Palms' restaurant chefs, who had also loaned me a crystal drinks dispenser until my newly ordered recycled glass ones arrived. There was nobody browsing in the library for the first time that day, a group having just left after borrowing a big stack of summer romance books between them and saying they were off to get some cocktails to go with them. I recommended they ask Dan, the bartender, to whip them up an I Capture the Cosmopolitan.

I heard footsteps coming up the staircase and readied my smile, keen for someone to have a glass of the iced tea so I wouldn't drink it all myself and then need to leave my post for a wee.

'Here it is.' I heard a voice that made my heart stop. Why was it so familiar? My mind rattled through the voices I associated with being here: Khadeeja, Layla, Sadeera ... No, no, no, it couldn't be ...

'Marianne?' Was that really her, or was there something in this iced tea? I stood up – and there she was. My best friend, here, in the Maldives, standing in my library as if we were in our own bookshop back home.

'Hi, Jenn,' she smiled.

There were about three seconds of shock before we ran to each other with open arms and streaming eyes.

Through tears, I babbled, 'You're here! You're not in America!'

'Apparently so,' she choked back at me. 'And you're crying – what's going on? You're too sensible to cry.'

'This is all good crying, right?' a voice said behind Marianne and I pulled back to see Drew, who gave me a wave.

'Oh, Drew, you came too.' This set me off again, for God's sake. 'What are you both doing here?'

When we'd slightly pulled ourselves together, Marianne asked, 'Do you take a lunch break?'

'Yes, I do. The library closes for an hour, in about twenty minutes.'

'Wait – library? Wasn't this supposed to be a bookshop?'

'I'll tell you all about it over lunch.'

'OK. Mind if we look around?'

I gestured wildly. 'Please do! Have a drink! Enjoy the books! Oh, hello, how may I help you?' I smiled at an incoming customer while quickly wiping my eyes.

For the next twenty minutes, as people came and went, I couldn't stop glancing at Marianne. She looked mega-tanned and her hair had lighter, sun-kissed streaks running through it. She had freckles, which always came out in the summer, but against the tan and lighter hair they seemed even stronger. Her eyes sparkled whenever she and Drew spoke to each other, and I wondered how I could ever have doubted them as a couple when they seemed so at one with each other.

When lunchtime came, Drew made his excuses, saying he was off to check into their room. 'There are about a million dishes I want you to try here – what would you like?' I asked Marianne.

'I want one of those fish tacos you're always putting on Instagram – yes, I have been Insta-stalking you – and I want to sit on the beach and feel the ocean breeze. Please.'

'Are you sure you don't want to sit in a restaurant? You must have just travelled a long way. The à la carte here is good.'

'No more big meals in restaurants.' Marianne laughed and rubbed her stomach. 'Well, at least until tomorrow.' She studied me. 'You look really well, Jenn. I haven't seen you this relaxed in a long time.'

I brushed her off. 'Believe me, I've still been the tightly wound Jenn you know so well for a lot of the time.'

'Maybe,' she answered. 'But there's something about you … You look like you're enjoying the challenges again, and enjoying the sunshine.'

'I am enjoying the slowing down,' I admitted. 'They say a change is as good as a rest, and I think I've been learning how to appreciate both. How long are you here for?' I asked. We grabbed the tacos and settled onto a quiet bit of the beach, under the shade of a coconut palm.

'Maybe about four nights. This place is expensive.' She laughed. 'Plus, I promised Evan I'd be back home by mid-June to relieve him of his duties, just in time for the summer events programme.'

'I would have come to you; I *should* have come to you.'

'No, I wanted us to come here. It seemed like the perfect next stop on our trip. Albeit a pretty convoluted one, getting here from Las Vegas. Besides, there's a bookshop, or library, here that I was dying to check out.'

I smiled and munched on my taco for a minute. 'Thank you for coming. You have no idea how good it is to see your face.'

'You too.' She spotted me looking at her finger for a second ring beside her engagement one. 'It didn't happen.'

'It didn't?'

'Not yet. We are getting married, though, you know. Drew and I are very much getting married.' She stuck her chin in the air as a final whisper of defiance. 'But I'm just not doing it without you.'

'Oh, thank God. I'm sorry I—'

She stopped me. 'No more sorries, and no regrets. We both said and did some silly things, but it's all in the past and I think we can be stronger now, right? Remember that feeling we had when school finished, and we had so much love in our hearts for each other, for our friends, and we felt unbreakable because we'd all experienced the last, big, scary, transformative, wonderful, crazy years together? That's still how we are. No matter what happens, we're family, we're linked, and it doesn't matter where we are in the world or what jobs we do or how old or young we are. Can't break us up.'

Marianne stood, brushing the sand off her lap, and gestured for me to stand too. She then knelt down on one knee, and I put my hand over my mouth.

'So I came all the way here, my dear friend Jenny, to this very hard-to-reach, but very perfect wedding paradise island in the Maldives, to ask if you would do me the honour of being my bridesmaid?'

'What? Here?'

'Yes. Ish. It's actually not legal for us to get married in the Maldives, but we can still have a vow ceremony, apparently, and then we just do the legal bit at home.'

'Hey, look who did her research!' I cried, impressed.

'All right, all right, is that a yes or not?' Marianne pinched my leg from where she was still on the ground.

'Yes, I would love to be your bridesmaid. A thousand times yes!'

In the words of someone very wise and close to me, there's no point in living life by some kind of imaginary rule book, so why the hell wouldn't we plan to have the wedding the following day? As soon as I got back from lunch, I called Khadeeja to tell her my friends had arrived and asked if there was any way I could arrange a super-small ceremony for my day off tomorrow. She said it was fine, and even graciously gave a discounted rate for Marianne and Drew. That evening, I raced to Marianne's room straight from work to tell her the good news, and we spent a while making plans, and I finally got to know Drew better, hearing all about their wild misadventures in Las Vegas and beyond.

'Oh, you know what's on this evening, if we hurry?' I said, checking my watch. 'The *Boduberu* performance on the beach. It's really great, and I know one of the drummers.'

Marianne raised her eyebrows. 'Making friends with the boys in the band, are ya?'

'It's not like that,' I said. 'He's taken, I hope ...'

We settled down at the side of the beach, even though I told Marianne and Drew they were proper, paying guests and were perfectly entitled to sit front and centre on the beanbags.

'Nope. I've been front and centre of a lot of action recently. Watching from the sidelines suits me just fine if you're here too.'

'We never threw you a hen do!' I suddenly cried, just as the group of men appeared and one lifted his shirt to mop his brow before banging a hand on his drum.

'No, this is brilliant,' she whispered, swirling her cocktail in her glass.

We watched the first half of the performance and I felt a swell of pride at how enthralled Marianne, and Drew, seemed. This, in a way, felt like I was showing them my island, and I wanted them to love every second here.

When the dancing and drums came to an elaborate flourish, signalling the end of the first half, I jumped up to try and catch a word with Rish during the break. 'I'll just be one second,' I said to Marianne and Drew.

'Hey.' I caught him by the arm, and he swung round so hard I nearly got thumped in the stomach with his drum.

'Bookshop Jenn!' he cried, pulling me into a one-armed hug and keeping the drum away from me this time.

'Finally, I want to know what happened!'

'When? With who? Just now? Who are your friends?'

'You know what I'm talking about,' I hissed.

'Oh, you mean the other night? When you ran out on our date? Well, I cried of course, Layla had to console me, the guests complained, it was a whole thing.'

'It was not, you idiot. What happened? Was Layla mad?'

'That you set us up? At first ...'

Uh-oh.

He continued. 'But then we *talked* ...'

'You talked? Hallelujah! Please tell me it wasn't just about work.'

'Nope, we did a lot of talking, about us, and then,' he leaned in close to me, that happy grin inches from my face, 'she let me kiss her.'

'SHUT. THE. FRONT. DOOR!' I screeched, banging his drum with my palm in excitement.

'Shhh,' he laughed, angling his drum away.

'So are you a couple now? Finally?'

'Let's not rush things, you know.' He became serious for a moment. 'How did you know, though? Before either of us even really knew?'

I tried to find the words, and catch them, before the dusting of sadness within me settled upon them and they came out coated. 'Because of the way you looked at her. And how she looked at you. I think someone looked at me like that once and I let it go because I was too afraid.'

'Afraid of what?'

'The risks, you know. Things not working out, not being able to predict the ending, getting hurt, hurting other people I loved ...' My eyes glanced at Marianne before I could stop them. She had forgiven me once. Would she ever forgive me for secretly falling for her brother? 'And you did know, you just hadn't admitted it to yourselves yet. I get that. As a very risk-averse person, I get the idea of self-preservation like you wouldn't believe.' He danced into my head again, Evan, like he always had.

Rish pulled me from my thoughts. 'I have to get back to it now, but we'll catch up soon, right?' He grinned and ran back across the sand, and I joined Marianne and Drew once again, shuffling close to her as I sat down.

'This is magical,' she whispered as the group were getting ready. 'Not just the music, but all of this, being on this island, being with you. Am I actually getting married tomorrow?'

'Yes,' I replied.

'Because I've been in this position several times over the past month ...'

'But now you have me to help make it happen.'

After the *Boduberu* party was over, there would be the monthly fireworks and dancing on the beach tonight. The sky was dark, other than a few mauve edges around the lowest clouds, and we rose from the sand and dusted ourselves off.

'You must be shattered after all your travel,' I said to my friends. 'Do you want to stay out or just catch up on sleep before the big day?'

Marianne stifled a yawn. 'No time to sleep.'

'This is Bounty Cove Cay,' I said. 'Relaxing *is* the aim of the game here.'

There was a high-pitched whistle followed by a burst of twinkling blue lights overhead from the first of the fireworks, and we all looked up and gasped, Marianne's arm linked with mine.

'Jenn?'

I turned from the fireworks to see Layla a few metres behind me, barefoot on the sand. She was in her skipper's uniform, and in the light of the torch flames I could see she was smiling.

'Hey, Layla, come and meet Marianne.'

'I will, soon,' she said.

'Oh my God,' Marianne gasped beside me, her voice cracking. I looked at her and a pop and fizzle of showering sparkles from overhead illuminated the tears that filled her eyes.

'What's wrong?' I asked.

'You came?' Marianne ignored me and asked Layla.

I turned, confused, until I noticed the shadowy figure standing beside my favourite island friend.

My breath stopped at the sight of Evan, here on my beach.

'Turns out I couldn't miss my sister's wedding,' he said, and then turned to me. 'Hey, you.'

'Heaven.' I breathed aloud. I meant to say 'Hey, Evan,' but I don't think anyone noticed.

I stepped towards him and he smiled, stepping closer to me too. What was happening? Was he here just for Marianne, or also for me? I didn't know the right moves, couldn't find the right words, but we still seemed to be getting closer to each other.

'I hope you don't mind that I'm here,' he said, not taking his eyes off me, and I realised he was still looking at me the way I remembered, despite all this time and all these miles.

'I don't mind one bit,' I replied, and I didn't wait any longer to take my risk. I reached for him, and he closed the gap between us, cupping my face in his hands, and kissed me like we were castaways.

Until Marianne's voice pierced through the fireworks. 'Ex*cuse* me?'

# Chapter 40

# The Maldives

Oops. Evan and I broke away from each other's lips and slowly turned to where Marianne was standing with her jaw in the sand, Drew was looking confused and Layla was looking between us and them, wondering what the problem was.

'Mari—' I started, but she cut me off, turning blazing eyes onto me.

'That did not look like a first kiss.'

'No ...' Oh God. 'I didn't want you to find out like this, we were going to tell you, but it happened just before I left—'

Marianne cut me off again, turning to her brother. 'What are your intentions with my best friend?'

Evan looked between the two of us, as if deciding what would be the best approach here. 'Um ...'

'She's not a toy, Evan. She's never been in love, you know. She's barely had a proper boyfriend.'

'Thanks, Mari,' I interjected.

She continued, pointing at her brother. 'Are you just having some fun with her?'

'No,' he said, and then he looked back at me. '*No.*'

'So, what is it? What's been going on?'

Time to be brave. I put my hand on her arm, moving away from Evan. 'It was a surprise to me too when this started, but a good surprise. We didn't say anything because, well, it literally happened when I was walking out the door, so we didn't really say a lot to each other about our feelings – is that fair?' I asked him.

'Yeah,' Evan agreed.

'The timing was kind of off. But for me,' I took a deep breath, 'Evan feels like everything, even when we're apart, even without me really realising what he means to me.'

Turning back to Evan, I shrugged. 'Sorry, but it's true. If that's not how you feel, then I'll deal with that.'

'Well?' Marianne prompted, her hands on her hips, glaring at her brother. 'What about you, numbskull, is she your everything?' Evan was about to reply to her when Marianne gestured to me. 'Tell *her.*'

Evan's eyes reflected the fireworks just like they had the sunsets at home; they were full of a warm fire I wanted with me all the time. He moved closer to me, slowly, slowly, forming his words.

'Every night you were away I thought about you. I kept a clock with the time in the Maldives in my room so I could imagine when you were waking up. So I could imagine keeping you warm if you were cool in the evenings. So I could imagine bringing you a drink as you worked hard, squinting over your laptop.'

I gulped. I'd never had anybody say things like that to me like before, and I suspected from the way his nerves were betraying him he'd never said them either. I was about to interject when he continued, taking my face in his hands like we were the only ones there, and looking down at me with those gold-flecked eyes.

'When I was out on the waves, I'd sit for hours just because being in the ocean made me feel like we weren't as far away from each other. And I'm glad you followed this adventure, but I'm still hoping you'll want to drift back towards me one day.'

I felt everything all at once, from the skin on my neck glittering against his touch to the soft ripples of the sand under my feet. Waves and whispers, fireworks and eyelashes, I brought my face close to him and told him, 'I never really drifted away.'

My morning view was a little different when I opened my eyes on my best friend's wedding day. Here I was in my bungalow, and beyond the transparent frosting of the mosquito net the walls were still white, the low Maldives sunshine already seeping in and creating pools of sunlight on my floor. The air was scented like coconuts, as it always was. The trees nearby creaked in the soft breeze with the sound of waking wildlife, as they always did. But inside my canopy, I wasn't alone. I had Evan with me.

Last night had been … well, you know that Katy Perry song 'Teenage Dream'? It was like that. Over ten years of feelings rose out of me and I kissed Evan like I'd always wanted to, all the way back to my bungalow. We undressed each other and though I'd seen the bare skin of his chest a hundred times, being close to it felt like the fusion I had always known needed to happen. And he seemed totally wrapped up in me, too, thankfully.

Anyway. I woke up pretty satisfied.

I liked watching his chest rise and fall, his breathing slow and in time with the gentle dawn waves beyond the window. I liked following the lines of his face, drinking him in. I liked that, like Rish, he had small crinkles at the corners of his eyes. I liked waking up next to him.

It turned out that Evan had spent the whole ferry ride over asking Layla questions about me, about my time here, about how happy I was, until she'd eventually asked him if he was some kind of stalker and he'd told her that no, his sister was my best friend, and that she and her fiancé had flown out in the hope of having a small wedding ceremony on the island. And the Book Nook on the Beach back home was closed – just temporarily, no more than a handful of days – until Marianne and Drew would be flying back. And you know what? That was fine with me.

He stirred, and I couldn't help smiling, but I closed my eyes, so he didn't feel self-conscious about being stared at in his slumber, like I knew I would.

I felt his fingers on my face, brushing at my hair. 'Wakey, wakey, beach babe,' he whispered, and when I looked up at him, he said, 'I feel like I'm in a Bounty advert.'

'Wait until you taste the coconuts,' I replied, and then wanted to bury my head in the sand at how whoppingly euphemistic that sounded.

He sat up, the canopy too low for his tall frame, looking around at his surroundings. 'Is the beach really right out there? And this is where you've been living?'

He had arrived at night, so he was waking up to morning in paradise. 'Yep, you want to have an explore?'

'Definitely. And a dip.'

'If you're up for it, I know a good way to combo the two things ...'

I was going to miss starting my day like this, so much. I tried not to think about my time here coming to an end – I still had a little over two weeks, and come on now, isn't it the exact opposite of living in the present to keep imagining how sad you'll be in the future not to be here, right now?

I was sitting on my paddleboard, my legs either side, dangling in the already warm Indian Ocean. Before me was my island, my paradise, and to my right, standing on his own board without a hint of a wobble, moving in circles, was my man. And to top it off, today my best friend in the world was getting married, and I was lucky enough to be a part of it.

Because of it being so last-minute, Bounty Cove Cay had arranged for the ceremony to be not on the main beach, but in the outer corner of the island beside the bungalows, which I actually thought was pretty perfect. It would remain quiet and intimate around there, especially at the time they'd squeezed us in, which was going to be shortly after sunset, when most guests had migrated to the restaurants, but the sky would be that beautiful cotton-candy pink and baby blue.

This meant that Marianne and I had the whole of my day off together to prepare, and I was going to start by using my employee discount to treat her to every spa treatment under the Maldivian sun (that had availability).

After paddleboarding, I stole my visitors for a breakfast of tropical fruits, fresh coconut water and *mas huni*, and then Drew and Evan took themselves off to explore while I spent some long-needed quality time with Marianne.

'You're not mad about me and Evan?' I asked for the millionth time, while we had a couple's massage overlooking the ocean.

'No. Surprised, though I don't know why because you always fancied him, but I'm not mad. I'm actually happy for you about all of this, believe it or not. Even when I was angry at you, I was still happy you were finally taking some time to live your life.'

'Thank you,' I said, reaching out for her hand but accidentally grazing the hip of the masseuse.

'Everything OK?' She lifted her head to look at me and the masseuse gently pushed it back down.

'Yes, just a little worried about the library. I'm hoping I've done enough.'

'You've done everything you can to give it life, now you just have to let it breathe. If it fails, it fails. The point is you tried, you took a risk, you had an experience and an adventure, and that's what you wanted, wasn't it? Really?'

That is what I'd wanted, she was right. 'I'm so glad you're here,' I said, by way of reply. 'But let's not talk about work any more. This is your wedding day, Mari!'

'I think it actually is this time, you know!' she said, with a laugh. 'About bloody time!'

'I don't know,' Marianne said, turning this way and that in the mirror, nerves in her voice trying to stay hidden. 'It seemed so right in Vegas, but here ... I feel a bit like I might blind you and Evan while you're watching the ceremony.'

She went to the window, where the sun was streaming in, and shimmied to show how she lit up like a disco ball in her short, sequinned wedding dress.

'I see what you mean, but it does look comfy, and nice and cool in this heat.'

'Oh, it is that. I stomped a two-hour walk back through the desert, from our demolished chapel to our castle hotel, in this thing.'

'How about ...' Leaving my thought dangling, I left the bungalow with a cry of 'Give me ten minutes!' and reappeared shortly afterwards to find her still in the sequinned wedding dress but lying in my hammock.

'Oops,' said Marianne. 'I was doing my make-up but just fell in.'

'All right, how about wrapping this around your waist over the sequin dress, keeping it loose and open at the front to make it one of those kind of long-short dresses?' I held out a sarong I'd just purchased from the gift shop, in the palest of blues with white turtle silhouettes printed on the fabric. 'I know it's not quite the right colour, but you know, "something blue" and all that. Plus, it was made here in the Maldives, so that could maybe count as "something borrowed"?'

'Actually, I love the pale blue.' Marianne admired it, lost in thought for a moment. Then she added with a smile, 'So creative.'

'I learned from the best.'

I watched her wrap the sarong around herself, and then tuck the pink rose I'd found for her into her hair. She looked beautiful.

'Now listen,' I said. 'If this isn't what you want to wear I'll see what I can do. I was also thinking that maybe we should pre-plan something for after, like a restaurant reservation, or—'

'Jenny,' she stopped me.

'I just want it to be perfect,' I said, knowing that voice.

'It already is, to me. And if it isn't to anyone else, then who cares? Who needs perfect? Let it go, and let's enjoy ourselves.'

Let it go. She was right. I'd nearly slipped back into old ways there and was being taken away from the moment. Still, I hoped she liked the wedding we'd pulled together for her. Being so last-minute, it wasn't quite going to be the all-out ceremony that Bounty Cove Cay would usually put on, but thanks to a few favours I'd pulled in, I thought it was going to be quite lovely.

When the sun dipped below the horizon, I popped out from my bungalow to check on the set-up happening on the beach, leaving Marianne alone for a moment.

Layla, being quite the jack of all trades, was going to be acting as the celebrant for the service, taking the happy couple through their vows and pronouncing them (not quite legally, but very much so in their hearts) man and wife. Rish would be on hand to play a traditional rhythmic beat on his *Boduberu* drum while the couple walked down the aisle, which was marked out with a scattering of pink rose petals, towards the palm-branch archway. Two white seats had been brought over for me and Evan to sit on.

As requested, Rish and Layla had drawn a big heart in the sand with Marianne and Drew's initials inside, just beyond the altar at the tip of the sandbank. And either side, also stencilled in the sand, were the names of both the mother of the groom and the mother of the bride. I knew Marianne would curse me for making her well up before she even reached her husband-to-be, but it felt right to have her mum here, beside her daughter.

I gave Layla and Rish a thumbs up, before scuttling back to my bungalow. Drew and Evan were getting ready in Rish's bungalow, and I rapped on the door on my way past.

'Hi, are you two nearly ready?' I asked, when Evan opened the door. He looked great in his cream shirt and linen trousers, but there wasn't time for ogling right now.

Drew appeared at the door and pulled me into a hug, which was so sweet and surprising I almost unleashed a few unexpected tears, again, but I pulled myself together and went to fetch his bride.

'Are we good to go?' I asked Marianne, coming in the room.

'I think so,' she answered. 'Am I doing the right thing?'

'Yes, of course.' I pulled her up from where she was sitting on my bed. 'Come on. God, you're always so scared of everything.'

My favourite part of watching my best friend's wedding (not the movie) was how they both couldn't stop catching giggles from each other throughout the whole thing, which kept setting Layla off, then me, and then the whole cycle would start again. How happy I was for her to know she'd found someone who made her laugh like that.

My second favourite part was sitting with my hand laced in Evan's, out here in the open, feeling unsure about what our future might bring but so excited to find out.

The ceremony drew to a close with Rish handing them each a fresh coconut, the tops lopped off by his own hands, which they were told to drink from, and then from each other's.

Marianne was in love, she was happy, and with Drew I felt as though I was seeing her build bricks of feeling and family again. I wish I'd never doubted them, but that was in the past. If she hadn't been busy smooching her new husband right now, Marianne would have told me to live in the present.

On that edge of sand, as the stars woke up and took their seats in the night sky, Rish propped his smartphone at the base of the coconut palm and the six of us danced at Marianne's wedding reception to a playlist of wedding classics. And it was paradise.

'Jenn? We've got something to confess,' Marianne said, just as we were all getting sleepy at the end of the night. She pulled out a cardboard sleeve, which I opened to see a photo of her and Drew leaning on the bonnet of a car, under an archway of neon bulbs that read *Welcome to the Little White Chapel Tunnel of Love*.

'What's this?' I asked.

Marianne took a breath. 'You know how we said the wedding here in the Maldives wasn't technically legally binding, so we'd need to pop to a registry office when we got back to the UK?'

'Yes ... ?'

'Well, that was all true, at least it was the plan, but on our last night in Vegas, since we had our licence and our flights out here booked, and all that ...' she looked at Drew, '... we thought we'd do the legal bit there and then.'

Drew cut in. 'But Mari made us swear that after the drive-through ceremony we were not to speak of it until after this ceremony, because she wouldn't consider herself married until after she'd done it here, with you.'

I started to laugh. 'Wait, so you're one hundred per cent properly married now?'

'Legally binding, bitch!' Marianne cried.

This was fantastic news. Weren't we all full of exciting little secrets to share, and didn't that make us all infinitely more interesting?

# Chapter 41

# The Maldives

I had to go back to work the following morning, so I left the happy couple, and Evan, in the capable hands of the best entertainment manager I knew, Rish, who would make sure they had a good time until I was done for the day.

It was a hot one out, and the library was busy today, with so many guests milling in and out, escaping the midday heat, that at first I didn't even notice Khadeeja walk up the stairs to the mezzanine.

'So, this is it,' she said to somebody beside her.

'Oh, I love it,' the woman enthused, and that's what made me look over from where I was helping a customer who loved historical romance find the next bodice-ripper to devour.

I tried to focus, but I could hear the mystery woman pattering away about all the things she liked about the space, and even better, I could hear Khadeeja agreeing with her compliments.

As soon as I could, I walked over. 'Good morning, ladies, may I get you a glass of iced tea while you browse?'

'Yes, please,' said the woman. 'You must be Jenny?'

I shook her hand, taking in her smiley face and her smart casual dress the colour of papaya and patterned with a turtle print similar to the one on Marianne's sarong. I liked her; she seemed sunny and nice.

Khadeeja said, 'Jenny, this is Aishath, she'll be managing Look from the start of next season.'

My heart stopped for a moment. Did that mean … ? As usual, Khadeeja had her poker face on, but the fact that Aishath had made the trip over here was surely a good sign.

I stopped gawping and beamed at Aishath. 'Hi, Aishath, welcome to Look, the new library at Bounty Cove Cay!'

'I love what you've done. How gorgeous to be working up here with this view,' she said, gesturing to the panorama of pool and beach and sea and sky before us.

'Thank you, it's been a challenge, but I hope it's been of some help. And I hope you don't mind running a library instead of a shop.'

'For sure. I'm really looking forward to taking this on, I think I can make it shine.'

'Actually, could I ask you a question?' I said. I wasn't sure how Khadeeja would feel about this, but I *was* sure it wouldn't do any harm now, at least not to Aishath and the library.

'Of course,' Aishath replied.

'Do you have any ideas for events the library could hold during this high season? I'd love to hear them – we both would, I expect.'

'I do, actually,' she beamed. 'I've been thinking about this. Creative-writing workshops, perhaps a writer in residence down the line ... I was thinking we could market the events through literary channels, too. I've been organising some information on those I could contact. But I've never held an event before. Perhaps I could email you some questions and some ideas and you could leave me with some tips on how I could get started?'

She was going to be great. 'Yes, I'd love to. The ideas don't come too naturally to me, I've come to accept that about myself, but for the execution I'm your girl.'

They left soon after, but not before Khadeeja had whispered to me, 'Could you pop to my office at the end of the day? I know you have your friends visiting, but this won't take long.'

I hoped it was good news and that she wasn't mad about me admitting my failings to the new literary manager. But it was too late now. Whatever happened, happened.

As requested, I found myself back in Khadeeja's office again for the third time in just over a fortnight. I hadn't had a lot of time to pull together figures, but I was armed with anecdotal evidence to support my case, should she say the library was going to close.

'Aishath seems lovely,' I said, taking a seat in front of Khadeeja's big white desk. Small talk was not my forte, so as nervous as I was, I hoped we'd get right into it so I could stop squirming.

'She is, she's going to be a great addition to the resort.'

'Does that mean ... ?'

Khadeeja smiled at me, a smile of genuine warmth, and I nearly fell off her fancy chair in relief. 'Yes, we're going to keep the library open. Good job, Jenny.'

'I'm sorry I wasn't as good as you'd hoped,' I said. God, I was such a Brit sometimes.

'You *were* good,' Khadeeja said, firmly but kindly. 'You just took a little while to show me your magic. I was hard on you, I know, but that's because I'm actually quite a bookworm, so I had a vested interest in making this work.'

'This opportunity has been ...' I struggled to find the words. 'More than you could know. I know I was brought on board to launch a new store, but I feel like I've learned so much too. I've relaunched myself, in a way.' I laughed at my own joke, so at least one of us did.

'I'm glad,' said Khadeeja. 'And I'm glad I hired you. Perhaps you could provide vacation cover for Aishath.'

I thought she was joking about that, but it didn't matter. She was glad she'd hired me. That was music to my ears. Not everything had gone perfectly or according to my careful plans, but actually, that was OK.

With the library, I felt as though I was leaving my mark on this island, in a small way. It wouldn't have been possible had Rish and Layla not put themselves forward to help elevate the ecotourism idea, or without Khadeeja's support, or Marianne's advice. I was lucky to work among people who could bring out the best qualities in each other.

Khadeeja stood up. 'Right, you aren't going anywhere yet, so let's keep up this good streak for the next couple of weeks, all right?'

'Yes, absolutely, for sure.' I got up and grabbed my bag while she led me to the door.

As soon as Khadeeja's office door closed behind me, I did a happy dance right there in the corridor.


A couple of days later, it was time for Marianne and Drew to head home.

'You're finally married now – don't you want to take a honeymoon? You could stay here a while longer?' I asked, sitting in their Island Paradise Villa at the back of the island while they packed up their last few belongings.

'We've had enough of a honeymoon to last us a while, to be honest. We're going to head home. Our home. Drew's going to move in with me when we get back, and stay a while, and what an adventure that will be.' Marianne winked at me. 'Besides, I have a bookshop to get back to, you know, you lazy cow.'

'Ha ha.'

'You, however, should take a week off.'

'I've been off for three months!'

'But soon you're going to be done working here and you should take some time *off* off. Doctor's orders. Besides, Evan flew all the way out here, so do this for him. I know he's my annoying older brother, but you seem to like him, so why don't the two of you fly over to Sri Lanka or something? That's pretty close.'

'I don't know ...'

'All right, well you make a few spreadsheets about the whole situation and then decide,' she teased. 'I think we're ready to go.'

'Do you like my hat?' Drew asked all of a sudden, pulling on a garish baseball cap covered in gold dice and red diamanté.

'It's very nice,' I laughed.

'New author photo?' He left the room ahead of Marianne and me, chuckling to himself, and we walked arm in arm to the jetty where they were going to take the ferry back towards the airport.

'We do work well together, don't we?' I said to Marianne. 'I'm sorry for trying to change you. I think you're just brilliant as you are.'

'Pfft, nobody can change me,' she grinned back, and then added. 'Back atcha, though. I do think we work well together, in business and in life, partly because we aren't striving to be the same person. If I wasn't me, I would never have had some of these amazing, scary, beautiful mishaps. I wouldn't have found myself partying near Coachella, or risking roulette in Vegas, or climbing almost to a summit in Zion. I wouldn't have seen a chapel get imploded or walked two hours through the desert heat in a wedding dress and trainers. I like spending time with me. But spending a lot of time with me sure as hell makes me appreciate all you do for me. Without you I wouldn't have been able to start a business or even have the opportunity to do all these things. I wouldn't have the know-how to keep a bookshop running. I wouldn't have a family to be the protective walls for me to climb, if you weren't here.'

'Oh, Mari ...'

'And you, if you weren't the goal-oriented, skilled, strong, determined idealist you are, you wouldn't have applied for that role. I certainly couldn't have managed it. I know you were nervous, but you knew you could do it all along. There was no way you would ever have quit on yourself. In short, thank you for being my bridesmaid, and my best friend,' Marianne said, pulling me into an enormous hug.

'Thank you for being you!' I said.

'You make me grow,' she added, with a fond look and a quick nudge.

'You make me brave,' I replied, meaning it. 'Oh, Lordy, are the tears coming again? What's wrong with us?'

'We'll be back in Blighty soon, with our stiff upper lips, and everything will be back to normal.'

But we both knew that wasn't true. This break, from the shop, and from each other, had changed both of us. Where before we'd got locked inside our own personalities and lost sight of the strengths we'd always loved in each other, now we had opened the window again.

I saw now how being a little more spontaneous, and saying a few more yeses, could open up possibilities I'd only dreamed about before. I would never not be a careful planner, but maybe I could complement it from now on by living a little.

No, things wouldn't be 'back to normal', they'd be better.

*

When they'd gone, I went to find Evan before heading back to work.

I collapsed into his arms. 'I feel quite blue.'

'I know,' he said. 'It's going to be hard leaving here, isn't it? This life suits you.'

I was glad he got it. It wasn't that I didn't want to go home. It was just that I didn't want home to be so far away from *this* home.

Evan kissed my forehead and I looked at him, all beachy and tousled, like I'd always known him, really. 'I didn't know how things would pan out with Mari and Drew, so I didn't book my return flight. Shall I stay until you're finished and travel back with you?'

I felt I should jump at the chance, because I didn't want him to go, but ...

This was my time, and I needed to protect it, and if he felt how I thought he felt – if he was the same Evan who'd encouraged me to take this leap earlier in the year – he would know that wasn't a bad thing. 'Thank you. But I started this on my own, I think I need to finish it on my own.'

*Goodbye, my island,* I thought, taking a final lap around the boardwalk, trying hard to imprint every tree, every curve of the beach, every grain of sand into my memory. Three months had gone too fast, but now it was time to go. I'd accepted it, but I was going to miss it every day.

'If you and Rish get married, you'll invite me, right?' I asked Layla as we walked the jetty to her seaplane one last time, that topaz water all around me.

'Whoa, it took us seven years just to get together, let's not rush things.'

'He said something similar – you two *are* a good match.'

As we boarded the plane, I whipped my head back round to take it all in, feeling that warm Maldives breeze on my face, and inhaling the scent of coconut and pink roses that had followed me here.

'Are you ready?' Layla's voice came through my earphones once I was settled.

'No,' I replied, my voice shaking.

'You'll be back, you know,' she said. 'Just as soon as you need a rest and to slow down a little, you can come back to Bounty Cove Cay. You'll always have a home here. And you can stay with me, so you won't need to pay the huge resort prices, ha ha.'

With that I felt myself tip back as the seaplane lifted itself into the air. As we were swept away on the Maldivian breeze, I watched my little glowing diamond island until it became part of a cluster of glitter in the ocean below me, never taking my eyes off it. I was heartbroken to leave, but it felt good to use my heart.

'Is he going to meet you at the airport?' Layla asked through my headset.

'Yes,' I said. Evan had respected my wishes and gone on ahead of me a few days earlier. It was nice to know that somebody else was going to be taking the lead in the planning and decision-making for a week. I could just relax and enjoy our time in Sri Lanka. Rish had given me some great tips for what to see and where to go. I'd miss him, my friend.

Knowing I'd be seeing Evan again soon, really soon, made this ending a little easier, because my new beginning was rising over the horizon, as slow and warm and unpredictably colourful as the Maldives sunrise.

# Acknowledgements

Hello and welcome back from your Maldivian island paradise and from road-tripping around the USA – how was your vacation?

On our descent back to reality, I'd like to say a few thank-yous. Feel free to grab a small bag of peanuts.

Huge island-sized thank-yous to the Penguin Random House team behind this novel. To Sonny, thank you for your vision and enthusiasm, and I hope we get to share some of those book-themed cocktails soon. Emily and Katie, thank you millions for your happy help and motivation. Extra dollops of thank-you to Caroline for the cracking copy-edit, Laurie for the perfect patience with me at proof stage, Darren for the marvellous Maldivian map, Joanna and Emma for the gorgeous illustration and book cover, Laura and Georgia for the sparkling publicity and Hope for being my marketing queen.

Thank you to Hannah and the Hardman & Swainson team for always being massive supports and absolute legends. Can I suggest Las Vegas for the next party? Just an idea …

Thank you, Phil, for calming me the hell down at the top of Angels Landing (and many, many other times). And thank you Kodi for being very cool and brilliant.

Thank you to my family and friends who listen to me bang on about new locations every time I write a book. Thank you, lovely, lovely Mum and Dad, Mary and David, P, L, B, R, J, R, E, P.

Thank you, Katie and Ross, for all the fun adventures in the USA that we've had over the years, and I hope we can have many more together soon.

Thank you, Al and Helen, for your beachy-keen advice.

Thank you to all the locations in the book for welcoming my characters and for being my inspiration.

Thank you, writer friends, bloggers, readers and everybody who makes this community the lovely, supporting beam of sunshine that it is.

And the biggest THANK YOU to the NHS for all their hard, hard work pulling us through such a tough time.

Love and sunshine,

Lucy xx